Blackness

Awaits

Blackness Awaits

Norma Jeanne Karlsson

Edited by Progressive Edits

Cover Design and Layout by
Ellie Kay Bockert Augsburger
Creative Digital Studios
CreativeDigitalStudios.com

Cover Image Copyright © George Mayer/
Dollar Photo Club "Nude woman with silver make-up"

Published by It's Publishing
PO Box 14402
Parkville, MO 64152

www.normajeannekarlsson.com

ISBN: 978-0-9911873-3-1
ISBN e-book: 978-0-9911873-2-4

Table of Contents

Dedication...

To the fierce and the loyal.

Acknowledgements

To my husband...it's difficult to find the words. You are the rock in my life that grounds me at each and every turn. Without you none of this would be possible. I never knew that love and partnership existed the way that it does with you and I take not one day for granted now that I have it. I love you more with every breath that I take. Thank you...for everything.

To my children. As we struggle through two of your special needs, I am in awe of your perseverance and fight. To my typically developing son, I fear you are sometimes left in the shadows as we struggle to push your brothers forward. But it never fails that you're always right in step trying to push them even harder. I am blown away at your capacity to love, and the acceptance you have for the difficulties of your brothers. Being a mother is my greatest triumph and I'm beyond rewarded watching you each grow and learn. The three of you are my finest accomplishment in life.

To my mother. Thank you for showering me with unconditional love. I write what I know and I know what I do about motherly love because of you. You've been at my side as I've struggled and fought for my children and without you I wouldn't be where I am with them today. You've given me the hope of a better life and a better future for myself and my children because you fought when most people quit. Thank you for teaching me to fight when all seems lost. Love, love, love you!

To Chris. I'm able to write these stories because of you. You taught me what friendship and loyalty are fifteen years ago and I carry that with me closer to my heart now that I'm an ocean away from you. I treasure each and every moment we've spent in each other's lives.

Without you I wouldn't have had the strength to have pushed through the loss that has touched my life. You pulled me from my own blackness and I am forever indebted to you for that. Best friend isn't a title that suits what you are in my life. You are a piece of my heart that burns brightly every day. I love you dearly.

To Ellie. You are amazing. Your talent stuns me more every time you unveil something you've created. Whether we're talking about scars and naked bodies or the benefits of whiskey over Valium, I enjoy every conversation. You have become my friend beyond my remarkable cover artist. Thank you for being a sounding board to my crazy and the filter to my ridiculous lack of imagination. I can't wait to see where we go next.

To Amanda. As a writer you always hope to find an editor that gets you...and damn if you don't get me. You have inspired me to surge forward when my writing fight was beginning to wane. The honesty you've provided has warmed my soul and challenged my brain. Thank you for pushing me to continue to create and loving my characters as much as I do. I think after a three and a half hour conversation I fell in love with you a little bit. Here's to creating more books together and a friendship that will stand the test of time.

To Vicky and Ruth. You ladies are brilliant! You have lifted my spirits here in Belfast when I was down and homesick. I don't think I could have written *Blackness Awaits* if it wasn't for you two and our never ending coffees (I blame you for my new addiction) and conversations. I'm thankful to have met you both and cherish our time together.

To the bloggers and reviewers. Thank you for your time and your words, even the negative ones. It's criticism and praise that challenge and reward me in this journey. Without you *Blackness Takes Over* would never have gotten to where it is. I hope those of you that love where I began will continue to enjoy where I go.

To the readers and fans. Is it possible to love people you've never met or spoken to? I think I do! The words of thanks and support you have offered have stuck with me like a chorus in the background every day. I could not and would not have written *Blackness Awaits* without you all rallying around me. The emails and messages you have sent have made me laugh and smile. To those of you that have found inspiration and strength from Shannon and her boys I can't begin to tell you how rewarding that is for me. As long as I have you I will continue to tell the stories of strong women that fight and conquer. I can only hope that *Blackness Awaits* entertains and invigorates all of you as much as *Blackness Takes Over* did. Thank you, thank you, thank you!

Prologue

The dreary run-down bar is the perfect place to meet. No one will recognize me or expect me to be here. Still, I circled the block five times before parking two blocks away.

Walking briskly in the crisp autumn air, I constantly check for a tail as I make my way to the bar. You wouldn't know it was a bar if you weren't looking for it. It's just a beaten wooden door like all the others on the face of a long red brick building. I pull the heavy door open, moving through the dingy bar to the back booth hidden from onlookers. There are only five other people in the bar, all drunk to the point of oblivion. A waitress, if you can call her that, comes up to the table and waits silently. Never asking what I would like, just waits. I order a pint of whatever is on tap...I won't drink a drop. The waitress returns with the pint, remaining silent as she sloshes beer on the table while carelessly plopping it in front of me before retreating again.

The door to the bar swings open. Here is the man I've been waiting for, Mancini. It's been just over twenty-two years since I've seen him in person. He's aged and worn from his life, but looks more lethal than the kid I once knew. Mancini is a stranger to me now and I must approach this cautiously. He calmly makes his way to the booth, drawing no attention to himself, and slides in front of me as we silently study each other.

"What have you got for us?" I question Mancini in almost a whisper. I'm outside my depth here and trying desperately not to allow my discontent to shine through the façade. I must control myself. He reaches in his inside jacket pocket and pauses studying my face discriminately. I remain still and allow the scrutiny,

1

knowing I have no choice in the matter. After several painfully slow moments, he pulls a large envelope from his jacket and slides it across the table.

"I think you'll be very pleased," Mancini says in a harsh cutting voice as he leans back stretching his arms wide along the back of the booth.

I slide a finger under the edge of the seal hoping this will finally put an end to my search. I pull out a newspaper article first. The headline reads: *Butch Rossi Granted Retrial.* I feel my brow furrow; Butch Rossi is not any of my concern.

"Read the caption," he directs.

Shannon Kelly, Guardian ad Litem for Mia Rossi, makes her way into the courthouse for preliminary hearings.

I look at the picture above the caption. It's been so long, could that actually be her? She's a woman now, not an eight-year-old little girl. She was a precious child, features not unlike those of the woman in the picture. Her face is being shielded by a man, a bodyguard. Why does a family attorney need a bodyguard? I reach back into the envelope pulling out a stack of surveillance photos and a fact sheet (of sorts) listing her personal information: address, phone numbers, facts about friends, and detailed information about her routines. It's the photos I focus on.

Her gorgeous green eyes glimmer in the sun as a large man with a huge tattoo across his chest chases her around their living room in one photo. Her wavy auburn hair shines under the lights of a night club as she dances with a dark haired man in the next. Her athletic body is misted with sweat as she races a colossal man for a basketball in another photo. Who are all of these men around her?

"Yeah, that could be a problem," Mancini replies to my unasked question.

"Do you have any information on them?" I ask with a pleasant tone. It's more pleasant than I've spoken to anyone in decades. I know I have to keep up this front to gain what I require.

"They've all lived together since they were teenagers. They're as dedicated to her as any of my men are to me. What we're plannin'...need to consider them," his tone is serious but his posture is still relaxed.

I go back to the stack of photos. This is her. I know it's her. Other photos show her with her boyfriend, a huge blond man with strange colored eyes and her bodyguard an equally huge dark and mysterious type. The bodyguard is not unlike the man sitting across from me.

"What about the boyfriend and bodyguard?" I ask in the same muted tone I've been practicing for weeks leading up to this meeting.

"The bodyguard is a nonissue." I raise my brow at that statement. How can a bodyguard be a nonissue? "Anyone hired to protect someone is a nonissue. Money changes everything," Mancini repeats in a growl cautioning me not to question further. I nod understanding how well money can influence the actions of others.

"The boyfriend is a bit of an unknown. Seems he may have a pregnant girl in Seattle. Still runnin' checks on that. If he's screwin' around on her," he motions at the photos of Shannon, "he's a fuckin' idiot. From what I've been told, she's grown into a woman you do not fuck around on," Mancini says the last part with a small smirk on his lips. Shannon's always had a way with men her entire life. Even as a little girl she could wrap any man or boy around her finger with just a smile. That's why I need a professional team for this job, immune professionals.

"We need more background on all of these men. I don't want any surprises. Have you put together a team yet?" I ask Mancini hoping he'll give an affirmative.

"Just about. Gotta make sure they're good with doin' a job with a woman," he explains sitting forward resting his forearms on the table.

"I didn't know gender would be an issue," I state trying to force the issue in a civilized manner when all I want to do is call bullshit.

"Some men aren't good with it. I need to be sure before we move in," he states firmly.

"I'm not requiring anything that's outside the norm. We need the best for this job and you told me you could make that happen. What do you need to move forward?" Mancini studies my face for a long time before answering.

"Double the fee and I'll put my guys together in the next few weeks," Mancini states. I nod my head in agreement sensing there's more to the deal. He bows his head glancing at his knuckles before returning his gaze. "We need quick and easy so I'll pull a crew together that can handle that. Once we've got what we need, I decide how this ends." Mancini's eyes are cold and intense with this last statement. His reputation for how he ends jobs flashes through my mind. I'd like some say in the matter.

"This affects you as much as it does me. If there's an issue with her being a woman...what if your men become weak when it comes to her?" I ask. A bad choice, I realize the moment the words escape my lips. All the work I've done to keep the typical me at bay faded to the back with that statement. My first mistake. Mancini leans forward crossing onto my side of the table pushing me to retreat to maintain any personal space.

"Weakness is a man terrified of an eight-year-old girl," he seethes. "And don't begin to remind me how this affects me. I'll hold up my side of this clusterfuck and you hold yours. My men won't have an issue with her. Fuckers don't have souls. I do this job I'll do it my way and in the end she's mine to deal with. Now, if you're waverin' on my ability, let me straighten that shit out for you. I'm runnin' this fuckin' show. You try to come at me

4

or send someone in to do the job behind my back...I'll take it as a personal insult. You're aware how I deal with insults right?" His gaze is menacing as he growls.

I'm convinced. He'll get this job done. I'm also certain I need to keep my responses in check. I'm normally the one running the show and Mancini is giving orders now.

"I'm aware of how you deal with insults. It was not my intention to offend or insult you. She has a way with people and I wanted to be sure she won't affect your men," I explain. Mistake two.

"Don't pretend to understand my men or me. I know you. I don't understand you, but I know you." This is a threat. "We'll get the job done and deal with her as I see fit. My men'll clean it up. Keep the fuck outta my way and I won't have to make any visits to Northside."

With that Mancini pushes back to his side of the table and spreads his arms across the back of the booth again. He just threatened my children (Northside is where they attend school). I know this and know there's nothing I can do about it. I knew when I made the decision to find her that I was risking everything. Mancini just reminded me of the weight of those risks.

"I'm not going to do anything that would endanger my family," I say quietly.

"Newsflash, you already have," he smirks in response. "I'll get you the rest of the details and keep you in the loop as much as you need to be. Give Katherine my best." With that he stands up and moves out of the bar as inconspicuously as he entered.

Mancini threatened my wife with his last statement. I don't understand this world or the men I'm now dealing with, but I know a threat when I hear it...that was not an idle threat. I glance back down at the photographs choosing the one where Shannon's smiling looking directly into the camera secretly capturing her radiance. I feel the slightest ghost of a grin play at the corners of my mouth. If only she knew...blackness awaits.

Part One

Chapter 1

Kavanagh

I'm going to commit murder. I can feel it in my bones, in my pulse, in each breath I take. I'm pretty sure O'Sullivan, Cal, and Aidan are on board with my plan. Kid went upstairs with Kellerman and twenty minutes later Taylor dropped his bomb. Kellerman got a fucking chick pregnant when he was in Seattle. I don't know specific dates on when he and Kid became a couple, but I know he was all over her shit and fully warned before he went back to Seattle in October. Yeah, I'm going to commit murder. We have to get Kid out of here before we beat his head in.

"Make sure Kid's not in the room for this shit," I say to whoever's listening. I get chin lifts in response. O'Sullivan has been cracking his knuckles and pumping his fists since we saw the first picture of Kellerman and that chick. She's cute...that's all I can say about her. She's nothing compared to Kid. Kellerman must be a fucking idiot. The blood is rushing past my eardrums with such force I don't hear Kid and Kellerman come down the stairs. I'm barely aware of the Army vs. Navy game on the TV. The four of us turn to look at them as Kellerman starts to talk.

"I beyond fucked up today guys," Kellerman tries to grovel. "I feel like total shit about it and I can assure you, I'll never let anything go that far again. I love Kid more than I can even tell you guys and I know you all love her just as much. I meant what I told Kav all those weeks ago. If I hurt her I'd deliver myself to you all willingly. I'm here and I deserve whatever you wanna give me. I was wrong." I stand up and move toward Kellerman never looking at Kid. Kid keeps her fingers

9

interlaced with his and I want to break everyone of his as they touch her. I won't do anything to him while she's here. I won't put her in the middle like those two pricks did earlier. I can feel Kid's eyes on me while the guys approach my back.

"Kid go to the office and talk to Taylor," I order without looking at her. Kellerman maintains eye contact with me, not in a confrontational way...he doesn't know what's coming.

"Kavy," Kid warns.

"Kid, we need Kellerman alone for a few minutes. You need to leave," O'Sullivan orders her from behind my back.

"Go ahead Kiddo. I'll be fine," Kellerman soothes her. I'm going to break that jaw he's working.

Kid turns to walk away, and I relax a little that she isn't putting up more of a fight. My relief was premature, because she stops and turns back around.

"Guys, I know this is a man thing that I'm not a part of. But you all are my family...Kel included. He's my future now too guys. I'm no cake walk to be with, but he's fightin' for me like only you guys have. Think about that before you do anything stupid," she pleads before turning and walking away. She won't feel that way after she talks to Taylor. I hate that she'll be hurt, but she deserves to know.

Once she rounds the corner and I hear the office door shut it takes everything I've got in me not to launch at this motherfucker.

"Pool house," I growl at him. He nods and moves toward the back door. I can't risk Kid hearing us so the pool house is the best place to get this done. Once Taylor dropped this shit storm at our feet he told us he'd explain things to Kid while we dealt with Kellerman. I don't know how long we have, but getting out of the house buys us more time.

We enter the pool house. It's one large open space with six oversized beds that house all the brothers when

10

they visit off to the right and an open kitchenette with a large breakfast table to the left. It's a light airy beach house feel not really the place to maim, but it will have to do. Kellerman goes in first followed by me, the guys trailing. No one says a word. Kellerman stops in the middle of the room. His head is held high, but I can see he's apprehensive. I'd be scared fucking shitless facing us in a room.

"We're gonna kick the livin' shit outta you," I inform him in a growl resembling English. "Then you're gonna pack your shit, get on a plane, and crawl back to Seattle." His face is calm and collected with the first sentence, strained and confused at the last.

"What're you talkin' about back to Seattle?" Kellerman asks.

"You think we're gonna let you stick around and go back and forth? Kid deserves better than that and you fuckin' know it," Aidan seethes, moving to my right. Aidan's a big motherfucker. I've never seen him as pissed as he is right now, scary isn't the right word.

"Back and forth?" Kellerman repeats.

"This is not Sesame Street motherfucker. You heard him," Cal jumps to his brother's side. Cal can go off the rails but it's rare. He's the calmest of our bunch, but he's hell on wheels when he gets going. O'Sullivan moves to my left and I can feel the fury oozing from every inch of him. He's a fighter through and through. I have no doubt that he can, and will end Kellerman. Kid's the soft spot for all of us and we would all gladly sacrifice anything for her.

"I'm startin' to feel like I don't know what's goin' on," Kellerman says as he looks at all our raging expressions.

"He explained it," O'Sullivan says motioning to me. "Don't see the problem." He's so furious I'm surprised he can form words much less sentences.

"I get the ass beating. I put my hands on her and shouldn't have. I'm down for whatever you four got planned. I'm not fuckin' leavin' Kid though. I don't know

11

what makes you think I would leave her, but I'm stayin'." Kellerman's confident as he talks. I have no doubt he'll take the beating, but he's not making Kid a stepmom or taking her away from us to Seattle that's for damn sure. She deserves the world not some slut's sloppy seconds.

"Fuck this shit," O'Sullivan roars and lunges at Kellerman. He lands a brutal right hook along Kellerman's jaw, snapping his head to the side. Kellerman stumbles but doesn't go down. O'Sullivan is a man possessed now that he's started. He grabs Kellerman's shirt to hold him in place as he repeatedly crushes his face. Kellerman doesn't fight back.

"Fight back you pussy!" O'Sullivan screams as he releases Kellerman's shirt only to connect a left cross splitting the skin below his eye. Stumbling back Kellerman falls to the floor. He's breathing hard as he stays down.

"Who's next?" Kellerman asks without a hint of snark. He's really going to let the four of us beat his ass. We'll kill him. He looks done after O'Sullivan; the three of us on top of it is too much. I have to be the voice of reason in the room as I see Aidan making his way toward him.

"He's had enough," I state firmly. Aidan snaps his head back to me with a look of shock on his face.

"You're lettin' him off that easy Kavanagh?" Aidan grumbles.

"He's gotta be able to walk through the airport."

"I'm not goin' to the airport," Kellerman mumbles spitting blood into his shirt. This sets me off.

I pick Kellerman up by the throat and pin him against the wall squeezing as I speak, "You will get your sorry ass on a plane. Today! She's had enough pain in this life, you motherfuckin' piece of shit." I squeeze harder the more I speak, because the more I speak the more infuriated I'm becoming. "If you think for a second I'm gonna let you take her from me, you're sadly mistaken. What she's learnin' today about you, you dickless fuck, is gonna wreck her. Get outta this fuckin' city today or we're comin' for you." I squeeze one more time before I let him drop. He slides down the wall gasping for air, coughing and choking.

"I'm not leavin' her," Kellerman gasps out. Aidan hurls forward and kicks him over and over and over in the torso.

"You fuckin' are!" Aidan screams as he lands his final blow. Kellerman falls to the side spitting out blood from what I'm guessing is some internal damage at this point. Maybe we are going to commit murder. This motherfucker seems intent on dying in our pool house.

"Not," Kellerman mumbles before he passes out.

"What the fuck?!" Cal bellows. "Is he insane? Why's he lettin' this go on?"

Aidan bends down and starts checking Kellerman's vitals. His doctor brain must have just kicked in gear. No pun intended (maybe a little pun intended).

"Guessin' his spleen is damaged maybe his liver too," Aidan explains without much concern in his voice while standing up. "We need to decide what we're doin' here."

"Wait for him to wake up. See where his head's at," I say. I can't put him over my shoulder and walk him out in front of Kid. He has to leave on his own. We all sit around the breakfast table and stare at Kellerman waiting for his pathetic ass to wake up.

Chapter 2

Kellerman

I come to in excruciating pain. These crazy motherfuckers know how to work someone over. My face is fucked. Blood dried all over and swollen based on the tightness I feel. My stomach is also fucked. Aidan must have kicked it through my spine. I push myself up to a sitting position cradling my midsection as I do.

"Sleeping Beauty has arisen fellas," Kav announces to the group. "Ready to pack your shit?" he asks me gruffly.

"Nope," I breathe out. I can barely catch a good breath at this point, but I'm not giving in. I have no clue why these guys think I need to go back to Seattle, but I won't leave Kid.

"O'Sullivan I think you knocked him stupid," Cal announces as he makes his way to me. "Get up and get the fuck outta our house. I'm done playin' games with you." He reaches down grabbing the neck of my shirt and hauls my ass off the floor. My legs are weak so I use the wall to keep upright. Cal leans into my face. "You goin'?" he seethes. I shake my head no.

He hocks back and spits in my face. I get the feeling they're pissed at me for something I'm unaware I did. I reach up with my hand and wipe his spit down my battered face.

"I'm not leavin' her," I state short of breath. "It's her house and she wants me here. I won't leave here unless she tells me." O'Sullivan laughs a sinister chuckle from the table.

"We're goin' easy on you compared to what Kid'll do once Taylor fills her in," he scoffs. Now I'm getting

15

pissed. What the fuck does Taylor have to do with any of this shit?!

"What the fuck does Taylor have to do with anything?" I implore Cal who has let go of my shirt but is still in my face.

"He's the one that found out your dirty little secret," Cal fumes. Secret? I don't have any goddamn secrets. Not from Kid and certainly nothing that would warrant this level of psychosis.

"Can you all stop speakin' in code and tell me what the fuck is goin' on? I don't have any goddamn secrets. If Taylor is in there mindfuckin' Kid we're gonna have problems," I inform them. Cal's scowl has lessened slightly as he tries to figure out if I'm lying. I look at the table to see similar looks on the guys' faces.

"Your baby's momma," Kav states plainly. Well that would definitely be a secret because I don't have kids.

"I don't have kids you guys," I huff. I can't believe they would think I would leave children behind in Seattle.

"You will in about six months," Aidan replies. I feel the blood drain from my face and my stomach turns more than it already was from the beat down.

"What?" I ask in a whisper. Cassie. Fuck, Cassie's pregnant. This shit just got a whole lot worse.

"I can see that you're finally startin' to grasp what's goin' on here," O'Sullivan chides. "Ready to pack now bitch?"

"I didn't know. She hasn't been in contact with me since I got back," I explain. How the fuck does Taylor know this shit and I don't?

"Well a wham-bam-thank you-ma'am will make them less likely to call you," Kav taunts. "Chicks don't like bein' the piece on the side." Piece on the side?

"What the fuck are you talkin' about Kav?" I can feel my patience running thin. Too much information coming in mixed with a lot of ball busting and an ass beating is

16

wearing me down. Kav stands up and trades places with Cal two inches from my face.

"I'm talkin' about you fuckin' that cunt while you were in Seattle after callin' dibs on Kid," he growls in my face.

"Didn't happen," I scoff.

"Look motherfucker I can see you're all fucked up and I don't wanna go to prison, but I will end you. We've seen the pictures. We know it happened." He bumps his chest into mine staring me down.

"I don't know what pictures you saw, but I haven't been with Cassie since I moved here. The first time," I clarify.

"BULLSHIT!" Kav bellows in my face. "Get Taylor now. I want this shit done!" Cal moves out the door and we all wait in silence. How is this happening? Cassie's pregnant? She would tell me. She wants me back and made that perfectly clear when I was in Seattle last time. If she was pregnant she'd be here or blowing up my phone. The door opens and Taylor walks in with that fucking smirk on his face that makes me fantasize about wrapping my hands around his neck.

"Don't you look pretty?" Taylor taunts. I glare at him but don't respond. I want those fucking pictures now. I push Kav out of my space and gingerly walk to the table where Taylor threw them down. I pick up the stack and race through them feeling sicker with each progression. I was pissed that night. I couldn't get a hold of Kid and once I talked to Kav and he told me she was with Taylor I flipped. Not my proudest moment. Cassie was there being all sweet and innocent (a rarity), asking if she could do anything for me. I mauled her. Things got heated, but I stopped before anything happened. I didn't fuck her that night.

"I know this looks bad," I state to the group. "We made out and shit got a little heavy but that's it. I stopped it."

"Last I checked chicks can't get pregnant from tonsil hockey," Kav snarks.

"If she's pregnant it's from a week before I came here. We hooked up then and that was the last time. I haven't been with anyone since I met Kid. This," I motion to the photos, "was a dick move on my part and I'll make it up to Kid. I need to talk to Cassie to figure the rest out," I say moving to the door. I will work this out with Kid. I can't lose her.

Taylor grabs my arm as I move past him. I didn't fight back with the guys, but I will go at it with this piece of shit.

"Get your fuckin' hand off me you meddling bitch," I snarl.

"Ooh, testy." Taylor mocks. "Just thought you should know it was my arms she fell into when she saw those pictures. My tongue that caressed her tears away. My kiss that left her breathless. She'll be fine without you." I see red and pivot on him faster than he anticipates. I connect my right fist directly with his temple and he hits the floor like a ton of bricks.

"Shit," Aidan says under his breath.

I move to the door, realizing I only thought these guys were my friends. I've been in this position before though, you think you have friends then the going gets tough and you're on your own. I can't believe they trusted Taylor without ever giving me the chance to defend myself.

"Thought you guys were my friends," I say over my shoulder. "Fuck you."

I make my way into the house to find Kid. I'm sure she's devastated. I can fix this...I hope she doesn't shoot me before I have the chance. I go to the office first. She's not here. I run up the stairs yelling for her, checking our room (it feels like our room, not just hers). She's not here. I check every bedroom and bathroom. She's not here. I run down to the basement hoping she's working off her anger. She's not here. Fuck she left. I run to the

18

garage. Her Shelby's here. All the guys' cars are here. I make my way back in the house. She left on foot? No way would Taylor let her leave on foot. Unless she took off while he was in the pool house. I rip my Nexus out of my pocket and hit her speed dial number. It starts ringing and I hear her BlackBerry in the kitchen. She left her BlackBerry. She left her BlackBerry? She would never leave her BlackBerry. Something's wrong. I run into the pool house just as Taylor is coming to.

"She's gone."

Chapter 3

Kavanagh

My world is moving in slow motion, a torturous lethargic motion that I can't break free from. The moment Kellerman burst through the door I knew something was wrong. I hadn't felt right for that last half hour, but I ignored it because I was focused on Kellerman. FUCK!

"She's gone," was all he said and we sprinted from the pool house. We all ran screaming from room to room. He was right, she's gone. Now we're in the office scouring all of the video from our state-of-the-art security system for some shred of a clue as to where she went. Kid wouldn't just take off. Not without her BlackBerry or letting one of us know or leaving a note or leaving a text…something. This is bad. My hands are shaking. The last time I shook like this I found Kid underneath Liam thirteen years ago in my bedroom broken and lifeless. This can't be happening again.

"Flower delivery," Taylor says bringing me out of my head.

"What?" I ask.

"There was a flower delivery. Look at the van." Taylor points at the monitor where a large white van with a flower logo pulls into the driveway. The driver gets out but keeps his face hidden from view beneath his hat. He rings the doorbell, again shielding his face from the camera on the porch. Kid answers and takes the flowers from him. He follows her in the house. There's no camera in the foyer so we lose visual.

"Try the camera in the great room. Maybe there's a view down the hall," Cal suggests urgently to Taylor.

21

Taylor pulls up that footage and scrolls to the correct time. It's a shitty image, but we can see Kid put the flowers on the table and sniff. She just stands there like she's stuck in time. A few moments later the delivery guy comes into view raising his hand up above her head and slamming it back down around her head or neck. The image is too far away to tell which.

"FUCK!" I roar. She goes limp falling back into his waiting arms. He scoops her up, carrying her out of the house. Taylor quickly shifts back to the other footage of the porch and then the driveway. The "delivery" guy carries her hurriedly out of the house to the van. The van door slides open and a pair of arms covered in black sleeves reach out for her. As the arms lean out so does a head and neck. His head is covered in a black ski mask. He pulls Kid into his arms roughly and then retreats with her into the van. The delivery guy quickly rounds the hood, climbs in and reverses out of the driveway at a normal pace. I watch the van leave our driveway, carrying the beat of my heart with it.

Shannon

I'm being carried. Cradled to a firm chest encapsulated by strong arms. My eyes flutter open to see a man I'm unfamiliar with. I look to my left to realize I'm being carried onto a plane, a small private plane. I try to wiggle and push against the chest I'm pressed into but my arms are heavy and weighted.

"Sit still," his voice commands roughly. I look up into his face. He's not looking down at me so I only have a view of his dark stubble covered jaw and his neck, which is thick and muscled with a tattoo on it.

"Please," I plead. I don't know what I'm pleading for with that word, but it's all that I can formulate.

"Don't worry," he says clinically. Uh, bull-fuckin'-shit. He's putting me on a plane after kidnapping me. Don't worry? Fuck him. My limbs are so heavy and I feel foggy.

I'm guessing I've been drugged. I try to wiggle free again to no avail.

"You're not goin' anywhere," he grumbles. He flops my limp body on a couch at the back of the plane. "Get the drugs," he says to someone behind us.

"No please don't drug me. I'll be good," I implore. I certainly won't be good, but I'm not going to tell him he's about to endure the fight of his life once I can move my fucking arms. Another person approaches and I can see the needle and syringe out of my periphery.

He nods at the syringe wielder. I feel the sharp prick in my arm and then the sting of the injection. He sits down in a chair next to me not looking in my direction. I flop my arms around myself trying to draw some comfort as the drugs take over. These arms are not my home. I'm not safe.

Kellerman

"Where the fuck were you?" I bellow at Taylor after watching the love of my life being carried away.

"Kellerman, that's not gonna help anyone right now. Stay focused," Cal chides me.

"I'm fuckin' focused. I wanna know how she's taken from her home and her *bodyguard* misses it," I sneer.

"I'd like to know too," Aidan pipes in. Until a few hours ago Aidan and I were on the same page regarding Taylor. I'm hoping in light of everything we're still on the same side.

"I was in the bathroom," Taylor answers blankly. I don't respond. Fighting with this fuckwad isn't going to get us anywhere.

"I'll call the police," O'Sullivan jumps up from the grey leather wingback chair he's surely ruined gripping the arms violently.

"They'll just slow us down and push us off her case," Taylor responds. "If we call them we have no control. If we work this ourselves, we determine how it goes down."

"We don't have the resources, Taylor," Kav scolds. "How are the five of us supposed to find her? We're what, an hour behind them? We need help."

"I'll call in some favors and you guys can call your families. We can do more on our own," Taylor says while typing away on the keyboard not looking at any of us. I don't like this. He's in the bathroom when she's taken and he doesn't want the authorities in on this. What the fuck? I look over at Aidan who seems to be thinking the same thing. Neither of us comments.

"The plates are fake. The flower company is fake. We need something to go on," Taylor says without looking at us again. He's in the zone. Maybe he'll be able to find her. I don't give a shit if this prick loves Kid, if he finds her I'll be forever in his debt. I can't reconcile in my head if he's a threat or a gift. Damn it this is beyond fucked up!

"Each of you start scouring the footage. Look for anything that's identifying," Taylor instructs. Aidan and I move to a laptop, Cal and Taylor work at the desktop, and Kav and O'Sullivan take another laptop. The six of us are silent. Aidan and I go through the final footage, Taylor and Cal take the indoor footage and Kav and O'Sullivan comb the beginning. I'm trying to keep my emotions in check as I see Kid's seemingly lifeless body carried from her house by some psycho.

"Keep it in check," Aidan says under his breath to me. I look at him and he's staring at my fists. My knuckles are white from pumping my hands mindlessly. I nod but continue fisting my jeans to relieve a small amount of tension as we both go back to the footage.

It's been forty-five minutes and no one has found anything. We're each looking at less than a minute of footage. If there is something to find I think we would have found it by now. I decide I'm going through it one more time and then I'm calling the cops.

I click through the video frame by frame. I've looked at this so much everything is blurring together. The delivery guy leans to hand off Kid when I finally see it.

"There," I whisper to Aidan.

"What?" he questions.

"His neck. What's that on his neck?" Aidan zooms in and takes a sharp breath.

"Mancini," he says barely above a whisper and all the Chicago boys gasp.

"FUCK!" O'Sullivan roars ripping his phone out of his pocket. "Dad," he says into the receiver. "Someone in the Mancini family has Kid."

Chapter 4

Kellerman

I don't know who the Mancini family is, but I'm guessing by the response in the room this is bad. Strike that, this is beyond bad, it's fucked.

"Let's get your face cleaned up while they figure out what to do," Aidan says to me. I look at him like he's insane. You think I give a flying fuck about my face right now?!

"I'm good," I scoff. He's part of the reason I'm in this condition at the moment.

"Kellerman, we're gonna have to go after her. You need to be at your best. You can't be out in public covered in blood with a gaping gash under your eye. Come-the-fuck-on!" Aidan demands as he stands up. I follow him to the kitchen silently. I notice a large vase of flowers on the entryway table. Fuckers actually brought her flowers. The last thing she heard about me before they took her was that I basically cheated on her and got the other woman pregnant. I can't run to her and beg forgiveness. She's somewhere alone with men that are doing God knows what to her, and I'm sure the thought of me is bringing her no comfort. I feel bile rise in my throat for the first time. I haven't let my mind wander yet. Wandering is painful.

"Run and hop in the shower. I'll stitch you up once you're done. There's gonna be a scar," Aidan informs me. I couldn't give a shit at this point. I don't respond other than to fly up the stairs two at a time to our room. I no sooner close the door when I'm enveloped in Kid's scent. She always smells clean. She's light and airy, not covered in lotions and perfumes. She smells like a bright fresh spring morning. My hands start to shake as the emotion builds in me. Kid's gone. Fucking gone and I'm standing here in her room shaking like a leaf. I stamp it down. I have to keep my shit together for Kid.

I climb in the shower and wash off in record time. I pull on jeans, a black thermal, a black hoodie, and fly back down the stairs. Aidan has laid out all of the supplies he needs and gets to work on my face silently.

"Fucked up today," Aidan breaks the silence.

"Don't," I warn. They did fuck up and I don't know where we all go from here, but this is not the time. Aidan lifts his chin at me and keeps working. Once my face is cleaned and stitched we head back into the office, or more aptly, the command center. All the guys are on phones barking orders, yelling, cussing, growling and grunting. It's like observing an alternate universe of high-tech cavemen.

"Care to fill me in on what you know?" I ask Aidan.

"The Mancini family is the largest crime syndicate in Chicago. All the 'soldiers' of the family bear a mark, a tattoo of a stab wound, on their necks. Shows that they bleed for their family. That's what you saw on the delivery guy's neck. I've worked on enough trauma victims to be familiar with it," Aidan explains.

"With Sully Senior being the Bureau Chief of the Bureau of Organized Crime in Chicago he'll surely be able to help," Aidan says as O'Sullivan ends the call he was on.

"Kav you got that plane waitin'?" O'Sullivan barks at Kav. Kav holds up a finger and receives a death scowl in return. After thirty seconds Kav hangs up.

"Let's roll out," Kav instructs. We all head into the garage piling into Cal and Kav's SUVs. The only thing anyone packed is the laptops and tablets we all had out in the office. I jump in with Kav and O'Sullivan while Aidan and Taylor jump in with Cal. Kav's driving like a madman and I feel better with every mile we gain toward the Downtown Airport. The tension in the car is thick, but I don't care. This isn't about us, it's about finding Kid.

"Look, Kellerman," Kav breaks the silence. "This situation is fucked. You don't have to be here. We've got this."

"Fuck you, Kavanagh," I fume at him. "You guys may have had her thirteen years longer than me, but she's my life. I'm not goin' anywhere until I know she's safe."

"Good," O'Sullivan and Kav say in unison.

"Fuckin' pricks," I snort. God these guys are a pain in the ass constantly testing me. The tension eases off a bit, but the silence remains. We pull into the airport and pile out running across the tarmac to a waiting Learjet 60. The six of us file in followed by two young pilots. I hope they at least have their licenses. The pilots have obviously been made aware that we're in a rush because as soon as our asses hit the leather seats the plane starts up and taxis to the runway. Once we're up in the air one of the baby-faced pilots comes into the cabin.

The pilot, whose name tag identifies him as Tanner (a twelve-year-old's name), brings two trays of sandwiches and follows with multiple bottles of water and soda. Aidan and I are in the forward facing seats at the front of the plane. Kav and Cal have their backs to us and O'Sullivan and Taylor are facing them. I'm as far away as I can get from Taylor but that's not saying much. We all eat without uttering a sound, willing the hour and twenty minute flight to Chicago Executive Airport to go faster. I'm sure the inside of this plane is nice, I don't notice. My thoughts are with Kid and how the hell we're going to find her.

"What's the plan guys?" I ask to no one and everyone after we polish off the food.

"Don't know," O'Sullivan answers. I turn in my seat to look at him. "I gave my pop everything we have. He'll give us the run down once we land."

"You should probably stay out of this as much as you can," Taylor sneers at me. "Not much you can do."

Before I can spout off something foul, Aidan pipes in, "He's the one that figured out Kid was missin' and found the mark on the fucker's neck. I'd say he's done everything so far." His tone is clipped and simmering under the surface, the giant is raging. Aidan is definitely team Kellerman.

"Whatever. Just keep him outta my way," Taylor instructs the cabin.

"You're not runnin' shit, Taylor. Back the fuck off Kellerman. He already laid your ass out once. Hate to see you suffer brain damage from another assault," Cal taunts. Cal is also team Kellerman. If I can get Finn in on this I have the Callaghan trio. Finn, shit...we should have picked up Finn.

"We shoulda picked up Finn," I say to Aidan.

"I called him. He's gonna stay in Kansas City and run down some leads first. He'll meet us in Chicago tonight or early tomorrow. He's so pissed it's best he's not on this plane," Aidan replies directing an accusatory eye flick toward Taylor. Finn is also team Kellerman. My Callaghan trio is complete, time to move on to another family.

"Just got an email from my pop," O'Sullivan announces. We're more than halfway through the flight at this point. To say it's dragging would be the understatement of the century. "Says he put together a small task force, keepin' most of our info to themselves not wantin' to tip anyone off that we're lookin'. Can't find a connection between Mancini and Kid. Families are pickin' us up at the airport."

"That's not a lot of information," Kav points out the obvious.

"Yeah," O'Sullivan agrees and goes back to whatever he was doing on the laptop.

This day is a clusterfuck of monstrous proportions. I have never felt as high as when Kid and I laid our shit bare, agreeing to move in together; and I've never felt as low watching her carried away on surveillance. Mix in there the beat down the boys handed me, Taylor making a play for Kid, and Cassie being pregnant, December fourteenth can go fuck itself. I need to talk to Cassie. Once we figure shit out I'll call her. The timing of this couldn't be worse. I need to be completely focused on Kid, not worrying if I'm going to be a father.

"We'll find her," Aidan says softly. I think he's talking to me but when I look at him, he's staring out his window. I don't respond. I can't consider the alternative to his statement.

I close my eyes willing myself to catch just a little rest before we touchdown. I know we're in for long hours and I need every ounce of energy I can gain. Just as I'm about to nod off I hear Kav start to talk.

Kavanagh

"Brian," I say to O'Sullivan. We never use each other's first names and I can hear my voice is pained as I say it. "This shit's wrong. What're we gonna do?"

"Don't freak out on me, Kav," O'Sullivan pleads; his tone just as pained.

"I'm not freakin' out. I'm bein' realistic. If Mancini has her," I pause and take a deep breath. "You know what we're gonna find and it's not Kid. Not Kid alive and not Kid okay."

"Don't," O'Sullivan growls at me. "Don't do that. We're gonna find her. Kid's strong and smart. She'll keep herself alive until we find her. Our families are not gonna lose her. We're not gonna lose her."

I want to believe him. I want to trust everything he's saying, but I know the truth. Mancini doesn't leave witnesses. He makes people disappear. He makes them disappear in a variety of ways that has my stomach turning as I think about the news reports in Chicago of dismembered bodies being found piece by piece throughout the Midwest. Dogs found having people's body parts in their stomachs. Kid can't be that. She has to be okay. She has to fight.

31

"She'll fight," I whisper to O'Sullivan. He cocks an eyebrow at me and smirks.

"Fuck yeah she will."

Chapter 5

Shannon

Ugh. I'm fucked up. I feel like I've been on the bender to end all benders. My head is killing me and my body feels like it weighs eight hundred pounds. I slowly open my eyes but find I'm in the dark, not just dark...blackness. There's not a speck of light to be seen. I close my eyes and will my body to ascertain where it is and what state it's in.

I'm fully clothed, all the way down to my panties. My boots (gun hidden in my boot) are gone. I'm on a mattress, no pillow under my head. My wrists and ankles are bound. It feels like rope, but I can't be sure. I think I'm in a bed and my ankles and wrists are attached to the head and footboards (hard to tell). I'm spread eagle. I test my binds and quickly realize I'm not wiggling out of this. I'll have to be let go or find something sharp to cut myself loose. In the blackness I don't see either of those things happening. I want to scream even though I know that would be foolish at this point. This is a nightmare come to life. This day is a fucking nightmare come to life. Butch is free and I lose a little bit of Mia, I fight with Kel, make up with Kel, find out Kel essentially cheated on me and got a girl pregnant, I make out with Taylor, I get kidnapped, and now I'm in blackness...fucking nightmare.

A door opens to my left and I put on an Oscar-worthy performance of drugged up sleeping kidnap victim. It's a male that has entered based on the smell of his cologne and the timber of his voice.

"She's still out..." His voice is harsh and deep, the same voice of the man who carried me onto the plane.

That's right, I was on a plane. Fuck these drugs have really jacked with me.

"He cracked her fuckin' head open so yeah, she's still out..." I don't hear any response so I figure he's on the phone.

"I'll get her up and talkin' soon..." I don't recognize his voice other than that of my drug-pushing kidnapper. His accent is Chicago or the likes.

He stops talking, but I don't hear him move. I don't panic. My years with Uncle Mick are screaming in my ear to be calm...I am. My pulse is even as is my breathing. I'm calm like a sleeping baby. All of a sudden I hear a scraping metal sound. I pretend this wakes me...if I was asleep it was loud enough to do the trick.

I flutter open my eyes. The light streaming in from the open door only exacerbates my headache. I look at myself and discover that I am, in fact, bound to a double bed that's a few feet off the floor. The head and footboards are metal and look like they come from an insane asylum (comforting). I'm tied to the furthest edges of them with light colored rope. Knots from a sailor it would seem. I'm not getting out of these. The room is maybe fifteen feet by fifteen feet, with a dresser and a lamp against the wall at the end of my bed, to the right of that heavy green paisley curtains are drawn across what I assume is a window though I can't see it or any light. The wall to my right has a door in the middle (closet?). There's a bedside table on the right of the bed with a lamp with no shade on it. The left wall holds my exit/his entrance and the cause of the noise that "woke" me, a metal chair that my captor is sitting in...studying me.

The man's hair is an inky black, cut short and disheveled. His eyes are deep brown surrounded in long dark lashes and a strong brow. His large nose has a sizeable bump and his face is long. His mouth is in a straight hard line fading into his dark stubble-covered jaw. There's a tattoo of some sort on his neck, but I can't make it out from here. He has broad shoulders and huge

34

arms. He's wearing black slacks and a light grey button down shirt (bit formal for a kidnapper). He's sitting with his elbows on his knees so I can't gauge much else about him. I try to memorize every feature. We stare at each other for what feels like hours.

"You're not scared," his voice is demonic, low and harsh. That was a statement not a question so I don't respond.

"That's new," he says more to himself than me as he stands from the chair and moves toward me.

"Most people panic when they wake up bound to a bed in a dark and strange place," he's trying to make me panic. I don't panic. I follow him every step of the way to my bedside with my eyes on his, he doesn't break our connection.

"This is going to be very interesting," he purrs stroking the back of his fingers across my cheek. I don't flinch. I want to slap his hand away and put a bullet in his head, but I lay there silently as he touches me.

"Shannon." He knows my name. "I need some information from you. Either you can tell me and we're done or I can make you tell me and this will be much harder." I consider my options carefully. The attorney in me is awake and ready to question.

"When you get the information from me that you want are you letting me go?" I ask pointedly.

"She speaks," he purrs and reclaims his seat in the chair. "I didn't say I'd let you go. I said we'd be done."

"By done, you mean you kill me?" My tone is harsher than I'd like but this is new for me, I'm trying.

"I didn't say I'd kill you."

"So you just get information and you have someone else kill me?"

"My job is just to extract information from you by any means necessary...the quicker the better." He enjoys what he does and he's good at it based on the look of confidence covering his drawn face. He glances over his shoulder quickly before returning his blank gaze back to me. I can see his face but not his eyes. I want to see if his eyes lack that bit of human, like Liam. I know that type of man. I need to know what I'm dealing with here. I know I'm not going to talk him out of anything. If I tell him what he wants to know quickly it gives people less time to find me. I'll need to stretch this out...I have to choose torture in order to have a chance to be found or escape. FUCK!

"What do you wanna know?" I ask. Let's see how long I can stretch this shit out.

"There is a safe deposit box in your name. I need to know the password to access it and where to find the key that opens it." His tone is light for a demon.

"I don't have a safe deposit box," I spit sharply. "I'm sorry I don't know your name." I wait for him to fill me in, but he leaves the room. I can see that beyond the door is a hallway all I can make out is the white of its walls, no visible exits. He's back a few moments later. He comes to my bedside and holds a piece of paper in front of my face. It's the signature sheet to a safe deposit box in my name from 1991, signed by my father. What the FUCK?! I have no clue what this is or that it existed. I haven't touched the trust my father left me. I never wanted that money...I wanted him. I also didn't want the witch (my mother) to show up asking for a hand out so I let the estate executor send "my" money to various charities. I don't remember anything about a safe deposit box.

"I don't know what that is. I've never seen it before. Obviously my father opened it in my name when I was a child without my knowledge," I huff. Well this torture choice just got easier. I don't know what he wants anyway.

"The people that want this have assured me that you know," he hisses.

"Well those people are fuckin' wrong," I hiss back staring at his dark eyes. "Why would I lie? You just told me you're gonna torture me if I don't tell you. I have NO desire to be tortured."

"You also don't wanna die. I told you once I have the information, you and I are done." Well played demon.

"Well stretchin' out my remaining hours being tortured and then killed doesn't sound like the way I'd like to spend my last moments alive. I'm guessin' you're good at what you do and I'm not gonna be rescued, right?" I posit.

"I highly doubt it." His devil grin is back and his eyes are dancing.

"So what point is there? I'm dyin' today either in a few minutes or a few hours after bein' brutalized...I choose the former." I state matter-of-factly. I'm trying to mindfuck him as best I can. I know the torture is inevitable, but I want to push it off as far as I can.

"Great." He smacks his hands together and rubs them vigorously. "Tell me what I wanna know and we can be done." He looks over his shoulder again before turning his gaze back to me. What the fuck is he looking at? Every time he says "done" I get the sense he's looking forward to that part. I'm going to lie and see if that buys me some time...surely an ass beating to follow, but time to be found or somehow escape.

"The password is Snuffleupagus and the key is in my jewelry box at home in my bedroom." There is no waver to my voice and I maintain strong eye contact. He furrows his brow at me and chews the information I've just given him.

"What kinda fuckin' password is that?" he asks, unbelieving.

"It's a Sesame Street character. It's for a kid remember?" I scoff like he's the idiot. He stands up and makes his way over to me, leaning so his face is close enough to mine to feel his breath.

"If you're lyin' to me...this gets very bad," he sneers.

"I'm not," I stand firm. His tongue flicks out and he runs it across my jaw and up my cheek. I don't blink. I don't panic.

"Mmmmmmmm," he purrs, "you taste as good as you look. I may have to rethink our arrangement. Maybe we won't be done so soon after all." This could be my way. Let him rape me for hours (the thought causes bile to rise) until someone finds me. I have to stay alive. First step was the lie...now I have to sacrifice my body. I don't panic. I smile, the fakest smile I've ever smiled, he doesn't know that though.

"I'd take that over torture and murder any day." My voice isn't strong but it's not shaking like my insides are. I just offered a demon my body...I don't panic.

He touches his forehead to mine pressing his hands on either side of my head and inhales deeply with his eyes closed. When he opens them I stare into their depths hoping there's a sliver of human there. Nothing...just like Liam. I know his game now.

"I'll make you a deal," he whispers so quietly I can barely hear his words. "If you're a good girl and don't fight. I won't let them kill you. I'll keep you for myself. I'll keep you safe." Safe?! Raped for life or murdered...not really a choice in safety. If I'm alive they'll find me. They will find me.

"Okay," I breathe out. A real smile pulls across his face, he's happy...genuinely. I'm going to vomit! I swallow back the puke response and smile back at him.

"Okay, Kitten," he purrs at me. He places a chaste kiss on my forehead and stands up. "I'm gonna go pass off the information you gave me. If it's good then we can move forward with our arrangement. If not, I still have a job to do." His eyes turn hard at the last part. I nod.

He turns on his heel and leaves the room shutting me in blackness again. I welcome the alone time. I start to think about everyone I love. I want their faces in my head and love in my heart right now. My boys must be so worried about me. "I'm okay," I whisper hoping they can feel me with them. I think of Kel. He's going to be a father. While this pains me more than I can consider, I push it from my mind and try to be happy for him. He'll be an amazing father. I imagine him laughing and

38

playing with a little boy that shares his golden hair and teal eyes. I feel pain in my chest but a smile pulls at my lips. I have to let Kel go.

Taylor...he loves me. He'll find me. I know he'll fight hard to find me. I feel comforted in the thought that he's out there searching for me. My heart is still with Kel, I can't just turn that off. If I can get through this and end things the right way with Kel, Taylor and I could have something. He could be my one.

I think of the rest of the amazing family that I have. My dads, both moms, my brothers, if I die they have each other...they'll be okay. I think of Mia having Butch, I'm so relieved she won't be alone anymore.

I come to terms over the next, hours I'm assuming, that I may not be here in the world much longer. While this revelation is devastating, I'm strangely okay with it. I'll fight as long as I can, but I get the feeling it's the first fight in my life I won't win. I have to be okay with this being the end. If I fight with everything that I've got and still lose, I'll die having no regrets. I'll have peace. I've lived a great life surrounded by love and support. It wasn't conventional but it was strong and unconditional. I will miss this life.

Chapter 6

Kavanagh

We land at Chicago Executive Airport and rush out of the plane to waiting SUVs and our families. Pop, Ryan and Adam are there and at the sight of them I almost lose it. I walk determinedly to them engulfing my brothers in my arms. I hear Adam let out a small sob and that's all it takes to steel myself. I'll be strong for my family. I squeeze them tighter before I let them go and turn to Pop.

"We're gonna find her, Pop," I say with no waver in my voice. He wraps his hand around the back of my head and crushes it to his shoulder. I take a breath remembering to keep my strength.

"You find her," he orders me. "I'll fuckin' bury every one of the motherfuckers that had a hand in this." Pop's pissed. Pop's scary pissed. I pull away from him and look up to see Dr. Callaghan having a similar powwow with Aidan and Cal. Sully Sr. isn't here but Collin and Hugh are, and they're animatedly filling O'Sullivan in. Kellerman and Taylor are avoiding each other like the plague and giving us space with our families.

"Dylan," Pop calls over my shoulder. Kellerman quickly makes his way over to us. Pop, Ryan and Adam all get a good look at Kellerman's face and I feel guilty as shit for the first time. He looks awful and from what I can tell, for no good reason. We have fucked up monumentally today. Starting with Kellerman.

"What happened to you?" Pop asks with an accusatory tone in his voice, presumably at me.

"Misunderstanding," Kellerman replies.

"Bullshit," Pop retorts. "You four get your asses in the SUV. We've got shit to do." We get our asses in the SUV. The others follow suit and we're off to make the quick drive to Highland Park where all of our families live. It's only a twenty minute drive, but every minute we're not moving toward Kid is another minute I feel like I'm failing her.

"What happened to your face, Dylan?" Pop asks again as he pulls onto the I-294.

"It was just a misunderstanding, sir. I'm fine," Kellerman replies again dodging the question. This is not going to go over well with my father.

"I didn't ask if you were okay, I asked what happened," Pop states pointedly. Time for me to intervene.

"We happened, Pop," I say softly. I'm going to get in trouble like a teenager in about two seconds.

"What the fuck does that mean, Aaron?" he bellows. I'm sitting next to him in the passenger seat and he cuts his eyes to me waiting for an answer.

"The guys and I thought Kellerman did something to Kid. Roughed him up before we got all the facts...while Kid got grabbed. O'Sullivan's handy work on his face, mine on his throat, and Aidan's on his body. Cal didn't get a chance to have a shot," I explain. Pop flicks his eyes to the rearview mirror searching for Kellerman to substantiate my claims. He must get it nonverbally because he moves his gaze back to the road without a word.

"You're tellin' me you're beatin' the shit outta Dylan for no reason while my daughter's bein' ripped from your home?" Those words cut through me like a scalpel, razor sharp leaving a slow bleed. He's right. We fucked up today and this is our fault.

"Yes," I reply to his question in a whisper. He roars and slams his hands into the steering wheel repeatedly as we all watch in silent horror. My father never loses his cool. He's the premier attorney in Chicago and

42

known for keeping his cool when all others would lose their shit. He's currently losing his shit. I'm terrified.

"Dad," I hear Adam shakily call from behind me. Pop stops and breathes heavily through his nose trying to calm himself down. After a few minutes just as we're pulling into our neighborhood my father turns to me.

"This isn't your fault," he says confidently. "We will find her." I don't look his way because this is my fault and I don't know if we'll find her the way we want to. "Aaron, look at me." I look his way as we pull into the Callaghan's driveway. His eyes are pained and furious.

"This isn't your fault. That wasn't about you, it was about me. She's my daughter and I'm scared outta my fuckin' mind. It's not your fault," he says reaching across the console to squeeze my hand. I look down at his fingers wrapped around mine. He's scared. The last time he was scared mom died. This is so fucked up. I can feel the tears leaking from my eyes, but I make no move to stop them or look at my father.

"Aaron, we'll find her," Ryan says from behind me gripping my shoulder. I can hear the tears in his voice. I can't be strong for them. I'm crumbling under the guilt. My door flies open behind my back.

"We're not doin' this," O'Sullivan commands. "Get your shit together, get outta this car and fuckin' help me!" I turn my gaze to him. He knew I was crying before he opened the door. He's pulling me out of myself like we always do for each other. I give him a quick chin lift, wipe my hand down my face and climb out of the SUV.

"We got this. Wherever she goes, we go," O'Sullivan says wrapping his arm around my shoulders. He's right. I won't quit until I find her.

Kellerman

Kavanagh just broke the fuck down and his dad had a maniacal shit fit. I'm officially the calmest of this bunch. Ryan and Adam look sick. I know they're older than Kid, but she's the momma bear to these guys.

43

They're lost without her. So am I. I follow behind the Kavanaghs into the Callaghan house, if you can call it that, it's really a mini castle. It's dark so I can't be sure, but I'm guessing there are acres of land around this enormous house. The driveway is long enough that I can't see the street from where I stand. I'm so far outside my depth with these people, Kid included. I don't come from money. I've made a good deal of it working my ass off, but I don't come from it. I come from a neighborhood where women and children are victims of hideous violent crime. I keep my head down and follow. It's no time to think about this shit. I need to get to Kid.

"Dylan, follow me to the kitchen," Dr. Callaghan says softly, although I can tell it's an order. I comply willingly.

"I just wanted to get a look at you for myself," he says as he starts poking around searching for damage I suppose. He pushes and prods my face and neck while I stand with my eyes closed willing this exam to go quicker. "Take your shirt off for me." I pull off my hoodie and thermal all at once. He starts moving his hands and fingers down my chest then rib by rib. He gets below my ribs and I wince a bit when he pokes around at the black and purple bruising. "Tender?"

"Yeah, a bit," I lie. It fucking kills.

"Aidan told me he was concerned about your spleen and your liver. I have to agree with him. I can't do a full examination here in the kitchen. I'd need to get you to the office to have a look under ultrasound to be sure, but I'm guessing you've got a hematoma within your spleen and possibly your liver as well. These aren't life threatening but you need to take it easy. No physical contact in your midsection for a while," he advises. I'm barely listening. I don't care what's wrong with me, after listening to Kav on the plane I'm worried what's happening to Kid as I sit in this fancy kitchen.

"Thanks for lookin' me over. I'm good," I say as I yank my thermal and hoodie back over my head. Just as I do, I hear heels clicking across the tile floor.

"What in God's name happened to you, Dylan?" shrieks Maggie O'Sullivan. She comes barreling up to me knocking Dr. Callaghan out of the way. "Who did this to you? You tell me right now!"

"Mags, he's fine. Where's Sully?" Dr. Callaghan asks referring to Sully Sr., but it reminds me that Kid calls O'Sullivan that. What if I never hear her voice playfully bantering with her boys or her cooing their endearing nicknames again?

"He's on his way here now with a mobile command unit," Maggie replies eyeing me over. "I know Brian's handy work when I see it, Dylan Kellerman. I'll be havin' words with him." With that she stomps out of the kitchen. Maggie O'Sullivan is going to kick her son's ass. I might want to watch that. Kid would love to see it. I lift my chin to Dr. Callaghan and make my way back toward the noise in the living room.

Chapter 7

Shannon

The door opens and the man enters. His eyes are dark with anger and something else I can't place. His shirt is off and his chest and abs are ripped all the way down to the man V. His face is nothing to write home about, but his body is in good shape. I suppose torturing people is a good workout.

"Kitten," he sneers, "you lied to me." I know. "Now I have to punish you for the lie and get the truth."

"I didn't lie," I lie.

"You're right." He grins a devil grin. "The password was good." WHAT?! "But the key's not in your jewelry box."

"It was in my jewelry box," I lie but try to feign innocence.

"It's not anymore."

"What if someone moved it or took it because I'm missing?" I'm pulling at strings here.

"My guy assures me that hasn't happened." Guy? Who the fuck does he have on the inside of my house? What if they're doing shit to the boys too? I feel vomit coming again…swallow it back. He comes to the headboard and unties one of my wrists from the bed but still has my wrist tied to the rope. I can't see what he's doing but my arm is being hoisted in the air. It's secured again and he does the same to my other arm. My body is now pulled in a seated position twisted at the waist because my legs are still attached to the foot rail. He moves to my feet, unties them and brings them over the edge of the bed in front of me. He unbuttons my jeans

47

and rips them and my boy shorts down my legs hard. I don't kick or provoke him. This is already going to be bad.

I can see now my ropes are on pulleys and hooks on the ceiling. Once my bottom half is naked he uses the ropes that are secured on the ceiling to stand me up. I stand as the rope pulls me forward to the center of the room and my arms move out from my shoulders and up above my head. My legs are barely able to keep their balance as I wobble. Once satisfied with my arm position he secures the ropes to a hook on the wall and again on the ground (I think the floor is concrete). He takes rope and ties my ankles individually and spreads my legs shoulder width apart, securing the ropes to other hooks on the floor. I'm now half naked and spread eagle vertically. He hasn't looked in my eyes this entire time. I would have thought he would want to watch my reaction but nothing.

He stands in front of me fisting his hands while looking at the ground. "It's time for your punishment, Kitten." The demon is back in his voice and his eyes, as he trails them up my body to meet my gaze. He reaches behind his back and pulls out a large serrated hunting knife. Bile is travelling up my throat as he slowly stalks toward me. I keep my eyes glued to the blade of the knife as he steps in front of me.

"Don't move," he commands in a low growl. I become a statue. He reaches for the hem of my pale green V-neck sweater and begins slicing up the front slowly and firmly. My breathing is metered as I watch the blade pass between my breasts ending at the neckline. He moves to each wrist performing the same slicing move toward my shoulders. Once my sweater is cut off my body he runs the flat of the knife across my bust. I watch the blade intently.

"Don't move," he commands again, panting harder than I had noticed. He grabs my bra between my breasts and slices it clean in half. Making quick work of the straps with the blade, he divests me of the last of my clothing. I'm now completely naked, spread eagle, and bound. There is no positive, no angle I can work.

He reaches for the buckle of his belt and undoes it slowly watching me every step of the way. He's going to rape me now. I'm trying to prepare for it. He said not to fight so I am doing everything I can to relax...easier thought than done. He walks around me and stands near my side outside of my field of vision. I can't see him, but I can hear his heavy breathing. I hear the sound of his belt being pulled through the loops slowly ending with a jingle of the buckle once it's free. Then all goes silent. I wait for him to make a move toward my body or unzip his pants, but it's silent for a long while.

I feel it before I hear it.

Pain is bursting through my skin like fire. My whole body tenses and lurches forward against my binds tearing the flesh where they hold me. This time I hear the *whoosh* of air before the belt cracks against my ass. The pain is indescribable. He's hitting me as hard as he can and I'm certain my skin is broken. He's hitting me so quickly that I can't recover between strokes. I'm screaming out in pain I'm sure of it, but I don't hear anything. All I hear is *whoosh, crack*. Something wet is sliding down my legs...blood. I have no idea how long this goes on, but my legs start to give out so he cracks my calves and thighs. The pain ravages every inch of my body. I can feel the searing tear of my skin, each slice the belt makes. Eventually it overwhelms me and I pass out.

I wake to my arms being wrenched higher above my head until my feet (untied now) can barely touch the ground. My head hangs to my chest and the back of my body shrieks in pain. He grabs my chin and rips my face up to him. I look hazily into his eyes. I see the demon twinkling in his dark pools of death.

"Tell me where the key is," he growls.

"I. Don't. Know." I pant between each word. He drops my chin and exits the room slamming the door, leaving my broken body in the blackness. I'm asleep again quickly, but immediately awoken by the pain of my wrists supporting my limp weight. I try to find a comfortable way to hang but there is none. This is no longer my punishment...this is my torture. As time ticks by I try to focus on my family, Kel and Taylor again. I try to figure out who the men that have me are. I think about my father, where this key could actually be. I had guessed the password without thinking but it makes sense now. Snuffleupagus was my favorite. I'm racking my brain, but I'm exhausted and passing out more and more. The ripping flesh on my wrists doesn't bother me as much anymore or I don't have the strength to care.

The door opens and the demon comes in wearing a light blue dress shirt rolled up at the sleeves and slate colored slacks. I thought the demon looked evil before, this is beyond evil. He's like death personified, lifeless and haunting. A new blackness awaits me.

Chapter 8

Kellerman

I enter the living room and it's a mêlée of over-communication. Everyone is talking and moving. I can't process anything other than these people are panicked. I'm not panicked...I don't know what I am. Lost, I'm lost. I take a seat in the fanciest red and gold patterned chair I've ever seen, careful not to put too much of my body weight on it for fear it will crumble beneath me. I look at the faces of people I know well and people I know very little and my heart breaks for all of them. They've lost their daughter or sister. The pain on all their faces is tangible.

"Dylan," I hear my name called by a female voice. I look up to see Mary Callaghan offering me a bottle of water.

"Thank you," I say taking the bottle from her. She takes the chair next to me, fitting it perfectly. She doesn't say anything as she studies the crowd as I was before she came over.

"Too much," she whispers. I look at her and see her blue eyes glistening with tears. "I'm tellin' you God, this is too much." She's pleading for reprieve for her family. I agree God, if you exist, this is too fucking much. Probably not the way to phrase it if I'm talking to God but there you go. I reach over and grab Mary's hand. She quickly wraps her tiny fingers around mine and grips them with a strength I didn't think her tiny body possessed. We wait.

The frantic commotion stops as Sully Sr. enters the house. His face is a mask of conviction. He's working.

"Collin, Hugh, you two outside to debrief with Saunders," he orders in a bark. Hugh and Collin move quickly out the front doors. "The rest of you listen up." The room stays silent as Sully Sr. commands. "We haven't found her. We've hit every safe house we know the Mancini family operates and a few that are from other groups. She's not there. I've looked through the footage and agree the perp bears the mark of Mancini, but we aren't findin' any connection there. We may have to pull in other resources like the FBI to get this done. I'm holdin' off on that as long as I can because that shit'll hold us back.

"At this point we've got file after file on any and every known associate of Mancini. We need you all to go through them for us. We're workin' with a small task force to keep this quiet. If they think there's a large-scale hunt goin' on they're more likely to cut their losses. That means I don't have extra bodies here so you guys have to be research right now." We all nod in agreement but no one utters a word. Going through case files is not what this group wants to do, but we'll do it if it can find us Kid.

O'Sullivan stands up and approaches his father carefully. Sully Sr. rings him around the neck in a rough hug before dragging him outside. The noise rises again as people discuss what we should do.

"Tables," I say. Mary looks at me and understands my single word suggestion.

"We've got card tables in the basement. Come help me bring 'em up," she says softly. We both stand and I follow her back into the kitchen and down a full story of stairs into the world's largest basement. "They're just over here." I grab seven tables on my own leaving her one. She tries to argue, but I just move away to climb the stairs. Once back in the mammoth living room I begin setting the tables up. Cal comes over and starts silently helping. Kav and the twins disappear in the kitchen and return with arms full of folding chairs. We all go about setting up our research area as the

52

O'Sullivan boys return with dollies of file boxes. We go about divvying them up and put our heads down to work.

I put my earbuds in and turn up Motörhead, flipping open the first file in front of me. I have no idea what I'm looking for so I read. If something seems connected to Kid, Kansas City, any of the guys, or a safe house I mark it and pass it off to one of the cops that keep checking in with us. I don't talk, I don't stop, I don't eat, I don't sleep, I do nothing but read and mark. I'm nauseas and in pain when I feel a hand on my shoulder. I pop an earbud out and glance over my shoulder to see Sully Sr. standing behind me.

"Come outside a sec," he says quietly. I look around the table to see only the original six of us that flew in from Kansas City are still at it. I have no clue how long we've been going, but as we step outside and the sun is rising I realize it's been a long time. I glance at my watch. She's been gone sixteen hours. I feel puke rising up my throat at the realization that we're eight hours away from the twenty-four hour mark. I stop in the front yard and heave up everything that's in my stomach. I wretch until nothing comes out before standing up and wiping my mouth with an offered tissue from Sully Sr.

"You're doin' the best research of anyone in there," Sully Sr. says as we stand in the driveway staring out at the mobile command center. "I know you're focused but you gotta take care of yourself too. Try and go catch a couple hours of sleep. We're movin' on some leads and won't be back until noon." I don't respond. I'm not sleeping. "Dylan, you gotta listen son. She needs you strong." I turn and meet his gaze. He's in pain but he's fighting to maintain control for the sake of his daughter. I give him a chin lift and turn on my heel back into the house. The other guys are gone from our research table and the rest of the families have taken their spots. We're working in shifts it would seem.

"Come in the kitchen and eat some oatmeal," Maggie orders kindly, grabbing my arm and leading me to the kitchen. "You eat. You sleep. You get back to it," she says as she guides me to the other guys surrounding a breakfast table made for royals. I sit in an empty seat as she slides a bowl in front of me with oatmeal and blueberries. Kav slides me a protein shake silently. He and I are both big and require a pretty large calorie intake. I lift my chin to him in thanks. I silently eat my breakfast and down my shake in ten minutes. Kav and I stand up at the same time. Mary comes in and takes our dishes before we can clean them up ourselves.

"You two follow me. I'll be back for you in a moment boys," Mary says addressing Kav and me first followed by O'Sullivan and Taylor. We follow Mary up the grand staircase at the front of the house. I imagine Kid sliding down the rail when she's here. She's still so much like a happy child, fun and full of life. I shake the thought off as we approach a guest room. "You two are in here. Beds are all made. Fresh towels and toiletries in the en-suite and fresh clothes laid out for you both. Get some sleep boys," she softly instructs as she kisses us both on our cheeks.

Kav walks in first and I shut the door after I enter. The room is regal I'm sure, but I see nothing other than the two beds. I start pulling off my clothes and fold into the sheets without a word to Kav. I'm not mad (okay I'm mad but it's not the time). I don't have shit to say to anyone. I'm falling deeper and deeper into myself. I did the same after Mia and Kathy. Working the crab boats was ideal because it wasn't social hour. I could work and keep to myself easily. I hear the water in the shower kick on and find the old crabber in me quickly falling asleep from pure exhaustion.

Shannon

"I need to go to the bathroom," I whisper my throat dry. He kicks a bucket at me. I try to maneuver my legs to get the bucket under me but it's pointless. My secret weapon of leg strength is gone. I look at the demon with pleading eyes. If he doesn't move the bucket and help

54

my legs I'm just going to piss all over myself and the floor. He looks at me and shakes his head before he releases the ropes holding my arms, my body crashes to the floor under my weight. The pain of my ass and legs hitting the floor jolts through me and I rise onto my knees to stop the contact with the ground. I push the bucket between my thighs and pee. There's blood. I don't know if it's from the damage to my back or if the demon damaged my kidneys in the beating. Either option is concerning. Once I'm done he pulls the bucket from beneath me. I stay on my knees unable to move.

"Time to put you to work," he sneers. I look up at him as he undoes his pants.

Stay calm and breathe Shannon. Steel your mind against everything. Uncle Mick's voice rings in my ears. My pain fades away and my breathing becomes metered and consistent.

The demon pulls his dick out and strokes himself in front of my face tauntingly, a mischievous grin pulling the corner of his mouth.

Don't fight until you know you can win. You bide your time until you can strike the final blow.

I'm stuck here. Wait it out, Kelly.

"Your mouth is so pretty," the demon purrs rubbing a thumb across my bottom lip. I don't look at his face. I look straight forward into nothingness. If I can force myself to have an out of body experience I'm more likely to survive. I push my mind away, my eyes close.

You are the center of your strength. You have the power in your life. Shannon, there isn't a fight you can't win.

My team never loses.

The demon moves toward my face and I can sense his dick loitering near my mouth. I force my mind to leave this body. He can have my body. I can fix my body.

"Open up. If you use your teeth for anything I'll use your face for throwing practice with my knife," he threatens. I open my mouth slightly preparing to be raped...he's gone. The air in the room has changed and I force my mind to kick back into gear. I open my eyes and the demon is standing a few feet away with a knife at his throat. The demon's eyes are trained on me flashing with rage. The man holding the knife to his neck is strangely familiar yet I don't know him. I sit silently and watch the two men.

"What the fuck are you doin'?" the new man seethes. His voice is thick and rough.

"Boss said make her feel this. I was makin' her feel it. What the fuck are you doin' here?" the demon responds flippantly. I hold my gaze on this scene trying to figure out what's going on. The man holding the knife to the demon's throat is staring at me intently. I know those eyes. Deep blue sapphires...I can't remember. He shakes his head no at me with the slightest of movements. He DOES fucking know me. I keep my gaze trained on him but make no attempt to talk or engage him as his simple body language requested.

"Boss? Don't know who you think your fuckin' boss is but he's standin' right here about to slit your throat before I go and sell your wife as a sex slave," the knife wielder growls. I gasp in shock at his threat. He raises a brow at my response.

"He rape you?" he asks pressing the knife deeper into the rapist's throat. I shake my head no. "Was he goin' to?" I stare at him not knowing how to respond. There's fury swarming in his eyes, fury I've seen only in my boy's eyes when they think I've been harmed.

"You walked in on the beginning," I whisper. I feel my stomach roll knowing I'm going to throw up in the near future.

"Why do you give a shit what I do to him if he was gonna rape you?" he asks inquisitively.

"I don't give a shit what you do to him. I give a shit what you do to his wife," I retort. I feel a little bit more like myself now.

"Why?"

"Because I'm in a room gettin' tortured and almost raped for something that has nothin' to do with me. I don't want that for anyone else's life," I state matter-of-factly. I hold the gaze of his eyes and see rage flaring. Maybe I've insulted him and his ways...I don't give a fuck! The drugs must be out of my system because I'm starting to feel a fight boiling within me. He holds my gaze a few breaths longer.

"Good," he says softly before dragging the knife quickly across the demon's throat. He begins to gurgle and falls to the ground lifeless almost immediately. It was a quicker death than he deserved. I watch as his blood pours onto the floor thinking I could have done a better job at making him pay.

"I hear you're pretty good with a blade. Do you not approve of my technique?" the guy asks me bringing my gaze back to him.

"It was fine," I say coolly.

"Fine?"

"Fine."

"Would you've done somethin' different?" he asks amused by our conversation.

"I woulda cut off his dick and fed it to him, then cut his anterior tibial artery and watched him panic and bleed out slowly," I offer calmly. It's the best I can come up with off the top of my head. This man is staring at me in wonder. I'm so confused by him that I decide not to try to figure it out. He's going to kill me or let me be killed. He's just another demon; a demon that just stopped a rapist, but a demon nonetheless.

Chapter 9

Kavanagh

I wait in the room while Kellerman takes a shower. We slept like rocks. It was only a four-hour nap, but I feel like a new man. Kid's been gone over twenty hours at this point. We're coming up on some scary deadlines here. No ransom requested. No threats made. No body parts mailed to us. We will find her. I have to believe that.

The water kicks off and Kellerman comes out wrapped in a towel still wet from the shower. He looks like shit. Dude is cut like no other, but his bruises are gnarly. His lower torso is black and purple. His face is swollen with bruising on his jaw and a decent black eye. The stitching under his left eye makes him look like Frankenstein. Kellerman's a good looking dude (not as good as me obviously), but he looks awful right now. He's fucked up. That shit's on me.

"How ya feelin'?" I ask quietly. I haven't tried to talk to him since we've been here. I don't think he's talked to anyone since we started researching.

"Fine," he answers blankly. He pulls his underwear up under his towel before letting it drop. He sits on his bed with his back to me pulling the clean long sleeved black T-shirt Mary left over his head. Kellerman's a big dude so I'm guessing he's wearing Cal's clothes and I think I'm wearing Finn's. I don't give a flying fuck. I'd put on a dress at this point (maybe not but you get my point).

"Man, I'm fuckin' sorry. I don't know what else to say here," I apologize as best I can.

"Don't worry about it," Kellerman says dismissively as he stands and pulls the new jeans up.

"Kellerman, seriously give me somethin'," I plead. This guy is starting to freak me out. He's a shell of who he normally is. All of the light is gone from him.

"Got nothin' to give, Kav," he replies in a whisper. He shoves all of his shit in his pockets and leaves without so much as a glance at me.

I follow Kellerman downstairs to find the room packed with more people than were here last night. Twice as many it looks like. Mary scoops her arm around Kellerman's waist and pulls him to the kitchen, no doubt to feed him. I follow them quietly.

"You're not havin' any problems are you?" Mary asks Kellerman. "Sully Senior said you were sick earlier and Robert was concerned about your spleen and liver. Be honest with me, Dylan. Do we need to get you into the office and check you out?" She's holding down his chin forcing Kellerman to look her in the face.

"I'm fine, Mary," Kellerman says softly. I can't tell if it's the truth or not. He doesn't look fine. She studies him a breath longer before releasing his chin and pushing him into a seat at the table.

"Eat," she commands her eyes now coming to me. I listen and make my way to the table. "When you finish come out and join us. Love you two." She pats my shoulder as she sets down a giant plate of roasted turkey sandwiches. She knows we can eat. We both smile in thanks and dig in. Kellerman doesn't utter a word the entire time we eat. Finn comes in and starts talking away at us so we both just listen. He didn't find shit at home so he flew in here this morning. He looks as bad as us. He's going to go bald from running his hand through his hair before this is over. Kellerman finishes his food and makes his way out to the living room.

"He's fucked up," Finn acknowledges immediately. I nod but don't say anything.

"Aidan and Ry filled me in. They feel like shit. Bet you do too. We find her, you guys fix that shit. Let it go for now," he instructs. Again I nod because there's nothing to say. Kellerman can hate me for all I care. I only want Kid right now.

Shannon

The man studies my face for a moment and then leaves without at word. He doesn't close the door behind him and that may be the worst torture I've endured yet. I'm no longer bound and my exit is clear, but I can't even stand up. I may be able to drag myself, but I'm guessing he'd catch me before I made much progress. FUCK!

He walks back in the room with a half smile directed at me, reaching down to my hands offering to help me stand up.

"I can't," I admit. I can't stand up. I'm dying on my knees as it is. There's no way I can hold my body weight.

"I'll carry you," he says softly moving around to my back. "It's gonna hurt though."

"It's been hurting," I snort. Does he think I've been at a spa in here?

"He went at you pretty good," he explains bending down. He undoes my wrists completely before hooking an arm behind my knees another behind my shoulders. I won't be able to support myself making this hard on him. I don't know if he'll be able to carry me like this. "Wrap your arms around my neck, Shanny." I do as I'm told. Wait...Shanny?

Before I can process that he scoops me off the floor and I scream in pain. It feels like every wound has just torn open in synchrony. I'm shaking from the pain and start to gag. He quickly carries me out of my torture chamber, into the hall and then directly into a bathroom to the left. It's not too big but it has a soaker tub that's filling with water. He gently places me in the warm bath causing equal amounts of pain and relief.

61

I'm still shaking in pain, my gagging has stopped.

"Take a breath, Shanny. You're all right now," he coos.

"Who are you?" I question studying his face intently now that we're in a fully lit room. His hair is a little long and wavy falling across his forehead, dark chestnut brown. His eyes are a deep sapphire blue. His face is angular and masculine, covered in a well maintained almost black short beard, and fucking familiar. He's about Sully's height and build. He's dressed casually in a long sleeved navy Henley T-shirt and loose jeans. The demon was wearing dress clothes. I can't make sense of this.

"I thought you recognized me earlier," he says with a little hurt in his voice maybe. I feel like I know him, but I sure as shit can't place it. Maybe, if we met on the streets and not in a torture chamber as I was about to be raped just before he committed murder (justifiable homicide), I could place his face.

"I do recognize you. I just don't remember who you are," I admit quietly. My stomach is no longer rolling and the water is soothing my aching body. I close my eyes for a moment.

"You're the prettiest girl I've ever seen that can hit a ball that far out," he says in a soft almost childlike voice and my eyes spring open. I stare at his face long and hard, and then I see it.

"Nicky?" I whisper. A sheepish grin marks his face. "Nicky," I repeat in a whimper trying to figure this out.

"Don't get upset. You're safe now. I've got you," he says softly grabbing my hand and squeezing it tight. I don't understand.

There was a boy in my neighbor's back yard one day. It was in the spring before my father died. My neighbors, Senator and Mrs. Grady, didn't have kids so I was surprised to see him out there. Being the social child that I was, I ran over to him. He was just sitting in the grass looking bored out of his mind.

"Wanna hit a ball with me?" I ask excited to have someone to play with. There are no kids in my neighborhood to play with (the kids that do live around here think I'm weird). He looks up at me and smiles his deep dark blue eyes shimmering in the sun. He's probably a few years older than me, but I don't care.

"Sure," he says in a shrug. He stands up and brushes off his jeans. "You gonna play in that dress?"

"Mother makes me wear dresses every day. I have shorts on under. Come on," I say pulling him by the hand toward my yard. He interlaces our fingers and takes the lead. When we get to my bat, glove, and bag of balls, he smiles at my gear.

"You wanna hit first?" I ask politely pulling my hand away from him.

"Nah, you go ahead." He moves out to the middle of the yard with my glove to shag the balls I'm going to hit. He's not out far enough, but I don't tell him that. I toss a ball high and crack it sending it soaring well beyond him. He watches the ball sail past before turning back to look at me.

"You're the prettiest girl I've ever seen that can hit a ball that far out," he yells back at me with a huge almost proud smile. I beam back at him. I don't care that he thinks I'm pretty. He thinks I can hit the ball far. "What's your name?"

"Shanny," I respond. I don't know why I told him that. Only my daddy calls me Shanny.

"I'm Nick," he yells throwing the ball back toward me. I catch it bare handed ignoring the sting.

"Move back Nicky. I'm just gettin' warmed up," I tease. He shakes his head at me with a broad grin before moving back.

63

"Please explain this to me. I feel like I'm goin' insane," I plead.

"That was the best five hours of my life, playin' with you. I never forgot that day. I can remember every single detail of it," Nicky says softly. His voice is slightly gravelly and deep, not a little boy anymore. "I was there that day with my uncle, Vito Mancini. I barely spent time with him when I was a kid but my mom was sick that day or something so he took me out with him."

"Nicky, this is not helpin' me understand why you're here. Did you do this to me?" Please don't let him be some crazy ass stalker.

"Fuck no! How could you think that?" He goes to drop my hand, but I cling to it. If he didn't do this then he can get me out of here.

"I'm freaked, hurt, tired and confused. Please just tell me what's goin' on."

"It's a long story and we don't have a lot of time before the rest of the team gets back. My name is Nick Scarso. I'm an enforcer in the Mancini Crime Family. My job is to extract information from people quickly."

I pull my hand free from his and turn my gaze to the water. The bathroom door opens quickly snapping my head back into place swiftly and every feature on Nicky's face changes. He looks like the demon only more petrifying. I cower down into the water further.

"Scar," the man (who I can't see because Nicky is blocking my view) at the door calls tentatively. "What happened to Tony?"

Nicky stands up slowly, his hands are shaking at his sides as he turns to face our visitor.

"What happened to Tony is about to happen to you. He got in my fuckin' way. Clean it up!" Nicky's voice is raw and powerful. The authority he exudes is totalitarian. I'm officially fucked. They've sent someone to torture me that knows me. Okay an afternoon of playing with a kid doesn't make him an expert in my life, but he knows me. He's not here to rescue me. He's here to get this done faster.

"Sure boss," the man relents softly. "You need at hand puttin' her under. Tony said she's a handful."

"If I ever need help with a buck ten bitch, fuckin' put a bullet in my head. Get that goddamn mess cleaned up," Nicky growls and the man scurries away.

I ease my gaze back to the water and wait. He's going to use this water to torture me. Apparently he's confident in his ability to hold me under water on his own. Uncle Mick never did water torture training. I'll have to use my skills from other things to make it through this. He did some water escape training with me the last few summers before I moved to Chicago. He sunk a car in the pond out on his land and made me swim down to it, buckle myself in, wait as long as I could and then release myself. Scary right? I can do this. Uncle Mick made sure.

Feel the burn in your lungs? It means you're alive, Shannon. Stay alive and you can do anything. Only death will stop you.

Nicky is standing staring at the empty doorway, continuing to block my view. I can hear a lot of movement outside the bathroom though. Moving a body is loud business it would seem. I take the time to focus my mind, concentrate on my breathing. My pulse is even and I begin to take long deep belly breaths, oxygenating my lungs. I won't have long to do this but every little bit will help. I should have kept up the training Uncle Mick put me through. I've kept constant with weapons and fighting but not other things, certainly not water escape. I can hear his voice in my head so clearly since I've been here. It's like he's with me.

Deep...long...breaths. That's it Shannon. Try four minutes this time.

I did the four minutes, got up to four and a half. No way can I hold my breath that long now. I keep taking deep breaths to the rhythm of Uncle Mick's voice. I'm focused.

"Shanny, look at me," Nicky's command brings me out of my own head. I don't comply. If he's here to torture information from me, I'm not going to be helpful.

"Scar," the same guy from before calls from the doorway. "Boss is on the phone for ya." The guy sounds winded. Carrying dead weight will do that I suppose. I keep breathing long deep breaths.

"Gotta move her," Nicky's voice is strained and rough. I don't look at him. I don't panic.

"I'll watch her for ya. You're not done in here yet, right?" There's a long pause in the conversation and I keep breathing. He's going to leave me with this guy. Nicky strides to the door swiftly.

"Don't fuckin' touch her. I don't want my dick goin' anywhere near where your's been." Nicky's threat is menacing and then he's gone. I'm naked, in a bathtub, alone with yet another demon. I keep breathing, deeper than I was. I feel no pain in my back or head, just air in and out.

"Shame really. I'm easier on pussy than Scar is," the man says with a laugh. Comforting.

I don't look at him or respond. I can feel myself detaching from my body. My mind is steeling itself in a cage within a cage. Survival is the only goal. I don't panic.

Chapter 10

Shannon

"Maybe I'll getcha after Scar," the man taunts. "I've heard he's a bigger fan of ass than pussy, so I'll workout whatever he doesn't."

I no longer have drugs in my system so I feel the familiar Shannon Kelly simmering under the surface. I'm still taking deep breaths and steeling my mind, but fuck if I don't want to drown this motherfucker. If he would just get a little closer...I could get him. Even weak I could take him. He's short and skinny, looks young too. I have only glanced at him from my peripherals...yeah I could take him. He takes a step closer to me and I stop taking deep breaths, focusing completely on his movement. I wait for him to touch me. If I can get his wrist, he's mine. Here the fuckwad comes.

He leans over, stretches his hand out, and dips it into the water. He's headed toward my crotch based on his trajectory. I bend my knees so it appears I'm being more accommodating. I still haven't looked at the guy's face. I'm watching his arms. Then he makes his grave mistake. He removes the hand that was supporting his weight on the edge of the tub to push up the sleeve of the arm snaking toward my body. I lash out reaching both of my arms around the back of his neck shoving him face first into the water between my bent knees. He has no leverage with his legs to heave himself out. I hold down his head and shoulders with my right leg. My left leg is under his body so I lock my ankles together over and under his body and squeeze. This isn't the way I constrict around the boys when I'm playing, this is strength I didn't know I possessed coursing through my muscles.

67

The man is thrashing and kicking trying to get his legs hitched the right way. He's pushing off the bottom and side of the tub with his arms but their slipping and sliding. I've got him. He's not going anywhere. I maintain pressure as bubbles surface and his fight wanes. This is not a scary movie, I don't let go when I think he's dead. I wait and wait and wait, then I check his pulse keeping my legs still around him. No pulse. I killed him. Releasing the pressure I push his lifeless body down to the end of the tub with my feet.

Then I turn my head off to the side, over the edge of the tub and puke. I just killed another human being because he was trying to touch me. I should feel guilty or sad or angry...I'm numb. When I've finished emptying my already empty stomach I lay my head back and wait for whatever is to come next. Whatever blackness awaits me I'll be ready.

Kellerman

I'm functioning. That's all I'm doing at this point. Kid's been gone over twenty-seven hours and we've made no progress in finding her. We haven't run out of files yet, but we're looking through lesser likely options now. I refused to get up and eat dinner with everyone else that's on my "shift" so Mary brought my plate out to my research spot (gifting me with a scowl of disapproval before she left). It's not like this is social hour for any of them either, I just have less to offer than they do.

I have (or maybe had) relationships with Cal, O'Sullivan, Kav, Finn and Aidan. I've been getting to know everyone else a little here and there before this shitstorm landed. I don't have anyone to depend on in my life. I've been on my own since my dad died. My mom took off when I was still in diapers. She came in and out of my life off and on until I was a teenager, haven't heard from her since. It honestly doesn't bug me. She wasn't cut out to be a mom, not her thing. Dad more than made up for her absence. I've got aunts, uncles and cousins dotted around the country but no tight

68

relationships. Being up in Seattle and the Bering Sea, family didn't much concern me. While my dad was still alive he and I were really close and I had a small group of friends (other fisherman), I was good with that.

Everything changed in my life after Kathy and Mia. Before that, I was really social, huge group of friends. I partied a lot and didn't pay much attention to things that mattered. I know I was young (classic excuse), but I was selfish and egocentric. When we lost Kathy and Mia, a switch flipped in me. None of my "friends" came to check on me, not even a phone call. I was at the hospital with my dad for days and he was the only person that cared how I was doing. After living in the same place my whole life, with a shit ton of friends, I was shocked how alone I felt. So I took off. I ran as far away as I could, trying to escape the guilt I felt and trying to become a different man.

I'm not sure I succeeded at becoming a different man. Here I am, closing myself off just like last time. I miss my dad so much right now. He didn't try to make me stay in Kansas City; he got my move at the time. I needed that space to heal. Dad let me have the distance in miles but our connection never faltered, we talked all the time. He got me through the grief and the pain that I felt. If he were here, Dad would help me get through this.

When the guys flipped on me in the pool house it felt familiar. They made no consideration for me and took Taylor's word (and half naked pictures) as fact. It looked bad, shit it was bad, but they should have talked to me. So I'm acting like a spoiled little bitch and pouting about it. I also don't have the energy to put into the necessary conversations; everything is going to Kid right now. That's all I can do.

I feel the pressure of a hand on my shoulder pulling me out of my pity party for one. I look up to see Mr. Kavanagh standing there with a soft look on his face. I pop one earbud out.

"You're still at it?" he asks the unnecessary question. I nod briefly before moving to get back at it. He pulls a chair up next to me stopping my progression toward isolation.

"You're pissed at the guys." It's a statement not a question.

"I'm fine," I respond coolly.

"You're a shit liar, Dylan."

"Mr. Kavanagh I really am fine. I just wanna find Kid."

"We all want that. You're strugglin' with more than that though. Aaron told me," he says softly. Thanks Kav. Now I have to deal with Kid's family knowing about my possible paternity issues. Clusterfuck is the kindest term I can think of to describe my current life circumstances.

"I'm not thinkin' about anything other than Kid right now, sir. I'll deal with everything else once we have her home."

He lifts his chin at me catching that I really don't want to think, much less talk, about this right now.

"You need any help. When the time comes, I'm all ears," he says sympathetically before standing and moving to his spot at our research area. I push my earbud back in (Metallica) and focus on the file in front of me. That was nice of him to say...maybe I'll take him up on that offer.

Kavanagh

My pop just walked away from the zombie that is Dylan Kellerman. He's getting worse if that's even possible. We're all wrecked, emotionally drained, pissed...you name it, we've got it going on. Kellerman has us all beat though, and he won't let anyone near him to try to help him. We're all shut out.

"He talk to anyone yet?" O'Sullivan asks as he claps me on the shoulder and motions toward Kellerman.

"Just said about ten words to Pop."

"Shit's on us, huh?"

"I don't fuckin' know, man. We're all a mess but him...it's different." I shrug and watch Kellerman methodically read, mark and set aside case file after case file. He could have a career in this...if that's a career.

"Think she's okay?" O'Sullivan whispers.

"No," I whisper back. "She's not okay." He sucks in a breath at my brutal honesty.

"I don't get it. Kid wouldn't hurt a fly," he huffs. I quirk an eyebrow at him and we both grin. "Okay. She would hurt, kill and maim but only out of necessity. She doesn't hurt anyone that doesn't have it comin'. She fights for the people that can't. I don't get it."

"This has to be about somethin' from Chicago. It can't be firm related, right?" He nods his agreement. "So then we got two options. It's from when she was a little girl, which seems unlikely, or it's from undergrad." I shoot O'Sullivan a knowing glance.

"Liam and Brendan? Why though, man? After all this time who would do this and have the resources to pull it off?" he questions rapid fire.

"I'm just talkin'. I've got no more answers than you. But I feel less and less confident the answers about who took Kid are in those fuckin' files. I think they may be in our past."

"Let's get the guys together and talk this through. If this is really about that night and what we did...we gotta do somethin' about it," he finishes turning on his heel to find our brothers.

If someone took Kid because of what we did to Liam and Brendan she's already dead (my stomach lurches at the thought). I can't figure out what Mancini would want with that though. If Liam sold drugs for Mancini back then it was small time. Why would he come after her now? Christ nothing makes a damn bit of sense! Every time I feel like I'm finding answers...I end up with more questions. More damn questions and no Kid.

Chapter 11

Shannon

"Shanny?" I hear Nicky's voice in the distance. I peel my eyes open to find him hovering over my body concern bleeding from his eyes.

"I'm cold," I croak. I must have fallen asleep after committing murder. Parasympathetic nervous system must have kicked into overdrive and made me tired (I paid attention in biology). The dead body is still slumped over the end of the tub. I feel nothing when I look at it.

"Let's get you outta here," Nicky says softly. He has a towel draped over his arms like you would for a baby that he easily scoops me into. Now that the adrenaline is gone I feel every movement, every fiber of the towel. The pain causes me to shake more than I already was from the cold.

"I've got you," he soothes into my hair as he carries me back into my torture chamber. I look down the hall quickly to see if I can find an exit, but all I find is the world's longest white hall with no visible exits. Perfect!

Nicky lays me on my side and I immediately roll to my stomach to remove any possibility of my wounds touching the mattress. Nicky moves around the room a bit as I keep my face cradled in my arms face down.

"I'm gonna treat these wounds now, Shanny," Nicky's voice is still soft and smooth. I thought he'd be mad I killed that guy, but he killed one too so maybe he's not attached to these people.

He starts putting something goopy on my legs first working his way up, I tense and yelp.

"Sorry."

How can a man be slitting the throat of a torturous demon one second and a soothing caretaker the next? He works his way up to my ass where the majority of the damage is. I squeal when he gets to the deeper ones.

"SSShhhhh," he soothes as he moves over them. I want to be soothed but all I am is on alert for the next beating or inevitable rape. I do get quiet though. He finishes on my lower back and stands up off the bed. I feel a large sheet-like fabric draped over my back, he smoothes it gently over my wounds.

"You'll be more comfortable now." I hear him sit in the metal chair next to my bed. There's tension in the room so I wait for whatever he's got planned for me.

"What happened in the bathroom?" Nicky's voice is choked with emotion. I turn to look into his face and I see sorrow. Why's he sad? Did I kill his brother or something? That would just be my luck right about now.

"He told me it was a shame you wouldn't let him rape me because he's easier on pussy than you are. Then he remembered you're more into anal than pussy so he figured he'd take whatever you left. He came over to the bathtub and tried to touch me. I touched him instead," I explain clinically.

Nicky runs his hand through his unruly hair just like Finn does. I bet Finn is bald by now from the stress of trying to find me.

"I'm sorry," he says in a whisper.

"About?" I ask curtly.

"Him sayin' that shit to you. Him tryin' to touch you. You havin' to kill him on your own." His tone is disbelieving, like I should know he's sorry for all of that.

"Don't worry about it. I'm sure he won't be the last before this is through." I give him an accusatory glare and then turn my face back to the mattress.

"I wasn't done in the bathroom," Nicky's voice is stronger and sounding more pissed.

"Great. You wanna try your hand with me in there? I feel like my chances are pretty good at this point. One down a few more to go," I snark into the mattress. If I could eat a meal I'd feel better about my threat. I'm sure I've been here more than a day with no food and no water. I should have drunk some of the bath water.

"Shanny, I need you to look at me," Nicky demands. I make no such effort. Fuck him and his band of raping torturing brothers. He lets out a defeated sigh.

"My name is Nick Cooper. I'm an undercover agent with the Domestic Crime Agency. I've been workin' undercover in the Mancini Crime Family since I was twenty-one. I'm here to keep you safe and get you home," he dictates forcefully. Okay that got my attention. I pivot my head and study his face. There's no waver or lie there, just his sad sapphire eyes.

"Are you schizophrenic?" I ask concerned. He barks out a loud laugh before smiling at me.

"No. I'm both the things I told you. The one I just told you is the real me and the first is my cover. You need to know both because while we're here I need to be Scarso. If they suspect anything is goin' on other that what's supposed to be, we'll both be in danger. That's why I acted the way I did earlier. He had to think I was the same old torturing murdering Scar."

"You forgot raping," I accuse harshly. Nicky quickly divests himself of his chair, leaning onto the bed his face inches away from mine.

"I have never in my life touched a woman that didn't want it," he growls.

"What, no doesn't mean no to you? Does it just mean try harder?"

"Jesus Christ you have a mouth. If I was what you seem to think I am what do you think mouthin' off like that would buy you?" Nicky slams his body back down into his chair glowering at me. My mouth can't seem to stop itself. I need to shut up.

"I don't know, Nicky. I'm new to this world of rape and torture. I'd hate to give you a wrong answer. I've learned what that gets me." Okay apparently I can't shut up.

"I'm gonna stop this before it gets outta hand for no reason. I'm NOT a fuckin' rapist. I had to leave you in the tub because I have to maintain my cover if I'm gonna keep us both alive. I'm sorry you had to defend yourself and that won't happen again while you're here. The team has been informed that you are to be left alone at all times and they won't disobey." He rakes his hand through his hair again before finishing his thought.

"I talked to my uncle and he filled me in and didn't all the same. The team here now has ten guys plus me. You and I have taken out two. If bodies keep stacking up we'll have problems so that needs to stop. What he didn't tell me is that there is a lookout team nearby as well as another grab team. He won't tell me because he's paranoid, as he should be, that if someone knows the locations of all the teams they can get you out.

"There's no cell service or internet here only a tapped landline so I can't get word to the DCA. I called into the agency that I was takin' a job but didn't have the location to give them. One of the team met me five miles out and I followed them here with no cell service the whole way. They've locked this shit down makin' it damn near impossible for me to pull you out. The only way out is to find what they want before they can get their hands on it. My uncle told me that there's a safe deposit box in your name that he needs access to with a key and a password. Said you already gave them the password but not the key. Do you know where it is?"

"I don't know where the key is. I didn't know the box even existed until I got here," I say softly. He's telling me the truth. Nicky's not here to hurt me, he's here to rescue me or at least keep me safe.

"We'll figure it out. Let's get you fed so you can rest and I can research," Nicky says picking up a bowl from the floor.

"You won't let anyone else hurt me right?" I need confirmation.

76

"No one will hurt you," he states pinning me with a confident gaze. Relief washes over me.

"I'm sure you're hungry. I've got some broth to feed you." He motions to the bowl and spoons me up a bite. I gingerly push up on my elbows and open my mouth to take a small taste of the warm liquid. Good.

"Thank you," I say softly. He smiles and offers me another bite. I take a little more this time.

"You're good with weapons?" he asks in a curious tone.

"I am," I tell him honestly. I take another bite. Who knew chicken broth could be so satisfying?

"Do you have a favorite?"

"Firearms. I enjoy knifes too. I can do some damage with a bat. I've trained with pipes, tire irons, crowbars...lots of unintentional weapons. I prefer a gun over anything though."

"How'd that happen?"

"My Uncle Mick that raised me after my dad died and my mom took off. He was a Navy SEAL. He put a gun in my hand one day after I hadn't spoken in a month. I hit the target on my first shot and was born again. That .22 brought me back to life," I explain with a fondness in my voice, not for the gun but for Uncle Mick. It wasn't that rifle that brought me back, he did and he's still keeping me alive today.

I finish off the broth and down a bottle of water.

"You doin' all right after what happened in the bathroom?" Nicky eyes me cautiously.

"Another thing Uncle Mick taught me was to control my reactions to things. That guy was gonna hurt me. I hurt him first. I don't feel anything but numb about it. I'm a bit of a heartless robot when it comes to situations like that. You slittin' that guy's throat in front of me didn't faze me either." Making sure I connect firmly with his gaze, he relents after a few moments.

"There are cameras all over this room, Shanny. I turn off the feeds when I'm in here but when I'm not they'll be on at all times and I won't leave the monitors for a second. I'll have eyes on you at all times. Once the team finds out you ended Bruno in the bathtub, I'm guessin' they'll stay away." He flashes me a big smile. "I promise I'll keep you safe," Nicky finishes emphatically.

"I believe you, Nicky," I respond quietly.

"I didn't know they had you. If I'd known they were comin' for you I woulda stopped it." His voice is clear and sincere. I wish he would have known. I nod my head and close my eyes. I'm completely exhausted from the past few hours of absolute crazy.

"I'll be back soon to talk. Get some rest," he coos. I don't respond as I'm shut away in blackness, feeling a little safer.

I see a figure standing over the space where my window used to be. I smile; he's going to save us.

Pop, pop.

I go limp...My chest hurts...I'm sleepy.

The fireworks have stopped and I hear sirens. The fire is getting bigger. I want my Daddy. I'm cold and my arms are moving slowly, but I try one more time on my belt. I push the button and pull on the belt as hard as I can, falling on top of him as it lets me go. I curl around him and say...

"Daddy, please wake up." My voice is small and shaky. I push on his face trying to wake him up. The fire is getting bigger and the smoke is getting darker. He coughs and blood comes out of his mouth. He wraps an arm around me and pulls me into his chest, it's making gurgling sounds.

"Shanny," he rasps. "Tell Uncle Mick we had a nice meal." Daddy's really hurt and not making any sense.

"Daddy, there's a fire. I'm cold." I start to shake from head to toe, hard.

"Tell Uncle Mick, Shanny. I'm so sorry baby. I love you," Daddy says and closes his eyes.

"I love you too, Daddy," I whisper and close my eyes. I'm tired.

I wake up to someone touching me with rough leathery hands.

"Got one!" a voice screams and starts pulling on me, pulling me away from Daddy. I cling to his jacket but his arms aren't holding me anymore.

"Come on sweetheart. I've got you," the voice says.

"No! I want my Daddy!" I cry and hold on tighter. I'm shaking harder now and I can't keep my eyes open.

"I'll get your Daddy next. Let's get you outta here." He pulls my hands away from Daddy's jacket and lifts me out of the car. I look back down at him. Daddy's sleeping.

I wake up screaming, a bloodcurdling scream, sweating and shivering at the same time. No. That can't be. I haven't been able to remember that conversation for over twenty-two years. It was so real I can still smell the burning oil, feel the smoke choking my lungs...I'm going to throw up. I scramble off the bed and empty my stomach on the floor. Well I try to empty my stomach, but I just wretch and dry heave. The door flies open and Nicky rushes in toward me. I'm naked on all fours on the floor.

I fly back onto my ass, scurrying toward the wall at my back curling my legs in front of me to shield myself. My whole backside is shrieking with pain as I collide with the wall, maintaining eye contact with Nicky the whole time.

"Shanny, calm down," he commands softly approaching me with caution. I'm shaking hard and feel my stomach turning again. "Let me help you get back in bed."

I don't respond I just sit in this spot quivering and running through the dream over and over. An arm reaches under my knees and behind my back as I'm lifted into the bed. I stay in a ball on my side convulsing violently, my mind in a haze. A heavy blanket covers me and I feel the bed dip. Nicky sits behind me in silence until my quaking stops and my breathing slows.

"It was just a dream. You're okay," Nicky soothes from behind me. Oh no I'm fucking not!

"I'm so far from okay I don't even know what that means," I whisper harshly. "It wasn't a dream. It was a fuckin' memory I haven't been able to have in twenty-two years."

"What kind of memory?"

"The day I died."

Chapter 12

Kellerman

Sully Sr. called the FBI this morning. Kid's been gone forty-eight hours now and we've been pushed from the case. No more files to go through or hiding behind the monotony of reading them. We've all been interviewed and re-interviewed and then again by different agents. They've decided not to announce her disappearance to the media yet fearing it could further endanger her life. The guys batted around the idea that this has something to do with Liam but once they talked it through they squashed that idea. We're back to square one at this point and I'm losing hope. I won't survive this. I can't survive without her.

"Dylan, come eat some dinner," Maggie calls softly. I've been sitting in the Callaghan's sunroom since the FBI got here.

"I'm not hungry," I respond without looking at her.

"You haven't eaten today. My daughter needs you strong and healthy so get your ass up and come eat!" she yells. I turn and look at her. She's mad, not mad at me, but I'm a convenient outlet.

"I'm not hungry, Maggie. Thanks for the offer though." She moves toward me and grabs my chin roughly.

"You do NOT get to give up. She's fightin' out there somewhere and you'll fight here for her. Get in that kitchen and eat some food or I'll..." She stops and a sob breaks from her throat. I wrap my arms around her, pulling her next to me on the floral sofa. I hold her in my arms as sobs wrack her body with violent force. We sit like that a long time until she calms down a bit, still shuddering and sucking breaths. She clutches onto my shirt still, clinging to me like I'm a life preserver saving her from the waves of sorrows trying to drag her down.

"Don't give up, Dylan. Please don't," she whimpers into my chest.

"I'll never give up. Not until I know there's nothing left to fight for. I promise you that," I murmur into her dark hair. Maggie tips her head up pulling off her glasses to wipe her tears away. I offer her a slight smile before loosening my grip from around her shoulders.

"Thank you. I needed that. Sorry I yelled at you, that...I...well..." she stutters.

"Don't worry about it." I meet her gaze to let her know that I'm fine. She can scream and cry at me as much as she wants. I don't mind seeing the release. I wish I could find my own actually. She lays her head on my chest again and we sit in silence as the sun sets on another day without the love of my life in my arms...instead I hold her mother as she silently weeps for her missing daughter.

Maggie eventually cries herself to sleep as I cradle her. O'Sullivan comes into the sunroom and carries his broken mother outside so Collin can drive her home. When O'Sullivan comes back in the house; him, the whole Callaghan trio and Kav cautiously enter the sunroom. They silently fill the floral seats around me but none of us tries to talk, we just sit.

My phone starts to vibrate in my pocket. I pull it out to see Cassie calling. I don't really want an audience for this conversation, yet I don't want to be alone (I'm a pussy).

"Hello?" I answer briskly.

"Dylan?"

"Hey Cassie," I reply softly.

"Dylan, I've been meanin' to call you. We need to talk about something important. You think you could fly home this weekend?" Is she fucking kidding?

"Look Cassie, I'm dealing with some crazy shit right now. I know you're pregnant. Is it mine?" She's sobbing now. FUCK!

"D-Dy-Dylan, I'm-I'm just...God," she snuffs into the phone. Okay that was not my finest moment. It's not her fault I'm in this hell right now. I need to keep it together.

"Don't cry. Everything will be fine, promise," I soothe into the phone. I glance around to see the guys all eyeing me curiously.

"I'm sorry," she chokes into the phone trying to calm herself. "This is just a lot." I wait to respond until her sobs quiet.

"I know. Can you answer my question now? You calmed down enough?"

"I don't know, Dylan?" she whispers.

"Don't know what? Don't know if you're calmed down enough or don't know if it's mine?" An important distinction I think. She's blubbering again. Girls cry and men freak. We'll do anything to make that sound stop. But I can't do anything to make her stop and worse, I don't care that she's crying (I'm officially an asshole of the highest order). All I can think of is Kid being tortured and never letting a tear slide down her buttermilk skin. She wouldn't.

"I don't know if you're the father," she stutters out between sobs.

"Okay, Cass. I know this is gonna sound harsh but hear me out. I'm not gonna be around until you find out. My girlfriend is at the top of my priority list right now and she'll stay there until I have a child to replace her position," I say as kindly as I can.

"Yeah, that was harsh. Well, if we find out the baby's yours will you come home?" she asks with a small amount of glee at the thought.

"Let's cross that bridge when we get there, Cassie," I respond. No fucking way is that happening. I'm not leaving Kid. I'll make it work somehow. "How long 'til you can find out?" I have no clue about this shit.

83

"I would have to have an amniocentesis or another thing called a CVS, if we wanted to find out while I'm pregnant. They're both dangerous for the baby so I don't wanna do them. I guess we have to wait until I have the baby," she explains clinically.

"I don't wanna have to wait until the baby's born to find out," I say a little short.

"Well I don't wanna lose the baby. I wanna keep it. I'm pretty sure it's yours anyway. I think you should come home and we can talk about it," she says with no emotion. Where are the tears from a few minutes ago?

"Not happenin', Cass. I'm in the middle of some shit right now." I'm getting shorter with each response.

"Shit more important than your child?" she scoffs. Wow, and so the manipulation begins. I knew she'd get here. It's her thing. Sweet and soft with you until you're lulled into a sense of safety then, bam, she hits you with the manipulative crazy shit. This is why we're not together. This is why I should have stayed the fuck away from her. Maybe Kid could get me custody if the baby's mine? That thought turns my stomach. What if Kid isn't around to help...no I can't go there. I need to get off the phone and figure out a way to find Kid regardless of the FBI being involved.

"If I knew it was my child we could have this conversation. We don't, so we're not. I need to get off here. Cassie, please do right by this baby. No matter if it's mine or not, do right by this baby," I implore.

"Dylan, what's goin' on? You're freakin' me out a little," she sounds human again.

"I'm just busy. I really need to go. Remember what I said," I remind her gently. "Bye Cass." I hang up before she can respond.

The eyes in the sunroom are still on me.

"Say what you gotta say guys," I instruct. Let's get this over with.

"Doesn't know if it's yours?" Kav's first out of the blocks.

84

"No."

"She keepin' it?" O'Sullivan's next.

"Yes."

"She pushin' you to go back to Seattle?" Cal chimes in.

"Yes."

"Convinced it's yours?" Finn joins the chorus.

"Yes."

"Refusin' to do the amnio and CVS?" Aidan's last to join twenty questions.

"Yes."

"Trap!" the five of them yell in unison. We all chuckle at that. First time I've laughed in days. It hurts.

"Seriously, when we get Kid back, she'll figure it out. It's her thing," O'Sullivan suggests.

"Don't really wanna drop this at her feet after what she's been through," I say softly. I can't imagine her wanting to deal with my shit, much less help, after whatever horror she's enduring.

"You don't, she'll kick your fuckin' ass," Kav warns. I smirk at that, knowing he's right. If I don't let her help me she'll definitely kick my ass.

"Let's get her first, then we'll figure out my train wreck of a life," I insist. They all nod in agreement and we go back to silence.

"I can't fuckin' sit here anymore. I'm goin' nuts!" Cal huffs standing up. "Tell me there's somethin' we can do." Cal looks around the room at each of us, willing us to fix this somehow.

"O'Sullivan," Finn perks up with an idea, "your third, ten times removed, cousin you called to deal with Liam and his friend." O'Sullivan nods confusedly. "He still less than on the up and up?"

"I don't know. He's not really around the tree at Christmas, ya know. But I'm sure he's not curin' cancer or anything," he snorts.

85

"Call him. See if he knows anything. See if he can find anything out," Finn rattles off excitedly. I can feel my pulse picking up strength at the idea. O'Sullivan studies our faces for a second and then pulls his phone out.

"My pop'll fuckin' kill me for this," he says as he puts the phone to his ear. We all wait with bated breath.

"Kieran?" he pauses for a long moment. "Hey it's Brian...Yeah man I know. It's been a long time...Not so good cousin. You remember that mess you helped with a while back?" O'Sullivan waits and listens to whatever his cousin is saying for a few breaths.

"Right, well you remember Shannon? Someone in Mancini's family grabbed her over two days ago. We got nothin'. My pop's got nothin'. And now the FBI is in on it and we're all sittin' here with our thumbs up our asses. Need your help again, man."

I'm sitting on the very edge of the sofa pleading for this person I don't know to help us. My adrenaline is pumping, my heart is pounding, and I feel a little flicker of hope beginning to spark within me.

"Yeah I know the place. Give us a half hour," he pauses again before standing up. "No fuckin' cops. I'll leave my brothers here...Later."

We all jump to our feet to go wherever and meet the criminal cousin. The six of us file out of the sunroom trying to look nonchalant. I'm doubtful it works but everyone is distracted so we're good. Kav lifts his chin at Ryan and Adam who fall in step with us as we head out the front doors. Taylor's nowhere to be seen and I'm thankful. I've avoided that prick like the plague since we've been here. I don't want him with us for this. He used to be a cop so I'm sure he wouldn't be welcome where we're going anyway.

"Where are you all headed?" Dr. Callaghan asks eyeing our group. Mr. Kavanagh and he are headed in the house as we're headed out. They were probably getting an update from the mobile command center that's still in the driveway.

"Gotta get the hell outta here for a bit, Dad. We're goin' nuts waitin'," Aidan lies. His father nods but Mr. Kavanagh continues to eye the group.

"What're your plans?" Mr. Kavanagh asks his sons.

"Gym," the three say in unison. Good lie. Mr. Kavanagh gives us a chin lift before tossing his keys to Kav.

"Thanks Pop." With that the watchful fathers move in the house.

"Where to?" Kav asks O'Sullivan as we make our way toward the cars.

"Brannon's in Canaryville," he responds and we split off. Kav, O'Sullivan, Cal and I hop in Kav's dad's Mercedes S-Class while Aidan, Finn, Adam and Ryan climb in Aidan's G-Wagon. We set a blistering pace headed down the I-94, riding in silence, each of us willing the car to move that much faster, hopefully toward Kid.

Chapter 13

Shannon

"With your father?" Nicky questions softly.

"Yeah. Haven't been able to remember my last conversation with him. I guess bein' left in a room by myself for hours on end my mind finally cut it loose," I say in a huff. Not the way I wanted to remember. "I need to go to the bathroom."

"I'll carry you," Nicky says standing up from the side of the bed. I don't want to be carried, but after my fit on the floor a few minutes ago I know I can't walk to the bathroom. He scoops me up like I weigh nothing keeping me wrapped in the warmth of the comforter striding out of the room and into the bathroom where I killed a man. I still feel nothing.

"Can I put you down? You think you can get yourself on the toilet on your own?" Nicky asks looking deeply into my eyes. I nod and he gently lowers my feet to the floor holding my torso to his chest. I get my footing and take a ginger step toward the toilet and find I can walk fairly well. He lets me go and I take the three further steps to the toilet on my own. I turn and Nicky is still in the bathroom watching me.

"You gonna watch?" I ask annoyed.

"No, I'll turn around." He won't even leave me in the bathroom alone. I may be a little annoyed, but I'm also a little happy he's watching me so closely.

"Any time now." I raise my brow at him. He smirks and spins. I drop the comforter and suck in a sharp breath between my teeth when my battered ass and thighs hit the seat.

"You all right?" Nicky questions making a move to turn.

"I'm fine. Just stings a bit." He stays with his back to me until he hears the flush of the toilet. I'm just tucking the comforter around me when he scoops me back up and carries me back to my torture chamber.

Once back in the room he eases me down onto the bed and sits next to me as I curl up on my side. I'm so tired. Who knew taking a piss could be this exhausting. I let my eyes drift shut for just a moment.

"Shanny, we really need that key. We're runnin' up on some deadlines here," Nicky says eagerly raking his hand through his chestnut hair.

"Nicky, I don't know where it is," I breathe out exasperated.

"If I don't do somethin' to you soon or get the information shit's gonna look more suspicious than it already does," he says pointedly. That gets my attention. I shakily push up onto my elbow staring into his deep blue pools.

"What does that mean, Nicky?" I ask sweetly and cautiously. He rakes his hand through his hair a few more times.

"I've got a reputation for bein' brutal and quick. You've been here for more than two days and I haven't done shit to you. This room is wired with cameras so the whole team knows you're just layin' in here. I turn off the feed when I'm in here but they can tell I'm not doin' shit when I'm in here."

"I don't know what to do. I don't know where it is. I've been thinkin' about it a lot and I can't figure it out. What do we do?"

"We're gonna make my team believe that I'm rapin' you right now," he says in a rasp. My eyes bug out and I push further away from him. "I'm not gonna rape you. But you're gonna scream and I'm gonna let you get a few good hits in on me. It'll buy us a good twelve hours. When we're done I'll give the team a bogus key location

90

to send them out lookin'. While they're gone you and I'll try to figure out where it really is."

"I have not a fuckin' clue where it is, Nicky. What if we can't figure it out? What happens when they come back without it?"

"We'll figure it out," he says demonstratively. "We need to get to this because I've been in here a long time." I hesitate for a moment and then nod in agreement to his plan. "Can you sit up?" I slowly but surely push my beaten body to a seated position. He reaches behind his head and pulls his T-shirt over his head. Dude's ripped. He's not Kel but his body is well maintained.

"Make it believable," he says with a smirk. I take a few moments to get my head around this situation. He's not going to hurt me. He's helping me. He killed the rapist for me. He's taken care of me. I now get to kick his ass. I lunge forward and connect my fist with his jaw snapping his head to the side. When his gaze snaps back to mine I can see the shock (I hit like a dude). I offer him a smirk and then start screaming at the top of my lungs. I hit him a few more times and claw his chest until I feel flesh beneath my fingernails. I become so entrenched in what I'm doing that I'm shocked when he grabs my wrists and throws me down on the bed pinning me beneath him. I'm panting and dazed. I look up into his eyes and see worry.

"Are you okay?" he asks almost panicked in tone.

"Yeah," I say on a short breath.

"You went somewhere else just then. You were screaming Liam." FUCK! That's not good for business.

"Sorry. It must have brought back some other memories." I try to sound unaffected but I'm freaked. He watches me for a moment and then releases his grip on me to stand up. I get a good look at him and I've done a number on him. His nose and lip are bleeding and his chest looks like a lion got a hold of him and used him like a scratch tower. I'm also completely naked again. I grab the comforter and raise it in front of me.

"I'm gonna have to take that. I wouldn't rape a woman and then give her a blanket," he informs me apologetically. I tentatively hand him the blanket and bring my knees up to cover myself from view as best I can. He swipes his hand over his face and chest a few times and then rubs his blood in the middle of the mattress. I quirk an eyebrow at him.

"Try to keep that spot between your legs when you lay down." I feel the blood drain from my face as I realize what he's asking of me and why. I nod, just barely. He studies my face for a moment longer then turns on his heel leaving me in the blackness. I lay down on my stomach feeling the wet spot of the blood between my legs. I close my eyes, willing myself to fall asleep knowing this could have been a lot worse. Maybe I'm not going to die after all.

Chapter 4

Kavanagh

We make illegally good time and pull up at Brannon's thirty minutes after we set off. None of us talked on the drive, too much nervous energy. I did rock some Five Finger Death Punch during the ride...mood music.

"Let's do this," O'Sullivan says and we file out of the car meeting the rest of the guys on the sidewalk. Brannon's is a hole in the wall and frequented by a rough crowd most nights. I push through the heavy beaten wooden door and scan the room. It's pretty packed for a Monday night, not overly full though. O'Sullivan spots his cousin at a table near the back of the bar. Kieran Delaney has led a rough life and it shows on his face and body. There are multiple scars on his face from fighting that are accentuated by premature wrinkling from a cigarette a minute habit. His frame wouldn't give it away but he's made a name for himself bare-knuckle fighting since he was fifteen. He looks more than ten years older than us when he's only actually three.

"Quite a crowd ya brought with ya Bry," Kieran says to O'Sullivan in his gruff whiskey and tar voice.

"Needed to get some air," O'Sullivan says taking a seat across from his cousin. The rest of us take seats around two tables on either side of them and wait. We sit in silence waiting for Kieran to give us some glowing piece of information that will lead us to Kid.

"Shannon still look as good as she did ten years ago?" Kieran asks throwing back two fingers of whiskey. Kellerman tenses across the table from me but keeps his shit together (barely).

93

"Better," O'Sullivan states plainly (he's not lying). "Tell us you got somethin'."

"Made some calls. This shit's buttoned up tight. Not Mancini's usual."

"We've figured that out the last two days, not findin' shit that'll help us," O'Sullivan huffs.

"His nephew, Nick...been gone a few days. Guy's always around, nasty motherfucker. Somethin' of an enforcer for the family." Kieran's face has grown dark and serious. This can't be a good sign. "His reputation...she's not good if he's got her. You'll be lucky to find her whole much less alive." The table is shaking and I cut my eyes to Kellerman to make him stop only to realize it's my hands that are quaking. I pull them off the table and scrub them over my face vigorously.

"Do you know where he'd have her?" O'Sullivan growls.

"There's an old warehouse up on Ashland that Mancini runs shit from, but it's not where he'd have her. Got a guy checkin' some places outside Chicago for me. You know why they took her?" Kieran questions, signaling the waitress for another drink.

"No," O'Sullivan moans.

"How'd they get her?"

"Took her from our house."

"From your house?" Kieran scoffs. "How the fuck that happen?"

"Quick grab while we were busy," O'Sullivan says under his breath glancing at Kellerman who's staring at the table like it's the map to Kid.

"Grabbed her while you were fuckin' your boy up?" Kieran asks studying Kellerman's stitches and bruises. O'Sullivan nods.

"Convenient." Kieran turns toward Kellerman and I see the mask of a fighter slip over his features.

"You distract 'em so they could grab my cousin's girl?" Kieran snarls. Slowly Kellerman lifts his head and turns his gaze to meet Kieran. Kellerman's eyes are boiling with fury.

"No," he growls in the lowest timber I've ever heard, "she's *mine*."

"Yours?" Kieran laughs. "Last I knew Shannon she didn't belong to anybody." I look around our group and see all my friends and brothers tensing wanting to defend Kellerman. He's our family now; we have each other's backs.

"Kellerman's her boyfriend. Didn't have shit to do with this," O'Sullivan explains hotly.

Turning his gaze back to his cousin Kieran continues to question, "How'd you all end up kickin' his ass while she's gettin' grabbed? Shit like that doesn't just happen, cousin."

"Her bodyguard wrongly informed us Kellerman cheated on her. We offered retribution."

"Okay and where was the fuckin' world's shittiest *bodyguard* when she got grabbed?" Kieran's getting pissed and his hands are pumping. He hasn't seen Kid in a decade yet she still has an effect on him. That's how she works. She touches you once and it marks you for a lifetime.

"Bathroom," Kellerman mocks. Kieran's gaze snaps to him and a knowing exchange occurs that I hadn't put together yet. Taylor.

"*Bodyguard* played you dumb motherfuckers. String his ass up...you'll find her." Kieran pauses and watches all of our faces cloud, except Aidan and Kellerman's. They always suspected Taylor. "Bring him to me. I'll get it outta him...free of charge."

O'Sullivan shakes his head.

"It's not Taylor. He's in love with her," O'Sullivan winces glancing at Kellerman. "Sorry, man. It's true though. He made a play for her right before she got grabbed."

"For a lawyer you got shit for brains," Kieran says harshly. "Kidnappin' a woman from her house that can

95

shoot the tits off an ant while kickin' the shit outta ten men at the same time, has a bodyguard, lives with you three, is connected to some powerful families in Chicago, and is datin' this motherfucker," he jerks his thumb in Kellerman's direction, "that's ready to rip my fuckin' head off for askin' if she still looks good...that takes inside information. That shit doesn't just happen."

O'Sullivan snaps his head over to Finn. "He get one over on you?" he asks coldly.

"Taylor passed all the checks guys. You know I wouldn't let anyone near her that didn't. There was nothin' on him, not even a question," Finn fumes at the accusation of wrongdoing.

"Then he's connected. Played you," Kieran says pointedly throwing back another two fingers of whiskey. "What's his name? I'll find out for sure, but I'd bet my left nut he served her up on a fuckin' platter for Nick Scarso to carve up like a Thanksgiving turkey."

"Shut the fuck up with that shit," O'Sullivan threatens. A fight between these two would be epic but we don't have time for that. They stare each other down for a few moments before Kieran lifts his head at O'Sullivan signaling a truce.

"Andrew Taylor. Used to be a cop," Finn informs Kieran. "How long to find out?"

"It'll probably be tomorrow at this point. I still say bring him here and I'll go to work on him, but if you wanna know for sure it'll take a little time. Go home and I'll call when I know," Kieran says with distaste in his mouth. He's a man of action...I like that.

"You put me in a house with Taylor, I'm gonna end up in prison," Kellerman seethes.

Kieran watches as Kellerman pumps his fists and clenches his jaw just at the thought of being in the same house as Taylor. "You can stay with me," Kieran offers, shocking the group.

"Thanks," Kellerman agrees without thought. I don't want to leave Kellerman with Kieran, but I really don't want Kellerman to murder Taylor and the look on his face tells me that's the likely outcome. The rest of us stand and offer Kellerman and Kieran fist bumps as we turn to leave.

"You good?" I ask Kellerman before I'm the last to leave.

"Fuck no," he replies angrily. I nod in understanding. He wanted Taylor gone weeks ago and now maybe because we allowed him to stay, Kid's gone. If Taylor was behind this he's a walking dead man...it'll be a race to see who wins the spot of executioner.

"Call if you need somethin'," I say evenly. I leave after he offers me a chin lift.

We all climb in the cars and head back to the Callaghans'. This ride won't be silent. We need a plan.

Kellerman

"How long've ya known?" Kieran asks me finishing a text then shoving his phone in his pocket after Kav leaves.

"Since the moment she was gone," I say gruffly. "Haven't said shit because I needed to find her and Taylor's been workin' his ass off to help. Shoulda trusted my gut."

"Always, man." He pauses for a long while studying his empty glass. "I saw Shannon the day after I cleaned up that mess. Came over to check on my cousin...nah that's a fuckin' lie, I wanted to see her." He lifts his gaze to mine showing he means no disrespect. I give him a flick of two fingers letting him know I'm good with his storytelling.

"Bry was always like a little brother to me. We weren't around each other a lot...family differences, but I was protective of him. When he called me that night, I'd never heard the dude so furious. I could hear the phone shakin' in his hand. The mess wasn't his issue, it was the girl. Never fuckin' thought he'd be that fucked up over a chick. So I wanted to see.

97

"I came over the next afternoon sometime. When Brian answered the door he looked sick. He didn't say anything to me just walked to a bedroom. I followed behind him thinkin' he wanted privacy. Walked in the room and there she was, Kavanagh wrapped around her back and Callaghan wrapped around her legs. I could see Brian had been in front of her and was anxious to get back." He stops telling his story to signal for another drink. I could use a fucking drink, but I won't do that right now. Kieran gets his whiskey and quickly throws it down his throat not reacting to the burn. He puts the glass back on the table and studies it hard for a few minutes.

"I've been a fighter as long as I can remember. Brian's been a fighter as long as I can remember too. We've both kicked the shit outta a lot of people, never fazed me. I can walk away from a fight and never look back at the man I've beaten bloody or worse. But when I saw her face swollen and disfigured, her fingers and knuckles scabbed from fightin', her body bruised and broken...that shit fazed me. There she was surrounded by these giant ass kickin' dudes sleepin' peacefully givin' them as much comfort as they were givin' her. Shit rocked my blackened soul to the core.

"I just stood there for a few minutes starin' at Shannon before Brian crawled back in bed with her. His body had been tense and agitated, but he slid in bed with her and she reached for him in her sleep. She fuckin' reached out and pulled him into her chest like he was a child. Never seen anything like it, man. All his tension faded away in an instant. I watched the four of 'em from a chair in the room for an hour maybe. I doubt they knew I was there, they were all asleep. After about a half hour she whimpered and those three constricted so tight around her I thought she'd break, but she just settled." Kieran looks up from his glass and I see it. Kid does this to people. She makes people feel shit they didn't know was possible. Her touch lingers for a lifetime.

"About a month later I met her for real, came to dinner at their place. I'm an ugly scary lookin' motherfucker to most and after what those fuckers did to her I was sure she'd be afraid of me. I was good with that. But she wasn't afraid of me. She was still fucked up from that shit. You could see a blackness behind her eyes but fuck if she wasn't the sweetest funniest damn person I ever shared a meal with. She wrapped her arms so tight around my neck when I was leavin' that night I didn't know where she found the strength in that skinny body. I saw her off and on while they were in school and she got brighter every time. I'm still a nasty scary motherfucker, but Shannon put a little light in me."

I never thought I could love Kid more than I already do but listening to this man, that's clearly not a pillar of society, be so affected by her...I love her just a little bit more. I feel the ghost of a smile drift across my face before Kieran finishes.

"I'll find her. I'll find her any way I can and when I find out who did this, bodies will drop. She's had enough in this fuckin' life and doesn't need whatever's happenin' to her. You need to prepare though. If Nick Scarso has her...we may not be bringin' her home. I'm not sayin' that shit to be a dick because it fuckin' wrecks me to even think it, but it's the truth. We don't get to bring her home...you're welcome to accompany me on the bloodiest revenge tour since *Rambo*."

Ghost smile is gone and my stomach is back to doing flip flops like there's a Romanian gymnast in there. Fuck this is bad.

"Thanks for tellin' me that story, Kieran. I won't turn into a chick on you, but I love Kid like I can't fuckin' explain. We don't find her...I won't be around to join your tour," I say matter-of-factly.

"I get you. I'm not sure how any of us are gonna get through that..." he trails off as his phone vibrates. He pulls it out and reads a text. His scarred up haggard face breaks into a full blown smile. "That was fast. *Bodyguard* isn't what he pretends to be." Kieran flips his phone around and there's a picture of a teenage Taylor standing next to an older man that looks very similar to him.

"Who's that?" I lean in to get a better look.

"That," he points at Taylor, "is the *bodyguard*. And that," he points to the older man, "is Vito Mancini. Bodyguard's birth name's Anthony Tarantino, Mancini's third cousin or some shit. Always trust your gut...Dude I don't even know your fuckin' name."

"Dylan. Dylan Kellerman." I'm in a haze so foggy I'm surprised I can even remember my name much less produce the words to speak it. "What do we do now? Go pull him outta the Callaghans' house by his nuts?" I'm raging.

"We're gonna have to be a little more under the radar than that. Cops and feds are all over the Callaghan's. I'm not exactly on the list of preferred visitors where law enforcement is concerned." Kieran laughs. "If we call Brian, bodyguard'll be dead before we get anything from him. Let me make some calls and see what I can come up with. You good on your own a few minutes? Not gonna go buy a hatchet and roll up to Highland Park?"

"I'm good. Just fuckin' help me find her," I plead in a grumble.

"We'll find her," he says emphatically...I actually believe him.

Chapter 15

Shannon

I wake to the door opening in the room. Not knowing who's entering, I lay perfectly still until a warm comforter falls onto my body. I turn my head to see a bruised and bloodied Nicky grinning and I feel myself grin back. He reaches over me and turns the bedside lamp on before sitting in the chair next to my bed.

"Convincing performance, Shanny. I sent the team on a wild goose chase that should give us a good six hours alone. I brought you some soup. You eat and we'll start talkin'," he says sweetly. I sit up on the bed wincing a little in pain but pushing through. I keep myself wrapped in the comforter as Nicky puts a tray in front of me with a bowl of chicken noodle soup, bread and Gatorade.

"Thanks for the food," I say softly.

"I'm sorry I haven't been able to feed you more. If I don't keep up appearances shit gets bad for both of us. That show you put on went a long way to keep our secret safe."

I nod and go about eating the soup. It warms me to my bones while the bread fills my stomach to the brim. I try not to chug the Gatorade, but I'm not all that successful. When I'm done Nicky starts.

"Who's Liam?"

"A ghost," I reply quickly and unaffectedly.

"Try again," he growls.

"Not really somethin' I feel like talkin' about, Nicky. Let's move on to business."

"I'd like to talk about Liam." I don't respond. I sit silently and wait for him to get the picture that I'm not discussing Liam. After about five minutes (I'm guessing) I lie down in the bed and close my eyes. No point sitting anymore.

Nicky crawls in bed behind me scooping me into his chest gently. I instantly relax into his arms. I need some comfort after everything. I feel safe here.

"Shanny," Nicky says softly.

"Hmmm?"

"Who's Liam?"

"The second to last guy that tried to rape me," I whisper. Nicky's body goes rigid and his arms constrict around me almost painfully.

"Tried?" he growls.

"I put up a pretty good fight and was found before he could finish the job."

He doesn't say anything else and neither do I. I just stay wrapped in his arms hoping he doesn't make me talk about Liam anymore. I don't want to think about him while I'm here. This is enough of a nightmare on its own. But goddamn if I don't feel safe in this Nicky's arms. I hear Uncle Mick's voice.

Always trust your gut, Shannon. Your instincts never lead you astray.

My gut tells me, Nicky will keep me safe...with or without the key.

Kavanagh

After a between car conference call, two stops at gas stations, and two hours passing we're finally pulling into the Callaghan's driveway. It looks no different to when we left, but shit has changed. I'm still reeling from the conversation (verbal smack down) with Kieran. We've worked out a strategy to make sure none of us goes off half cocked. I hope it works.

102

The seven of us walk in the house to be greeted by Mary. She looks like shit. Her face is drawn and lifeless sporting blue eyes with huge dark circles beneath them. Her blond hair is piled on her head in a crazy mound of mess. She's wearing sweats. I've never seen her in anything other than a perfectly put together outfit. I wrap my arms around her and give her a firm squeeze causing her to squeak.

"You boys hungry?" she asks softly as I disentangle myself from her.

"Aren't we always?" I say with a smirk, hardest smirk to put on my face.

"Where's Dylan?" she asks in a menacing tone. She probably thinks we killed him and dumped the body.

"He's at our place, Mary," Adam interjects with our agreed upon lie. "Needed some alone time." Her face drops into a sad scowl.

"He's still mad at you boys, isn't he?" she shoots an accusing look at Cal and Aidan. It's a good excuse that we didn't think of. I'll roll with it.

"We're not his favorite people right now. We fucked up," I say regretfully.

"Watch your mouth," she scolds smacking my arm (I think she smacked me, barely felt anything). I don't think she really means it. We cuss like truckers all the time. Kid's worse than us.

"Sorry."

She glares at all of us a moment longer. "Come get some dinner. Taylor, Collin and Hugh already ate." I feel relief that I won't have to eat at the same table as Taylor. Why I didn't make the Taylor connection earlier I don't know. He protected her so fiercely for weeks on end, I never thought he'd hurt her. Fuck her? Yeah that was definitely in his plans, but to hurt her...I never considered it. Now we have to act like we don't suspect him until we have proof. After that all bets are off.

103

Kellerman

My palms are sweating, my heart is pounding, blood is whooshing past my ears blocking out all the noise in this bar, and my mind is racing. Taylor did this. Taylor fucking did this! I'll kill him. I'm going to beat him to death or choke him to death or set him on fire or cover him in honey and watch a bear chew his face off...yeah I'm flipping out.

Kieran's been gone a while and the steely disposition I had when he left me has faded. If he doesn't come back soon I can't be held responsible for my actions.

"Whoa," Kieran says as he flops back into his seat from earlier. "Take a breath man." I do what he says since I'm hanging on by a thread here. I breathe deeply through my nose and out my mouth a few times with my eyes closed. I need to keep my eyes open because every time I shut them I see visions of killing Taylor.

"Here's the plan. We lure the *bodyguard* out. Get your boys to tell him we know Nick Scarso has her and watch his play. My guess is he'll fuckin' panic like the bitch that he is and lead us right to her. Once we have her...we fuckin' end him and whoever else did this," Kieran snarls the last part.

"Let's move on this shit now. We're better off hidin' from cops and feds at night," I say sternly.

"Fuck yeah! I got some boys comin' down to give us some backup and firepower. I'll call Brian and get this show on the road." He pulls his phone out and pauses for a second. "We'll have her before sunrise." A well and true smile breaks his face as he hits the call button on his phone.

I'm coming Kid.

Chapter 16

Shannon

Nicky sits up behind me on the bed and pulls me into his lap. I snuggle into his chest relieved my body feels better.

"Shanny, look at me," Nicky commands softly in my hair. I lift my gaze slightly and look into his sapphire pools. Damn if I don't see sincerity and nothing else. "What's goin' on with you and your bodyguard?" My eyes bug out at that question. Left field much?

"Uh...what?"

"Your bodyguard. Your file made it look like...I got the sense he was more than an employee."

"They sure have a lot of information about me."

"My uncle had them start lookin' for you around your birthday. Took 'em about three weeks to end up in Kansas City. Someone watched you until after Thanksgiving, gatherin' information for the grab."

"That's unnerving," I huff. I shift off his lap so we can talk easier.

"Yeah it is."

"Why do you wanna know about Taylor?" Why isn't he asking about my boys or Kel? His gaze shifts from mine and I get nervous. Has he done something to Taylor?

"You seem close with him," he prompts.

"I am close with him. I've spent all my time with him for weeks after the death threat your people sent," I scoff.

"No one here sent that threat, Shanny. Mancini had some guys run it down when you got it. That's outside this shit show."

"FUCK!" I yell. Can my life get anymore fucked up right now?

"Don't worry about that now. Let's deal with this first okay," he soothes.

I steel myself before I launch into my story.

"That dream I had. It must have the answer in it, but I can't figure it out," I say quietly.

"Tell me about it and we'll talk it through together." That makes me smile. Karl would be proud of me. I'll talk it through with Nicky like I talk cases through with Karl. I can do this. It's not a whiteboard and coffee but it'll do.

"Like I told you, my Uncle Mick raised me after my father was killed in a turf war shooting. I was shot too and then shipped off to live with him. It's a long story but that's the short version." He nods looking confused, but I keep going.

"Uncle Mick wasn't a conventional parent. It was good though and a lot of useful training it turns out." I give him a wry smile, but he doesn't return it.

"And the lack of emotion?" Okay that sounds harsh but it's true.

"Yeah. Anyway in the dream my dad told me to tell Uncle Mick 'we had a nice meal' as he was dyin'. It wasn't a dream...that's what happened. But I don't think I ever told Uncle Mick because I just remembered it while I was here. And I have no fuckin' clue what it means," I moan and throw my head back. This is so damn frustrating.

"Did you ever talk to your Uncle Mick about that day, the shooting?"

Only once.

"Only once."

"Think back on that day, Shanny. Think about the weather, what you were wearing, what you did, where you had the conversation. Think about everything you can remember." I close my eyes and lay on my side curling into a ball to try to retrieve one of the most painful memories I have other than Daddy and Liam. Nicky puts a soothing hand on my bare shoulder and I let his warmth fill me. I need to feel safe to do this.

We're walking across the field together. I have my .22 rifle over my shoulder and Uncle Mick is carrying targets and extra ammo. This was Uncle Mick's gun when he was a little boy. That makes me feel special. My birthday is next week and I'll be nine. I asked Uncle Mick for a .22 handgun. He said he'd think about it, but I know he'll get it for me. I'm good at shooting. It makes me happy. I'll get good enough so that no one can ever shoot me again.

We get to our spot and Uncle Mick walks out to the hay bales and sets up five targets while I set up my rifle. I cleaned it last night, excited for today. When he gets back to me I'm ready to shoot. I line up my shot and squeeze the trigger. I hit the eight. The rings on the target start at six on the outside and move to a ten at the bullseye. An eight's not a bad start, but I can do better. I load another round and slide the bolt.

"Widen your stance just a hair, Shannon. Bring that elbow up," Uncle Mick corrects me softly from behind. I do what he says and line up my shot. BULLSEYE! I scream it in my head, but I don't react. He's teaching me to stay calm. It's really hard. I line up another shot.

"Shannon?" Uncle Mick questions before I squeeze the trigger.

"Yes?"

"Can you tell me about the day of the shooting?" I pause and fire. A seven. I load a round and quickly slide the bolt.

"I told you I don't remember," I say angrily. I shoot a nine. Load and slide again.

107

"Just tell me what you do remember about that day. You don't have to try to remember anything. Just talk about it while you shoot," he says nicely. I'm being mean. I just get so mad now…I didn't get this mad before. I fire…bullseye again.

"We were goin' to a Cubs game. That was our special time." I load, slide, and fire…bullseye. "Daddy had a meeting before the game so I went with him. It was boring and I had to wait alone. We were there a long time." I load, slide, and fire…bullseye. "When he was done we left. I got to throw a penny in a pretty fountain at the office building first, then we left. Daddy wasn't happy." I load, slide, and fire…bullseye. "Then all the shooting started. I thought it was fireworks. I don't remember much after that." I shrug. I don't think that was much of a story for Uncle Mick.

"Did your father say anything to you that you remember?" I load, slide, and fire…center of the bullseye.

"No." I load, slide, and fire…center of the bullseye.

"Did you get any food or go for milkshakes?" I pause and think. I load, slide, and fire…center of the bullseye.

"We had a nice meal." I load, slide, and fire…center of the bullseye.

Uncle Mick slides his hand on my shoulder and squeezes tight.

"Good girl, Shannon. Switch targets now." I nod, load, slide, take aim at the target to the left, and fire…center of the bullseye.

If I wasn't shooting I'd be crying right now. I don't want to think about that day. I remember more than I'm telling Uncle Mick, but I don't want to talk about it. It makes me hurt all over. I can't remember what happened after I got out of my seat belt. I've tried every night before I go to sleep and I can't remember. Why can't I just remember?

Holy fucking shit! I told him. I jump up and look straight into Nicky's sapphire eyes.

"I told him!" I squeal.

108

"Good girl, Shanny," Nicky compliments and offers me a big grin. I grin back. Then it drops.

"I still have no fuckin' clue what that means," I huff.

"Talk it through with me."

Chapter 17

Kavanagh

O'Sullivan just took a call from Kieran. He ran upstairs and locked himself in the bathroom to take the call. My heart is pounding as I stare at the staircase trying to make O'Sullivan appear with good news.

"How was the gym?" Taylor comes up to me from behind. My whole body goes tense, but I will it to relax. I can do this. I'm the king of bullshitting.

"Fuckin' needed that release, man. How was the nap?" I ask lightly.

"Needed. I was wiped. Any news from the feds?"

"Nah, just more hurry up and wait. I'm goin' fuckin' nuts!" I am going nuts so my tone is genuine, motivation not so much. I sit on the couch and he follows. I really wish one of the guys would come help me out, but I know they're avoiding Taylor so they don't fuck up our plan. Who would have thought I would be the calmest of our bunch? I'm not the calmest...I'm focused.

I hear O'Sullivan thunder down the stairs and out to the sunroom where all the other guys are. Taylor turns a questioning brow at him but doesn't follow.

"What's that about?" he asks me trying to see O'Sullivan from around the corner.

"No clue," I lie. That was good news running (like a girl) through the room.

"Haven't seen Kellerman." It's a question not a statement.

"He's at my brothers' place. Needed some alone time or some shit."

"Huh," he scoffs.

111

"What?" I ask harshly. Keep it in check Kavanagh.

"Figured he'd cut out on Shannon, just thought he'd last a little longer," Taylor says in a full of himself smarmy tone. I take multiple deep breaths before I respond. If the guys don't get in here soon...Taylor's a dead man. Our plan was to relieve anyone stuck with Taylor after three minutes. They're not coming to intercede...fuckers.

"He just wanted a few hours on his own to get his shit together. The beat down did a number on him and he doesn't like feelin' like he can't do shit," I growl.

"He's a pussy," Taylor scoffs. "So he got slapped around a little. So what? Put your big girl pants on and find your girlfriend...or soon to be ex."

I stand up to cave his skull in when Cal and O'Sullivan walk in. Thank FUCK!

I give them a knowing eyebrow raise to indicate I'm hanging on by a thread with this motherfucker.

"You two wanna join us where we don't have an audience?" Cal asks politely. I haven't seen his dimples in days and his bright eyes are getting duller by the hour. But right now those fairytale eyes have a sparkle of fury in them that gets me excited.

Taylor stands up and we all silently move into the sunroom where all of our brothers are, except Collin and Hugh. We can't risk their jobs and they will surely be pissed at us for taking that into consideration.

The chairs and couches in here are yellow and pale green with flowers all over them. We have picked the girliest room in this huge house to hang out in. I'm sure that means something, but I don't have the time to analyze it. Once the four of us sit down, O'Sullivan starts in.

"I called a guy I know today," he lies. "A guy that I thought might know something about stuff like this." O'Sullivan does a good job of convincing Taylor based on his determined attention. "Turns out he does. He knows

112

who has Kid. Now we need to decide what we do with this information."

"Who has her?" Taylor is out of the blocks quick with his question, almost foaming at the mouth.

"I think we should decide our move first. Do I tell the feds or do we go this alone?"O'Sullivan questions seriously.

"Why wouldn't we tell the feds?" Finn asks...that was not a real question. They planned this conversation before we got in here. If Taylor wasn't so intent on the name he'd notice the lies around the room because we're shit actors. But he doesn't.

"You see how slow they are with shit. What if they don't move on this information fast enough and we lose her?" O'Sullivan points out.

"That's good thinkin' O'Sullivan," Taylor interjects. God he really did do this!

O'Sullivan's eyes flare at the comment, but he reins it in. Aidan is sitting next to me, fuming. His fists are pumping and he's panting short hard breaths. I turn my gaze to him and give him a look that says "keep it together". Aidan closes his eyes and tries to meditate himself back to normal (that's what it looks like anyway).

"All right so we sit tight on the name and wait for my guy to call back. They got a lock on a possible location and are scoutin' it out right now. We should know soon." I really wish what O'Sullivan just said was true, but I can see he's lying and it's painful for him. If we were really this close to finding Kid we'd all be frantic. Taylor doesn't notice again.

"That's good. Maybe we should do some background on the people that have her. Who is it?" Taylor asks too eagerly. O'Sullivan smiles before he answers knowing we've got Taylor right where we want him.

"Nick Scarso."

You know those scenes in movies where everything stops around a person and all you can hear is a ticking

113

clock...that's me right now. My gaze moves through the room of stopped emotions seeing every eye in the room on Taylor and his reaction is priceless. I can almost hear his brain screaming fuck. His eyes are closed in defeat, his hands show the slightest tremor, his breath is short, and his throat is bobbing trying to swallow the pill we just shoved down it.

Time picks back up and the room remains silent. I slap my hands together loudly causing Taylor to jump and me to chuckle internally.

"Well let's hope your guy calls soon. I'm ready to get this shit done!" I bellow excitedly.Everyone in the room agrees with similar levels of enthusiasm, not Taylor.

"You good?" I ask Taylor with fake concern in my voice. "You don't look good."

"Nah...I'm...I...Just shocked I guess," he stutters and stumbles over his words.

"It's good to have connections," I state suggestively, but he doesn't pick it up. He's dazed and confused and trying to formulate a plan. I figured he'd have his phone out texting Mancini or Scarso or something, but he's just sitting here like an idiot.

Finn sneaks out of the room and I block Taylor's view, not knowing what Finn is doing. I'm sure it's something he doesn't want Taylor to see. A few minutes later Finn comes back and offers O'Sullivan a chin lift indicating success with his plan. Taylor's wheels are still spinning until he abruptly stands up.

"Gotta take a piss," he says absently and leaves the room. I want to follow him but that would be super fucking weird so I stay where I am. Once Taylor's gone a few minutes we huddle.

"What's the fuckin' plan?" I ask enthusiastically.

"Kieran's idea. Lie and tell Taylor we know who has Kid and hope he leads us to her. Finn put a tracker on Adam's car so we can follow him," O'Sullivan explains.

"How do you know he'll take Adam's car?" I ask hoping they have planned this shit out.

"Only one pair of keys by the door. He'll take 'em," Finn responds knowingly. He pulls his phone out and messes with it then holds the screen so we can all see it. A little blinking light on a map. It's moving.

"Time to move out ladies," Cal commands. We all rush to the front door. It's after midnight so the house is pretty empty now that the feds have taken over. We make a clean getaway. All of us pile into my dad's S-Class and Aidan's G-Wagon like we did earlier. I get Aidan on the handsfree and we pull out of the driveway.

"He's headed West on Half Day Road," Finn's voice filters through the speakers. I race in his given direction.

"What about Kieran and Kellerman?" I ask the car.

"They're on conference too," Aidan informs me.

"We're rollin' your direction," Kieran's voice comes through. "Got three guys and some firepower with us. You guys dodge the feds and cops okay?"

"Yeah the house was pretty empty actually," O'Sullivan informs him.

"Good."

We ride in silence for a while before Finn's voice breaks the silence. "We're about seven miles behind Taylor. He's on Illinois twenty-two now." I punch the gas a little harder. I don't want to be that far behind him. I know we need distance so he doesn't make us, but I want to be close. The silence resumes...we're coming Kid.

Kellerman

Kieran's plan is working like magic. His guys that are following us are three rough, hard, ex-cons that are packing enough heat to make Kid jealous. This is going to be...intense. Kieran's almost giddy at the idea of exacting revenge on Kid's part. I'm fucking terrified that we're driving into an ambush and Kid won't be there. We left Canaryville as soon as we filled O'Sullivan in so according to Kieran we should be intersecting the guys in about fifteen minutes if Taylor stays on his current route.

Since we have no idea where Taylor's going we could be on the road for hours or he could stop before we catch up. I'm hoping for the former so we can be there to stop whatever he's planning.

"I'm headin' North on fifty-nine," Kieran informs the guys on our extended conference call.

"Taylor just turned onto North Old McHenry Road. We're headed to the country," Finn's voice comes through the car. I really wish I knew Chicago. I'm lost and have no clue where we're going or if we're close to the guys at all. Kieran's GPS isn't helping me, but I can tell he's happy with the development.

"We'll intersect with you guys in ten minutes tops. Let's hope he's movin' out further. Less witnesses," Kieran says followed by an evil cackle. He's bloodthirsty for sure.

For the most part we're riding in silence other than to get or give updates. The silence is edgy. I'm trying to keep as calm as I can, but I can feel the adrenaline kicking up a gear every mile we turn. Kieran's flying down the highway with a car full of guns and ammo. I'm a little nervous what will happen if we get pulled over, but I don't ask him to slow down. I want him to speed up.

"We're on North Rand Road. Where's he at?" Kieran asks as he smashes the throttle a little harder.

"Hang on," Finn responds. Kieran grumbles as we wait. "He's on Rand now too. Where're you at?" Adrenaline is screaming through me now!

"Cuba Road."

"He's about five miles ahead of you and we're about five out from him. We should meet up soon."

Five miles. Five minutes away from him. This is really fucking happening. I close my eyes and will this car to move faster...take me to Kid.

Chapter 18

Shannon

"We've been at this for hours, Nicky!" I yell stomping my heels into the bed like a child. We have gone over every restaurant and meal I ever had with my father...nothing. Nicky put more salve on my backside a few hours ago, then we ate some sandwiches, we talked about the guys for a while, we went to the bathroom, but other than that all we've done is talk about two brief twenty-two year old memories. I'm wiped and frustrated and in the middle of a full blown temper tantrum and Nicky is laughing at me.

I glare at him and he laughs even harder. His laugh is deep and raspy, it makes me smile.

"Jerk," I huff after he calms down.

"I've been called worse," he jeers. "Let's try one last thing and then we need to get a new plan."

"One more," I warn. His team is coming back soon and I don't know what we're going to do then.

"Where did you have milkshakes with your dad?" he asks simply.

"At the kitchen bar. It was our treat, my mother fuckin' hated the mess we'd make," I say through a smile.

"Where would you have a sit down meal?"

"At the dining room table. That almost never happened though. I still have that table. Uncle Mick got it in the will. I thought it was weird because he was only family by marriage, but it's a beautiful antique table..." I stop mid-sentence. The table...a nice meal...Uncle Mick... "It's in the table, Nicky," I whisper.

Gunfire...I hear gunfire outside.

"FUCK!" Nicky bellows jumping up from the bed. "I missed the deadline. That's a new team comin' to grab you. Put this on." Nicky rips his long sleeve T-shirt over his head leaving him in a white tank and jeans. I fly out of the bed no longer in any pain as the adrenaline kicks into high gear. I pull his huge shirt over my head and roll the sleeves up.

"Gun Nicky," I demand with my hand out.

"I've got one piece on me. I need to go get a visual on what's goin' on. I'll come back for you with your piece. Get under the bed."

This goes against every instinct I have, but I do as Nicky says. I crawl under the bed like a child afraid of the boogie man.

"Hurry," I implore. He slowly moves out the door into the hallway. I'm in blackness again. Alone and unarmed while men are coming to take me. I'm pissed. I breathe calmly thinking of Uncle Mick.

Never let them take you without a fight.

Oh I'll fucking fight.

The gunfire is getting closer, louder, more constant fire than brief bursts. I breathe and listen. I can use this bed as a barrier if they get in here. The door flies open.

"Shanny," I hear Nicky and let out a huge breath. I quickly scurry out from under the bed and make my way to him. He's still in his tank, no injuries. "We need to move you."

"Gun!" I demand loudly.

"Couldn't get to 'em. They're on the other side of the house. I can get you out come on," he says holding his hand out to me. Hand in hand we approach the door, before I'm stopped by a familiar sight.

"Taylor?"

Kellerman

We met up with the guys perfectly. I'm a little in awe of how perfectly. We were driving (illegally paced) down the road and then I saw Kav at an intersection. We pulled our caravan off the road and supplied everyone (that can operate one) a gun. As soon as that was done we were back on the road. Taylor has stopped. So either he made it where he was going or we'll catch up to him and make him take us to Kid, either way this is coming to a quick end.

Kieran just pulled onto a dirt road behind Kav and Aidan. It's either a road or a long ass private drive because I see no signs of life. My stomach is in my throat and I'm clutching my pistol tightly. I see a flicker of light over a hill and to our right that looks like headlights. All four of our caravan turn off their headlights and creep toward the lights.

I have two extra pieces on me. My plan is to find Kid and put a gun in her hand (maybe two). I'm good with a gun and so is Finn, but the rest of the guys are average at best. Kieran and his boys are comfortable with guns, but I'm guessing they're less about precision and more about destruction. Kid can out shoot anyone I've ever seen. I know Taylor beat her by two millimeters to get his job (I cringe at the thought) but Kid creamed his ass in shots on target...she never missed. If she's whole and has a gun, all will be well.

Kav takes a sharp turn into the fields heading toward an old farm house. We all follow. As we creep slowly toward our target a large SUV tears up the road toward the front of the house. Who the fuck is that? We park at the back of the house surprised to see Adam's car empty with the door open near where we parked. Then gunfire erupts hitting the cars. We all scatter and I run toward an open door at the back of the house. There's a light dusting of snow frosting the fields around us and the moon is reflecting off of it making it a little easier to see at almost 5:00 a.m.

Before I reach the door I'm brought down hard from my right side by a tackle. My gun flies from my hands as I wrestle this guy as best I can in the dark.

I don't know if he has a weapon, but I'm not waiting to find out. I roll him to his back, sit on his chest and wail away at his head. I continue until he's no longer moving. Satisfied he's not coming back anytime soon, I jump up snatch my gun from the snow and haul ass to the door.

I scoot in quietly my back to the wall, my gun at the ready. I look like something out of a cop show. I don't know what I'm doing, but I want my back against something solid and my finger on the fucking trigger. As I move through the house I can hear voices. One sounds like Kid and I pick up my pace silently, letting my ear guide me to her.

I make my way down a stairwell leading to the world's longest hall in the basement and see Taylor's back in a doorway. A man (I'm guessing Nick Scarso) is in front of him facing me. I move quickly down the hall creeping quietly as the gunfire enters the house. I get maybe twenty-five feet behind Taylor when I hear her.

"Taylor?"

Shannon

"What the fuck are you doin' here?" Nicky spits at Taylor.

"Two birds, one stone, Nick. Gettin' rid of you and takin' her," Taylor sneers and then smirks that Taylor smirk. I don't understand. Does he know Nicky? It sounds like they know each other. How is that even possible? He's here to rescue me. I knew he'd find me, but I can see him training his eyes on Nicky. He's going to kill him. Everything moves slowly. Taylor raises his gun toward Nicky as Nicky returns aim. I drop Nicky's hand and throw myself in front of his body wrapping my arms around his neck. I hear multiple pops and look up into Nicky's face smiling into the blackness.

Kellerman

Scarso recognizes Taylor. I fucking knew it. Gunfire starts going off like crazy upstairs drowning out whatever is being said and then it happens. Taylor raises his gun simultaneously with Scarso. Then she's there. She throws herself around Scarso like a shield.

"Nooooooo!!!!" I scream running toward her. I see it, her body quakes as each shot hits her. I raise my gun, firing it at Taylor's back running full speed toward them. Taylor's body jars as the bullets penetrate his body, and then I'm hit. One of Scarso's rounds hits, dropping me where I stand. He screams a feral cry cradling Kid to the ground as I lay two inches from the man that just murdered Kid. With one last look upon her body I fall into the blackness.

"See you soon, Kiddo."

Chapter 19

Kavanagh

I fly down the stairs to the basement. It's the only place I haven't been yet. We finally dropped maybe fifteen guys outside, Kieran and his boys doing most of the work (happily). I don't give a shit who's dead or if I spend the rest of my life in prison. I have to get to Kid.

The rest of the guys are hot on my heels as I hear the whoosh of helicopter propellers. I believe the cavalry has arrived. I get to the bottom of the stairs and stop. There are bodies lying lifeless at the end of a long fucking hallway at the entryway to a room. I sprint down the hall. Kellerman's down. Taylor's down.

"Nooooooo!" I scream flying into the room to find Kid wrapped around a man like a blanket. She's drenched in blood. "Aidan!" I scream. He flies in pushing me out of his way. I fall on my ass and stare at her lifeless body. She's pale and limp. Her eyes are fixed open. I roll to my left and puke. She's gone.

"Get the fuck up!" Aidan screams. "Get out to those choppers, get me a spinal board, and tell them to get ready to move to Northwestern!" He goes back to C.P.R. on Kid and I race down the hall noticing my brothers with Kellerman. O'Sullivan is sitting with Cal in the hall, heads cradled in their hands.

"Help me!" I command. Both jump to their feet and fall in stride next to me. I run out to see Sully Sr. running at us fury on his face. I cut him off before he can waste any time.

"She's bad. Aidan needs a spinal board and a lift to Northwestern, now!" I scream over the whir of the helicopters. He wastes no time barking into a radio. Two teams of whatever they are go flying past us with spinal boards, Sully Sr. in step with them. The three of us stand there in silence. I taste salt on my lips and realize tears are streaming down my cheeks. Cal's face is also tear-streaked. O'Sullivan is a mask of pain. No tears, just devastation.

Aidan comes tearing out of the house with four guys carrying Kid on a board. I watch as her body goes past. She's gone. I can feel it. She's not here anymore. I watch the shell that used to carry my heart float past me and I crumble to the ground is sobs. A medical helicopter lands just as she passes me. The team carrying her followed by Aidan, sprint to it and disappear inside. It takes off in a matter of seconds. She's going back to Northwestern Memorial Hospital where this all started. She'll be in the same hospital she was as a little girl fighting for her life. This time she won't win.

"These two can go to Centegra Hospital. If they need moved from there the hospital can sort it out," Sully Sr. yells at EMTs. I look up to see Kellerman and the man Kid was wrapped around being wheeled into waiting ambulances. Finn's on the ground leaning against the house with a gunshot wound to the shoulder. Kieran and two of his guys are talking to cops or feds (I'm not sure which).

"How the FUCK did this happen?!" Sully Sr. bellows. I try desperately to get my brain in gear to figure out what I just saw.

Kellerman in the hall face down inches from Taylor also face down. Kid wrapped around the front of some dude, arms around his neck. None of this makes sense.

"Taylor's dead!" Sully Sr. yells over the vortex of noise around us. Good! He fucking did this to her. I wish I could have been the one to pull the trigger.

Cal drops to the ground next to me as Ryan and Adam come to us and follow Cal's lead. O'Sullivan stands unmoving watching the chaos around us, while we sit watching the fading lights of the ambulances in silence. Pure...dead...silence.

126

Kellerman

"Dylan," I hear my name being called. An angel is calling my name. Heaven's not a bad place.

"Dylan you're out of surgery can you open your eyes for me?" she calls a little louder.

Surgery? Fuck me I'm not dead. KID?! My eyes fly open scanning around the room as I try to sit up.

"Whoa, whoa big fella take it easy. Lie back for me," she says softly. I do as she asks because the pain in my leg isn't going to allow me to go anywhere. She pushes a button raising the back of the bed higher so I can sit up a little.

"Kid?" I question with a dry harshness from the desert in my throat.

"I wasn't aware there were any children waiting for you," she remarks walking around messing with things around me.

"Shannon Kelly?" I ask, grabbing her arm so she'll stop and listen. "She was with me," I explain hoarsely. Fuck I need a drink.

"Just you two brought in. No one else," she responds.

"Us two?" I clear my throat as I ask. She hands me a pink cup filled with water. I gulp it down quickly handing it back for a refill. She passes me the refilled cup and starts to talk again.

"Two of you rolled in at the same time. He's already been sent to another facility. You're the only one left," she explains. "I'll be back in a few. Rest."

I lay my head back against the pillow and try to figure out what's going on. I have the last image of Kid in my head throwing herself in front of Nick Scarso, protecting him. I don't understand. Why would she give her life for that monster?

127

"I see you're up and at 'em," a child (Doogie Howser) in scrubs says to me as he approaches. "Surgery went well. Your femoral artery was nicked but we got it closed up just fine. The bullet made a clean exit. In six to eight days you'll need a follow-up appointment. I'll send some recommendations home with you at discharge. Until then, relax and heal. You need anything press the red call button and your nurse will see to you." With that he's gone. That was a strange interaction with a fifteen-year-old that saved my life (probably not fifteen but close enough).

Shot in the leg. Nicked femoral artery? That could have been a lot worse. I need to get out of here and find Kid. I hear a clamor outside the recovery room before the doors slam open. The Kavanagh twins barrel toward me wearing scrubs, my nurse charging in behind them.

"You ready to blow this popsicle stand?" Ryan bellows. "Need to get you to Northwestern."

"Let's go," I say trying to sit up. It's a wasted effort.

"As I already told you, he hasn't been discharged. He's not even out of recovery yet," the nurse rants.

"Guessin' he doesn't give a shit," Adam replies to the nurse. "Need to get you to Kid," he says to me his gaze full of seriousness. That's all it takes. I sit straight up and start unhooking myself from every monitoring device stuck to me. Alarms are sounding off behind me in an un-harmonic symphony. My surgeon comes in the recovery room at a sprint. His eyes crazed as he watches me.

"He's leaving. These two asked him if he was ready to go and now look at him. He's in no state to be travelling," the nurse explains trying to push me back and reattach stuff to me. I just keep pulling.

"Doctor Kelso?" Ryan interjects.

"Yes," the surgeon responds staring at me in horror. He's too young to have dealt with crazy like this. It'll be a good learning experience for him.

128

"Doctor Kelso. Mr. Kellerman would like to release himself from medical care at this facility. We understand this will be against medical advice and he is willing to sign this AMA form and leave as soon as possible. There's a private ambulance waiting for us outside." Ryan's one hell of an attorney. Adam slides a form in front of me and I sign it without looking.

"We good?" I ask Dr. Kelso reaching down to rip out my IV. I pause, waiting for his answer.

"Everything is in order," Dr. Kelso says quietly as he reads the form I just signed.

"Don't!" the nurse screams and smashes her hand over mine before I can divest myself of my IV. "Let me take it out for you." I nod and wait. She takes it out quickly and bandages me up. Adam rolls in a wheelchair and he and Ryan help me down into it.

"Thanks Doc," Ryan yells over his shoulder as he sprints with the wheelchair down the corridor.

Once we're outside I see they weren't lying about a private ambulance. Two workers climb out, transfer me to a bed, and wheel me into the back. Once I'm in, Ryan and Adam climb aboard and slam the doors. The ambulance worker sitting behind my head pounds on the wall two times and the ambulance lurches forward.

"I'm going to start an IV and do a check on your vitals Mr. Kellerman," the ambulance worker, whose name tag identifies him as Chuck, informs me. I don't care what he does as long as I keep moving toward Kid.

"She's alive?" I ask whichever will answer.

"For now. It's not good Kellerman. Pop told us to get your ass there fast," Ryan says, his voice scared. She's alive. Okay, I can work with that. I let out a huge sigh and let the pain medication take me to dream about Kid...alive.

129

Part Two

Chapter 20

Kellerman
December 23, 2013

The funeral is today. One week has passed since we found the farm. One week since my life stopped. Cassie keeps calling me. I let it roll to voicemail every time. My mailbox has been full for five days now. I haven't checked one message. The voice I want to hear won't be there.

I've talked to every law enforcement officer under the sun in the last week. The FBI has been around the most. I'm not surprised. We stepped into a shit storm no one knew was swirling. Not that any of us have been given any details; only that this is an ongoing investigation and we'll get more information soon. I don't care. I've been told I'm not being charged for shooting Taylor. I acted in self-defense (defense of Kid) based on Illinois law. Also, I'm not the one that killed Taylor, Nick Scarso is. We've been given no information on him. Actually, when we we've asked we've kindly been told to shut the fuck up about him. I'm still lost on that whole night. I can't put the pieces together to make that scenario make sense, so I've stopped trying for now.

"You gonna go to the funeral?" Kav asks. His face is gaunt with dark circles under his eyes. His broad body has lost muscle. He's not eating or working out, just slowly withering away. He's no different from me.

"Can't do it," I respond quietly.

"I get that," Kav says as he flops his body in the chair across from mine.

"You goin'?" I ask.

"Nah, can't do it either," Kav says shaking his head as he stares at his lap. "I'm gonna run down and grab a drink. You want somethin'?"

"Water."

"Cal and O'Sullivan just got done eatin'. I'll be back in a few," he says as he climbs out of the chair. I give him a chin lift in response.

I sit in silence like I have been for the last week. I'm comfortable here. No sound. No thought. Just numb. Then it happens.

She squeezes my hand, just a flick of her fingers. I squeeze back hard, mindful not to break her hand.

"Kid," I call softly, moving to her face. "Kiddo, can you hear me? Please, if you can squeeze my fingers again." She does. Again just a flick of movement but she does. My hand begins to shake and my brain kicks into gear. "Kiddo, can you open your eyes and look at me?"

Nothing happens for a long time, no movement, no finger flicks, no eyes open. They told us this could happen. It's a slow process and we don't know what kind of damage was done. Kid was shot four times; three in her back causing massive blood loss but luckily no organ damage and the fourth in the back of her head, causing a lot of damage. Scarso cradled her head with both hands including his hand holding his gun. This caused the bullet to slow and change trajectory. The bullet stopped in Kid's skull. Unfortunately, from the impact Kid's brain began to swell and she was put in a medically induced coma for four days. They brought her out of the coma two days ago but she still hasn't regained consciousness, a common occurrence according to Dr. Callaghan.

"Please wake up, Kiddo," I plead. "Please."

Her stunning green eyes flutter open and land right on mine which are now streaming tears (very masculine tears). I reach over her and press the nurse call button never leaving Kid's gaze. She looks scared and I don't know what the fuck I'm supposed to do.

"You're okay, Kiddo. I just called your nurse," I explain. Her nurse hurries in the room. "She's awake."

"I see that," the nurse coos.

Kid's eyes stay planted on mine as the nurse moves around doing God knows what. I just hold those emerald jewels with my eyes, trying to reassure her silently.

"Doctor Callaghan is on his way," the nurse informs us and continues to check monitors and Kid's vitals. Cal breaches the doorway and his eyes fall to Kid.

"She's awake," I inform him. He stands still for a moment before taking off down the hall.

"Hope you're ready for visitors," I say smiling at Kid. The corner of her mouth turns up slightly.

"You boys have to let her rest. She's awake now, but that doesn't mean she's back to a hundred percent. This will be a long road," the nurse chides me. I know that. I also don't give a shit. She's awake. I hear their feet pounding the floor before they enter the room.

They're at her bedside opposite me in a flash. Kav leans over and nuzzles his face into her neck like a child to a mother. She weakly runs her hand around him rubbing his hair and face, comforting him. She never lets go of my hand. Eventually, Kav stands back up and wipes at his eyes. Those are happy tears he's wiping away. O'Sullivan's next wrapping his arms under hers and around her back smashing his face into her chest. His shoulders are shaking and I hear a sob break free from his chest. I think the rest of us have all cried and sobbed and God knows what else while we waited, not O'Sullivan...his time is now.

Kid lets go of my hand and runs both of hers up his shoulders and squeezes him with everything that she has. Once his quaking stops he stands up and kisses her forehead. He walks to his chair (we all have our spots in her room) at the foot of the bed and plops down next to Kav. Cal just stands there staring at her and her at him. It's like they're talking but none of us can hear it. He pulls his chair over to her bedside and holds her

141

hand rubbing her knuckles with his other hand. Her breath hitches at this and she searches for my hand with her free one. Kav and O'Sullivan pull their chairs to the bed too, Kav next to me and O'Sullivan next to Cal. They both put their hands on her legs looking at her waiting. That's when her tears start to fall.

There's no sound or shudder from her, just tears streaming down her face as she looks at each one of us...holding her as best we can. The four of us offer her silent strength as tears slide down her face. She holds my gaze one more time and falls back to sleep.

The four of us sit in anticipatory silence. We all want to wake her back up, but none of us is willing to disturb her. Dr. Callaghan walking in the room brings us all out of our daze.

"Well this is a familiar scene," he sighs, "that I never wanted to walk in on again." I don't know what he's talking about. I look at him puzzled. He hasn't seen us like this with her. He clears his throat, "The day after she was attacked when she was younger," he explains to me, "I came to see her and found her in my son's bed each of these guys holding some part of her." That's right. Kieran told me the same story. This is how they comforted her after Liam. I feel blessed and sick all at the same time: Sick that she would ever in the past or now need this and blessed that I'm one of the people comforting her.

"Just like that day though boys," he chides, "I need to see my patient." They all start to peel away from her slowly moving their chairs. I stay; meeting eyes with him letting him know I'm not moving. He nods at me and starts trying to wake Kid softly.

"Kid? Can you open your eyes for me sweetheart?" He rubs her arm up and down a little and her eyes flutter open. She looks into his eyes and an emotion flashes across them, she looks self-conscious. "It's all right sweetheart. You're okay. I've got you," he soothes her like a father to a young child not a doctor to a patient. She holds the tears at bay and smiles as best she can at

142

him. He looks her over carefully but quickly before sitting on the edge of her bed brushing a piece of her hair back.

"Kid," he starts softly, "you were shot four times, three shots in your back and once in your head. The shot to your head did not penetrate your brain but the force of the bullet cracked your skull and caused your brain to swell. We've had you in a medically induced coma to allow your brain to recover from the swelling. Your wrists had deep lacerations, and you had many lacerations covering the back of your body. Those are all healing nicely."

"Thank you," she pushes out grimacing in pain her usually cool silky voice harsh and raspy. The first words she's said and she's thanking someone. She's some kind of amazing.

"I love you, Kid." He leans over and kisses her forehead just as Aidan runs in the room, his sneakers squeaking as he skids to a stop. His scrubs are bloody and his brow is covered in sweat. I'm guessing he ran here from surgery. He's panting and looking at Kid with intensity.

"She's alright, Aidan," Cal calls to his little brother. Aidan walks over to the bedside and leans his tall ass over and kisses her forehead. She reaches up cupping his cheek and closes her eyes. She's exhausted from being awake and told how fucked up she's been. She falls asleep before Aidan pulls back. Aidan and Dr. Callaghan leave the room a few minutes later and the boys resume their chairs around her bed. I lay my head on the bed next to our clasped hands and sleep with her for the first time in a week. She's back and I'll never let her go again.

Chapter 21

Kellerman

News of Kid waking up doesn't take long to make the rounds. Her family has been on a rotation of visiting while she's been here. Now that she's awake everyone is here. No one is waking her up or bothering her. They all just want to be near her for when she comes to on her own again.

I don't know what kind of room Dr. Callaghan has Kid in but it's not a regular hospital room, it's huge and can fit all of us easily once the guys roll our beds out of the room. Even with all of these people here it's pretty much silent in the room, all of us waiting for her to wake up again. I never move from my perch at her side clinging to her hand. Even when Mr. Kavanagh and Sully Sr. try to convince me to take a walk with them, I can't leave her. I haven't left this room once since I've been here. Not knowing if or when she'd wake up I couldn't risk not being by her side so I've sat in this chair for a week. The worst fucking week of my life.

There's a waiting room of sorts directly across from Kid's room. Her family is regularly going back and forth between the rooms, waiting for her to wake up again. Mr. Kavanagh comes in and sits on the other side of her bed taking a turn holding her hand, staring at her face. He looks better than he did while Kid was missing, but just. His salt and pepper hair seems to be a little more salt than pepper in the last ten days and there maybe be a few more frown lines creasing his face. But now, sitting watching his daughter his face is warm and soft.

"My wife and I always wanted a daughter. Don't get me wrong we loved our boys, but we always wanted a daughter. After the twins were born Anne was so busy with the boys we decided to stop trying for our little girl for a while. Then Anne got sick and having a little girl was no longer an option." His voice is easy and I think he's telling me this story, but he's just gazing lovingly at Kid's peaceful face.

"One day I got a call from Aaron that he had met someone and she was moving in. I was shocked and worried. He was only eighteen and didn't have a great track record with girls. Two weeks later I came to the townhouse to have dinner. Kid had cooked us an award winning pot roast dinner. She was breathtaking. The love that she poured into everything: school, the boys, telling a story, cooking that meal, giving me a hug...I knew right then that she was my daughter. She may not have come from me, but she was mine. Her father was a lucky man to get eight years with her. I know I'm blessed to have had the last thirteen. She's what people in this world hope to be." He sighs and looks at me.

"I don't know you very well Dylan, but what I do know I like. The fact that you worked your ass off to find her and haven't left her side for a moment tells me the level of commitment you have to her. The fact that you haven't been scared off by this fucked up situation or the people that did this tells me you're willing to fight for her. The fact that you share her with the boys tells me you accept her family for what it is. The fact that she keeps squeezing your hand in her sleep tells me you're her safe place. I know you love my daughter and you have my blessing with her. No more calling me Mister Kavanagh...it's Pop," he finishes softly before looking deep into my eyes. "Keep her safe Dylan."

"Pop," Kid whispers. He and I were staring at each other so intently we didn't notice she had woken up. His head snaps to hers, as quickly as mine does. She's staring at him with adoration.

"Ah, Kid," he murmurs into the back of her hand as he pulls it to his face. "I love you so much." He kisses her hand and leans in to kiss her forehead. "You've got a hospital full of visitors, Kid. You wanna see 'em now or would you like a few minutes?"

"Few minutes Pop," she whispers. He gets up to leave the room. "Pop." He turns back at the sound of her voice. "You're a great father. Thank you for loving me like you do." I see tears in his eyes as he winks at his daughter.

"I love you," she whispers.

Pop smiles broadly with love before leaving the room. We're alone for the first time in over a week.

"Hey," I whisper.

"Hi," she whispers back with the best she can do at a smile. She pulls at my hand signaling she wants me to come closer to her. I stand up and move my face close to hers so I can hear her easily.

"Will you hold me, Kel?" she murmurs. Hell yes I will, but I don't know how I'll manage it. Her backside is still healing and her bed was clearly designed for one person only. I scoot in next to her snuggling into a space a child could barely fit. My 6'5" frame makes this bed feel like doll furniture. I run my arm beneath her neck and she rolls onto her side her face grimacing in pain. I help her scoot over so she can nuzzle into my chest with her hand on my abs as she sighs. I have never been so comfortable being uncomfortable in my life. I kiss her hair every few seconds.

"I love you, Shannon Kelly," I say purposefully. "I'll never let another day go by without telling you that." I squeeze her into my chest as much as I can without causing her pain.

"I love you too," she says in the strongest voice to come out of her yet. My heart is pounding against my ribs so hard I'm sure it'll cause bruising.

"Get outta that bed!" the nurse yells at me from the doorway. We both snicker.

"Busted," she giggles lightly. I climb out of the bed before the nurse stabs me with a scalpel. I reclaim my seat and hand holding duty. I feel a thousand pounds lighter now. The love of my life is back. I'm going to marry this girl and make her the mother of my children. Those are two things I never thought about until she walked into Mia's room in October. She made my world tip on its head. Kid brought me back to life.

Shannon

After Kel is threatened out of my bed the family starts pouring in to see, hug and kiss me. I've never been showered with so much love and affection by so many people. It's overwhelming. Kel sits next to me holding my hand as everyone makes the rounds to me. He's polite and affable, though I know he really wants me all to himself.

Both Maggie and Mary cry and cry as they hug and kiss me, telling me they're having a tracking device embedded under my skin. I may not argue with that. Ryan and Adam sit with me and tell me an interesting story about busting Kel out of a hospital in McHenry a few minutes after he had surgery. I laugh at most of their story until I realize Kel was shot and had surgery. I've lost a week, during which some crazy shit has gone down. Finn comes in and sits with me. He's got a sling on his left arm and tells me he was shot in the shoulder. He didn't have to have surgery though. He tells me some of the things going on, but really he just sits with me. As much as I want to see everyone I can't stay awake for long periods of time. I'm in pain, my head is killing me, and I'm exhausted like nothing I've ever experienced. I wake from my most recent nap as Pappy, Collin, and Hugh enter my room looking bleak as they make their way to my bed. Everyone leaves the room.

"Kellerman we need a minute," Pappy orders softly.

"Sir, I appreciate that but I'm not goin' anywhere. I'll put my earbuds in and turn the volume up to give you all the privacy you need, but I'm not leavin' her," Kel says strongly. Pappy studies him for a second before he nods in agreement. Kel kisses my hand before he puts his earbuds in and blasts what I recognize as Eminem. He got that from me. I smile at him before I turn to my visitors.

"Kid," Pappy's voice breaks as he leans down to kiss my cheek.

"I'm okay, Pappy," I say pushing my face into his throat. He holds himself there for a few moments composing himself before he pulls back. Collin and Hugh both take turns laying their heads on my chest and sobbing just like Sully did. I hug them each tightly (as tight as a weakling can) before letting them go. The three of them pull chairs up to the side of my bed. While they do, I steal a glance at Kel. He's staring at our intertwined fingers, no doubt going deaf from the music pounding his eardrums. I squeeze his hand and he looks up into my face. I give him a soft smile before turning back to the O'Sullivans.

"There's a lot to go over, Kid and you're in no shape to go through everything but there are a few things we need to go through now. You okay with that?" Pappy asks. I nod.

"Taylor's dead. Another man died at the scene that was helping the guys find you. His name was Kellan O'Shea and his funeral was today," Collin informs me. I nod. I feel like I should know who Kellan O'Shea is, but I can't place him. He died trying to help save me and I don't even know who he is. Once I'm better I'll figure it out and reach out to his family.

I'm not surprised Taylor's dead. I feel sick that he's gone, tears prick the back of my eyes but no tears fall. I don't remember everything from that day, but I remember him being there. I'm waiting to hear if Nicky is dead too.

"Do you remember what happened?" Collin asks tentatively.

"Most of it. Some things are a little fuzzy. I'm not sure what I can tell you," I admit not wanting to put Nicky at risk if he's alive.

"We know about Scarso if that's what you're worried about," Hugh says softly. I'm not sure what they know or if Nicky is alive. I need to tread lightly. If he's alive his uncle will kill him if I say the wrong thing. If he's dead...I don't want him to be dead.

"I don't have the energy to tell you about everything that happened while I was there. But, I'll tell you how it ended. Scarso was with me when we heard gunfire. He was tryin' to get me out of the house because he believed another crew was sent for me. Before we could leave the room I was held in, Taylor came in. Scarso and Taylor seemed to know each other. Then Taylor drew on Scarso. I didn't have a weapon so I threw myself in front of Scarso. That's the last thing I remember," I huff the last part because I still can't get a grip on how any of this makes sense.

"Why would you do that, Kid?" Collin asks in a pained tone. "Why would you put yourself in front of him after what he did to you?"

"I don't know if I can tell you guys that part. It's complicated," I say quietly not wanting to offend them.

"It's okay, Shanny. You can tell 'em," Nicky's voice calls from the doorway.

Nicky looks like a different human being. His hair is light blond and cut short like Kavy's. His eyes are a new (fake) deep almost black brown. His face is clean shaven. I know it's him though. He's smiling sheepishly at me.

"Nicky," I push out in a whisper feeling a lump in my throat.

"Gentleman, I'm agent Nick Cooper you'll know me as Nick Scarso," Nicky explains. "She's had a long day and shouldn't have to explain the events that have taken place. Any questions you have I'd be happy to answer. Some details still must remain confidential at this point, but I'll give you what I can," he states confidently striding toward my bed.

Pappy, Collin and Hugh are dumbstruck that Nicky is in this room.

"I'd offer to shake your hands but mine are in quiet a state at this point," Nicky says holding up his bandaged hands. I scan the rest of him to see he's favoring his right arm, but that's all I can see. He looks good, safe. Pappy stands in front of him before Nicky can get any closer to me.

"Did you do that to her back?" Pappy seethes.

"No, but I blame myself for it," Nicky admits.

"You motherfucker!" Hugh screams standing up then lunging at Nicky. I squeeze Kel's hand pulling him hard. His head flies up to meet my gaze sensing my stress he pulls his earbuds out.

"I'll fuckin' kill you," Hugh continues to scream lunging against Collin and Pappy's grasp. Kel stands up and quickly rounds the bed in a limp jumping in front of Hugh.

"Hugh, man, don't do whatever you're doin' in front of Kid. She's had enough," Kel instructs coolly with the right amount of threat in his voice. Nicky is standing still watching Kel intently.

"That motherfucker kidnapped her, let her get beaten to a pulp, and then let her take four bullets for him. He's lucky I don't have my goddamn gun!" Hugh bellows. Kel's expression changes. This is bad. All in one movement Kel pivots, rocks back, and lands a fist to Nicky's jaw. Nicky stumbles back as Kel advances on him. Collin, Hugh and Pappy are trying to get Kel under control (barely making an effort) but he's throwing them back so hard they're not able to. I need this to stop.

"Kel stop, PLEASE!" I yell but he doesn't hear me. I don't know what to do. So I do what I've always done. "KAVY!!!!" I scream at the top of my lungs as Kel lands another fist to Nicky's face. Kavy comes tearing into my room shaking and heaving, trying to figure out what the fuck is going on.

"Make him stop, Kavy," I say in almost a whimper. Kel is continuing to pummel Nicky while Nicky just stands and takes it, never raising a fist. Kavy rushes at them ripping Nicky backward by the shoulder throwing him to the floor then wrapping his python arms around Kel walking him backward toward my bedside. Sully and Cally run in with the same freaked out faces that Kavy had. They stand over Nicky menacingly, obviously identifying him as my threat.

"Kellerman, stop," Kavy breathes out roughly not letting Kel go.

"He did this," Kel growls. That stops Kavy dead in his tracks. Kavy looks over at me and I know if I don't start talking Nicky is going to die in this room with my boys beating him to death.

"Don't touch him...any of you!" I command. "Nicky are you okay?" I ask since I can't see him behind Cally and Sully.

"I'm good, Shanny." Nicky laughs lightly. He's good.

Kel, Kavy, Sully, Cally, Hugh, Collin and Pappy are staring at me like I've sprouted another head. Time to explain.

Chapter 22

Shannon

"What happened in that house is a long story that I don't have the fuckin' energy for. But I'll tell you this. Nicky kept me safe. He saved me from...a lot and I don't want any of you to do anything to him," I instruct firmly.

"Kid, we're fuckin' strugglin' here. You're givin' Scarso a free pass after what he did to you. What's goin' on?!" Kavy's voice is pained and confused so I figure he needs something to move this along.

"I met Nicky when I was a little girl," I say softly. "We spent an afternoon playin' together when I was eight. He was the first kid to play with me and not think I was weird. He was the first boy to hold my hand and tell me everything would be okay. He was my first kiss. Nicky was my first real friend."

The faces in the room have changed from fury to confusion and a little pain. My boys don't like to share and Kel doesn't want to think about anyone kissing me other than him, even if it was a ten-year-old little boy. I smile at their faces and laugh. Nicky takes a few steps toward me, keeping his distance from my boys, but looking right in my face with adoration.

"What?" Kavy starts. "What the fuck? I don't understand. Somebody give me more than what she just did. You sure she doesn't have brain damage?" Kavy asks Pappy. I chuckle at that.

"I don't have brain damage, Kavy. And even if I did, I'd still be smarter than you," I snark. He glares at me before a ghost of a smile crosses his lips. "You wanna quit huggin' Kel now? Unless there's something you two need to tell me." Oh yeah, the snark is back! That gets

153

me a snort from Kavy and a smirk from Kel. Progress. Kavy unfolds his arms and takes two steps toward me.

"Once you're back on your feet, I'm kickin' your ass," Kavy says softly as he kisses my forehead. I smile. I'd like to see him try and kick my ass. He stands up and moves to a chair at the side of my bed. We're lucky the rest of the family is out to dinner. This would be difficult to explain to them.

"Kel, you wanna sit down?" I ask softly. He doesn't respond just makes his way around my bed scooping my hand into his as he takes his chair. His knuckles are bloody and he's shaking with adrenaline. My beautiful man, protecting me. He does have a fresh new scar under his left eye. Note to self, ask about that later.

"Why doesn't everybody sit down and we can get this over with so Kid can get some rest," Pappy instructs. I think Collin, Hugh and Pappy would have been happy to let Kel beat Nicky to a pulp. They weren't doing a lot to stop it. I get that. I'm a mess and they blame Nicky. I'd want to kill anyone that did this to them too. They all take chairs around my bed. Nicky takes the one across from Kel and picks up my hand looking tenderly into my eyes. Kel squeezes my hand and growls at Nicky. I mean a literal growl like an animal produces.

"Easy there big fella," Nicky says but doesn't drop my hand.

"I agree with Kellerman. Get your fuckin' hands off her," Kavy warns from the seat next to Kel.

"You got yourself quite the pack here, Shanny," Nicky says with a smile dropping my hand and turning to face my pack. Nicky explained to me that I needed to get a pack (a wolf pack) of friends when we played that day. He told me that's how you stayed safe in the world. I guess I listened later in life. It's strange how that one afternoon playing with a boy affected so much of my life.

"Why does he keep callin' you that? It's gettin' on my fuckin' nerves," Kavy growls. He's jealous and protective right now. It's cute. I grin down at him.

154

"My dad called me Shanny and so did Nicky. I called Nick, Nicky. I'm guessin' that's why I gave you all the nicknames you have. It's how I show love," I say softly. I never really thought about that until now. I just called them those names after Liam's attack. I didn't think about it, I just did it. Kavy's face is soft now just like the other boys'. Kel is still seething, glaring at Nicky. I turn and look at him pulling on his hand to get his attention. He looks at me, his face going a little gentler.

"I love you, Kel," I whisper. He pulls my hand to his mouth and kisses my palm.

"Oh God, knock it off you two. Nobody wants to watch that shit," Cally snarks with a giant dimple wielding smile on his face.

"Fuck you, Callaghan," Kel murmurs into my hand.

"Think Kid might get jealous you try fuckin' me," Cally retorts.

"Hey, I might wanna watch," I say with a huge grin.

"Kid, give us just a day with you back before you start in on us, okay?" Sully pleads. He's not ready for the snarky me. I smile and nod because I get it. He almost lost me and just wants me safe right now, not mouthy. I'll give him until tomorrow.

Kavanagh

Kellerman is ready to commit murder. The rage seeping from his pores is palatable. I don't blame him. I'd be pissed too, fuck that, I am pissed too. He's just raging enough for the whole room right now. I love this dude. Yeah, I know that doesn't sound like me but it's true. He's so dedicated to Kid he's putting me to shame and that's saying something. He won't leave her. We've all tried to get him out of this room...not happening. He was so dark when she was gone, it's good to see some light back in him, but he's still shaken. We're all still shaken.

Nick fucking Scarso is here. I didn't see that coming. Kellerman was going to beat that guy into hamburger meat and then keep going. Again, I don't blame him. I'm glad I pulled him off though. Kid doesn't need that shit right now, and Kellerman knows it. It's the only reason I could stop him.

Now Scarso is here and apparently has some long lost connection to Kid. He's pissing me off looking at her the way he is. I'm ready to hear what this motherfucker has to say.

"Get talkin'," I order. No kind requests here.

"As I was explaining earlier, I'm agent Nick Cooper with the DCA. I was undercover in the Mancini Crime Family under my birth name of Nick Scarso. I'm limited with what I can divulge at the moment, but I'm happy to fill you guys in on what I can," Scarso explains nicely. I stare at him with a look that says get fuckin' talkin'. Dude is seriously testing my patience.

"As Shanny said we have history, but that wasn't known before she was taken. I did not know of her abduction until twelve hours after she was grabbed. I was called in to take over an information extraction job. I recognized Shanny upon entering the premises and took over ensuring her safety. I believed Shannon Murphy to be dead. For reasons that are currently being investigated it seems her death was faked at the time her father was killed," he pauses looking at Kid. Her eyes are bugging the fuck out, but she doesn't comment.

"About five months ago Vito Mancini had men begin to search for Shannon Murphy. It took them several weeks to locate her. Once they did they spent several more weeks following her and collecting information," he pauses again to check on Kid. She must already know this part of the story because she looks blank. The rest of us are becoming varying levels of irritated and confused.

"Mancini ordered the grab and had it carried out by a team of his men. The beating and torture she received were not at my hands nor was I present when it

156

occurred. It was carried out by one of Mancini's soldiers."

"Where's the *soldier?*" Sully Sr. interjects in a menacing growl.

"He was retired after a later incident that again I'm not at liberty to discuss," Scarso responds harshly. Kid gasps and we all look her way.

"Kiddo?" Kellerman asks softly.

"I'm okay," she lies. "Go ahead, Nicky."

"There was a standing deadline to extract information from Shanny of sixty hours. When that deadline came and went, another crew would be movin' in to reduce risk. I was in the process of preparin' to move her when the ambush occurred. That ambush was orchestrated by Andrew Taylor as you all knew him. His birth name was Anthony Tarantino, Mancini's third cousin."

"WHAT?!" Kid screams.

"Kid, calm down. You can't get your blood pressure up," Cal soothes. Everyone sits quietly waiting for Kid to calm down and to get her shit together. We knew this or at least some of this. Kid's hearing it for the first time and there is betrayal and pain covering her beautiful face.

"Explain that shit to me," Kid seethes glaring at Scarso.

Scarso clears his throat and quietly begins to explain, "Tarantino, uh...Taylor was raised by his aunt in Kansas City and then started workin' for Mancini. His background as a cop is real, though I don't know the details on all of that. I can only assume he was workin' for Mancini inside the force. While his men were watchin' you they reported back to Mancini. From what I've learned, when you put out feelers for a bodyguard Mancini sent in Taylor. He was just there to keep close tabs on you and feel out the guys. He was there to keep you alive too. I told you the threats against you were real

157

and not from us," Fucking shit! Someone else is threatening Kid? I'm locking her in her bedroom when we get home.

"Lockin' you in your bedroom when we get home," O'Sullivan grinds out at Kid. I laugh one hard bark out loud. Great minds think alike! Kid snickers. Fuck I missed her laugh.

"I'm sorry to say this but he did have genuine feelings for you, Shanny. He was in pretty constant communication with the team. He told them things had gotten personal with you. The grab leader was on the phone with him the day of the snatch right before you walked in to talk to him. He said if you didn't answer the door that meant he was claimin' you and shuttin' the job down."

"You've got to be fuckin' kiddin' me?" Kellerman sneers. "You're tellin' me not only was he makin' a play for my woman, but because she turned his ass down he allowed this shit to happen?!" Scarso nods. "That motherfucker's lucky he's dead!" Okay, that rage I was talking about earlier, it's ramped up a bit now. Normally, this is where Kid would step in and calm him down except I think she's more pissed than he is. FUCK!

"Kid, I think this is enough for today. You just woke up and you're not healthy yet. Let's do this another time," Collin suggests calmly.

"He kissed me. Told me he loved me. Told me he'd wait for me to figure shit out with Kel. I laid bound to a bed knowin' he'd be lookin' for me and felt comforted by that! When he walked in that room, I thought he'd come to rescue me!!" she wails.

Kellerman stands up abruptly and moves with purpose (and a bit of a limp) into Kid's bathroom slamming the door shut. The scream that follows I can only describe as gut-wrenching. He sounds like an animal, feral and primed to kill. I look to Kid for some guidance. Her face is completely pale. She wasn't thinking about Kellerman when she said that shit and now she feels guilty. I'll do anything in the world to get that look off her face.

"Kid, he'll be fine. That's not on you," I soothe.

"Kavy, please," she softly pleads for me to make it stop. We can hear his fists pounding the tiled walls. He's going to fuck me up when I walk in there, but I'll take it for her. I stand up, Cal and O'Sullivan follow. Reinforcements are a good thing to have right about now. I walk to the door of the bathroom and pause a second before I open it. What I see before me cracks my heart in two.

Chapter 23

Kavanagh

Kellerman is on the floor continuing to hammer his left fist into the wall. The entire wall is shattered. Maybe an eight foot squared wall, tiled three quarters of the way to the ceiling and not a one intact. The classic white hospital tile is dripping in bright red anguish-filled blood. Kellerman's hands are ruined, bones broken, skin gone, agony seeping from the wounds. I take a tentative step toward him, pausing when his eyes cut through me. I thought his screams were feral, his eyes are haunted. He's finally broken. I look back at my boys and indicate with my chin for them to shut the door. I don't want an audience for whatever goes down. O'Sullivan shuts it and he and Cal take steps so they're right at my back.

Kellerman is still driving his fist into the wall, but softer and more repetitive now. I take another step and end up at his feet my boys just behind me. I crouch down to his level and he lunges at me with the strength of a lion. I fall back on my ass, Cal and O'Sullivan bending down to catch me from falling flat on my back. I'm on my ass on the floor of a hospital bathroom with a 6'5" 260 pound man in my lap fisting my shirt, shaking uncontrollably, sobbing like a baby. Cal quickly scoots around me and wraps his arms around Kellerman. O'Sullivan does the same from the other side and we sit there in the man hug to end all man hugs...the four of us weeping.

Kellerman

I broke. Picturing her laying bound to a bed seeking comfort in Taylor searching for her broke me. He didn't love her. I don't give a flying fuck what Nick Scarso (or whatever his name is) says. If he loved her she never would have been laying on a bed, bound, waiting for him to rescue her. She's been kidnapped, beaten, tortured and betrayed. The betrayal I just witnessed streak across her face caused pain in my soul I didn't know had nerve endings. I slowly start to get my breath back and my shaking under control. I'm sitting in Kav's lap like a toddler with O'Sullivan and Cal surrounding the rest of my body. They've all stopped crying but are still holding me with supportive force. I release a deep breath and pull my head out of Kav's rock hard chest. I open my eyes and meet Kav's to see concern and love (manly love) pouring from them.

"Thanks," I croak. My throat is wrecked from the screaming and sobbing. O'Sullivan drops his arms but leaves a hand on my calf. Cal drops his and leaves a hand on my shoulder. Kav leaves one hand wrapped around the side of my neck.

"That's how she deserves to be loved," Kav says forcefully squeezing my neck. I nod but don't say anything for fear I'll start crying again and I'm pretty sure I'm about to grow a vagina at this point from all the emotional upheaval. I take a minute before I speak.

"The last thing she heard about me was that I cheated on her and got another woman pregnant. We haven't talked about it yet so I don't know where her head's on that shit. Taylor, or whatever the fuck his name was, made a move on her and told her he loved her before she got snatched. She wasn't waitin' for me to save her. She was waitin' for him," I explain softly.

"Man, I get that's fucked up. It. Is. Fucked. Up. But that asshole's gone. Your baby momma situation will work itself out, you didn't cheat on Kid. She'll see that and you two will work on this shit. Don't let Taylor take anything else from you. And if you can't do that, then don't let him take anything else from Kid," O'Sullivan beseeches me.

162

"If she leaves me you guys have to promise to keep her safe. If Scarso is tellin' the truth and those death threats made on Kid are from someone else you have to keep her safe," I order gruffly.

"Don't man. Stop yourself from goin' there. You're not goin' anywhere. She's not leavin' you so get that shit outta your head! One thing at a time right now. Let's focus on gettin' Kid healthy and whole first. Nothin' else will happen to her. We'll watch her night and day. You've already been doin' that and so have we. We won't stop no matter what," Cal commands. I've never heard him that serious ever. I don't think I've heard him say that many words before period.

"Now. You're a fuckin' mess," Kav points out. He's right. I'm covered in blood and still bleeding. I'm guessing a few of my knuckles are broken. The bathroom is fucking wrecked. That's going to be a fun bill to pay! "Get in the shower and we'll get Aidan to come look at your hands."

The four of us stand up. We're four big guys in a small bathroom. It's a tight squeeze. Jesus there's blood everywhere.

"Thanks guys. I really mean that. I don't know what else to say, but I needed that. The release...and the comfort," I say quietly looking at my tattered hands.

"It's what we do. We're family," Kav says smacking my shoulder twice followed by the other guys. I nod as they make their way out of the bathroom.

Shannon

I don't care what Kavy says, that shit is on me.

"I can't believe I just did that," I admit in a whisper.

"Kid, this has been rough on all of us. I think Kellerman took it worse than any of us, if that's possible. He was wrecked when you were gone. He worked endlessly, doing anything he could to find you. He

163

wouldn't talk to anyone, barely ate or slept. You'd think him recovering from his beating he woulda needed more rest, but he didn't," Hugh explains.

"What beating?" I ask sternly. Blank faces look back at me. Oh no. They're telling me. I arch my brow waiting.

"I don't know all the details, Kid. Maybe you should talk to the guys," Hugh dodges.

"Don't you fuckin' dare, Hugh Jacob O'Sullivan. You tell me what you know!" I demand.

"Kid, I'm serious, I don't know. He was fucked up when he got to Chicago. He took a beating, I know what that looks like. I don't know anything other than that."

"Pappy?" I question. He looks like he knows.

"Kid, let's not go through all of this right now. You need rest. I shouldn't have let this go this far. We'll come back tomorrow and finish with Scarso," Pappy instructs in his fatherly tone.

"Stop callin' him that!" I screech like a spoiled brat. My emotions are making me a little crazy. I'm blaming the drugs. "His name is Nick Cooper. And I need to talk to him alone for a minute," I say quietly.

Pappy studies me and Nicky for a long moment.

"Okay, Kid," Pappy relents. "But not too long. *Cooper* can come back tomorrow and we'll finish this conversation. No damn arguing," Pappy demands. I nod. He's right, I'm beyond wiped. I napped most of the afternoon but my energy is zapped at this point. I close my eyes. "We'll see you tomorrow, baby girl." Pappy kisses my forehead.

"Love you," Hugh says kissing my cheek softly.

"Be back in the morning, Kid," Collin says kissing the tip of my nose. I finally open my eyes to see their adoring faces relaxed. They have killed themselves to find me and get me well. I love my family.

164

"Thank you guys. Thank you for searching for me. Thank you for loving me. I love you all so much, I'll never be able to say it enough," I say gently.

"You're the best piece of all of us, Kid. Doesn't work without you," Hugh says with a strangled voice trying to hold back his emotions. I smile and nod as they turn away to leave.

"Gentleman, I'll explain this further tomorrow if you like but for now you need to know that Nicky Scarso died in the firefight at the farm," Nicky says professionally.

The O'Sullivans stare long and hard at Nicky. If they knew everything that Nicky did for me it wouldn't be so difficult, but I'm not in any condition to go into details right now.

"Cooper?" Pappy growls low and menacingly. "You fuck with her anymore, I'll end you."

"Noted," Nicky replies confidently. The O'Sullivans leave. I can't hear anything in the bathroom anymore. I'm so worried about Kel. If I could go to him I would. Maybe Nicky would carry me in there.

"Shanny, I know this is hard. I can't begin to apologize to you for not gettin' to you sooner or figurin' out a better way to get you outta there. I want to make this right but I'm not sure I can. Tell me what I can do for you," Nicky agonizes.

"Nicky this is gonna take time. You can't fix this, nobody can. I appreciate you comin' here and tryin' to sort shit out for us," I say as my eyes flutter shut.

"I'm sorry I had to bring up the *soldier*," his voice is pained. My eyes fly open.

"Don't. Please, I can't. Kidnapping, beating, being shot, betrayal I can deal with all of that right now. I can't deal with the almost rape. I will, I promise, just not today." Nicky nods his head leaning over me he presses his lips to my forehead.

165

"I need you to give me details about what's goin' on. The key, Nicky. Please tell me you found the key," I plead. Nicky squeezes my hand and smiles broadly, his fake brown eyes alight.

"I got the key. That key is currently causin' a world of hurt for a lot of people, Shanny. Nothing is public yet, but what we found in the safe deposit box is gonna end the Mancini Crime Family and Governor Grady," Nicky explains with a smile.

"What? Governor Grady...what does he have to do with this?"

"The day you and your father were shot I was at the house you and your father visited. It wasn't an office you went to it was Grady's house. I saw you throw that penny into the fountain and I ran to you, but you were already driving away by the time I got there. Your father had mountains of evidence against the then Senator Grady and Vito Mancini. I'm guessin' he was there to try to broker a deal or something. We don't know yet. But what we got will put everyone involved in prison for life Shanny. You did something amazin' figurin' out where that key was," Nicky beams.

"I didn't do much, Nicky. You're the reason I figured it out. You guided me to the memories and thoughts," I say smiling brightly at him. I know he didn't do anything to make me remember (dream) the conversation my last moments with my father, but I still remembered it while he was there. As heartbreaking as it is to remember it's infinitely better than not having the memory.

"It was all you. I just pushed a little when you couldn't get there on your own," Nicky says sheepishly.

"Bullshit, Nicky. You did a lot for me. I would have never figured that out without you. I'm glad it worked out and I don't have to worry about anyone comin' after me again," I say in a relieved breath. "Can I ask you something?"

"Anything."

"What's the DCA? I've never heard of it."

"It's an offshoot of the FBI. We work covertly with little to no red tape on domestic issues. Drugs, human trafficking, organized crime, things like that."

"You're Jason Bourne aren't you?" I ask in a feigned fangirl voice.

"Somethin' like that," Nicky says in a cocky tone followed by a sincere smile.

Nicky stands up and presses a soft kiss into my cheek.

"Thought I lost you again," he murmurs into my skin before pressing another kiss to it. "I'll be by tomorrow to go over some more stuff." Nicky stands to leave the room but I stop him.

"Nicky," I call. He halts his retreat turning back to face me. "Thank you. You kept me alive and safe. No matter what happened to me this wasn't because of you. You're not to blame."

"Why'd you do it?" he questions in a whisper, making his way back to my bedside. Nicky sits in the chair and studies my face long and hard.

"Do what?"

"Throw yourself in front of me?" he asks quietly studying his hands that are bandaged and mangled.

"I just did," I say with a shrug. I don't know why I did it. I just did. Taylor was going to kill him and I couldn't let that happen. If I'd had a gun I would have shot Taylor. I wouldn't have killed him, but I would have stopped him. "What happened to your hands?"

"When you jumped in front of me I wrapped my hands around your head. The bullet that got you went through me. Doctor told me that it changed the trajectory of the bullet enough to stop you from getting the full brunt of the bullet."

"So you saved my life."

"No Shanny, you saved mine." His eyes (I hate the fake brown) get soft and I see how much pain he feels for what happened to me. I realize I want him in my life. I don't know how much, but I went through something that only he knows. I feel deeply connected to him. If he hadn't come to the job there's no doubt I'd be dead right now and probably would have gone through horrors before that end.

"Can I still be in contact with you even though you're a super secret agent?" I ask lightly.

"You can do whatever you want. I still feel like the bad guy though. I've done some really fucked up shit in this life...feel like a monster. So, you don't want me around, I'll take that. You want me around but not often, I'll take that. You want me in your life in any way, I'll take that. Just knowin' you're alive and safe, I'm good. There's no pressure Shanny."

I reach out and grab his arm trying to avoid his mangled hands. He places one of his bandaged mitts on top of my hand and smiles reluctantly at me.

"You were not the bad guy. You killed the bad guy...for me. I get that you think you're a monster, but a monster wouldn't have saved me. A monster wouldn't have tended to my wounds. A monster wouldn't have fed me. And a monster surely wouldn't have wrapped his hands around my head to stop a bullet. You may have been a monster in the past as Nick Scarso, but I met Nick Cooper in that torture chamber and he's a good guy," I say emphatically with a firm(ish) squeeze of his arm.

"I didn't stop Bruno in the bathroom with you," he whispers painfully.

"Don't you fuckin' dare. You didn't know what he was gonna do. You were tryin' to keep me safe. That situation was fucked! I don't blame you for that," I scold him. I can tell by the look on his face I've done nothing to alleviate his guilt. I'll keep trying.

168

"I didn't know I was gonna stop a bullet when I wrapped my hands around your head. You shocked the shit outta me and it was the only thing I could think to do to protect you," Nicky murmurs guiltily.

"Well you just made my point, dummy. You were tryin' to protect me." A small grin plays at his lips.

"You're the most amazin' woman I've ever met. If you didn't have that behemoth in the bathroom that obviously loves you better than I ever could, I'd make a play for you," Nicky admits strongly.

"Kel's it for me, but I appreciate the compliment." I smile sweetly.

"I know you've got a lot of support and love around you, but if you ever need anything call me. I'd do anything for you." He writes his number (very slowly given the state of his hands) on a notepad and hands it to me. He stands up and lingers for a moment. Then he bends over and presses his lips gently to my forehead. "I'll see you tomorrow," he murmurs into my skin. Then he's gone. He saved my life and inadvertently helped me remember things I've desperately wanted. Nicky's my friend.

I close my eyes finally alone in my room. The boys are still in the bathroom. All is quiet. I quickly drift to sleep thinking about Kel and his broken teal eyes.

Chapter 29

Kellerman

I wash myself as best I can in the shower, my hands quaking in pain the entire time. As I step out of the small cubicle I see fresh clothes sitting on the sink. The guys must have brought them in for me. I dress as quickly as I can with my battered hands (pretty damn slowly). There's still blood everywhere so I have to be careful where I step. The cleaning staff is going to love me. Once dressed I tentatively poke my head out the door, not knowing what reaction my presence will garner. I let out a sigh when I see Kid sleeping with the guys all sitting around her like a protective shield.

"Hey man," Kav says standing up. He takes a few steps toward me like he's approaching a wounded animal, slow and cautious. He stops a few feet away assessing me from head to toe. "Aidan called a hand specialist to see to you. He's gonna meet you downstairs somewhere when you're ready. Information's written down out at the nurse's station."

"Thanks, Kav," I say quietly so I don't wake Kid up. "She doin' okay?"

"Been asleep since we came out," Kav whispers and shrugs.

"I think I'll head down to the specialist now. I'll let you all know what happens." I turn on my heel and leave the room quickly. This is the first time I've left her room since I got here last week. It feels like I'm entering a new world, a dark new world where I'll be alone. Kid doesn't need the stressors of my life hanging over her right now. A possible father and kind of cheater, that's not what she deserves in life. I need to let her go. She needs to heal and reclaim her life.

I make my way down to some offices and wait for the hand specialist. It's well past office hours so he's definitely doing a favor for Aidan. The door to the waiting area opens and Aidan's large body fills the doorway. He lifts his chin at me as he crosses the room, sitting in the chair opposite me staring at my battered hands.

"Fucked those up," he says in a grunt. I nod. "Look Ry told me what happened. We knew Taylor was bad, but I'm sure hearin' what Kid felt about him was brutal. Dude wasn't dead we'd be huntin' his ass down."

"Never been so pissed someone's already dead that I wanna kill," I scoff.

"Don't bail on her," he orders. "I can see it in your face. You think you'll be doin' her a favor, you won't. You'll just hurt her more and she doesn't need that. You man up and stick."

"Aidan, why the fuck do you even want me around? You all beat the piss outta me not too long ago. You wanted my ass back in Seattle. Nothing's changed. I still might be a father. I have to consider what that'll do to Kid. If I leave now she may hurt in the beginning, but she'll heal without havin' to deal with all my bullshit. If I stay and have to choose between her and a child, things are gonna get real messy."

"Look we were wrong. I know you haven't let any of us say anything, but we were in the wrong. I'm so fuckin' sorry. We have a tendency to go off half-cocked when it comes to Kid. What we did with you was outta line. I don't blame you if you're pissed at us, shit, I'm pissed at us. Don't let that fuck with you. If the baby is yours, we'll deal with it, together, in the family. I want you around because you're part of this family. That's the reason we were so pissed at you. We thought you'd pulled the wool over our eyes. We weren't just pissed that we thought you fucked Kid over, we thought you fucked us over too."

172

"I get why you guys did what you did. Now that I know about Taylor, he had an agenda and it worked all of us. Not gonna lie though, you guys takin' his side without any thought for mine sucked." Aidan's head drops. I don't want to be mad at them. I'm not mad at them, I'm hurt. After the bathroom crying circle I feel a little better though. Maybe these friendships can be resurrected.

"I don't know what to do about my shit. I haven't talked to Cassie since that night in the sunroom. She keeps callin' and I don't pick up. I'm such a prick. She could be pregnant with my baby, and I'm not even pickin' up the phone for her," I huff.

"You don't cut yourself any slack do you?" Aidan questions with a smirk on his lips. "This is not a normal situation. It's not like you've been watchin' a game and havin' some beers instead of pickin' up the phone. You've had some serious shit goin' on. I think she'll get that." I doubt that. "And I'll say this again, I'm sorry. You're my friend and I shoulda given you the benefit of the doubt. Won't make that mistake again." I give him a slight nod. I don't know what to say. I don't know if I'll be around to even have a friendship with him or the guys anymore. "Doctor Wick should be here in a few minutes. I've gotta go wrap some things up. Think about what I said before you make any decisions."

"Thanks for callin' this guy. Not really what any of us need right now," I say as he stands up.

"No problem. See ya later."

As Aidan makes his way out of the room I sit and run through everything he said and didn't say. I know he's right in some ways, but he's wrong in others. I need to get my head straight. I reach in my pocket and pull out my Nexus. I hit the call button and put it on speaker phone. I can't hold my phone to my ear my hands hurt so bad.

She picks up halfway through the first ring.

"Dylan!" Cassie squeals.

"Hey, Cass," I say quietly.

"Dylan, oh my God! You were shot. You've been all over the news. I can't believe you went to that house. What were you thinking?!" She's so shrill I turn the volume down to dampen the effect.

"I'm okay Cass," I soothe. I can hear her sobbing. I'm sure pregnancy hormones aren't helping her with all of this.

"I can't believe you did that. I'm pregnant. What if you died? What would I tell our baby? I can't do this alone!" Now she's hysterical. I don't know what to say so I just sit and wait for her to calm down. I was selfish. But when Kieran figured out who Taylor was I had to go. I didn't think about abandoning my maybe baby either. I'm a selfish prick. I just wanted to save Kid. I didn't think beyond that, definitely not father of the year material.

"I'm serious, I can't do this alone. I need you to come home and help me. I'm a wreck. My hormones are all over the place and I'm pukin' my guts out all day and all night. I need you. Please," she whimpers.

"Cass, I'm sorry you're strugglin'. I need to figure some shit out before I can make any decisions," I explain gently.

"No! You can't have any more time! I need you now. Get on a plane!" Okay, that was a mood swing. She's growling now.

"I can't sit on a flight right now. My leg's not ready for that yet."

"Fly private. You can move or lay down or whatever you need to do." Fuck she has an answer for everything.

"I have a job in Kansas City, Cass. I can't just take off to Seattle."

"They have jobs here, Dylan. You can find one, I'm confident in your abilities to provide for our family." Wow now she's completely robotic. She sounds like a possessed "Stepford wife". That's not far from what she is in reality. Her father owns a fleet of fishing vessels and he has spoiled her rotten. Four months with her and I knew I couldn't keep up with her high maintenance. She liked to party, go out as often as she could, and shop until her credit cards were screaming for her to stop. It wasn't really a problem because I was out at sea most of the time we were together. She was just something to do on land. I should have stayed away from this crazy!

"Cass, I need to work stuff out with Shannon. We haven't talked about anything yet. You don't even know if the baby's mine. I told you I didn't want to get involved until I knew," I say a little harsher than I want.

"It's yours Dylan. It has to be."

"Why's that?"

"Because."

"Great reason."

"Don't be a dick. It's yours. I was only with the other guy once, and it wasn't the right time of the month," she spits.

"I need proof. I wore a condom, Cass. How can it be me?"

"Condom's aren't a hundred percent. Maybe it broke or something."

"I'd know if it broke. I took it off."

"I don't know what to tell you. It's yours. So get your ass on a plane and come home. Your son or daughter needs you!" She's getting teary again. I have whiplash from the violent mood swings.

"I'll call you tomorrow and we can talk about it. I need to go now. I have to see a doctor right now."

"Fine. You can go but you better call me!" she growls.

"I'll call," I promise.

"Bye, honey," she says quietly.

"Bye, Cass."

I hang up and toss my phone into the seat next to me. What a shit show!

"Didn't want to interrupt," I hear a voice to my side. I snap my head up to see a nicely dress older man. "Sorry."

"No. I didn't hear you come in. Sorry you had to hear that," I apologize.

"No worries. I've got five children. I know how it goes." I nod embarrassed that he heard any of our conversation.

"When's the due date?" he asks pleasantly. "Sorry, I'm Dean Wick. Aidan Callaghan asked me to see you." He goes to extend his hand to shake mine before assessing the damage I'm sporting.

"I'm not really in the position to shake your hand. Thanks for comin' in to see me after hours," I say guiltily. I pulled this man away from his five kids because I had a temper tantrum.

"I just told you I have five children, this is a reprieve," he jokes. "Let's get some images of your hands and then we'll see where we're at." I nod and follow him into a small x-ray room. I put on the heavy apron and sit still while he captures multiple images of my hands.

"Have a seat in the room next door while I get these processed," he instructs.

I move into the next room and wait silently. He comes in a few minutes later lining up the images side by side on a large light box affixed to the wall. He looks them over silently circling things and making notes in a chart.

"Well you did quite a number on yourself. You've got what we call a boxer's fracture in your right hand. You can see here your fourth and fifth metacarpals are fractured." He indicates toward the image where I can see what look like breaks in the bones. "In your left hand you also have a boxer's fracture but only in the fifth metacarpal. I think we can just tape your left hand but your right will need to be splinted. We also need to dress the abrasions to avoid infection." I nod. Not much to say to that. He leaves the room and comes back a few minutes later with some stuff to get me set up.

176

"I'll start with the abrasions. I have a product here that's like a second skin. It adheres to your skin and stays in place until the healing process is complete," he explains as he starts cleaning my hands. Fucking hell that hurts. I sit still and watch him work. This reminds me of when I had to fix Kid's hand after she beat the shit out of that creeper at Bar. I hated that it happened at the time but taking care of her and holding her in my arms that night was pure pleasure. It was our beginning.

"I know it's not my place but are you having issues with paternity?" Wow that came out of left field. Normally I'd tell this guy to fuck off, but he's here taking care of me as a favor so I rein it in.

"I guess you could say that. The woman I was talkin' to is my ex. I just found out she's pregnant. She doesn't know if I'm the father. She doesn't want to do an amnio or some other thing I can't remember. I have to wait until the baby's born to find out," I say humiliated.

"That's not true," he says confidently.

"I'm sorry?" I don't know which thing I said was wrong.

"You don't have to wait until the child is born and she doesn't need to have and amniocentesis or a CVS," he explains.

"Really? She said that those were the only options."

"Most people think those are the only options. The medical industry is always changing and innovating with new techniques. There's a new non-invasive blood test that can determine paternity. The fetal cells are carried in the mother's blood. Once a routine blood draw is performed it can be analyzed for DNA testing," he says with a smile seeing the relief flooding my face.

"Can that test happen at any time?" I ask hoping it can be done tomorrow!

"I think after ten weeks. I'm not sure on those details, but I can get you in touch with a lab here that does the test."

"That would be great. Thank you so much," I say smiling from ear to ear.

"Not a problem."

Once my second skin is in place, Dr. Wick tapes my pinky and ring finger together on my left hand. I have to keep it taped for at least two weeks. My right hand is sporting a very attractive black splint that looks like an overworked bowling glove. My pinky and ring finger are held stable by the splint and the glove holds my palm and wrist in place. It's uncomfortable. Teach me to fight an innocent wall.

I'm going back to Kid's room. Aidan was right I was thinking about taking off tonight, but I can't do that to Kid. I at least need to talk to her first. If she asks me to leave I will, but I'm not just going to take off. The old me would do that, I'm not him anymore.

Chapter 25

Shannon

I wake up in the hospital room in a sweat. I was having a nightmare. My breathing is labored and my heart is pounding. I squeeze my left hand to draw some comfort from Kel, but my hand is cold and empty. Kel's not here. I push the button to raise the back of my bed up slowly. The guys are all in their little beds around the room. They look so big in those tiny things, giants in doll furniture. I get a bit of comfort seeing them here with me. My pain meds have worn off, but I'm going to wait before I ask the nurse for more. They make me foggy and I need to think.

Taylor did this to me. While he didn't order the kidnapping, he allowed it to happen. He told me he fell for me and when I didn't return the sentiment he handed me to who he knew was a torturous monster. I feel sick at the idea of Taylor's hands on me. Motherfucker is lucky he's dead. I can't believe I went off about Taylor in front of Kel. It was stupid and selfish on my part. There's part of me that wonders if I did it on purpose. Kel cheated on me (kind of cheated), and now there's a baby coming. I don't understand why he's here, yet I'm happy he is. Why am I happy my kind of cheating boyfriend is by my side? I need to call my old therapist, quick.

"Kiddo," Kel calls from the bedside. I jump. "Jesus. Sorry. I didn't mean to scare you."

"It's okay. I was just lost in my head." I look at his hands and gasp. "Shit! Kel, your hands." I reach out to grab his thick wrists and pull his hands toward me to inspect them. They've been covered in some skin like material, taped, and splinted.

"I'm all right," he says softly pulling his hands away from me. "You mind if I sit?" He's so tentative he's making me uncomfortable. I don't speak I just nod to his chair. Once he sits I start in.

"Kel, I—" He cuts me off before I can get going.

"I know you just woke up and went through a nightmare before that, but there are some things I need you to know now." I sit silently and let him continue. "I did not sleep with Cassie when I was in Seattle. We did the things you saw in those pictures and that's fuckin' awful enough but it went no further. I was pissed you weren't answerin' your phone and you were in your room with Taylor. I had a lapse in judgment and if you hate me for that, I get it. But I need you to know I didn't sleep with her. I haven't been with anyone since I laid eyes on you in Mia's room."

My heart sings at this information. He didn't sleep with her! He made out with her and maybe copped a feel but he didn't fuck her. The relief I feel is so immense I can't describe. I go to say something, but he continues.

"Got some bad news though, Kiddo. I slept with her right before I moved home and she's pregnant. She doesn't know if it's mine, but she's convinced herself that it is. I asked her to get a paternity test done. She's refusin' to get an amnio or the other test they can do. She says I have to wait until the baby's born."

"That's fuckin' bullshit Kel," I rage. "There's a maternal blood screen that can be done. It's non-invasive and can be done early in the pregnancy. She refuses and I'll file a motion to compel her to do so. And if that baby's yours and you want custody, I'll fight my ass off to get that for you," I rant. He launches himself at me.

"I love you so fuckin' much!" he bellows with his face in my neck. Smashing me beneath his massive body I wrap my arms around his shoulders and squeeze him tight. I'm sure I smell like a dumpster, but I don't care. He feels good against my body.

"Told you so," Kav mumbles from his doll bed. I feel Kel start to shake with chuckles. "And just some advice for the future...no glove, no love."

Kel snorts before he retakes his seat in his chair.

"Thanks for the advice, but apparently that's not a hundred percent, or that's what I'm waitin' to find out," Kel scoffs.

"Wait, you wore a bag and she's sayin' it's yours? I call bullshit," Kavy scoffs right back.

"Have to wait and find out I guess." Kel shrugs.

"That kid comes back as yours I'm guessin' that chick went mental and stole your swimmers from the condom," Kavy says as he sits up in his miniature bed, tattooed chest blazing. I stare at our clover and get tingles. My family.

"What're you talkin' about Kav? That's crazy!" Kel quietly yells.

"Fuck yeah its crazy. Happened to a dude I played rugby with."

"Kavy you're freakin' him out. Jeez," I scold.

"Could she really have done something like that?" Kel asks me.

"It happens, Kel. I doubt she did that though. Again, if she did, I'll fight to get you that baby," I spout confidently. This I can deal with. This is my world, my comfort zone. Maybe even a welcome distraction. I need to have Finn start doing background on her tomorrow. Kel's told me about her and she sounds like a piece of work.

"All right, I'm goin' back to sleep. You two keep the moanin' to a minimum," Kavy teases laying back. Kel and I both chuckle. Kavy's asleep in about ninety seconds. I swear he can fall asleep anywhere at the drop of a hat.

"Okay, now it's my turn," I say to Kel squeezing his hand gently. "I did cheat on you. I made out with Taylor and he got a little handsy. I'm so fuckin' sorry. I was sad and mad and hurt and he took advantage, but I allowed it. I did stop him though because even in that moment where I thought you had done something cruel and heartless, I still loved you."

"This day has included too much of you talkin' about kissin' other dudes," he growls. "I don't give a shit what happened with you and Taylor." I arch a brow at him. "Okay, I give a shit. A big shit. But it doesn't matter now. He's gone and you're safe. That's all that matters. I have you back." He raises my hand and kisses my palm. I wince at some pain in my head and he drops my hand like his lips just seared my skin.

"It's not you, Kel. My head hurts," I say softly. He reaches up and hits the nurse call button. She answers on the intercom and he barks that I need some pain medication.

"You can be nice when you ask," I chide.

"Don't like seein' you in pain." His voice is gruff as he picks my hand back up. His hands are really fucked up. I can't believe he did that to himself.

"Do your hands hurt?" I ask gently.

"Little," he says dismissively.

"Don't do that again. I couldn't get to you and you were in pain. That was torture for me and now that I know what torture is actually like, I don't want to experience that ever again literally or emotionally," I say sternly. His face wears hurt from my statement. I'm such a dick lately (blaming the drugs). The nurse comes in before either of us says anything else. I get doped up and she gets on her way, rolling her eyes at my garden of sleeping men.

"I'm sorry I hurt you today. I broke. I've been drowning since I realized you were gone and I hit my breakin' point hearin' you say you were waitin' for Taylor to save you. I don't care how you got through those days. It's not about me. I shouldn't have gone off like that. I never wanna be the reason you're hurt," Kel says in a whisper.

"We're a mess. All we keep doin' is apologizing to each other. Enough of that. I love you. This is gonna be a rough road and we need to be there for each other. We'll both have moments where we crack and break, but if we lean on one another we'll make it through. Promise me you'll lean on me before you attack a bathroom again," I instruct.

"I promise," he says assuredly. "Promise me you won't shut me out. I get how hard this will be, I can take it. Just don't shut me out," he requests. He knows me so well. It's what I want to do. I want to shield him from what happened to me and shield myself by denying it happened. I won't do that though. I'll heal and survive and face the demons lurking in the shadows of that house.

"I promise," I state firmly.

"Can I kiss you?" he asks sweetly.

"No."

"No?" he asks shocked.

"I don't know the last time I brushed my teeth, but my mouth feels like I ate a wooly mammoth's ass," I exclaim. He doubles over in a heaving laugh. I follow right along with him wincing at little shots of pain. When he's done he stands up and goes into the bathroom (be careful not to piss him off tiles). He comes back out with a toothbrush and two cups.

"Brush," he instructs handing me the toothpaste covered toothbrush. "Spit," he says holding an empty cup in front of my lips. "Swish," he says handing me a cup of water. "Spit," he repeats putting the spit cup in front of me again. Ah, fresh and clean. "Better?" he asks pleased with himself.

"Better." I smile. He sits on the side of my bed and leans his face into my space. His breath is heating my lips and I'm trembling in anticipation.

"I love you," he whispers and with passion he captures my lips. His soft plump pillows work eagerly across mine, tasting and savoring every inch of my mouth. Kel's tongue slips out and I willingly open my lips meeting my tongue with his. He tastes like heaven, spearmint mixed with Kel. A moan creeps up my throat and he intensifies the kiss massaging my tongue with his. His hands move down my chest, the rough calluses catching on the fabric of my hospital gown. He gets to my breast and my breath hitches. Kel stops kissing me and drops his hands pulling away from me, regret marking his face.

"No Kel, don't stop. I don't want Taylor to be the last man that's touched me. Please," I beg. Not just Taylor but the almost rapist. I want Kel to be the last man to have his hands on me. He hesitates a moment and then comes right back to me. His mouth more insistent and possessive, his hands pinching and rolling my nipples on the outside of my gown. I reach up and slide the shoulder of my gown off. It's not tied in the back because of my wounds. Easy access! His hand gently pulls the gown under my breast and he begins to palm me like a teenager copping his first feel. He runs his thumbs across my now achingly hard nipples. I arch my back pushing into him and a growl emotes from deep in his chest. His tongue darts in and out of my mouth as he nips at my lips constantly working his hands. He keeps working at me until I'm ready to move this along. But Kel begins to slow the kiss and release the pressure on my breasts. He drops his face into my neck both of us panting hard. He rights my gown back into place ever so carefully.

"Spank bank full!" Cally yells. All five of us break into cleansing tear-filled laughter.

Chapter 26

Kellerman

Kid made me sleep in her bed last night. I can barely fit in this bed alone much less both of us, but I wasn't denying her. After our make-out session, I wanted to be close to her. It took every ounce of self-control I possess to stop that where it ended. All I wanted to do was rip that damn hospital gown off her and bury myself to the hilt inside her until she begged me to stop. Yeah, I need to quit thinking about that. I woke up about ten minutes ago with a handful of tit and morning wood that still aches. It'll be a long cold shower this morning.

I gently peel myself away from Kid, trying not to disturb her sleep. Her garden of giants, sleeping in beds made for gnomes are snoring loud enough to wake the entire hospital. I stand up and stretch my arms above my head wincing at the pain from being stuck in the same position all night. My leg hurts the worst in the morning and now my hands are in the fray. I'm a hot mess. I amble away grabbing some clean clothes before heading into the bathroom. The blood is gone as well as the tile mess that was on the floor, but my wall of destruction remains. In the light of day I feel like a complete douche.

The weight of the world has been lifted off my shoulders after talking to Kid last night. I wasn't sure what her reaction would be, but as always I was floored by her dedication to me. I have no doubt that she'll be by my side through this whole maybe baby situation. Now, I can focus on her. I want to get her well and get her home. It's Christmas Eve and I'm realizing I don't have anything here for her for Christmas...hasn't been a priority. I step into the small shower and let the cool water run over my tense muscles. I haven't worked out in a week and a half. I've done pushups and crunches, but my leg hasn't allowed for much beyond that. The guys and I usually hit the gym hard for at least an hour and a half every night. We'll all be sore when we get back to it.

I climb out of the shower, dry off and quickly (my version of quickly with jacked up hands) pull my clothes on. I try not to be away from Kid long. Bathing was not even part of the program until a few days ago. I creep back out of the bathroom to see the sleeping giants have arisen. We're foul creatures. The farts and burps bubbling around the room are enough to make me roll my eyes as I make my way to my woman. Her sleepy eyes are fluttering open.

"Mornin'," I murmur against her forehead before sitting in my trusty chair. She gives me an annoyed stare. Kid is not a morning person, even doped up on pain killers. I don't know if she's allowed coffee yet. I should check so she'll quit looking at me like that. I switch my gaze away from her and over to the boys.

"Kav, can I talk to you a minute?" I ask. He's sitting on the end of his bed scratching...everything. His tattoos ablaze only in his boxer briefs, dude doesn't care that we aren't at home. He sleeps how he sleeps. At least that's what he told the nurses the first night here. Some of these girl's faces when they've walked in the room in the mornings have been beet red. The man has no shame.

"What's up?" he asks standing up.

"Maybe put Hulk away and talk outside?" I suggest. I don't need to see any more of the outline of his dick than I already can.

"Jealous?" he snorts.

"Very," I snark. I glance up at Kid and her eyes are closed but the grin on her lips says she's listening. Kav pulls on a pair of sweats and a thermal nodding his head at the door. Once in the corridor he winks at one of the nurses I'm sure he's going to fuck before we leave here.

"You good?" Kav asks turning his attention back to me. "Not as good as you could be based on your performance with Kid last night," he teases. I roll my eyes.

"I'm good, dick. I need to go shop for Kid. Obviously, I don't have Christmas shit here. Now that she's awake I wanna get her somethin'," I explain.

"Yeah the guys and I talked about it last night. We're gonna go out and pick some stuff up for her this afternoon. Family'll be here all day so we can slip out and she won't be alone," Kav says eye fucking the nurse some more. I'm guessing this is the longest he's gone without pussy. He may spontaneously combust.

"I need a jewelry store," I say. That gets his head snapping back to me.

"You thinkin' about puttin' a ring on it?" His face is shocked.

"Kav, we've been together two months. Come on," I scoff. That's nothing but a lie. I'd ask her to marry me now if I thought she'd say yes. With all her shit going on combined with Cassie, not really proposal time.

"When you do that shit, you better come correct," he warns.

"And what's your version of that?" This should be good.

"Fuck you Kellerman. You know what I mean. She deserves a rock the size of the moon and a proposal at the Super Bowl half-time show. Not to mention you have a lot of people to ask for their blessings. Come correct," he enunciates the last part. I shake my head at him.

"Well I'll get on mining moon size diamonds," I snark. He scowls at me before being distracted by his nurse again. Attention span of a toddler.

"We'll head out when the O'Sullivan clan gets here. Safer," he mumbles distractedly.

"Sounds good. You gonna head down for breakfast? Or you gonna cover her in syrup and have a breakfast buffet?" He shoves my shoulder wearing a shit-eating grin.

"I'm gonna talk to Kid's nurse and see if she can eat some real food. She's lost so much weight lately I wanna stuff a pound of bacon in her mouth," Kav grumbles. He's right; Kid's really thin right now. She was losing weight before this with all the stress of Butch's trial, now it's worse.

I break away from the now increasingly uncomfortable mutual eye fucking and head back into the room. O'Sullivan, Cal and Kid are all cracking up when I walk in. The sound of her laughter is intoxicating. I prowl over to her and capture her mouth in a hard kiss, halting her chuckle. Smiling broadly as I pull back from her.

"I'm next," O'Sullivan claims.

"Okay, but just one," I say leaning toward him. He palms my face and I sit back in my seat snickering.

"I never thought I'd have this again," Kid says quietly. There's a ghost of a smile on her lips but despair in her eyes.

"Kid," Cal soothes. "You'll always have this. Where you go, we go."

"I was sad, guys. At some point I came to terms with the fact that I was probably gonna die," she whispers.

"Kid?" Kav calls from the doorway no doubt he just heard what she said. His eyes hold as much despair as hers.

"I didn't give up, Kavy. I was gonna fight, but I knew it was a fight I'd lose," she admits dejectedly. God this is going to be a long road back to healthy happy Kid. I keep my emotions intact. No more going off the rails for me.

"You wouldn't have lost. Your team never loses," Kav says sweetly coming to her bedside.

"I was gonna lose, Kavy."

"Didn't happen. Never gonna happen," Kav spouts confidently wrapping his gigantic arms around her shoulders, crushing her to his chest.

Chapter 27

Kellerman

"Aaron, you're gonna smother her," Pop chides from the door. Kav pulls back and presses a hard kiss to her forehead before addressing his father.

"Mornin', Pop."

"Mornin'. Go help your brothers," Pop orders. Kav nods and heads out the door.

"Hoppin' in the shower," Cal informs us.

"Quick. I need to grab one too," O'Sullivan replies. Cal offers a chin lift and disappears into the room of destruction.

"Mornin', sweetheart," Pop coos running the backs of his fingers along Kid's cheek. "Sleep good?"

"Yeah, Pop," she says back smiling brightly at her father. It was strange at first trying to figure out all the relationships she has with these intertwined families. Now it just seems normal that she has three fathers, two mothers, and nine completely fucking crazy brothers.

"Jesus Christ, will you carry some of the weight, bitches?" Kav sneers. Ryan, Adam and Kav are carrying a Christmas tree into Kid's room. Or I should say, Kav is doing most of the carrying while Ryan and Adam watch.

"I'm carryin' the decorations," Adam points out.

"Yeah, and I'm still sore from my date last night," Ryan teases. Kav hoists the large fir into the room and leans it against the wall.

"Pussies," Kav says under his breath before he flops on his bed. Cal comes out of the bathroom and O'Sullivan takes his turn.

"You brought be a tree?" Kid whispers to Pop.

"Ryan and Adam's idea," Pop says proud of his sons.

"Best part of Christmas is watchin' you around the tree, Kid," Ryan says softly kissing her on the cheek.

"Couldn't miss it," Adam finishes with a forehead kiss.

"Love you guys," Kid murmurs into Adam's neck.

"Now, you can't decorate so you instruct and we'll follow," Pop says clapping his hands together.

After two hours there is a fully dressed seven foot tall fir in Kid's hospital room. There are presents under it now that the rest of the family has shown up. You'd never know what we'd been through the last ten days if we weren't in this room with Kid stuck in this bed. It feels like a normal Christmas Eve.

"Now, I know they're bein' cautious with food, but you're too thin," Maggie says pointedly after Kid refuses a Christmas cookie the size of her head.

"Ma, I don't feel great. I can't eat that, I'll get sick. I kept the smoothie down this morning but that was pushin' it. I'll gain the weight back. I'm okay, don't worry," Kid urges. Everyone fussing over her is starting to take its toll.

"I'll always worry," Maggie says softly pushing a tear from her cheek. She and Mary cry so much it's a wonder they're not constantly dehydrated.

"Ma," Kid soothes.

"I know. I know. Love you," Maggie coos and kisses her daughter's cheek lingering a moment before exiting the room, to surely cry her eyes out on Sully Senior's shoulder.

"What'd you do now, Kid?" O'Sullivan chides from his bed where he's been immersed in some game on his tablet.

"Just bein' my marvelously extraordinary self," Kid snarks.

"All right gentleman, if you all can clear out for a few minutes I need to see to my patient," Sheryl the nurse states firmly as she rolls a cart in the room. Most of Kid's brothers are in here so one by one they clear out. They won't go far. I stand up and place a chaste kiss at the edge of Kid's mouth and follow the group. As I leave the room Sheryl pulls the privacy curtain and gets to work. I'm guessing she's changing bandages on the bullet wounds. She'll need plastic surgery to remove the scars from her beating. Kav already talked to a surgeon who assured us it can be done once she's ready. Not soon e-fucking-nough!

"I hear you're visiting the jewelry store, Dylan," Mary says quietly from behind me. There are no secrets in this group.

"I am," I respond with a grin as she makes her way around me. She's starting to look like herself again. Her blonde hair is smoothed back from her flawlessly aged face. The bags and dark circles are gone from beneath her ocean blue eyes. Her slacks and red sweater make her look like a Christmas card has come to life. Doc is a lucky man.

"Always a good choice," she says kindly, though I can tell she wants to say something else. "I met Robert when Aidan was six months old. There was this gorgeous man standing in the baby aisle of the grocery store with three little boys, all of which were screaming, as Robert tried to load the cart with diapers while having Aidan in a baby carrier, Ryan on his hip, and Finn in the cart seat. That scene would have made most men wanna rip their hair out and run screaming in the opposite direction. Robert had a smile on his face. I melted." I smile because I don't have any idea why she's telling me this story, but I'm happy to listen.

"A lot of things changed in my life that day. I didn't know it then but I became a mother, a wife, a future grandmother, and a future mother-in-law in the baby aisle of a grocery store. Then about seventeen years later I got the daughter I always hoped for. My life was complete when we got Kid. She was the missing piece in our family we didn't know was gone. I have the feeling you'll be involved in some of those future roles I was blessed with twenty-nine years ago and reinforced thirteen years ago. I'll be nothing but pleased to have you included in our family, Dylan," she says softly patting my cheek two times. I have not a clue how to respond to that. I'm afraid she thinks I'm proposing.

"Mary I appreciate that more than you know, but anything that may be in our future is a long way off at this point."

"Oh Dylan, you just keep telling yourself that," she mocks and shakes her head walking away. Okay, that was weird. I didn't know that Cal's mom died when they were that young. Dude doesn't talk about that shit. He doesn't talk about much actually. The way I understand it, he only really talks to Mary and Kid. Not bad choices for conversation companions.

"You wanna head out?" Kav asks moving next to me. "Nurse'll be a while and the rest of the family is all staying until after we eat Christmas Eve dinner."

"Let me just tell her I'm headin' out."

"Grab our coats too would ya?" I offer a chin lift and head into Kid's room.

"Hey Kiddo, a couple of the guys and I are gonna head out for a bit. We'll be back soon okay?" I explain through the curtain as I move around the room gathering up the guys' coats.

"Okie dokie," she says loudly. She's so fucking cute when she says shit like that, I chuckle. "Don't laugh at my old lady saying," she feigns offense.

"Be good, Kiddo," I instruct moving toward the door. "Love you."

"Love you too, Kel," she purrs in her raspy sexy voice. On that note it's time to go before I do something sexually inappropriate in front of Sheryl and the rest of Kid's family. I may have let out a growl as I make my way out the door trailed by Kid's giggles.

"What?" O'Sullivan asks grabbing his coat from me.

194

"Your sister," I grunt. A Cheshire grin sweeps across his face.

"Pain in the ass right? Or should I say a pain in the dick?" I snort and shove his shoulder, though I can't disagree with him.

"Quit fondlin' each other," Cal snarks. "Let's move." So off I limp into the Windy City to find the perfect Christmas present. No pressure.

Chapter 28

Shannon

"How's that?" Sheryl asks as she eases the nightgown over my shoulders.

"So much better," I groan in relief. I've had a sponge bath, my hair washed and conditioned, my bandages changed, and am now in a soft jersey nightgown Mary bought me. I feel like a new woman. My catheter (medical device of the devil) was removed shortly after I woke up yesterday. I've since had the lovely experience of using a bed pan. I'm healing well and off all the weird drugs so I finally get to get out of bed and pee. Whoo hoo!

"You'll have to just let your hair air dry, honey. The wound at the back of your head is still healing," she explains as she cleans up around me.

"It is not a beauty contest around here. I'm good with air dried hair." I snicker.

"Tree's gorgeous by the way."

"Thanks. I just sat in bed and barked out orders. I could get used to this."

"Somehow I doubt that," she remarks, brow raised. She's right. I can't wait to get the hell out of here and back to my life. I grin in response. "Now get some rest. I'm gonna keep your family outta here a little while so you can sleep. Let your pain medication do its work. If you need me, call me. Do NOT get outta that bed on your own," she orders sternly.

"Promise," I respond crossing my heart. I wonder how long she'll be able to keep my family out of this room. I should time it, but I can feel my eye lids starting to droop. Who knew having someone wash and take care of all your needs could be so exhausting? Sleepy time it is.

"Shanny," I hear calling in the distance. A warm hand holding mine squeezes ever so slightly. I flutter my eyes open to see my long lost friend smiling at me.

"Nicky," I rasp hoarsely. "What time is it?"

"A little after four," he answers. Wow I was out a while. The room is empty besides Nicky and me. Sheryl must have some kind of long distance wasp spray she uses to keep my family out. I'm impressed. "How're you feelin'?"

"Better than yesterday. Still tired, but I got cleaned and changed earlier and that made a big difference," I beam. It's weird sitting here talking to someone I thought I'd never see again. Even weirder the circumstances that have brought us back together. Today has been harder than yesterday. More nightmares and thoughts of the almost rapist and everything he did to me. The bathroom incident hasn't bothered me yet, I'm not sure it ever will.

"I know this is hard for you," he says reading my mind. "You strugglin' with stuff?"

"I don't know, Nicky. You're right this is hard. Hard actually doesn't begin to cover it,. I've been through another trauma before and it took a lot for me to get back to myself. I'm here recovering, thankful to be alive, and on some great drugs but when that relief fades and the drugs are gone, I know how this goes. There is a blackness awaiting me."

"I know about what happened thirteen years ago," he mutters softly.

"What?!"

"Your house was bugged, Shanny. From what I can tell Mancini's crew didn't listen too much and I don't think they listened to that part. It hadn't been flagged as listened to. I listened after you were here though. No one else in my agency has or will hear that," he explains quickly.

"Fuckin' shit," I huff. "The pool guys right? The crew that came to winterize the pool?" I knew those guys were shifty. Teach me to trust a cute pool boy again or answer the door for a flower delivery. When I get home I'm permanently attaching a gun to my hand. He nods. "This is what I'm talkin' about, Nicky. That's some dark shit."

"I won't lie to you. You ask me anything I'll tell you the truth. The truth is not pretty and it'll be hard to hear, but I won't lie to you."

"Don't ever tell me Taylor loved me again. That backstabbin' prick passed me off to them knowin' what they'd do. He led me to slaughter. He tried to take me from Kel and when that didn't work he was willin' to sacrifice my life. I did nothing to deserve that," I whisper before finishing. "That shit that went down yesterday about killed Kel."

"Kellerman? You're worried about him in all this?" Nicky scoffs. Okay it's lesson time.

"Yes, I'm worried about him. I'm worried about my whole family. They went through a trauma just like I did. Theirs was different, but it was scarring nonetheless. You met me when I was eight and had a privileged life. I'm not the same person anymore. You know what happened when I was eight and apparently what happened when I was seventeen. That shit changed me. I'm not complainin' because I love who I am and the family I have now, but I'm different. So get me when I say they mean everything to me. Knowin' that my life bein' in danger hurt them, pains me worse than what was done to me." There's an edge to my voice, but he needs to understand how I work.

"You're not different," he says smugly. I raise a brow at him and wait for an explanation. "You always loved fiercely. You refused to leave your dead father as you were losin' your own life. You told me you took care of

199

your Uncle Mick until he took his last breath. You asked a little boy to play with you and gave him your first kiss because he asked you for it. And you threw yourself in front of me without thought to protect me from bein' shot after everything you went through. You're not different." Okay maybe not that different, but I am different.

"I'm different. I don't trust people anymore. I don't sleep feeling comfortable and safe unless I'm in Kavy's arms or as of late Kel's. I'm so terrified to let anyone close enough to love me I almost ran Kel off the day that they grabbed me. Yes, I'm still fiercely loyal and probably more so, but a girl that takes comfort in knowing how to kill someone with her bare hands and relishes in her weapons skills is not the same girl that you knew."

"Point taken," he acquiesces.

"I'm not havin' a great day in my head today. Strugglin' with Taylor and I can't really talk to the guys about it. They're too pissed. I'm havin' some nightmares about the almost rapist too," I whisper. I feel like such an idiot for believing anything Taylor said. I'm generally a good judge of character, but wow I was off the mark with that one. Pretty bad time to make that mistake.

Nicky's face is marred with sorrow, not pity, but painful sorrow.

"You have to cut yourself some slack with Taylor. He played you all and that was his job. Don't carry that guilt. And Bruno...that motherfucker is dead, Shanny. He can't hurt you! I know that won't help you forget what he did, but he's never comin' near you again. You need to talk to someone though. Can't leave this shit to fester. Have you told your family, Kellerman?"

"I haven't said anything. I don't want to tell anyone. They've dealt with so much already because of me I don't want to add to it," I admit guiltily.

"Don't make those kinda decisions for them. They love you and are here to support you. It'll be hard, but carryin' that shit on your own will be devastating. I'm here for you and you can talk to me about whatever you need to. I'm not goin' anywhere," Nicky finishes emphatically with an attempt at a hand squeeze. Kel and him could be hand injury twins.

"What do I do about Taylor? I'm questioning my sanity at this point. How did he get that over on me? I knew he wanted me, but I truly believed he had feelings for me. Then he sends me off to be tortured, raped, murdered? How could I be so damn blind?" I'm an idiot!

"I wasn't gonna let anything happen to you," Nicky says strongly.

"Taylor didn't know that."

"No he didn't. But I want you to know it. I wasn't gonna let anything happen to you."

"You didn't let anything happen to me," I remind him.

"Bullshit!" Nicky spouts. If I didn't know any better I'd think Kavy was sitting next to me. So I offer Nicky a Kavy worthy glare.

"It's true, Shanny. If I'd been there the whole time you wouldn't have takin' that beating or the hanging. And I sure as shit wouldn't have had to pull him off you before..." Nicky trails off. "And then the bathroom. Fuck Shanny I let shit happen that never shoulda even come close to you!" he yells at himself.

"Why is it that I always have men in my life carryin' guilt around like priceless Louis Vuitton luggage they can't take their eyes off of?" I huff. "Did you order the kidnapping?"

"No."

"Did you beat the shit outta me, order it, have any say in it?"

"No."

"Did you leave me hangin' afterwards?"

"No."

201

"Did you come into that room and plan to rape me?"

"NO!"

"Did you leave me in that bathroom thinkin' I'd have to kill someone to keep myself safe?!"

"Fuck no!!"

"Then fuckin' quit with the guilt shit!!"

"Okay," Nicky relents softly.

"Okay."

Round two of rid Nicky of guilt seems to have been more successful. Nicky keeps holding my hand and starts filling me in on some legal proceedings that are starting after Christmas. Nicky's touch is soft and soothing, but I can tell it's doing more for him than me. He still feels guilty. That won't go away but maybe someday it will be less intense for him. He may have shit to feel guilty about in this life...I'm not one of them.

Chapter 29

Kavanagh

We went out of control shopping. Yes we're men and shopping is not our idea of a good time, but shopping for Kid is different. She loves holidays and presents so we always make a big deal out of all the holidays. This one we may have lost our minds a little bit. The four of us can barely carry all of the stuff we bought back up to her room. As we walk down the corridor to Kid's room I notice everyone is still milling around the waiting area outside her room.

"You guys went out of control," Maggie admonishes us. She's not wrong. We set down all of the bags and boxes in the waiting area. I turn around and see Cooper (I've been warned to use the correct name or suffer the wrath of Shannon Kelly weapon extraordinaire) sitting with Kid...alone. I see this about two seconds before Kellerman sees it giving me about half a second to intervene before he ruins some other part of his body. The bathroom can take no more abuse.

"Man, keep it together," I urge with a firm hand on his shoulder. Finn walks over to offer some back-up.

"We've been watchin'. She's good, Kellerman," Finn explains softly.

"She was kidnapped, beaten and almost killed. I don't want him near her and I can't fuckin' believe any of you do either," Kellerman bellows to the group. He's right. I don't want him near her either, but I know Kid. Her and Cooper have history, she's going to have him around. I'll admit I'm jealous. She had someone before me that was her friend. I don't give a shit if he was a little kid, and it was for one afternoon. He had her before me. I'm possessive of her and what we have. Caveman? Yes. Alpha male? You bet your ass I am. She's my best friend, my sister. I share her with the guys because they've got as much claim on her as I do, but this fuckwad...no.

"Let's go," I growl. I got myself worked up with all that. I push her door open and stalk in. Kid clocks my mood before I'm two steps in with Kellerman, Cal, O'Sullivan and Finn right at my sides.

"Kavy," she warns. "Easy." Kellerman and O'Sullivan growl while Cal and Finn snort in disgust.

"I'm guessin' there's a room full of angry men behind me," Cooper says knowingly as he pivots his head to witness his telepathic abilities.

"Damn skippy," I spout.

"I'm gonna head out, Shanny. I'll be in touch," Nicky says as he stands up moving toward her and kisses her cheek. Kellerman is shaking next to me so hard I can feel the floor moving beneath our feet. As Cooper moves toward us we stand in his way, a wall of testosterone. "Can I talk to you a minute?" he asks me. That was unexpected. I look at my posse and they're all thrown too. I give him a curt nod and turn on my heel to exit the room. This should be interesting. Once out of Kid's room he motions with his arm for me to follow him. We go to the end of the hall into a stairwell outside the ear shot of the family. I could get a good ass whipping in on him in here and no one would hear it. I'll keep that in mind.

"I get that you all hate my fuckin' guts," he says honestly. "I'd hate me too if I were in your position. The thing is there's no way in hell you all can hate me more than I hate myself. If I coulda stopped this or made it easier on her I would've. I did the fuckin' best I could but it'll never be enough in my mind. If I hadn't shown up, let me give you a picture of what that woulda been. They woulda beaten her, raped her, tortured her, starved her and then they would've cut her into pieces and shipped her to you guys. I can tell by the look on your face the thought makes you sick, well it makes me fuckin' sick too because it's true.

"I don't need to feel good about what I did...I don't. I feel like shit about it. But Shanny says she wants me to stay in her life. I'll stay away from you guys and respect whatever boundaries she puts in place. I'm not makin' a move so you don't need to alert her gladiator boyfriend. I'm tryin' to do the right thing here. The only thing that's felt right in my entire damn life is doin' right by her and I promise you I'll keep doin' right by her no matter what. I love her. I've loved her since the day I met her and I'm guessin' you know how easy she is to love and that shit didn't stop the day she died twenty-two years ago." We stand there in silence for a minute or so before he speaks again.

"I'll let you get back to your family now. I just wanted to make my position known. From what I can tell you're the alpha of that pack." He stops and waits for my response. I'm a little floored by his honesty, but I recover quickly. Damn straight I'm the alpha, although Kellerman is the alpha of Kid's pack now. Scratch that, Kid's the alpha of our pack and lets us pretend to be the alphas of the pack.

"I appreciate you tellin' me that. I don't know if it makes a difference, but I appreciate it. She's my best friend. She's my sister. I almost lost her and you had a hand in that. It'll take me and the rest of us a while to get all this shit straight. Kid wants you around, I think you get that we don't get much say in that. She runs shit around here. That said, we think you're hurtin' her or makin' shit worse for her we'll cut you up and ship you to yours in pieces so she doesn't have to worry about you anymore," I warn in a blank tone. A ghost of a smile creeps across his face.

"We get all this sorted out. You and I are gonna get along just fine," he snorts as he walks out the doors.

Kellerman

We had an awesome day shopping (yeah I know). We're all pretty comfortable spending money in general, but spending it on Kid, that's a treat. The guys bought her everything she loves from Chicago. I could see the ghosts of crazy teenagers in them while we were out. Shopping was good therapy for the guys. I promise I'm not turning into a chick. I found the perfect Christmas present. No lie...it's perfection. I was riding on the high of our day until I saw Cooper in Kid's room holding her hand gazing at her softly. Yeah, happy mood is gone.

I'm sitting silently holding Kid's hand, while Cal, O'Sullivan and Finn talk her ear off. Kav left to talk to that prick, Cooper. I hope Kav puts his head through a goddamn wall. I wouldn't call myself a violent person normally, but lately I feel like I'm in a constant roid rage. So I sit silently, maintaining calm on the surface, while fierce fury boils within me.

"Kavy?" Kid calls as he enters the room. She's worried that my silent wish came true.

"All good, Kid," he assures her. Moving into the room further. "Don't know what you want us to do with him. Need some guidance."

"I know. Why don't you bring everyone in and we can talk?" He nods and exits the room, returning with the rest of the family. Once everyone has taken seats or leaned against walls Kid starts.

"You all know Nicky was a boy I only met once, but that one time was pretty important to my life. That was a long time ago and I'm a different person now. I love you all. You're my family and you know how much that means to me. My life wouldn't be what it is without each and every one of you. Nicky's the only thing left from my life before you guys. You all know me and love me, but you only know the new me, the damaged me. He knows the innocent me that was her daddy's princess. Having him around reminds me of that girl that's gone. He reminds me of my father, brings back memories I thought were gone.

"I'm not kiddin' myself. I know the road that lies in front of me. I have a lot of healing to do. I know what this journey looks like and I know I won't be alone. I think havin' Nicky around could help me. Yes, he was around for the trauma, but he wasn't part of it for me. He kept me safe and alive and..." she stops and takes a shuttering breath. We all wait in anticipation of what she needs to say.

"The *soldier*," she says looking at Sully Sr. who nods in recognition. "Nicky intervened before he assaulted me...sexually."

No, no, no, no, no, no, no! I'm screeching on the insides, but I don't utter a sound. Kid keeps her eyes trained on Kav so I do the same. He's shaking from head to toe staring at Kid, silently pleading for her to take those words back. I know there are other reactions going on based on the weight of the tension in the room, but my eyes are trained on Kid and Kav. Kav stands quickly and makes his way into the bathroom. I know his plan. Kid's hands are shaking. I look at her, but she keeps her gaze trained on the closed bathroom door. It's my turn to step up. I give her hand a squeeze and make my way to the bathroom. O'Sullivan just threw a chair so the room is distracted trying to rein him in. I push the door open and find Kav on all fours, puking his guts out. I make my way over to him, handing him a towel.

"Thanks," he mutters shakily. I sit on the floor and lean against the wall of destruction while he gets himself together. He flops down on his ass next to me and we sit in silence. The room behind us is not silent. People are sobbing, yelling, cussing and just about every other manageable thing you can think of. Kav and I are silent. Are there words for this situation? They did a rape kit on Kid when she got here. That was not a piece of information I wanted, but Aidan gave it. He said she wasn't raped. What did Cooper intervene on?

"It's my fault," Kav whispers. "If I woulda stopped and thought for two fuckin' seconds instead of listenin' to Taylor they wouldn't have gotten her." The anguish in his voice makes my insides curl.

"It's not your fault," I whisper back. "It's mine. I fucked up in Seattle. I fucked up the day they grabbed her tryin' to force a conversation she didn't wanna have. I fucked up not removin' Taylor when I knew he wanted her. This is on me." He doesn't respond and I don't say anything else. I'm right and he knows it.

"I haven't felt this for thirteen years. This pain in my body that penetrates every cell," Kav says softly. We're both staring at the wall in front of us, not chancing a look at the other. "It's not your fault, Kellerman and it's not mine. It's Grady and Mancini that are responsible." I nod not knowing if I believe him, but agreeing those two motherfuckers set this in motion.

We sit in silence a long while before Kav lets out a brief chuckle.

"This bathroom is fucked up," Kav comments motioning at my wall of destruction.

"You ever need any help remodeling you know who to call," I joke.

We stand up and make our way to the door. Kav pauses so I open the bathroom door and all eyes are fixed on us. Apparently, they were waiting for us. I step back and let Kav go ahead of me. Kid is scanning his body with her eyes for any damage he may have caused himself. She looks relieved not to find any.

Kav walks straight to her climbing over the foot of her bed. He smashes his body into the tiny space next to her (he's mostly on top of her) engulfing her roughly in his arms while smashing his face into her neck. She doesn't even wince at the pain, just wraps her arms around him closing her eyes. I watch them for a moment before I scan the room.

Most of the eyes in the room are red and swollen, watching Kid and Kav intently. There are a few smashed chairs lying in the corner. O'Sullivan, Cal, Finn and Aidan are sitting on the floor against the wall heads hung low to their chests. Maggie is curled in Sully Sr.'s lap sucking in shuttering breaths. Mary and Doc are next to them in the same position. Collin and Hugh are a shade of green sitting in chairs near her bedside. I'm guessing they'll be puking soon. Ryan and Adam are leaning against the window behind my usual chair, their shoulders smashed together tightly for support. Pop's in my chair with his hand on Kav's back his head hanging in his other hand. They feel her pain. I feel her pain.

I don't know what to do with myself so I just stand in front of the bathroom and wait. Kid's face is soft and peaceful with Kav wrapped around her. He gives her that peace. I should be jealous that it's not me, but I'm not. She finds comfort in his arms in crisis and has since the first day they met. I want her to have peace and comfort no matter where it comes from. I think she's fallen asleep now. Her breathing is even, so is Kav's...sleeping together like they always have. I clear my throat quietly.

"We should let them sleep," I whisper to the room. There are quiet rumblings of agreement as everyone moves from their spots of anguish toward the door. I pause for a moment and look upon her sleeping face. I love her. I'll protect her from now on, at any cost.

Chapter 30

Kavanagh

My body is stiff like a log. I must have fallen asleep. I groan and move to push myself up realizing my arms are wrapped around a small warm body. Kid. Oh God, Kid.

"Hey," she whispers running her hand over my buzzed hair.

"Hey," I murmur into her chest. I must be crushing her and she's already in enough pain without my heavy ass sleeping on top of her. I languidly push myself off of her allowing her breathing and wiggling room. She slides over indicating she wants me to fit into the place next to her. I've seen Kellerman do this so I know it's possible, but looking at it I'm not sure how. I smash myself in the sliver of space and Kid wiggles into my side laying her head on my chest. We lay together silently comforted by the warmth of each other's bodies.

"I never feel safer than when I'm in your arms, Kavy," she admits quietly. I squeeze her and smooth her messy auburn hair away from her perfect face.

"Think Kellerman might take offense to that," I say softly in a joking tone.

"Your arms are the first place I felt safe. You'll always be that for me, even though Kel offers me safety and comfort now. You'll always be my first," she explains looking up at me with those bright green eyes oozing love.

"You know next to you is the only place I'm at peace," I reply. I never sleep as peacefully as I do when she's next to me. She can be in her spot on our couch not even touching me and her presence brings me a calm I've never found in anyone else.

211

"I love you," she murmurs her voice full of emotion that she won't let spill.

"I love you, Kid," I respond with the same choked sentiment.

"I wasn't plannin' on talkin' about the *soldier*. I haven't begun to deal with any of that, but I wanted you guys to know that Nicky saved me. Something far worse was gonna happen to me than did because he stepped in."

"First, you can tell me anything and everything about whatever you want. It's not your job to shield me from stuff. I can take it. Yeah, it killed hearin' what you said but that's because I love you so fuckin' much the idea of you bein' hurt like that causes unbearable pain. But the idea that you would carry that yourself kills me, Kid. Never do that. Second, I'm glad that he saved you. Glad doesn't begin to describe. I still blame him for you almost dyin'. I get that you have history with him and went through some crazy ass shit with him. I'll do whatever you need me to do. If you need me to be cool with him, I'll give you two the space for that. I just can't promise he'll be any part of my life."

"I'm strugglin' too, Kavy. I'm smart enough to understand that Mancini and Governor Grady were willin' to do anything to get me. What happened to me was horrible but nothin' I can't heal from. I'd be dead, Kavy. These people were willin' to kill me to get the information they wanted. Nicky made sure that didn't happen. Taylor was a wildcard nobody expected."

"They did a rape kit on you when you were stabilized. It came back clean. You wanna tell me what happened?" I ask tentatively knowing I have to keep my shit fully in check for her response.

"He got his dick near my face, enough for me to feel violated not enough for me to feel sorry for myself. Women out there get a hundred times worse than what he gave me. I'm lucky," she explains quietly not looking at my face.

"You are the most amazing person I've ever known. Only you would have something truly horrific happen to you and be thinkin' you're lucky," I say pulling her chin up to look at me. "You want me to call Doctor Schrader? It'd be good for you to start talkin' about this." Dr. Schrader is Kid's therapist from when Liam attacked her. The woman is a Godsend. She pulled Kid out of the blackness that took her over back then; maybe she can stop it from even coming this time.

"I think that's a good idea. I don't think I can give the family the details I just gave you. They're gonna wanna know though. Can you tell them? I know that's a lot to ask—" I cut her off.

"It's nothin' to ask. I'll do it. Don't worry about us. We've got you." She nods and settles deeper into my chest. I could stay here all night, but I'm guessing our family is freaking out and needs to see us. Just as I'm about to get up Kid's door opens.

"Sorry, I didn't want to interrupt. I just wanted to check on you guys," Kellerman says softly. I can tell by the look of concern on his face he's telling the truth. What man in the world would have his girlfriend sleeping in the arms of another man and not show one speck of concern or jealousy? Kellerman. He gets us and lets all of us be who we are with Kid. I don't know how he does it but he does and that's the reason he's made for Kid. She needs a man that gets us and doesn't care, not only doesn't care but is happy to be a part of us. I almost killed him a few days ago. I don't know what the fuck I was thinking then, but I was wrong. He loves her like she deserves to be loved and I'll kill myself trying to make things right between him and me.

"We're good, man," I say rolling away from Kid. "Didn't even realize we fell asleep until I woke up. We needed that."

"I knew you guys needed it so I cleared the room out. That was about two hours ago though, so I thought I should check on you," he explains looking beyond me at

213

Kid. My back is to her now so I don't know what her reaction is, but Kellerman doesn't look happy.

"Let's step out for a second. I need to talk to everyone," I say moving to the door. Kellerman pauses looking at his feet and then turns on his heel to leave. Once he's gone from the room I look back at Kid and she's silently gazing out the window.

"Be right back, Kid," I tell her. She nods but doesn't look at me.

Shannon

I couldn't look at him, at Kel. When I went to a survivors group after Liam, women talked about this. I never experienced it because I was single then. I'm not single now and this is different. I'm terrified he won't want me now or if he does he'll look at me like I'm broken. FUCK! I need to talk to Dr. Schrader and fast. I grab the hospital phone and dial her old cell number. I hope she hasn't changed it.

"This is Doctor Schrader," she answers promptly.

"Doctor Schrader this is Shannon Kelly," I say softly. I haven't talked to her in years but we kept in touch long after I stopped therapy.

"Shannon, how are you?" she asks with the appropriate amount of concern. I've been informed that some version of what happened to me is in the media so I'm sure she knows.

"Not great," I answer honestly. "I could really use a session with you."

"I'd be happy to see you, only I'm out of town for the holidays."

"I completely forgot," I say sheepishly. "Why don't we set something up after the holiday?"

"No, that's not necessary. I can't meet in person but we can talk now if you'd like just to get the ball rolling until I'm back in Chicago."

"That would be great if you have the time."

"I've got plenty. Tell me why you called."

"Hold on just a second. I need to do something quick," I say reaching for the nurse call button.

"Sure."

I press the button and wait until Sheryl answers. I ask her to keep my family out until I tell her it's okay to let them in. She, of course, agrees.

"Okay, I'm back now."

"It's good to hear your voice, Shannon. Tell me why you called tonight."

I launch into my story. Every single bit of it.

Chapter 31

Kellerman

She's closing me out, wouldn't even look at me. I can only imagine what this is like for her so I'll be patient and understanding. I need to be those things for her, even if it pains me. Kav's explanation about what happened to Kid was...I don't have words. Agony in every cell of my being about wraps that up. We're entirely silent as a group. No one knows what to say or do. We just sit and let the reality of what Kid's dealing with sink in. I know it could be worse and now I'm thankful for that prick Cooper, but the idea of what was going to happen to her is excruciating.

We're all sitting out here because Kid asked the nurse for some privacy. I can see she's on the phone but that's about it. So we all sit here until we can go sit in there with her I suppose.

"Hello Chicago," rings merrily from Karl's voice down the hall. Just the sound of his voice brings a slight grin to my lips. He's a good development. He's been working his ass off while Kid's been here. Managing her case load between the two of them is one thing, but him on his own...I don't know how he's done it. "By the looks on your faces something has happened so fill me in so I can look like shit too."

Kav fills Karl in and he looks like shit for about two minutes.

"All right people. I know this is horrible. Everything that we now know is horrific, but she went through it not us. She needs us to be strong so she can heal. Button up your emotions and give her the strength she needs. No more sad pained faces. You need to cry, freak out, punch something or whatever else...you do it on your own away from her. And her bathroom doesn't count as away from her," he says pointedly glaring at me. "If she's worryin' about us and how we feel, she'll never deal with this the way she needs to. Think about her before you think about you."

"You're our Christmas gift," Maggie says pulling him in for a full on mouth kiss. He indulges her, dipping her low before releasing her back to her husband.

"If you're all gonna welcome me like that, I'll need measured breaks," Karl snarks. We all chuckle and life seems to fill a little bit of the black hole that we're living in.

"Mr. Kellerman?" I hear Sheryl call from the nurse's station.

"Yes," I respond wondering why she's calling my name. I approach her with an eyebrow raised.

"Shannon would like to see you alone. Don't test me," she warns the rest of the group thinking about trying to join me. Sheryl is kind of scary. I nod and quickly make my way into Kid's room. I shut the door and pull the privacy curtain around her bed. If she wants me alone she gets me alone.

I sit down in my chair. She's staring out the window again. It's dark out so I don't know what she's looking at, but I let her look. I don't grab her hand or say a word, just wait.

"I called my old therapist," she explains calmly. "Kavy suggested it after I told him what happened to me. I was gonna wait until I was discharged to start therapy, but after I saw you I needed it right away." That doesn't sound good. If I make her feel like she needs emergency therapy maybe I need to clear out.

"I'm scared, Kel," she says finally turning her head to meet my gaze. Her eyes are terrified. I can't hold back anymore. I reach and grab her hand as best I can with my taped and splinted fingers. I try to convey with my eyes that she's safe with me.

"I was single when Liam attacked me so I didn't expect this. I wasn't prepared for it, that's why I called Doctor Schrader." I nod a little to encourage her, hoping she can't see that I'm freaking the fuck out right now.

"I'm afraid you won't want me now that you know what happened. Or worse, if you do want me it'll be different now. Maybe you'll treat me like some damaged property you're stuck with, because you'd be an ass to leave the girl that was tortured and almost raped," she says wincing at the harshness of her words.

"Doctor Schrader talked me through a lot of this. Now I'm talkin' to you because you deserve a chance to leave if you can't do this. I won't blame you and I won't let the guys do anything to you if you go. But if you're goin' I need it to be right now," she says emphatically.

I pause for a moment to get my words and tone right. If I don't do this the best way it could go badly.

"Just go, Kel. It's fine, really. I'm in so much pain already what's one more ache?" She mistakes my silence for defeat. Fuck choosing the right words and tone. Here goes nothing.

"I'm not goin' fuckin' anywhere. I will not leave you. I will not be pushed away from you. I will not allow anyone or anything that happened steal one more moment of this life from me. You are mine. You're the only thing in this life that makes it worth livin' for me. I love you. I love you so fuckin' much I don't have words to explain it to you. I don't give a shit what that motherfucker did to you." She drops her head at that statement and I grab her chin pulling it back up to meet my intense gaze.

"I don't give a shit what that motherfucker did to you. The only thing I care about is you healin' from it. You're just as perfect in my eyes today as you were the day I met you. No, that's not true, you're even better today than you were then. We'll get through this together. I promise." I stop talking and she pulls me so hard I ram into the side of her bed causing me to wince.

219

"Sorry," she whispers in a giggle. I wrap my arms around her tightly, hovering above so I don't smash her broken body. She sweeps her arms around my neck and kicks her legs out knocking my knees from beneath me. I fall, crushing her body. "I want you close." I nod and remain where she's got me.

"I love you, Dylan Kellerman. You are the only man I ever want in my life again. Thank you for everything you just said. Thank you for loving me like you do. Thank you for never giving up on me. Thank you for being you." I smash my lips against hers in a kiss that I'm sure is too rough, but I can't pull back. I eagerly push my tongue between her lips and she gladly grants me passage. She tastes like strawberries and Kid. Heaven. I work my mouth against hers nibbling and caressing every inch I can get to. A soft moan breaks from her throat and I move. Never leaving her mouth I climb on top of her, she quickly spreads her legs to accommodate me. I pull her nightgown up exposing both tits. Perfect. I lean down and capture a nipple in my mouth suckling softly while working the other between my thumb and finger, pulling and twisting. Kid moans and arches her back into me feeding me more of her.

I start to kiss a trail down her stomach listening for any hesitation she may have. Her hands plunge into my hair encouraging my journey south. When I get to my destination I pause and look into her hooded eyes.

"Are you okay, Kiddo?" I ask with my voice full of want. I'll stop if she tells me, without question.

"I'll be better if you finish what you started," she says in her heavy sex voice. Green light!

I cover her with my mouth licking and lapping at her folds like a man starved for forty years has just been given his first meal. I press my tongue into her opening and she bucks and thrusts against my face. Moving to her clit, her legs begin to shake with her impending orgasm. I stroke her vigorously with my tongue, flicking tirelessly. I could do this for hours. The taste of her coating my throat and the smell of her saturating my lungs, there's nothing better in this world. My dick is so hard I'm afraid it may explode, but I won't take this that far. She's not ready for that.

I move my hands under her ass to tilt her up to my face a little more. Her bandages are gone but scabs still remain. She doesn't protest in pain or discomfort so I keep my hands on her cheeks and work my tongue in circles and lines. Kid's hands yank and pull at my hair harder and harder as her hips roll faster and faster. I remove one hand from her ass and drive one finger straight into her and that's her undoing. She cries out shaking and calling my name. I remove my finger and lap up all of her juices until she finally stills her hips and loosens her grip on my hair.

I kiss each of her inner thighs causing her to shudder. I lightly feather kisses up her abdomen and across each tit before travelling up her neck and jaw. She captures my mouth in a heated passionate kiss licking herself from my mouth. I slow the kiss and pull back to rest my face in her neck, trying to keep my weight off of her as much as I can. Keeping my dick completely away from her so she isn't uncomfortable.

"Fuck, that was good," she mumbles into my hair. I chuckle. "I missed you, Kel."

"I missed you too," I murmur into her neck.

"Didn't expect you to go down on me after that conversation. Thought I might get a kiss."

"I aim to exceed expectations, Miss Kelly." She laughs a deep belly laugh warming my heart.

"It smells like sex in here," Karl calls from the other side of the curtain. Kid and I both burst into laughter as I pull her nightgown down covering her perfect body. I climb out of the bed and go into the bathroom of destruction to clean up as Karl pulls back the privacy curtain. His eyes are dancing with mischief as he glances between the two of us.

"Spill," he commands Kid as I shut the door snickering. Karl is definitely our Christmas gift.

221

Shannon

Holy shit balls!!! That was unexpected and fucking amazing. In a coma one day and coming hard the next. Whew, I'm warn out. Karl is here! This day has gone from shit to great in warp speed.

"Spill," Karl orders as Kel shuts the bathroom door.

"What're you doin' here? It's Christmas you should be with your family," I chide as Karl sits in a chair next to my bed.

"Come on. You know I don't do well with anyone but my sister. She's got a new boyfriend and is doing Christmas with his family. I'm NOT spending Christmas in my parent's house without my sister. Plus, you're my family Shannon. You're the closest person to me, wild horses couldn't keep me from you," he says dramatically, but I know his heart is behind those words. "Now, spill!"

"Just a little reconnecting," I feign innocence.

"Uh huh, did he reconnect his dick to your lady parts?"

"Karl!" I screech and roll my eyes. "I'm in no condition to be havin' sex. I just woke up yesterday."

"Hey, I don't know the rules about what to do and not to do after crazy ass shit like you went through. But if I woke up and that man was at my bedside, we'd be reconnecting every body part multiple times...loudly," he says pointedly.

"You need a boyfriend," I instruct.

"I'll get right on that," he snarks. He's quiet for a moment before talking again. "Scared the shit outta me," he whispers.

"Scared the shit outta me too," I admit quietly.

"You know I love you right?" he asks sweetly his pale blue eyes twinkling.

"As much as I love you," I state emphatically.

"Well I wouldn't go that far. You're dysfunctionally dependent on me and unhealthily obsessed with my love life." He moves straight back to snark. He's good for my soul.

"That's very true. I'm not sure how I functioned in life before you strolled in," I snark right back.

"From what I can tell it was on sexy men that you wouldn't touch and a lot of double *A* batteries," he says before falling into fits of laughter which I follow gladly.

"You two all right?" Kel questions moving from the bathroom toward my bed. His teal eyes are smiling along with his gorgeous face. He fixed his hair that I spent a good amount of time disheveling. He's wearing a cable knit charcoal sweater and perfectly fitted dark wash jeans, he looks gorgeous. I've missed looking at him. Dr. Schrader was right. Talking is the best way to heal. I didn't talk after the Liam attack. I kept everything to myself other than talking to her, and it consumed me. I won't do that this time. I want to be free of this, so this time I'll talk.

Chapter 32

Shannon

As Kel makes his way back over to his perch at my side Karl's gaze hardens. His pale blue eyes crinkle up at the edges and his shoulders rise a bit. He's annoyed.

"What happened to your face?" Karl asks Kel harshly. Good question.

"Long story. How was your flight?" Kel dodges.

"My flight sucked. What happened to your face?" he asks again more annoyed.

"The guys and I had a misunderstanding. Nothing to worry about now," Kel says dismissively as he takes his usual seat at my side.

"You know what happened?" Karl asks me.

"No, I don't. I was informed there was, and I quote 'a beating', but that's all I got," I inform Karl. We both pin our gazes on Kel waiting for him to fess up.

"You two are relentless," Kel concedes. "Taylor informed the guys that I cheated on you with Cassie and got her pregnant. That gifted me quite the beat down and the opportunity for you to get grabbed." He explains it quickly and I get pissed faster.

"KAVY!" I scream. Kel and Karl both sit back in their chairs at my sudden outburst. Kavy dutifully comes sprinting in to my room.

"What?" he asks breathily.

"Did you and the guys beat the shit outta Kel?!" I fume. His eyes are bugging out of his head and staring at Kel, hoping for him to make me calm down. Not fuckin' likely. "Quit lookin' at him to protect you and answer my goddamn question." His body goes limp and his gaze hits his shoes.

"Yes."

"You fuckin' asshole! Are you kiddin' me with this shit? Taylor really got us all good, but you didn't even have the brain to talk to Kel first. I at least had the brain to talk to him first!" I shriek. Aidan, Sully and Cally trail in behind Kavy upon hearing my rant. They're in for it too.

"Sully you did this," I accuse pointing to the scar under Kel's eye.

"Yes."

"What did you do Kavy?"

"Choked him."

"Aidan?"

"Kicked him."

"Cally?"

"Spit on him."

Spit on him?

"You spit on him?"

"Yeah, I spit on him," Cally admits like he's telling me he chopped off Kel's pinky. I burst into fully belly pain inducing laughter. He spit on him! Everyone in the room just stares at my apparent lunacy until I calm down.

"Any of you ever so much as think about puttin' a hand on him you'll deal with me. He and I have an issue that's between us. I'll sort him out and vice-a-versa. Do NOT touch my boyfriend again!" I shout.

"Kiddo," Kel soothes. "It's okay. I'm fine. They did the right thing at the time. Their job has always been to keep you safe from assholes. That day I looked like a supreme asshole. They shoulda talked to me first, but that's not really how men operate. We like action." I growl and look back to my scolded brood.

"You guys are lucky I'm stuck in this bed," I warn softly with no real threat to my voice. "And how do you guys always get Kel to calm me down? It's not fair."

"He's part of the family now," Kavy informs me. "And we have a strict code of bros before hos—" Kavy gets cut off with a tissue box to the face. Point me, zero Kavy!

"Are you insane?" Sully asks Kavy looking at me warily.

"It's the only time we can mouth off to her. She's stuck and can't retaliate," Kavy informs Sully with a shrug.

"Problem with that logic. She's got a memory and she won't be stuck much longer dipshit," Aidan scoffs at Kavy. Kavy shrugs his shoulders again and starts to turn his lips up.

"I'll take my chances." Kavy smiles my smile at me.

"That's an ass kickin' I'd like to watch," I hear a familiar voice call from the door. I look past Karl to see a rough scarred up ruggedly sexy Kieran Delaney smirking a crooked smile at me.

"I'll make sure to get you front row seats, Kieran," I beam at him. This man has always given me a little light. I know he's bad news, but there's something about him that's always made me think he'd do anything for me. I don't know why...I felt it the first time I met him when he came to our townhouse for dinner. Even now he doesn't look at me like I'm broken in a hospital bed. He's looking at me like I'm at home on the couch getting ready to watch a game. I need some of that lightness in my life right now.

"Woulda come yesterday, Shannon. Funeral held me up late," Kieran explains moving to my bedside. He looks down at Karl and quirks an eyebrow. I don't usually have anyone around but the family.

"Kieran this is my friend Karl," I introduce politely. Karl stands from the chair next to my bed and extends a hand. Karl is gay but Karl is not a pussy. He's never been intimidated by my guys or the creeps we've had to deal with at work and not by the truly terrifying presence that is Kieran Delaney.

"Karl this is Kieran Delaney the long removed crazy cousin of the O'Sullivan boys," I introduce dramatically. Kieran eyeballs Karl's hand before grabbing it in a firm handshake that I have no question is equally returned by Karl.

"Shannon can you ever possibly be acquainted with a man that's not an alpha male on the prowl to constantly protect you?" Karl asks in his usual snarky tone while maintaining eye contact with Kieran who's trying not to laugh.

"I'm like a tractor beam for them Karl. I wouldn't know what to do with a beta male bein' needy and wanting. And last I checked you fit the profile right along with these Neanderthals," I snark pointedly. Karl releases Kieran's hand and flops back into the chair at my side.

"And don't you forget it. I run this shit," Karl snarks and we all break into muscle cramp inducing laughter.

As we calm down Cally, Sully, Kavy, Aidan and Kieran take up chairs in a circle around my bed, joining Karl and Kel. I feel a talk coming.

"Kellan O'Shea was your friend?" I ask Kieran starting to put pieces together.

"Yeah. You met him once at that barbecue you guys had after graduation," Kieran explains quietly. I got someone killed and I don't even remember the guy's face.

"I'm really sorry, Kieran. I'll get in touch with his family as soon as I can. Did he have a wife or children?" I ask in a whisper.

"He had a woman and a daughter. Baby's young...six months or something."

"Don't you dare, Kiddo," Kel warns. "You are not allowed to start takin' blame for shit that had nothing to do with you."

"Are you fuckin' kiddin' me Kel? He's dead because of me. There's a baby that'll never know her daddy because

228

of me. A woman that'll never be in her man's arms again because of me!" I bellow.

"Shannon," Kieran commands my attention from the other side of the bed. "O'Shea went into that night knowin' what we were gonna encounter. We all did. He was there because he met you once and knew you were worth the risk. He fuckin' told me he knew you were worth the risk. When I called him and asked for some weapons to help me and the guys out he said he was in when I told him it was for you. He knew what Mancini's men were capable of and didn't bat an eye. That decision was his and his alone. It's a shame his woman and daughter won't have him but he wasn't a guy that was gonna see eighty anyway. He went out with his boots on doin' something good for once in his life. You carry no guilt for that. None!" Kieran's voice carries such finality to it that I can't find the words to argue.

I turn my gaze to Cally. "You set up a trust fund for his family, Cally. You make certain they want for nothing. They live in a good house in a good neighborhood with a good car. The widow doesn't have to work unless she wants to. That baby goes to whatever school and university she wants to."

"Definitely worth the risk," Kieran murmurs quietly. I turn my gaze back to him. I was right, Kieran would do anything for me.

"Now I'm realizing I don't know how this whole mission 'rescue Kid' went down. I'm ready for that story. I have the feelin' it's gonna piss me off so give it to me now while my pain meds are in full effect," I order steeling myself against what I'm figuring is a story about my boys risking everything to find me.

Kavy starts the story from the moment I was taken until they got to Chicago. Sully fills in the pieces in Chicago until the FBI were called in. Kel fills in the pieces while he was with Kieran and Cally fills in the pieces where they tricked Taylor. Kieran gives me the rundown of the ambush and nobody talks about what happened in the house.

"Somebody tell me what happened in the house and after please," I ask exhausted by the bevy of emotions I've gone through up to this point. The men I love are officially insane. Lucky doesn't begin to describe what I am in this life to have them. Aidan clears his throat.

"Well you know what happened with you, Taylor and Cooper," Aidan says with grains of fury in his voice. "Kellerman was in the hall and tried to get to you but ended up takin' a bullet to the leg, nicked his femoral artery, as Cooper got two shots off. One hit Taylor the other got Kellerman. The rest of us came down just after and found all of you. All four of you were down. Ryan and Adam tended to Kellerman while Kav and I came to you." There's a long pause and all the faces in the room are solemn.

"I started workin' on you and Kav got me some FBI agents to transport you from the house. Apparently, Sully Senior had put a tracker on my SUV knowin' we were up to somethin'. When he realized we had left he notified the FBI and a medevac team. Saved your life havin' them there that quick. I lost you five times," Aidan's voice breaks. He brought me back to life five times. Five times. My breath hitches as does the rest of the room's as I'm certain they didn't know that either. Kel's hand is shaking in mine, but I keep my eyes trained on the shimmering blues of Aidan.

"Five fuckin' times," he says through quiet tears. "I begged you to come back to me the last time. I begged and pleaded for you to just fight one more time for me. Once more in this unfair goddamn life to please just fight. Just one more fight. I was losing and needed my sister to win for me." I feel one hot tear roll down my cheek as I watch my baby brother struggle through the memory of begging me to live. "You're the best piece of me. My life doesn't work without you in it. I couldn't do it. I couldn't save you. I tried so fuckin' hard, but I couldn't do it. I had to make you fight." His tears are flowing with force now, as are mine.

I have no words, no thoughts, nothing to express the emotions flowing through me. I sit straight up in my bed and extend my arms out to him. I need to be in his arms now.

In a flash Aidan launches into my arms pulling me down to the bed and crushing me into his chest. A shaky sob breaks from his throat and I squeeze him tighter trying to show him how much I love him and how thankful I am that he brought me back to life, made me fight.

The room around us is silent a long while as Aidan calms back down and his tears abate. I hold him as firmly as my weak arms will allow until his grip on me begins to relax.

"Thank you for savin' my life. Thank you for makin' me fight. Thank you for not givin' up on me. Thank you for lovin' me. I love you baby brother," I murmur into his chest. I tip my head up to look into his red and swollen bright blue eyes.

"I love you too," Aidan whispers pressing a long gentle kiss into my forehead.

"This is worse than the fuckin' funeral," Kieran says in a rough huff sniffing back what sounds like tears.

"No shit," Karl remarks in the same sniffy tone as Kieran. "If I'd known we were havin' a cryin' circle I woulda grabbed a box of Kleenex on my way in. Is my mascara runnin' Kieran?" That gets a nice cleansing laugh from the room. God I love Karl! He's not wearing any damn mascara by the way.

"Kellerman I'm not sure how you're sleepin' in this bed with her at night," Aidan says peeling himself away from me. "I'm sore after ten minutes."

"Felt good bein' in her arms those ten minutes though, didn't it?" Kel asks a smirk playing on his lips.

"Nothing better in the world, man," Aidan agrees as he reclaims his chair at the end of my bed.

I look around the room and as suspected there's not a dry eye in the place. What I hadn't noticed was the rest

231

of the family had come in at some point during this. My fathers, mothers, and the rest of my brothers are all standing looking at me with love and adoration. There's no pity from what they learned earlier about the almost rapist. They're just happy I'm alive.

"All right now that everyone's in here and everything's out on the table I want to say thank you to each and every one of you. You all did so much to find me and save me that thank you doesn't do it justice. But it's all I have. So thank you. I love you. No more fuckin' cryin'!" I beam. After a brief moment of smiles and snickers the tension leaves the room.

The boys get up and mill around getting ready to set up for Christmas Eve dinner. Kel keeps his perch at my side. I doubt he'll ever feel comfortable leaving me again and I'm okay with that. Maggie and Mary take seats across from him and offer him glowing smiles before looking at me.

"I talked to the Nazi, Sheryl," Maggie informs me with a roll of her chocolate eyes behind her glasses. "She told me that you can eat what you feel comfortable with." She looks at me with a hopeful gaze.

"Got some pumpkin pie?" I ask sweetly. Her face beams as she runs from the room no doubt to bring me an entire pie to eat.

The boys start setting up card tables in my room to make one very long table. They lay table cloths over the tops and set the table with pretty Christmasy plastic plates and dinnerware. The parents start carrying in copious amounts of food. Maybe I will eat something. Once the table is filled with food and family, I release a huge sigh of relief. Kel looks up at me from his chair at my bedside. He won't even leave me to go sit at the damn table.

"Happy?" he asks hopefully.

"Yes."

Chapter 33

Shannon

I wake just as the sun peaks over the horizon. It's Christmas morning. Usually, I'd be making a fuss running around cooking and stuffing stockings, but I'm here in bed with Kel feeling happier than I've felt in weeks.

"Dylan," I hear a shrill voice call. I turn my head toward the voice to find a petite blonde standing in my door shaking with fury glistening in her steely blue eyes. Her hair is a mess, face drawn and pale. She looks sick.

"Kel," I say nudging him awake.

"Mmm," he replies hoarsely without making a move to get up.

"Kel you need to wake up," I command while sitting the back of the bed up. The crazy chick is making her way into my room and she looks possessed. I really wish I had my gun.

"Dylan!" she shrieks at the top of her lungs. Kel and all three guys spring straight up in their beds. If this wasn't so fucking weird I'd be laughing.

"Cassie?" Kel asks rubbing the sleep from his eyes.

"What the fuck?" Kavy calls from his doll bed. He's not wearing clothes, underwear maybe. My boys are all sitting up assessing the situation and trying to see if the chick looming at my bedside is a threat to me. I'm trying to figure that out myself.

"You didn't call. And now I find you here, in bed with *this* while I'm carrying your child. You're such a fucking prick!" She squeals and swings her arm clumsily to

233

smack Kel. I quickly intercept her wrist before she makes contact and pull it down to the bed.

"Keep your fuckin' hands to yourself," I growl. Sully is now standing behind her shirtless and panting.

"Cassie, you put your hands anywhere near Shannon again, I'll personally put you outta here on your ass," Kel threatens in an ominous tone. I release her wrist and she glares at me. Bring it on bitch!

"You're threatening me? I'm the mother of your child," she says stomping her feet like a toddler. She'll make an outstanding parent.

"This bitch is insane," Sully snorts from behind her. Kel shakes his head and stands up from the bed approaching Cassie. Sully flops in a chair next to where she's standing, waiting for what her next move is.

"Are you gonna let him talk to me like that?" she huffs at Kel.

"He's a big boy. I think he can manage his words on his own. What're you doin' here?" Kel prowls toward her. He's pissed, but he's trying to pull it together.

"I fly here all night, on the most God awful private jet I've ever been on, to get to you on Christmas morning and find you in bed with this slut and then you allow this heathen to speak to me like I'm trash? Who are you? Where's the Dylan I fell in love with?" Kel is seething, but Kavy is up out of bed and ready to pounce. I see Kel give the go ahead nod as he takes a seat on my bed to watch him work.

"Hey Tinker Bell," Kavy coos sarcastically tapping her on the shoulder. She turns and stumbles at the glory that is Aaron Kavanagh standing before her in only his tight boxer briefs. This should be fun. "You say somethin' like that to or about Kid again, I'm gonna help her outta that bed and watch her kick the shit outta you. I don't know who the fuck you think you are but you are not welcome here. You think you're carryin' Kellerman's baby well good for you. That," Kavy points at me and her gaze follows but quickly returns to Kavy, "is his woman. She is number one in his life. Not you. You never fuckin' will be. That kid you're carryin' turns out to be his you still won't be shit." I'm not sure if she's going to cry or explode based on the scarlet color of her face.

"Who the fuck are you?" she yells. "Is this really the company you keep now?" she turns her back to me as she asks Kel. "If these are the people you're spending time with maybe I should consider keepin' the baby away from you. Maybe I'll just go back to Seattle and call my attorney and get that process started now before this filth can corrupt my child. I mean seriously Dylan, she was kidnapped from her home and this one," she indicates to Kavy with her head, "is threatening to have her assault me while I'm pregnant. I suggest you put some clothes on and get on the plane with me home so that you can maintain a relationship with our child. If you stay here with this trash you won't ever see this baby." Wrong fucking choice.

I sit up on the edge of my bed, throw my legs over the side and hop to my feet. Adrenaline is coursing through me so I feel no pain and there is no waver in my step. This chick is short and I'm towering behind her back. Sully, Cally (who's now on his feet at my side), Kavy and Kel are all gawking at me dumbfounded.

"Listen to me and listen good," I command sharply at her back causing her to spin away from Kel to face me. "You're gonna submit to a maternal blood screen so we can find out if that baby is Kel's. If the child turns out to be his I am gonna fight with everything I've got to have custody removed from you. See while you may think I'm trash, I know you are. I had you looked into and I know that while you've been pregnant you've smoked weed, drank alcohol and snorted coke." Her face has paled ten shades since I began, but I'm not finished.

"You try to keep this child from Kel and I'll come after you myself. And I promise you I won't be using words the next time we communicate. Sit your ass the fuck down now while I call someone to come draw your blood.

I see you're thinkin' about tryin' to run. My suggestion is you stay put so my boys don't have to grab you and hold you down." Cassie is shaking from head to toe; Kel is shaking too (with fury).

"You're doin' drugs while you're pregnant? What the fuck is wrong with you?!" Kel bellows. She flops dramatically into a chair.

"It's not that big a deal. It was early in the pregnancy. Bein' alone and knocked up was hard," she says as she shrugs like it's nothing.

"You do know you're sittin' in a room full of attorneys right?" Cally asks from behind her bugging his eyes out at me. Yeah this bitch is stupid.

"Why does it matter? You think any judge is gonna listen to you all and not me? It's my baby, biology always wins," she scoffs.

"Wow, Kellerman you took a huge step up movin' on to Kid," Sully teases. "This one is cute at best, but fuckin' dumb as a rock. You lucked out findin' Kid. You coulda been stuck with this shit the rest of your life."

"Tell me somethin' I don't know O'Sullivan," Kel replies shaking his head. I need to sit down. I move into the bed as though it's easy, even though that couldn't be further from the truth. I press the call button and ask the nurse to send up someone to draw some blood. She hesitates before she complies. I'm guessing somewhere out at the nurse's station there's a note from Doc that says do whatever I say. We all sit in silence a long time before Crazy starts to talk again.

"If I find out it's yours and you won't go back to Seattle with me I'm havin' an abortion," Cassie threatens. All my boys' eyes bug out and I sit up a little straighter. That was a threat I wasn't expecting. I'm trying to formulate a response when Kel speaks.

"You try to abort my child and I'll kidnap you and lock you in a fuckin' basement until you deliver. Then I'll feed you to the lowest scum of the earth I can find. You fuckin' threaten me again and you'll learn real quick what type of man I am," Kel growls sounding smarmy. Okay that was quite a warning.

"Yeah, not a real bright move Tinker Bell," Kavy grunts.

"You can threaten me all you like, but I know that you can't prevent me from having an abortion. Woman's right to choose," she says flippantly.

"You have no idea what we're capable of," Cally threatens. I can see all of our attorney brains are working overtime trying to come up with a solution to her threat. The problem is she's right. I could file an injunction to stop her from having an abortion but it won't hold for the term of the pregnancy. FUCK!

"Dylan, I'm guessing you can tell I'm right by their silence. So, would you like to come home now?" her voice is completely devoid of anything human. Kel looks at me trying to come to grips with her threat and what to do.

"Don't know if it's mine," Kel grumbles in frustration.

"It's yours. I had the maternal blood screen two weeks ago. Got the results yesterday," she says in a flourish pulling out an envelope from her handbag. Shit! "It's a good thing your DNA was on file. You remember giving a sample when that murder happened at your neighbor's? Came in handy." Wow this chick is an absolute cunt!

Kel hands the envelope to me without even looking at it. I rip it open and read quickly. It's Kel's baby. I feel acid rise up my throat stopped only by the melon sized lump forming. I look at Cassie and she's beaming from head to toe with her victory. I look at Kel and without a word he knows the answer. He scrubs his mangled hands vigorously across his face.

"I'll wait for you to get dressed," she says clinically pulling her phone out to completely avoid having to look at anyone. We're all silent. She's got us all where she wants us.

"If I go back to Seattle you won't do drugs, drink or do anything else to endanger the baby," Kel commands forcefully.

"Of course not, honey," Cassie replies sweetly looking up from her phone lovingly into his face. This bitch is completely whacked (women like her give a bad name to our gender as a whole). "Just a few stipulations though. You break off all contact with *Shannon* and the rest of these people. We live together and once the baby's born we get married. I don't want a wedding when I'm all fat and disgusting. If you break any of these rules, I'll either have an abortion or tell the cops that you beat me so that I can get full custody."

This is not happening. This cannot be fucking happening. I can't do anything. Kel can't do anything. My boys can't do a goddamn thing. She's taking him from me! I don't expect him to leave his unborn child for me. I won't let him. He and I know what it's like to be alone in this world and I can tell Cassie is no different from my mother. Without Kel, this baby doesn't stand a chance. If he lets her go and she has an abortion Kel will carry that guilt for the rest of his life. I can't do that to him.

"I'll give you five minutes to say your good byes," she states and moves from the room quickly. Kavy, Sully and Cally are stunned stupid. I sit forward and wrap my arms around Kel's neck pulling him in tight.

"I don't wanna leave you," he whispers into my neck.

"I don't want you to leave me," I whisper back. "You have to go though, Kel. We'll figure this out somehow. You have to play her game right now. I can't do anything to stop her." I release Kel's neck and he gently eases me into his lap crushing me into his chest.

"This can't be happening. I can't do this. How am I gonna do this?" Kel pleads.

"You record everything she does or says," Kavy orders. "You get every piece of evidence you can that she's an unfit mother for the next six months. The whole time pretendin' to be exactly what she's askin' for. You buy a burner phone and keep in contact with us so we know where we're at. She goes into labor...we're on a plane to Seattle to have that baby taken from her."

"What if she's not an unfit mother?" Kel questions quietly.

"She already fucked up doin' drugs and drinkin'. She's a shit person on the surface. That means deep down there's somethin' worse. You'll find it. We'll find it," Kavy spouts confidently.

"Kiddo?" I turn and look up into haunted teal eyes.

"Kavy's right. You make it your mission to find dirt on her. Anything and everything. I'll get you the baby Kel I promise. We'll be okay," I assure him sweetly pressing a kiss to his cheek.

"She'll want sex," Kel mutters.

"I know," I sigh. This fucking sucks!

"Can't do it," he states firmly.

"You'll do whatever you have to," I command sitting up to look in his face. He's in pain. His life is being held hostage and there is no foreseeable escape. Maybe I'll shoot her after she has the baby. "You better get goin'." Kel hesitates for a moment before placing me back in bed. He leans over my face and captures my mouth in a searing achingly sad kiss. I work my mouth and tongue in concert with his, drinking in every last memory. He slows the kiss and rests his forehead against mine. His teal orbs open and my heart shatters.

"I love you, Shannon Kelly," he says with a firm gaze his eyes broken.

"I love you, Dylan Kellerman," I respond with a waver in my voice. We hold each other's eyes a breath longer before he stands. He quickly pulls on jeans and a T-shirt, shoving the rest of his stuff in a duffle bag. He gives the guys each a chin lift before looking at me.

"Bye, Kiddo."

"Bye, Kel." He's gone.

Part Three

Chapter 34

April 28, 2014

Shannon

I haven't heard from Kel in five weeks. I'm worried. Struggling doesn't begin to describe what he's been since he left Christmas morning. We've only talked on the phone once since he left. Talking is too hard because Cassie is a fucking leech. She never leaves his side. The one time he called me he was in the bathroom with the shower running. We talked for four minutes before she started banging on the door insisting to be let in. So now Kel only texts. It's difficult too but more manageable. Five weeks is scary. The longest he's gone without texting before this was three days. I have no way to contact him without jeopardizing the safety of the baby. He buys a new phone every time he contacts me so it's not like I even have a number to call him at. This is bad.

I walk out my front door to be greeted by Rodger's warm smile.

"Morning Shannon," he coos.

"Morning Rodger," I coo back.

"Hey Shannon," Thomas calls in his deep bass voice.

"Hey Thomas," I say as I fold into the back seat of the S-Class.

Thomas (the security guard from my building that watched me the first day I was in danger back in October) is my bodyguard now. He doesn't live with us, but he's always with me if I'm not at home. I don't mind it. I actually like it. I've had a constant shadow since I came home from the hospital, and it suits me just fine. I've been in therapy with a new doctor here in Kansas

City. Dr. Wells is an older woman that reminds me of a grandma you don't want to fuck with. She tells it like it is and that works well for me. I'm healing.

We ride in comfortable silence to One Kansas City Place. When we get to the building Thomas escorts me in an elevator and then to my office. Karl is waiting for me like always.

"Good morning, Shannon. Here are your messages. We've got a busy morning at the courthouse," he informs me following me into my office. I head to my desk securing my gun in my safe and flop down into my Donghia chair. Thomas leaves my office closing the door behind him. He's a silent giant.

"Still no word?" Karl asks taking a seat opposite my glass and mahogany desk from me. I shake my head. "There has to be a good reason, Shannon. He wouldn't just drop off the map for no reason."

"Doesn't make it any easier," I whisper. My door slams open and Kavy, Sully and Cally charge in. Thomas follows with a curious look on his face.

"Look at this," Kavy orders shoving a phone at me.

They're trafficking drugs –Kellerman

"That's it? That's all he said?" I ask hoping there's more somewhere else.

"That's not it, Kid," Sully says softly. He hands me a piece of paper and cringes as I read the headline.

Fishing Magnate George Yates Announces Daughter's Wedding

George Yates and his wife Camilla are pleased to announce the upcoming nuptials of their daughter Cassandra Yates to fiancé Dylan Kellerman. The forthcoming event will take place at the Yates' family home on Mercer Island August 2nd. The happy couple is expecting their first child...

I drop the paper and slam my head onto my desk. This bitch is one for the record books. I pull my head up and look at the announcement again. There's a picture of Cassie and Kel standing next to each other. There's water behind them and the sun is shining on Kel's golden hair. He's grinning at the camera with a shimmer in his teal eyes. Cassie has an arm around Kel's waist and his is resting around her shoulders. Her other hand is resting on the slightest baby bump with her head tipped up looking lovingly at Kel's face. They look like the perfect couple. My stomach rolls.

"I need a drink," I say to whoever will provide some booze. Kavy slides a glass of whiskey in front of me. I toss it back and relish in the burn. "What's the text mean?"

"We don't know. We're assumin' her family is usin' their business to run drugs between countries. Finn's lookin' into it," Sully informs me with a squeeze of my shoulder.

"He doesn't love her, Shannon. This is just a means to an end. Keep sight of that," Karl says softly. I nod and swallow back another shot of whiskey.

I run my hand over the necklace that Kel gave me for Christmas. It's a large round intricate Celtic knot pendant covered in pavé diamonds with one large round diamond at the center. It's my family swirling around me. I haven't taken it off since Kavy fastened it around my neck in Kel's absence.

There was a Celtic knot theme to my Christmas. The rest of my family all got versions of our clover tattoos. Aidan has ten clovers running down his spine (each of us represented), Ryan and Adam got tribal designs on their right calves the clover in the center, Finn got the same small clover on the inside of his left bicep that Cally has (Finn's afraid of needles too), Hugh started a large half sleeve years ago and added the clover to cover his shoulder, and Collin put the clover in the center of his chest (similar to Kavy's). The shocker was my parents. Maggie and Mary both got small clovers on the inside of their left wrists, Doc got the clover and a further Celtic design on his right shoulder, Pappy added the clover below a military tattoo he has on his upper right arm, and Pop got the exact same clover as mine on the underside of his forearm. Everyone in our family wears our clover now. We're always together.

"I know he doesn't love her. It still fuckin' hurts," I say sharply. Karl nods.

"Have Finn get in touch with me once he knows something. I'm gonna head to the courthouse," I say in business mode letting everyone know I'm okay.

"You may wanna brush your teeth first. Hate for anyone to think you've become a lush," Karl chides. I smile and head to the bathroom to freshen up. Thomas follows silently behind me waiting for me to finish my business. When I come out Thomas has that look on his face like he wants to say something but doesn't want to all the same.

"You can always talk to me Thomas," I encourage.

"What your man is doin' is honorable. Not a lot of men would do that. Some of us are forgotten before we're even here," Thomas says softly as we move through the corridor to the elevators and a waiting Karl. Whoever forgot Thomas is a goddamn idiot. Thomas has become my friend. He's a different kind of friend from the guys and Karl. He's not involved in my every conversation or butting in constantly, he's just there on the periphery for when I need him. He's a welcome addition to my life.

"Whoever forgot about you is a damn fool," I state pointedly. He laughs and his deep boom makes my chest reverberate. I smile. We reach Karl and step into the elevator.

"The Smith's mediation got pushed back," Karl informs me. He keeps updating me as we make our way out of the building and to an always waiting Rodger. I push thoughts of Kel to the back of my mind. I need to concentrate on work. No, I need to be distracted by work.

Kavanagh

Kid looked devastated when we showed her that damn wedding announcement. This Cassie bitch is one

246

sick fuck. That text and link to the article is the first contact Kellerman has made in five weeks. I should be pissed at the dude, but I'm worried. I don't know what his situation is or how he's coping, my guess is shit is bad. Kellerman took a job with Cassie's dad when he got back. He's running operations for the Yates fleet. Cassie works for her father too in accounting so she's able to keep close tabs on Kellerman at all times. She hasn't drank or done anymore drugs since they returned to Seattle according to Kellerman. Cassie is nothing but a glowing first time mom now. It's scary how easily this woman can turn the crazy off and on. It also means we don't have shit on her to get the baby. Unless Kellerman's text is true.

Ring, ring

"Kavanagh," I answer my Nexus curtly.

"Hey man," Finn responds.

"Please tell me you found somethin'," I plead.

"This is beyond our reach is what I found. If the Yates' are traffickin' drugs they're proficient at it. We're gonna need some help. We get the authorities involved this will become a DEA show. That's not a bad thing except there's a baby and a wedding date looming," Finn says with a huff.

I spin my chair around and gaze out at the Kansas City skyline. My office is the exact mirror image of Kid's (without all the girly touches). As I stare, a crazy idea comes to mind that just might work.

"I'm gonna have Kid call Cooper," I tell Finn. He's silent for a long while. Kid talks to Cooper a lot from what I can tell. She hasn't seen him since we left Chicago right after New Year. I can tell talking to him gives her something we can't...I hate it.

"It's a good idea," Finn admits. "That guy still rubs me the wrong way though."

247

"Me too but we'll deal if it means gettin' Kellerman away from that crazy bitch. Kid needs him back." Finn growls something about okay and then we hang up. I can deal with Cooper if it means getting Kellerman home. Kid is fighting so hard to keep everything together. She goes to therapy and talks about what happened to her. She didn't talk about the Liam attack like she does the kidnapping. She genuinely seems to be healing. I know it'll take months if not years for her to be herself again, but she's not shrouded in blackness.

No trial dates have been set for Mancini or Gov. Grady. There's a mountain of evidence that the State's Attorney has to get through first. Gov. Grady is out on bail but Mancini and some of his cohorts are behind bars being held for other charges (drugs). Mancini was the real threat to Kid's safety; Gov. Grady was just the purse strings. I don't really give a shit what rolls they each played. I'll just be happy when it's all done and over with.

We hired Thomas before we even got back to Kansas City. Cooper assured us that he was trying to run down the threat that was made against Kid at Thanksgiving, but we weren't willing to take any chances. Thomas is a brick wall of "don't fuck with me" so I feel pretty confident she's safe for now. None of us has let down our guard though. This clusterfuck from hell with Kellerman has not helped in any way.

The Kellerman thing is what's weighing Kid down. I don't think she's gained a pound back since coming home. Her hip bones stick out, you can count each vertebra down her back, and her shoulders and collarbone are pressing sharply against the skin. She doesn't look good. Kid always looks good but she doesn't now. She barely eats, works out twice a day and sleeps clinging tightly to my chest every night.

I'm banging chicks at warp speed to get them out of the house so I can get to Kid quickly. She can't sleep unless I'm there. I don't make her wait long. I'm only

248

fucking the bare minimum of three a week at this point. It's a sacrifice that's necessary. I had an overnight trip in March that I couldn't get out of. Kid slept with Cal and O'Sullivan that night. She's never alone anymore. Not even at night. Sometimes I sit in the bathroom while she takes a shower. Until we contain the death threat she's constantly watched. She doesn't fight it either. Thomas follows her to the bathroom here in the office and if he went in and stood by the stall Kid wouldn't complain. She's not scared, she's smart. She knows there's still danger lurking and this time she won't be caught unsuspecting. She carries two guns and a knife at all times. If someone is stupid enough to come at her...it won't end pretty for them. Kid doesn't panic.

Chapter 35

Kellerman

I found it! I've been living here for almost four months and couldn't find a goddamn thing. Finally, yesterday I was going through some purchasing orders and fuel invoices, there it was. Extra stops are being made to and from Canada and between Mexico and California. The only thing I can find is extra fuel being purchased and strange bait and supply purchases. I'm not in my element with this shit so I'm hoping Kavanagh and the boys can get to the bottom of this and quick.

When I texted Kav this morning from the bathroom with the water running it was the first communication I'd had with them in five weeks. Cassie has surgically attached herself to my ass. I'm never alone. Half the time when I'm taking a piss she stands at the door and talks to me. It's exhausting. The reason I wasn't in touch for so long was because I got the distinct feeling I was being watched. I could never actually see anyone or find cameras, but I felt it. Cassie is a live wire of crazy so I have to be careful. If she catches me I have no doubt she'll follow through on her threats or worse.

Our "engagement" was just announced in the *Seattle Times*, making my week just wonderful. People keep congratulating me and asking where we're registered. I have no clue because I didn't know we were engaged. I never asked and sure as shit didn't buy that gargantuan ring Cassie's wearing. The picture they ran with the article was taken at a work party three weeks ago. I am officially living in hell.

"Honey," Cassie calls, it's like nails on a chalkboard amplified. She strolls into my office for the fifteenth time

251

this morning. I don't look up at her or respond. "Daddy says they'd like us over for dinner this weekend."

"'Kay," I say blankly still not looking at her. I hate her, actual pure unadulterated hate. I didn't know I was capable of feeling this way about someone I once cared about, but I do. I hate her.

"And the decorator called about the nursery again. She doesn't seem to understand the difference between cerulean and cobalt. Can you believe that?" she says truly offended by the idea. I have no clue what she's talking about. "Well I think I may need to hire a new decorator. Maybe a team instead of just one person. What do you think?"

"I don't care, Cassie. Do what you want," I murmur to my desk.

"Well you should care. He's your son. Don't you want him to have a nice nursery? He'll spend a lot of time in there with the nanny. I don't want all his baby junk cluttering up the house," she points out. Dear God she can't wait to get my son out of her and pass him off to the nearest hired hand.

"Whatever is best, Cassie," I placate her. I just want her voice to stop and her presence to be gone. If I could rip my son from her body now I'd do it. She told me the other day she felt like her body was rejecting the baby. Like the baby was a foreign object that should be removed from her before it causes her harm. Mother of the year! I just have to hold on for eleven more weeks. I can do eleven more weeks if I get my son and Kid back. I don't know what I'll do if that doesn't happen.

Shannon

"Cooper," Nicky answers my call swiftly.

"Hey Nicky," I coo.

"Hey Shanny. What's up?" his warm voice massages my ear. We talk all the time, but I haven't gotten used to how warm his voice is. He's not my guys or Karl or Kel...it's just different. He's helped me so much to heal

252

and struggle through the things that happened in that house. I love him and am happy he's my friend.

"I need you," I say softly.

"What's wrong? Are you safe?" His voice is alert.

"I'm fine. Don't freak out on me," I chide. "It's about Kel."

"Is he okay?" his voice is calmer but there is still a hint of government operative.

"He's as good as he can be. He thinks he found something."

"That's good. What is it?"

"He thinks the Yates' are traffickin' drugs," I say emphatically.

"No shit? Well I'd say that's somethin'. Sorry I haven't been able to help out more. I've been swamped lately."

"It's not your job to figure this shit out, it's ours. That said, I could use some help. From what Finn found they're good at what they do and it's not gonna be easy to pin this on them. On her."

"You need someone to dig around unnoticed?"

"I don't know. The guys just asked me to call you and see if you could help out. Maybe come to Kansas City and see what we've got? I know you're busy so if you can't it's fine. I'll try to find another covert three letter acronym agent that's known me my whole life," I feign guilt giving.

"I'll be on a plane soon. I can get to you by tomorrow evening. You know I'd do anything for you. If this gets you Kellerman back and his baby away from that crazy bitch, I'm in," he spouts confidently.

"You don't know how much that means to me. Thank you, Nicky," I say softly.

"No need to thank me. Love you, Shanny," he says tenderly.

"Love you, Nicky."

Please let him be able to find something! I move out of my room and join the guys downstairs, Finn included. They're all sitting in front of the TV on our massive sectional watching baseball. I flop down in my spot on the couch, Sully sweeping an arm around my shoulders tucking me tightly to his side.

"Nicky will be here tomorrow," I announce. Sully stiffens and then relaxes before speaking.

"That's good," he lies.

"I know you guys don't want him here in our house or anywhere near me. I understand that, but he's the only person that can help us right now. I need Kel back. We've only got eleven weeks to get shit hammered out and that's not a lot of time."

"We're fine, Kid," Kavy assures me. "Just takes us back. We'll be good tomorrow." I nod and turn my body closer to Sully's to absorb some of his heat. I'm freezing all the time.

"Cold?" Sully asks pulling me into his lap. I nod and snuggle in. "Need to get some weight on you, Kid. Your ass is diggin' into my thighs like daggers." I move to push off his lap and he tightens his arms around me, holding me captive. "Nope." I settle in and watch the game.

I'm thin right now. I'm not thin, I'm wasting away. I can hardly eat, I'm working out like a fiend, and I sleep for shit unless I'm smashed against Kavy, Sully or Cally. I need Kel. I'm not dependent on him or weak without him, I'm lost. If our relationship had ended normally I'd be fine. I would have been sad for a while, but I would have moved on (that's my story and I'm sticking to it). This is like being stuck in purgatory. I can't move on because he's still mine, but I can't stop existing because he's not here. So I go through the motions and wait. I still have fun with the guys and do everything else I would normally do. Oddly enough, I'm happy. I could be happier though and that sucks. Knowing there's another level of joy that I can't reach sucks.

I still see Mia every week. It's like a small connection to Kel that makes it even more fulfilling than it already was. Butch is doing well. He got a job at the local GM plant and seems to be building a life on the straight and narrow. He texts or calls me with updates every day. Kel was right, I didn't lose Mia. Maybe Butch could help us. I know that sounds crazy, but he was a distributor for the largest meth manufacturer in the Midwest. He may be able to give us some ideas where to look for proof of drug activity.

"You guys think Butch could help us?" I ask the guys.

"What do you mean Butch?" Cally asks shocked.

"He knows the drug world. He might be able to give us some inside information about trafficking drugs," I explain getting more excited the more I think about it.

"That's not a bad idea, Kid," Finn chimes in. "You think he'd go for that?"

"All I can do is ask," I say with a shrug. My shoulder jabs Sully in the chest and he winces.

"You have GOT to gain some fuckin' weight. Your shoulder just bruised me. That's not normal," Sully chastises me.

"Don't start in on me now," I plead and roll my eyes. I sit up in his lap and look into his chocolate eyes. They're stormy and about to let loose on me.

"Nope, I'm done keepin' my mouth shut. You look like shit. You look like a skeleton draped in skin, it's gross. You are gross! You are the most stunnin' woman the world has ever known and it's time to get that back. You're gonna have a baby here in eleven weeks you need to be able to care for. No baby is gonna lie on your boney-ass body and be comfortable. Plus, you need to be able to stand in front of a judge and look fit and healthy

255

so you can get custody. You don't look either right now," he informs me harshly.

"O'Sullivan," Kavy warns.

"Fuck that Kav, she needs to hear this. I know you're strugglin' without Kellerman, but this has gone on long enough. Get your shit together and get back to yourself. He tries to come home and fuck you he'll end up in the hospital from your hip bones givin' him internal bleeding." I snort at that.

"A pound a week. That's the goal," Sully orders.

"Okay," I concede. That argument was too good to try to fight against. He's right.

"Okay?" Kavy questions.

"Okay," I repeat looking at Kavy with a panty dropping smile.

"Kellerman come home and give you some while we weren't lookin'?" Cally asks.

"No," I huff seeing where this is going.

"Well whatever happened keep doin' it so we don't have to fight you all the goddamn time," Kavy instructs. I flip him off with both hands and climb out of Sully's lap.

"Who wants Five Guys?" I entice them with burgers and fries.

"Me," they all clamor in unison.

"Let's go," I say turning on my heel headed toward the garage.

Sully just said I'm going to have a baby in eleven weeks. I haven't thought of that. I know that sounds bizarre, but I've been so focused on healing myself and getting Kel back I didn't think about his baby coming too. How the fuck could I have missed that? I didn't miss, but I haven't been counting on it. If Kel doesn't find anything juicy on Cassie I don't get a baby or Kel. I don't even know what Kel's having. I need to get a nursery together. Fuck I need baby supplies: diapers, bottles, a crib, a changing table and a whole lot of other shit!

We all pile into Cally's SUV and head to Five Guys. I turn around in the passenger seat.

"We need to turn the guest room into a nursery. I need to start shoppin' like yesterday. I have no clue what I'm doin'. How could you guys let me slack for this long?!" I reprimand them in a high squeaky voice.

"There she is," Finn says in a laugh. "There's our Kid."

"Fuck you, Finn. You just bought yourself baby proofing duty," I scold with an eyebrow raised.

"Who knew tellin' you that you look gross would have such a positive effect on you?" Sully snarks from behind me. I launch over my seat at him and pull his hair like a girl. "Ow, ow, ow! Let go, fuck. I didn't miss this part of you." I let him go and sit down in my seat.

"Yes you did!" I exclaim.

"Yes we did," they all agree.

Chapter 36

Kavanagh

Kellerman: Tell me you found something.

Kavanagh: Nothing yet. Cooper's coming in today. Kid's calling Butch too.

Kellerman: Butch?

Kavanagh: His past profession may help.

Kellerman: Didn't think of that.

Kavanagh: Neither did I. Kid's idea. She's on a fucking mission.

Kellerman: I need to text her. I can barely get away from Crazy long enough to text you.

Kavanagh: No shit? It's 6 here, meaning it's 4 there. Sleep much?

Kellerman: You'd never sleep if you had to sleep next to this bitch.

Kavanagh: You want me to wake Kid up so you can talk to her?

Kellerman: Let her sleep. I'm guessing she's not getting a lot.

Kavanagh: If I move away from her she's wide awake. It's unreal.

Kellerman: I fucking hate that. 11 more weeks man.

Kavanagh: Yeah Kid just got that memo last night.

Kellerman: What?

Kavanagh: I've told you she's been struggling. Can't eat. Working out all the time. Weighs maybe a buck 10.

Kellerman: Yeah.

Kavanagh: Last night O'Sullivan laid it out for her. Told her to get her shit together. That a baby's coming in 11 weeks and she needs to be at her best. Totally flipped her out!

Kellerman: Again...what?

Kavanagh: She's been so focused on her therapy and getting you away from CRAZY that she didn't think about you coming home with a baby. It's not like she doesn't want the baby she just misses you.

Kellerman: I guess I'm around the baby shit all the time it's all I think about. If I could rip that baby out of her body today I would.

Kavanagh: Well when you get here Kid'll have it in order. She shopped online last night until 2 in the morning. I had to rip the laptop out of her lap and hold her down to make her sleep.

Kellerman: LOL that sounds like her.

Kavanagh: She's back. It's like the old Kid again. Your baby did that!

Kellerman: I can't wait to get him home to you guys.

Kavanagh: Him? You're having a boy?!

Kellerman: Fuck that's right I haven't talked to you guys. Yeah it's a boy!

Kavanagh: That's awesome! Kid is gonna freak!!

Kellerman: The succubus is awake. Gotta go. Tell Kid I love her.

Kavanagh: Will do.

Kellerman's having a boy. Kid will love that. She'd love a girl too but she's used to boys. Now she can quit freaking out about if green is actually gender neutral. That's a conversation I never want to have again. She snuggles tighter into my chest and I squeeze her firmly. I remember not too long ago getting elbowed and kicked if I was wrapped around her too tightly, now she can't get enough contact.

She really is like the old Kid again. She ate a double burger and large fries for dinner, then came home and polished off a pint of ice cream. She'll have her weight back up in no time. Who knew O'Sullivan calling her gross would make her so happy? When she gets her hands on Kel's baby she'll be like a new woman. I can't wait to see that.

Kellerman

Cassie is standing up out of bed when I come into the room.

"What were you doing?" she asks in an accusatory tone.

"Takin' a shit," I lie.

"Do you really have to be so gross?" she asks climbing back into bed.

"Just bein' me," I say sarcastically.

"Come back to bed and warm me up," she commands. She knows that won't happen though. I haven't laid a hand on her and I won't. I'm forced to sleep in this house, in this bed, but I won't fuck her.

"I'll pass," I say climbing into my side of the California king allowing for plenty of individual sleeping space.

"Come on, Dylan. How long are you gonna hold out on me? You know I suck a mean cock. Don't you want your dick sucked?" she asks in a sex-filled voice. That voice just made my balls retreat into my stomach.

"I'd love to get my dick sucked. Just not by you."

"So we're gonna get married and never fuck? You're gonna spend the rest of your life celibate?"

"Yup," I pop my *p* replying cheerfully.

"I can't live a life without sex, Dylan. I need to get laid," she chides.

"So get laid. I don't give a shit what you do."

"So you're tellin' me if I bring a guy home to fuck you won't care? You'll just happily allow him passage?" she scoffs.

261

"If you can find a guy that wants to fuck a twenty-nine week pregnant crazy chick with ankles the size of her thighs, by all means have at it."

"You are such a fucking asshole! Why can't you just let this shit go?" Cassie screams in her shrill voice. Nails on a chalkboard!

"You mean why can't I let go of the fact that you're blackmailing me with my child? Huh, I don't know why Cassie. You tell me," I snark.

"This relationship will never work like this. You need to grow up."

"I'll live my life and you live yours, that's how this fake as fuck relationship works."

"What kind of an example will that be for our son?" She lays on the guilt. Little does she know MY son will never know her or her psychotic ways.

"The only one you'll be able to provide," I say demonstratively.

"You'll change your mind. You'll need sex and love eventually and I'll be here waiting to provide it." Crazy as ever.

I pull the blankets up to my chin to keep any part of me away from her. I sleep under a different blanket from her. I also sleep in a long sleeve shirt and pajama pants. If I could find a chastity belt I'd wear that too. I can't believe I ever put my dick in her. Eleven more weeks, I can do eleven more weeks.

Shannon

Ding, dong.

I run to the door and find Nicky standing there with a huge smile on his lips. I jump and wrap my arms around his neck.

"Jesus Christ, Shanny eat a doughnut would ya?" he says as he runs his hands over my protruding spine.

I let go and push back from him.

"Don't start. Sully gave me a tongue lashing last night. I get it," I warn.

"I knew I liked these guys," he says moving in our house. The guys were right this is a little weird.

"No ski mask this time?" Kavy asks from the hallway. I know it's not necessary to point out that Nicky has never been here nor was he one of the guys wearing a ski mask. Here we go.

"Left it at the hotel," Nicky replies without missing a beat. Kavy smirks and offers a nod. Male communication is so fascinating.

I lead Nicky into the kitchen where Cally, Sully, Finn and Kavy are all piling their plates sky high with Gates Barbecue.

"Got a bit of everything. Load up and we'll talk," I instruct Nicky. I pile a plate to the brim with brisket, fries, beans, coleslaw and bread. I'm shooting for a pound and a half a week of weight gain.

"She always eat like that?" Nicky asks the group as we sit around the breakfast table.

"Only since O'Sullivan called her gross last night," Cally says with a dimpled smirk. Nicky chuckles.

"She had the strangest motivation as a kid too. When we were playin' that day I was tryin' to convince her that she could fit through the dog door on her guest house. She kept refusin' sayin' she'd get stuck. Finally, I told her she probably couldn't because she had a really fat head for a little girl. She plowed through that door and locked it so I couldn't get in for fifteen minutes," Nicky says with a smile.

"Served you right." I look around and my boys' faces are softer. They see what Nicky brings me.

"You know she played volleyball in college?" Sully asks Nicky. Nicky nods ripping pieces of meat from a rib. "Well there was an annual mud volleyball tournament

263

that the frats did. Only men allowed. It was for charity so Kid wanted to play. Some guy told her that she could play if she could prove she could compete with men on the same level. Kid asked 'Are you callin' me a girl?' The dude told her if she didn't know she was a girl he could show her. Kid tackled him and held him to the ground until he admitted she was a man and he was a little girl." The whole table is in fits of laughter. All of us remembering and Nicky hearing it for the first time.

"Served him right," I say looking around the table at happy smiling faces. This feels good.

We continue to eat and tell stories, mostly about me. When we're done eating we all clean up dinner together and then head into the great room to get down to business. After Finn and Kavy explain what we know Nicky gives us his insight.

"I've dealt quite a bit with drug cartels through the years and this stinks of them. We need a man inside the operation. I have a guy that's been working another mission that just finished; he'll be perfect for this. Once we find out how they're runnin' the drugs we can send him into the operation to collect intel. Shouldn't take more than a month for him to get what we need. It'd be different if we were tryin' to take down the cartel, that's a long process. Takin' down traffickers is pretty simple. The thing you have to consider is the cartel will not take kindly to the Yateses bein' arrested. My guess is they'll be taken out so they can't rat. I know your man hates this chick but she'll very likely end up dead. You think he's down for that?"

"I don't know. That's pretty extreme don't you think? You really think they'll kill her and her father?" I ask shocked. I don't know why I'm shocked, but I am.

"I think we could try to put them in protective custody and that almost never works. The reason these cartels continue to run, is they leave no one behind to rat. These idiots climbed in bed with this cartel they knew the risks."

"Look I hate this bitch, but dying for takin' Kel away from me seems a bit much. I don't know that I could live with that," I say honestly.

"Could you live with Kellerman marryin' her and havin' his baby mixed up in cartel business?" Nicky asks pointedly. I blanch. "He's workin' for Yates. He could already be in danger. You need to leave emotion at the door and think safety right now. That wedding announcement went out in the news. You think the cartel didn't see that?" FUCK! Okay now I'm pissed. She could have put Kel's life at risk...the baby at risk.

"Send your guy in. Try to keep Cassie and her father alive if you can. Can you get Kel clear of the cartel?" I ask hoping he can.

"We can get Kellerman clear. In a company as big as Yates there's always a way to cover tracks. We'll draw any concern away from him. He hasn't been there long enough to garner any attention. We'll use him in the media as the duped fiancé," Nicky explains in a confident tone.

"You don't think the cartel will come after the baby, do you?" I ask cautiously.

"Nah, killin' kids isn't really their M.O." I breathe a sigh of relief at that. I'm going to have the baby strapped to me 24/7 to keep it safe.

"Do you think green is gender neutral, Nicky," I ask sweetly completely changing the subject. The guys in the room moan and throw their heads back in disgust.

"What?" Nicky asks thrown by the reactions and change of subject.

"Do you think green is gender neutral?" I repeat enunciating clearly.

"Kellerman is havin' a boy. Paint the fuckin' room blue!" Kavy shouts. My eyes bug out of my head.

"What do you mean he's havin' a boy?" I ask Kavy harshly.

"I forgot to tell you. He said he was havin' a boy when I texted him this mornin'."

"You forgot to tell me?"

"Yeah."

"You forgot to tell me?"

"That's what I said."

"You forgot to tell me!!!" I scream and lunge at him. He easily catches me, but I land a good punch in the middle of his chest causing him to gasp. I wrap my legs around his waist and start to squeeze. He's immediately tapping out, but I don't let go.

"Anything else you forgot Aaron Kavanagh?" I ask using as much pressure as I can manage.

"No," he breathes out in a whisper. I hold the pressure a moment longer then I let him go. He falls back on the couch heaving his lungs.

"Fuckin' shit Kid. You're stronger than you used to be," Kavy complains still catching his breath.

"That was some show," Nicky compliments me.

"I'm always glad to entertain," I say with a smirk.

"Stay away from her legs if you know what's good for you," Cally warns Nicky.

"Noted," Nicky responds shooting me a look. Nicky and I have talked about me drowning that guy in the bathtub. I haven't told anyone else. He told the feds he did it to protect me and it was swept under the rug (kind of scary the power secret three letter agencies have). The other members of Mancini's team that lived through the ambush know I did it, but I doubt they'd be believed if they decided to tell. I still feel nothing about that incident. I feel no guilt, no remorse...just nothing. I'm sure that's an indication that I'm pretty jacked up, but I'm not complaining. I don't want to feel anything about that whole time in my life. I'm good like this.

266

We spend the rest of the evening going over the Yates information while Nicky makes calls and sets up meetings and other secret shit. It's weird being friends with someone that can't really tell you what they do or how they do it. It's kind of cool too. My BlackBerry vibrates on the counter. I grab it to see a text.

Kellerman: You're gonna have a son in 11 weeks. I love you Kiddo.

Kid: Love you too, Kel. See you soon.

I'm going to have a son in eleven weeks!

Chapter 37

May 21, 2014

Shannon

We have a system. Nicky's guy (still don't know his name) was sent in by the DCA a little over three weeks ago. Sent in where? We don't know. Secret mission or covert op or whatever this is, leaves me and the boys in the dark. We're all more than okay with that, because the intel that's coming back to us is completely fucking whacked.

So here's how it works. Nicky's unnamed operative is undercover within a shipping company somewhere that's somehow connected to all this shit. He must be undercover as an accountant or something because he sends Nicky daily account information from the shipping company. Every evening Nicky sends me pared-down intel, I then take that intel and meet with Butch at the hospital. I visit with Mia and Butch goes through the accounts and whatnot, giving me his insight. I send Butch's notes back to Nicky when I get home and we start again the next day.

Great system right? I have no fucking clue. I don't know if we've found anything helpful for Kel. I'm convinced the stuff we're looking at is a front for drug trafficking, but I don't know if it links back to Cassie. Nicky is keeping typically quiet, only telling us our work is good. Nicky agreed to let us run through the intel because his team is swamped with missions right now and ours would fall to the bottom of the pile according to him. When I asked Butch to help he jumped at the chance saying he feels indebted to me for everything I did with Mia while he was away. I informed him he's not indebted to me because I love Mia and thus went a round-robin of "I need to thank you" and "no thanks necessary". Anyway, he agreed and has been instrumental with help.

"Shannon, come take a look at this," Butch says from the table at the end of Mia's bed. I put down the horrid magazine I was reading to Mia and make my way to him.

"What's up?" I ask flopping into the chair next to him. He looks at me over the top of his reading glasses. His rough scarred face is soft and gentle as he smiles a fatherly smile at me.

"You've put on some weight," he says softly.

"You callin' me fat, Butch?" I joke.

"You should see her put food away," Thomas says chuckling from the seat next to the door that he silently occupies every night. "She ate three chicken breasts, half a pound of sweet potatoes and a salad the size of my head for lunch today. Put me to shame."

"That's impressive," Butch says to Thomas his eyes bugging out a bit.

"I've gained seven pounds and I feel like a new woman," I admit with a smile directed at Thomas. He feeds me lunch every workday. He's a former football player turned bodyguard that loves his body, so he cooks to keep it healthy. I no longer skip meals or inhale salads on the run. Thomas makes me sit down every day and eat at a normal pace. Needless to say, my guys love him and think he's the Holy Grail of taming me. I cook in the evenings and on the weekends, and I can proudly admit, the guys were right. I looked gross and it was time to get my ass in gear. It's fully in gear now.

"You look good, Shannon. I'm glad to see you comin' back into your own. I was worried," Butch says softly pulling his glasses from his face, his hand rubbing my forearm.

"I didn't mean to worry anyone, but I get that's the effect I was havin' on everyone around me. I'm okay Butch. I was okay before too, I'm even better now though," I explain putting my hand over his. Bizarre as it is, Butch has become important to me. To think only a few months ago I wanted to have him in prison and as far away from Mia as I could muster. I enjoy spending time with him and watching him with Mia. He loves her the way that my father loved me; it beams from every inch of him. That beam warms me too.

"Okay, enough mush," Butch orders. "Look at this. Hidin' drugs for this company is all about bait. A fishing vessel or vessels purchase bait from some company. We'll call it company A. Company A orders the bait from a local fishery. Then our shipping company, company B, ships the bait supplied by company A to the fishing vessels. Here's where they're hiding the drugs. Company B still has bait every time they return to port, yet they deliver a full order of bait for the next round. They aren't comin' back with bait."

"How can we tie this to Yates? Company A and B aren't their companies." I'm hopeful we can find a connection because at this point I feel like all we're doing is damning a shipping company.

"That's what I just found. Yates fishes for the bait, delivers it to Company B, and picks up anything that isn't sold," Butch says with a half grin. "Woulda found it sooner but they're good at coverin' company names. I found it here on the port manifest. I guess they haven't paid off the port officials. The other thing that strikes me as odd is who ships bait? If you're a fisherman don't you catch your own bait or buy something locally?"

"Good question. I'll ask Kel when he texts." My face gets soft at the thought of Kel and I thumb his pendant. He's been in contact more since the five week drought. Every few days I get a text from him checking in or telling me he loves me. We don't talk shop. He made it clear that he wants none of our time intruded upon by this situation and I'm fine with that. He talks to Kavy about business.

"You ready for the baby to come home?" Butch asks stacking up the papers for me.

"Don't get her started," Thomas warns. I offer him a glare in return.

"I'm gettin' there. The nursery is painted and the guys spent last weekend putting together the swing, the bouncer, the stroller, the crib and moving furniture around until I got it how I wanted it."

"Yeah it was a fun weekend," Thomas snarks.

"Hey," I scold. He smiles a sweet smile at me.

"She's gonna be great at this. Never seen a woman pay so much attention to puttin' a crib in the warmest part of the room. She had temperature gauges on every wall findin' the best place. Baby's won the lottery of moms." Now Butch offers me a sweet smile. I look at my hands embarrassed. I know I've gone overboard, but I want everything to be safe for the baby.

"Don't do that," Butch orders tipping my chin up with a finger. "You're gonna be great at this. You do what's in your gut, Shannon. Look what you've done for Mia, you're good at bein' a mom. Doesn't matter how that baby gets to you."

"What if he doesn't get to me?" I ask before I can stop myself. That's the fear ruling my mind. If we can't make this drug trafficking link stick, I won't have a baby. I won't have Kel. Thomas stands up gliding across the room in two steps. He crouches in front of me forcing me to look in his hazel eyes.

"You're gonna get your baby and your man back. Life has thrown you enough shit, it's time it threw you some good. You are a fighter, Shannon and if this angle doesn't work you'll keep fightin'. We're all here fightin' for you too. We believe in you," his deep voice is soft yet powerful. I nod in agreement.

"Every time I've ever thought about a future something fucked up has happened and ripped it away from me. I'm scared," I whisper as Thomas leans in and wraps his gargantuan arms around my body pulling me into his chest. Brick wall doesn't begin to describe him.

"You're safe now. I swear to you I'll keep you and your family safe. Don't be scared," he murmurs into my hair. I just sit there in his arms allowing the safety he provides to wash over me. I know he'll keep me safe. "Let's get you home." I nod.

Thomas stands and moves to gather my jacket. I look over at Butch who looks equally worried and happy. I grin at him before standing.

"I'll head out too," Butch says handing me the papers. We kiss Mia and tell her we'll see her tomorrow before following Thomas to the elevators.

"Love you, Shannon," Butch whispers into my ear as we near the elevators. He's never said that to me before. I look into his face and see familiar familial love gleaming from his eyes.

"Love you too, Butch," I whisper back. He wraps his arms around my shoulders pulling me into a crushing embrace. We stand like that until the elevator dings. He lets me go leading me into the elevator with a hand on the small of my back. I have three fathers, two mothers, nine brothers, a cousin (Kieran is ever present), a Karl, a Thomas, a Nicky and now an uncle (Butch). Yeah, he's my uncle. My family keeps growing. If I can just get my man and the baby here I'll be complete.

We push out of the doors into a cool spring night. It smells like rain, damp and heavy.

"I'm over here," Butch says indicating he's parked to our left.

"We're this way," I nod toward the parking garage in the other direction. Butch offers Thomas a chin lift and squeezes my arm before turning toward the parking lot.

Thomas leads me down the path to the parking garage when I hear tires squealing in the distance. I pause for a moment trying to see who's in such a hurry. I make out an old Cutlass flying into the parking lot where Butch is parked. My pulse calms as I pull my gun from my bag, drop my bag and take off running. Thomas pushes me behind him and sprints across the street.

The gunfire erupts from the car in rapid succession before we hit the curb (not aimed at us). I turn up my pace as does Thomas running toward the taillights of the Cutlass. The car makes a quick bank across a grassy divide to get back out on the main road. I stop, line up my shot and fire four shots. I land each shot blowing out the two passenger side tires, the car spins out of control and crashes into a large maple tree. I sprint toward the car with Thomas, who again moves in front of me shielding me. Three guys pile out of the car running in different directions. I shoot the closest one in the knee and take off after the guy that peeled out of the backseat. Thomas leaves me to chase the driver.

"Stop fuckin' runnin'!" I scream as I gain ground on the kid. He's a kid, a teenager. "You don't quit runnin' I'm gonna start shootin' again!" The kid drops to his knees and puts his hands over his head. I have no way to secure him. What the fuck do I do now? I put my gun to the back of his head. "Don't move," I seethe. I look behind me to see Thomas carrying the driver toward me, unconscious.

"Fucker wouldn't cooperate," Thomas huffs dropping the driver's body on the ground like a sack of potatoes. "Get to Butch. I got this," he instructs. I take off running toward Butch before Thomas finishes his sentence. I hear sirens in the distance and two guys in scrubs are on Butch.

"Butch!" I wail dropping to my knees next to him.

"Ma'am please step back," scrub-wearer orders. I ignore him and stay where I am. Butch is covered in blood. I can't tell where he's shot, but there are multiple wounds in his chest. He's coughing and gurgling blood. I grab his hand and try to stay out of the scrub-wear's way. Of course he gets shot outside a children's hospital. They can't treat him here.

"Take. Care. Of. Mia," Butch gurgles out between coughs looking into my eyes.

"No, Butch you fuckin' hang on. You hear me! You don't leave her!" I yell leaning toward him. He closes his eyes. "BUTCH!"

"Ma'am we really need you to move!" scrub-wearer two growls pushing me aside. An ambulance just pulled into the parking lot and Butch is quickly loaded in, I climb in unasked. I don't give a shit if this allowed or not.

"Hospital?" the ambulance worker asks me as the ambulance speeds off.

"Truman," I respond quickly knowing it's only a few blocks away (across the street really) and the best place for a gunshot victim. They work on Butch at a fevered pace but they're losing him. They start C.P.R. and I close my eyes. I can't watch him die. He can't die. This is too familiar...too painful.

The ambulance screeches to a halt and multiple people are outside waiting for Butch pulling him out and rushing him in. I jump out of the ambulance to follow only to be stopped by a hospital employee.

"Are you family?" the woman asks me.

"He's my uncle," I reply without hesitation.

"This way," she directs me to a waiting room. I look down at my burlap colored linen pants and white button down covered in red bloody patterns. My hands and arms are stained with Butch's blood, getting dry and itchy. I don't move to wash off or change clothes. I sit in silence and wait.

Chapter 38

Kavanagh

O'Sullivan, Cal, Finn and I fly into the emergency room at Truman Medical Center.

"Butch Rossi," O'Sullivan barks at whoever is standing near us. I scan the room and see Thomas standing near some chairs. I grab O'Sullivan's arm dragging him toward Thomas, and I pray Kid is with him.

As we approach I see her. She's sitting in a chair covered in blood staring at her hands.

"Kid," I whisper dropping to my knees in front of her. Her head comes up and her eyes meet mine. She's furious. Not what I was expecting. She stares at me for a moment and then extends her hand toward me with a folded piece of paper clutched tightly. I take the paper and unfold it carefully. It reads: *Let sleeping women lie or you'll be next.*

I read it again and again trying to make sense of it. My brow is tightly furrowed and I can feel O'Sullivan, Cal and Finn reading over my shoulder trying to make this connect for them as well.

"They thought I was meeting Butch to find Kathy's murderer. He's here because of me," Kid explains blankly. Sleeping women...Mia and Kathy. FUCK! "A nurse brought that to me a few minutes ago. I figured it was something about Butch so I ripped it open and ruined any chance of forensics with all the blood on me. Not that there would be any."

"Shooters are in police custody. They'll get somethin' outta them," Thomas booms from above me. He's not covered in blood. What the fuck happened?

"What the fuck happened?" I ask in disbelief. I take the seat next to Kid, O'Sullivan following to her other side. Cal and Finn take the seats across from her. Thomas continues to stand watch.

"Heard tires squealin' and she took off," Thomas explains. "We got there too late to stop the drive-by, but Shannon took out their tires when they tried to make a run for it. She capped one in the knee, chased another down and held him at gun point while I got the driver. Just kids, man. Stupid fuckin' kids. KCPD has already come and gone. No charges against me or Shannon. Just a visit downtown to give a statement tomorrow." Kid is seething next to me. She wants to hurt someone, make someone pay for this and not the kids they got already.

"I kept the shooters while Shannon went to Butch. Dude's in bad shape. Still in surgery," Thomas says shortly as he scans the room on high alert.

"Kid, let's get you cleaned up," Cal says tenderly. He's the calm gentle giant. Kid nods and follows him to a bathroom or something. I don't fucking know. I scrub my hands over my face trying to make sense of this shit.

"They didn't come at you?" I ask Thomas.

"Nah, straight at Butch."

"She was safe?" I ask in an accusatory tone. Thomas turns his gaze from where Kid is behind a door with Cal toward me. If I was a weak man I'd be scared (I'm not admitting to being scared, just so we're clear).

"She was safe. Behind me at all times. Shots she took, I had her covered. She's precision with a gun. She was NEVER in danger," he growls at me. I give him a chin lift. If he says she was safe, she was safe. "That's a concern." Thomas says indicating his head toward the threatening note.

"Fuck yeah it is," Finn scoffs grabbing the note. "Looks the same as the note from Thanksgiving. It's gotta be someone from Butch's old life, his old boss Pedowski or another distributor."

"So now we have to worry about this and the Yates shit. Jesus fucking Christ!" O'Sullivan bellows. Kellerman needs to know and so does Cooper. At least I can call Cooper.

"Cooper," he answers in a gruff huff.

"It's Kavanagh. You got a minute?" I ask as pleasantly as I can right now (so not very).

"Yeah."

"Kid was involved in a drive-by tonight," I explain clinically.

"WHAT?! Is she okay? Where are you?" his voice is at high alert and I can tell he's now moving quickly.

"She's fine. Caught the shooters. She capped one chased down another. Thomas got the last. They fucked Butch up though. You know who Butch is right?" I ask realizing he may not know.

"Yeah I know who Butch is. You're sure she's all right?"

"She's as good as to be expected. Fuckin' pissed as all get out. Got a threatening note while she was here in the waiting room. That did not help her mood."

"You know who the note's from?"

"I'll give you Finn. He's more up to speed on that shit," I say handing the phone to Finn. Finn explains the note and the history behind the threats. I quit listening when Kid comes out of whatever room she was in, clean and wearing scrubs. She doesn't have on shoes either, just socks with grips on the bottom. She looks like a little kid. Cute as hell.

"She's walkin' up now. You wanna talk to her?" Finn asks Cooper, then hands my phone to Kid.

"Hello?" she asks.

"I'm good Nicky. Not a scrape on me," she huffs.

"Took out their tires. They crashed. Guy in the passenger seat had his gun still in his hand and was runnin' at us. Took out a knee. Went after the other guy, he stopped when I threatened to shoot him too. Thomas

279

had to knock the driver out to bring him back," she's so calm when she explains it. Kid doesn't panic. I can see her even, steady breathing. She's a freak of nature.

"Uh huh...Yeah...Don't know...That would help...Okay," she answers and responds to whatever Cooper is saying. "Love you too, Nicky. See you tomorrow." She hangs up and hands the phone back to me. We all look at her waiting for some information.

"Nicky thinks he can contain this threat easily. He's comin' here tomorrow to work on that. And no, he didn't explain shit. Never does," she scoffs throwing her head back against the wall. O'Sullivan reaches an arm around her neck pulling her close to him. I'd like to do the same, but she can only be held by one of us at a time. I grab her hand and interlace our fingers while Finn and Cal stretch their legs to rest against hers. Touching her brings us comfort. Always has. Always will.

Kellerman

I can feel something's wrong. I know the baby is fine because Cassie is asleep on the couch and I can see the kicks now. Baby's fine, must be Kid. I quietly move from the living room into the kitchen. I can see Cassie from here in case she wakes up.

Kellerman: Kiddo you good?

It's been half an hour and no response. Shit's not good. She always texts right back. It's only 10:30 p.m. in Kansas City. She's not asleep yet and if she was the text would wake her up. Time to text Kav.

Kellerman: What's wrong?

Kavanagh: Man you telepathic or something? Drive-by at Children's tonight. Kid's good. Butch is BAD!

Fuck me. I knew something was wrong. Goddamnit!

Kellerman: She's not answering texts. You sure she's good?

Kavanagh: She's talking to a doctor right now. Butch update. Her bag got left at the crime scene. Probably

280

doesn't have her BB. I sent Karl to grab it for her before he gets here.

Kellerman: So this was about Butch not Kid?

Kavanagh: No. About Kid too. Got a threatening note here in the waiting room. Same like Thanksgiving. Cooper's on it. Thinks he can squash the threat. Coming here tomorrow.

Christ how much more can she have going on in her life? Once this shit is over we're taking a year long vacation to a private island.

Kellerman: Glad Cooper is on it. Keep Thomas on her ass!

Kavanagh: No need. Thomas is on her ass and pissed! Almost as pissed as Kid.

Kellerman: Good to hear. Got some news for you to pass on to Cooper for me. Cassie and her dad have a meeting tomorrow. I'm not invited. That's fucking strange considering she hasn't left me alone for more than thirty seconds since I've been here.

Kavanagh: Yeah that's weird. You know where the meet is?

Kellerman: A shipping company. TUG Shipping. Think eyes should be on that meet.

Kavanagh: Agreed. Look I think Butch's out of surgery. I'll pass this on to Cooper. Keep in touch so I can fill you in on Butch.

Kellerman: Kiss Kid for me. Tell Butch I'm thinking about him. This fucking sucks!!

Kavanagh: Will do, man. This definitely sucks!! Later.

Kellerman: Later.

"Dylan?" Cassie moans from the couch.

"Yeah," I grunt from the kitchen.

"My back hurts. I can't wait to get rid of this thing. Ugh," she complains sitting up. I fist my hands trying to keep calm. I hate her, fucking hate her. Whatever

281

Cooper and his team are digging up will put her in danger once she's arrested. I could give a flying fuck. If that makes me a heartless bastard so be it. She's a monster. She hates my son. Talks about him like he's some evil parasite she needs to rid herself of. She's hired two nannies. TWO! She scheduled a C-section because she doesn't wish to go through labor, she says. She's an abusive neglectful mother and her child isn't even here.

No one knows about her blackmail. Everyone thinks we're a perfect shiny couple getting ready to welcome our son to the world. If anyone could see her behind closed doors they would die from shock!

"You need to stay in your office tomorrow while I'm out. Daddy's scheduled some conference calls for you to take while we're gone," she informs me. "Stop moving you little shit!" she yells at her stomach. Hate her!

Chapter 39

Shannon

We've been at the hospital all night. Butch made it through surgery but crashed again twice overnight. The shooters did a number on him. They got both of his lungs, liver, and spleen. It's just a waiting game at this point. Karl and Thomas stayed with me last night plus my boys. Karl brought me some jeans, a T-shirt, a hoodie and some Jack Purcells, so I'm no longer in scrubs. My hair is in a messy bun on top of my head and I'm makeup free. I look dynamite! Karl also went to Children's Mercy and found my handbag. Luckily the hospital staff had found it and held it so I don't have to deal with identity theft on top of my list of shitty life happenstance. Poor Kel had texted me, feeling something was wrong. Luckily he got a hold of Kavy. By the time I could text him back he'd gotten rid of his burner phone. He takes no chances.

I stand up and stretch in the Critical Care waiting room, our sleeping quarters for last night. Fuck I'm sore! Thomas senses my movement and jumps up. I give him a look indicating he can calm the hell down. He smirks and joins me in stretching.

"Shanny," Nicky's voice calls from behind me. I turn and smile at him. He moves quickly, pulling me roughly to his chest. I wrap my arms around his waist and wait for him to get his fill. When he finally lets me go he pulls me into a chair and sits next to me holding my hand.

"Fuckin' scared the shit outta me," he huffs his fake brown eyes ablaze.

"Had that shit under control," I assure him. I did. Uncle Mick was in my head and I was calm, cool and

283

collected. That's where I shine in this life, under pressure with a gun in my hand.

"Badass," he accuses. I nod in agreement. "I can't tell you what I'm workin' here, but you won't have another threat like the one that was here last night."

"Nicky, that sounds a little too good to be true. You're tellin' me you can come in and just make shit go away that's been followin' me for months?" I question, quirking an eyebrow at him.

"I can't tell you how, but I can assure you that no one that was part of last night will come after you again," he says definitively.

"Okay so I just have to worry about the Yates shit."

"You don't have to worry about that either."

"Since when?" I ask shocked.

"Since I just said. You think I'd let anything harm you? We're workin' the case hard to get to the bottom. I won't stop until we get Kellerman and that baby back to you," Nicky says softly.

"I can't stop worryin' about it until they're here. You tell me to get on a plane and pick them up then I'll let it go, until then it's a constant worry for me."

"Okay," he relents. "The threat in Kansas City is gone. So let this go."

"Okay. Will you explain that to me some day?" I ask quietly.

"Yeah."

"Okay."

"I need to head out to deal with this shit. I'll come around later to talk through this thing with Kellerman," Nicky says as he stands.

"Oh fuck, Nicky. Last night Butch found the drugs or at least how they're coverin' it up. Here," I stand and move to my bag to give him the papers, "these are the notes from last night."

"This is good," he says scanning the notes. "I'll look 'em over while I'm out. Kav texted me some intel from

Kellerman last night too. It's all gonna work out. Love you," he says kissing my forehead before leaving the room.

I turn back to see all my guys watching me. A room full of love.

"I'm gonna go see Butch. You guys should go home. I'm good," I say strongly.

"You know that's not gonna happen so save your breath," Karl chides. "I'll go down and get coffee and breakfast." I smile and nod at my friend. He's right, waste of my breath.

I head into Butch's room. This is a depressing sight. Butch is on a ventilator, chest tubes coming from each lung, and other wires and tubes are attached to him. His face is ashen and drawn. He looks weak and Butch has never looked weak. I sit next to his bed and gently wrap my fingers around his. I start to talk. I talk to him the way I talk to Mia. I tell him about what happened and what's going on now. I talk about Kel and the guys. I just talk.

"Shannon, foods been here a while. Come eat," Thomas orders from the door. I give him a chin lift. I kiss Butch's hand before heading back to the waiting room. I plow through two bowls of oatmeal, two bowls of fruit, and a gallon of coffee (close enough) before I feel normal.

"Less gross than you were a few weeks ago," Sully informs me taking the chair next to me.

"Well you're just as gross as you were more than thirteen years ago," I snark. He chuckles and kisses my cheek. I lay my head on his shoulder and close my eyes for a moment. I just need a little rest.

"Kid wake up," Kavy commands loudly.

"What?" I moan.

"Kid you really need to wake up and see this shit," Cally says in my ear. I'm laying against Cally now? I must have been out cold. I open my eyes to a breaking news story running on the TV.

285

"Alleged methamphetamine manufacturer, Gregor Pedowski, has been killed in an apparent house explosion. More details to come. Stay tuned," the reporter says.

Holy SHIT! Nicky blew up the guy responsible for my threats. I look around the room and all eyes are on me. My eyes are orbiting my head from bugging out. Holy shit. Meth houses blow up all the time. It's a good move. I still cannot believe this shit. He was just here talking to me like a normal (normalish) person. A few hours later a house has been blown up, and now I'm safe. This is not normal.

"Your boy doesn't fuck around," Kavy says in a chuckle.

"No shit," I huff.

Ring, ring

"Hello?" I answer.

"Hey Shanny," Nicky say swiftly.

"Nicky," I start but he cuts me off.

"I'm assumin' you've seen the news. Can't talk about it. I also can't make it back to you today. Somethin' came up I need to get back to. You're safe, Shanny. I'll be in touch later today."

"Okay. Thank you. I love you," I say because I don't know what else to say. I'm not sure the correct protocol for extending gratitude for committing murder on my behalf (again).

"Love you," he says softly and hangs up.

Kellerman

I'm alone for the first time in months and all I want to do is call Kid. I'm not going to though. I'm assuming the whole office is bugged. I have no clue how crazy Cassie is, but I put nothing past her at this point. So I sit in my office and wait. I hope her and her father are fucking up today. I hope they finally do something so we have enough proof they're drug traffickers to get my son the hell out of here. Eight weeks. I open my home page on my computer and there's a breaking news story out of Kansas City.

Meth Manufacturer Killed in Explosion

I read the article quickly and find the name of the manufacturer Butch worked for. This has to be connected to Butch getting shot. I don't know how but that's too much of a coincidence. I hope Kid didn't blow up the house. I wouldn't put it past her with as pissed as Kav said she was. I got a new burner on the way into work today. It's pretty easy now. There's a gas station that I stop at on the way here. Cassie stays in the car while I fill up for gas and go in to pay. I buy a phone and she fucks around on Facebook in the car, she has no clue. The guy that works at the gas station thinks I'm some kind of spy. He asked me a few months ago and I gave him a bland no comment type response feeding the illusion. It works out well him thinking that, he'll never tell anyone that comes asking about me or my purchases because he thinks he's in on something covert (whatever works, right?). I buy three phones at a time and hide them in my gym bag. Cassie's never going in there.

I can't call Kid, but I'm going to text her. I go to the bathroom, check over the top of every stall, and then lock myself in the last one.

Kellerman: How's it going, Kiddo?

Kid: Kel, my life is fucking crazy! I'm fine though. You?

Kellerman: Cassie and her dad are at their meeting so I'm alone. Doesn't get much better than that for me right now.

Kid: Word. Butch is hanging in there.

She just texted "word". She's too cute and such a dork sometimes. I chuckle under my breath as I text back.

Kellerman: That's good. Any idea how long he'll be in the hospital?

Kid: Long time I'm guessing. They jacked him up. Both lungs, liver and spleen. He's on a vent right now. They want to get him off it soon though.

Kellerman: Fuck that sucks. You been there all night?

Kid: Yeah.

Kellerman: You have to take care of yourself, Kiddo.

Kid: I know. I'm good. Promise.

Kellerman: Saw the news. You have anything to do with that?

Kid: I didn't blow up that house! What do you take me for?

Kellerman: You. Pissed and exacting justice.

Kid: If I could have done it I would have, but I didn't. I'm sticking my tongue out at you!

Cute as hell dork. I miss her so damn much it causes actual physical pain.

Kellerman: I wish I could hear your voice. I don't trust that this whole place isn't bugged. She probably had a tracking device implanted under my skin while I slept at some point.

Kid: Don't risk it. We're almost there. Butch found some stuff last night that's good. I think we've almost got them Kel!

Kellerman: No SHIT?! I have to get back for a conference call now. I'll text later and you can tell me about it.

Kid: Okay. I love you. Keep safe.

Kellerman: I love you too. Don't shoot anyone unless you have to.

I stalk back into my office hating Cassie more with each step. I get on the conference call and pretend to engage while fantasizing about my year on an island with Kid and the baby. The guys will never let that happen, but damn if it isn't a good fantasy.

Chapter 40

Kavanagh

I have officially had enough of hospitals. If I never have to see one again it'll be too soon. It's late afternoon and after Cooper's pyrotechnics us guys are breathing easier for the first time in months. We all figured Pedowski was behind the threats against Kid after that note last night. We should have seen it sooner, but we've been distracted with this Yates shit and the Chicago mess. Cooper just won major brownie points with us.

Buzz, buzz.

Kellerman: Something's up. Cassie came back from the meeting and is acting stranger than normal.

Kavanagh: Like how?

Kellerman: Too excited. She's in her office talking on the phone a lot. Can't hear what she's talking about, but she looks REALLY happy. You think she made us?

Kavanagh: No clue. How could she have?

Kellerman: I'm afraid she's had someone watching me. What if that's who they were meeting with? Fuck if I'm made we got serious problems brewing.

Kavanagh: Don't freak out. Just act normal and see what she does. If she's trying to build the "battered wife" story she'll start picking fights with you and fast. DON'T take that bait!!

Kellerman: I'm good. I won't crack. Not now.

Kavanagh: You see the news?

Kellerman: Yeah. Kid's whereabouts accounted for?

Kavanagh: LOL yeah she was with us asleep when it went down. If I didn't know that I'd have thought she did it too. She was raging! That scene today was compliments of Jack Cooper.

Kellerman: Never thought I'd say this...I'm starting to like that guy.

Kavanagh: Me too. He's trying to fix everything for Kid. He was here this morning before going commando and told Kid that he thinks your shit will be ironed out soon. Kid's not buying it though.

Kellerman: Me neither. Until Cassie's behind bars and me and the baby are back in KC, I'm not buying shit.

Kavanagh: Agreed. I'm gonna go grab Kid and make her eat some dinner. She's gained some weight back, no more concentration camp Kid.

Kellerman: Good. I don't want to be impaled by hip bones when I get home.

Kavanagh: No shit. Nothing worse than fucking a twig.

Kellerman: That's your sister and my girlfriend you're talking about.

Kavanagh: And?

Kellerman: You have no shame.

Kavanagh: Can't wait for you to get home so I can get laid on a more regular basis. I'm running on fumes!

Kellerman: Don't give me that shit. You know the last time I got laid?

Kavanagh: Point taken. How have you stayed away from Crazy all these months?

Kellerman: Easy. I wouldn't touch her with your dick!

Kavanagh: Thanks for that. You definitely upgraded with Kid.

Kellerman: Tell me something I don't know.

Kavanagh: I have a mole on my left nut.

Kellerman: LOL Sick fuck!

Kavanagh: Let me know what happens with CRAZY.

Kellerman: Will do. Kiss Kid for me.

Kavanagh: On it. Later.

Kellerman: Later.

I walk into Butch's room to find Kid having a full blown conversation with him (he's out cold, so it's a one-sided conversation). I stand at the door and listen to her babble away at him. Everything she does is filled with so much love. Even the way her hand is laying on his is loving and affectionate. She's talking about baseball; you'd think she was reciting a love poem by the tone of her voice. When you see her for the first time it's her beauty that stops you in your tracks, it's unparalleled (trust me I've tried to find anything close to her). Then she hits you with the wit and humor, she's constant entertainment. Then she unarms you with her fierceness, her loyalty and commitment to the things she loves is beyond compare. But the thing that ties you to Kid and never lets you go is her love. She loves in the way that all great artists try to capture yet never succeed. She's the embodiment of unconditional love, not the emotion, the state of being. I am forever in awe of her.

"Take a picture it'll last longer," Kid chides me.

"Can I get some naked ones?" I question brows raised.

"Yeah, I'll get right on that," she snarks. "You've seen me naked enough to have my image permanently etched in your brain, pervert."

"Etched in the front of my pants by my dick."

"You ever wonder why you can't get a girlfriend?"

"Nope," I reply popping my *p*.

"It's because you're disgusting. And a pervert. And you stare at me too much. Every chick you bring home thinks I'm yours. Not really the way to find something permanent," she informs me.

"You are my something permanent, Kid. Don't want what you and Kellerman have. I'm good like this and you know it." She rolls her eyes and stands up from her chair next to Butch.

"I know you're good. Maybe you could try two rolls in the hay before you send 'em packin'?" she suggests as we walk back to the waiting room.

"Why the fuck are we talkin' about this? You worried about my dick all of a sudden?" She punches my arm, hard.

"I'm just talkin', jerk. A baby's comin' home. Shit's gonna change." She flops down at the table in the waiting room patting the seat next to hers. I gladly take the invitation.

"I know. I can take the kid to the park and lure in unsuspecting women. It'll be great!" I exclaim. I already have it planned out.

"You're not takin' the baby to catch women. That is now a house rule," she dictates.

"You're no fun, you know that. You gonna turn into one of those crazy obsessive moms? Disinfecting everything, calling the pediatrician every time he cries, no cussin' in a hundred mile radius of his baby ears, makin' home made organic food you grow yourself, weaving your own cloth diapers, makin' him take ballet, wearing scary mom jeans and Christmas sweaters?"

"Yup," she pops her *p*. "And you'll take him to ballet and wear tights with him."

"My dick looks good in tights."

"Why am I not surprised you know that?"

I shrug. My dick looks good no matter what. Tights would just give onlookers a better view, duh.

"What're you two talkin' about?" O'Sullivan asks as he sets down two huge trays of food.

"My dick," I say grabbing a plate with some kind of meat and potatoes piled high.

"Glad I missed that," Cal says setting down an equally ridiculous amount of food.

"No shit," Finn chimes in setting down a tray of drinks.

"No comment," Karl says carrying in a tray with chick food. I roll my eyes and get back to my food. Thomas takes a seat next to Kid and starts piling up a plate for her. It's twice as much food as I have.

"She has arms, Thomas. She can make herself a plate," I scold.

"She's had a rough few days," Thomas growls. Okay big guy.

"Thanks, Thomas," she thanks him sweetly while glaring at me. Fuck shoot me why don't you. I didn't know him making her a plate of food was so important.

"Spends all her time takin' care of people. She could use some of that in return," Thomas says pinning me with his gaze.

"They take care of me, Thomas. Just not makin' me a plate of food," Kid says protectively but sweet at the same time. He nods and turns to his own plate of food. I get it. We take care of Kid in our own ways. I'm her protector. O'Sullivan is her entertainment. Callaghan is her comforter. Thomas is apparently her food preparer. He gives what he can and that's important to him. I get that. I stepped into his space.

"Sorry, Thomas. No sleep makes me a cranky bitch. Thanks for takin' care of her," I say quietly.

"No thanks necessary," Thomas grumbles with a chin lift. Note to self, don't get on Thomas's bad side. We all eat in companionable silence. A family meal is a family meal for us no matter where we are.

After we finish dinner and clean up our mess Kid tells us she's going to go visit Mia and we should go home. Butch isn't doing well at trying to come off the ventilator so they're holding off until tomorrow. She feels comfortable leaving him for the night. Thank God because my body needs a real bed. I'm not keen on the idea of her going to see Mia even if Pedowski is dead. I know I won't win that fight though. Thomas will keep her safe (and fed).

Kellerman

"Dylan, it's time to go," Cassie calls from my office doorway. She's beaming. Not a healthy pregnant glow, a mischievous light like a serial killer has before they capture their prey. Shudder.

"Yeah," I mumble. I walk out the door and Cassie sweeps her arm around mine holding my bicep. I'll have to disinfect that area tonight.

"Oh Cassie you're just glowing," beams one of the secretaries as we pass. "You two have got to be the most radiant couple I've ever seen. That baby will be a bona fide heartthrob." I use my super human strength to keep my eyes righted in my skull.

"I can't wait to get my hands on him," Cassie lies through her fake teeth.

"Just be careful of Irish twins," the secretary warns. What the fuck is that?

"I'm sure keeping Dylan at bay will be a task. Maybe the next one will be a girl," Cassie gleams and wiggles. She's talking about another baby? Please get me the fuck out of here.

"You two have a good night," the secretary says rubbing Cassie's belly. I've never done that. I wish I could enjoy the kicks and rolls, but I refuse to enjoy my son through her. No touching.

"Oh we will," Cassie says in a suggestive tone. I pull my arm from her as soon as we round the corner from onlookers.

"Ugh, I can't imagine havin' another baby in less than a year. That'll be hard on me," Cassie moans.

"What the fuck are you talkin' about?" I ask perturbed at the line of thought.

"Irish twins," she says like that should mean something to me. I raise a brow at her to explain further. "You are so clueless about some things. Irish twins is a

296

term used when someone has two babies in less than a year."

"Thanks for the vocabulary lesson. And you don't have to worry about that happenin'."

"We're getting married a few weeks after this thing is outta me. It would make sense to end up knocked up again. At least if it was a girl I could enjoy it a bit. This one is useless to me until he can get a job and take care of me," she says completely serious. Have I mentioned I hate her? I grind my teeth and don't respond. Eight more weeks and I'll be through with this. Breathe.

Chapter 41

Shannon

Butch has been home a week, at my home. I know, shocker. He's alone and needed someone to look after him. I hired a nurse to come in during the days and see to him while we're at work. The guys didn't care. I think they were happy I wouldn't have to run around so much in the evenings this way. So our house is full between gunshot victim and nursery.

I cut out of the office early today. I was tired from a shit night's sleep. I tried to sleep without any of the guys, bad idea. I was awake or semi-conscious all night. I should try a weaning process instead of cold turkey. I'm just nodding off when my BlackBerry rings. I should have turned it off. I don't recognize the number. Maybe I should just let it roll to voicemail and I can deal with it tomorrow.

"Shannon Kelly," I answer swiftly.

"Kiddo," Kel sounds crushed. I fly out of my bed and start pulling on clothes.

"Kel, what's wrong?" I ask fully alert.

"I'm gonna lose him," he murmurs almost imperceptibly.

"Kel, you're scaring me. What's wrong?!" I ask pointedly.

"I don't know what's happenin'. Something's wrong with Cassie and the baby. They're doin' an exam now. There's so much blood," he whimpers. FUCK!

"I'm on my way. I'll be there in four hours. Kel, I love you. Everything will be okay," I say hastily as I run frantically around my room trying to get my shit together.

"Hurry," he murmurs and disconnects.

"THOMAS!" I scream at the top of my lungs. I can hear him vaulting up the stairs as I shove shit into my bag.

"Shannon?!" Thomas bellows blowing into my room gun drawn scanning every inch. Butch comes hobbling in behind Thomas looking beyond concerned.

"Get the jet ready. Something's wrong with the baby," I instruct. Thomas has the phone to his ear before I stop talking. I have had a jet on stand-by for the last month not knowing what to expect. It's a three and a half hour flight into Boeing Field which is right down the I-5 from Swedish Medical Center. I'll be there in four hours.

"Shannon can I do something?" Butch asks.

"I'm fine Butch I just need to get out of here. I'll call when I can. Get a hold of your nurse for me and ask her to come by in the evenings," I say in heavy breath. "Love you." I kiss his cheek and take off down the stairs.

"Love you too," he yells at my back. I sprint to the front door and out to the driveway where Thomas and Rodger are waiting for me. I slide in the back and Rodger has us moving at an illegal pace. Thomas is on the phone, but I'm not focused on him or what he's doing. I thumb Kel's pendant, willing the universe not to take this baby. Not after everything we've been through.

After breaking the land speed record Rodger pulls onto the tarmac and I sprint toward the jet. As I'm ducking into the plane I hear the squeal of tires as Kavy's SUV growls to a stop on the tarmac. Kavy, Sully, Cally and Finn jump out and run at me. I climb inside and buckle into my seat on the Learjet 45. I'm concerned that the pilots look to be twelve years old at best, but I can't wait for a new crew. Tighten my seatbelt.

There are two seats facing each other on either side of the aisle and the same arrangement repeated at the back of the plane. I take a forward facing seat and wait for the guys to get in theirs. Thomas climbs on and then Rodger. I raise an eyebrow at him.

"You need someone to drive you guys in Seattle. None of you are in the head space for that," Rodger answers my unanswered question.

"Thank you," I say as he passes me to take a seat behind me. Kavy sits facing me, Sully sits across the aisle from me and Cally sits facing him. Finn climbs in the seat against my back. Rodger sits facing Finn while giant Thomas stretches his legs out across the aisle from Rodger. The cockpit closes quickly after the cabin door and we're moving. Please let this plane move fast. We barely taxi before we lift off. I let out a breath and relax my grip on the chair.

"Kid, what's goin' on?" Cally asks sweetly.

"I don't know. Kel didn't know. Said something was really wrong and there was a lot of blood. Thinks he's gonna lose the baby," I explain in a whisper looking at my hands.

"Fuck," huffs Sully.

"I can't do this," I mumble. I'm breaking, hitting my limit that I didn't know existed.

"Yes you fuckin' can," scolds Kavy. "You will not stop fightin'. You don't know how. Use this flight to rest and get your shit together. Your son needs you!" Okay so much for breaking down. I nod and close my eyes. They pop back open quickly.

"We don't have anything from Nicky to get the baby from her—" Kavy cuts me off.

"Called Cooper on the way to the airport," Kavy informs me.

"Yeah saw my life flash before my eyes while he tried to dial," Sully huffs.

"Quit bitchin' O'Sullivan. You're fine," Kavy chides Sully.

"Cooper sent all your work and his operative's intel. Special Agent in Charge of the Seattle Division of the

DEA is securing a warrant as we fly. They've got enough to search the shipping company and Yates plus hold Cassie and her father. Don't worry," Kavy instructs softly.

"And while Kav was tryin' to kill us, I called Ma. She's gettin' everyone on a plane," Sully tells me giving Kavy the stink eye.

"Thanks guys. I wasn't really thinkin' on the way out. Just wanted on this plane," I say guiltily.

"That's what you shoulda been thinkin'. We got you," Cally says brightly showing me some dimple. Sweet Cally. The cockpit door opens and one of the twelve-year-olds comes out. His name tag identifies him as Tanner (fuck me even has the name of a twelve-year-old).

"You guys sure know how to make a quick exit from Kansas City," Tanner says in a manlier voice than I expected. I want to check under his arms for evidence of puberty.

"We're in a rush again," Kavy explains.

"Again?" I ask.

"He was our pilot to Chicago," Sully explains. Yeah this guy will definitely think we're a little strange.

"This group looks better than the last," Tanner says laying down trays of cheese and crackers flicking his gaze to me.

"We always look better when she's in tow," Cally says kindly smiling a full dimple smile at me with twinkling fairytale bright blue eyes. I'm sure the last trip was a nightmare. I feel sorry for Tanner.

"Can't disagree with that," Tanner says nicely, not perversely. I give him a giant panty dropping smile and he blushes. Oh to be young again. "Wheels should be down in three hours. I'll be back in a bit to check on you." He shuts himself back in the cockpit quickly.

"Kid he has to fly the plane. Don't do that," Kavy admonishes.

"I smiled, Kavy. I didn't flash him." I roll my eyes.

"That smile is trouble for men and you know it. He's a teenager. You could give him a heart attack!"

"Shannon, don't smile at the pilot," Thomas grumbles from behind me. I turn around to glare at him but his eyes are closed. "Not a fan of flyin'."

"Thomas you didn't have to come. I didn't know," I apologize.

"I'm fine. Don't smile at the toddler flyin' this tin can," he orders.

"Okay." No more smiling at the pilot.

We land in Seattle safely and early. The seven of us tear out of the terminal to find a rented SUV waiting for us. A pleasant man hands Rodger the keys and we're off, racing up the I-5. Rodger seems to know where he's going so I don't try to instruct. I call Kel again and again but it's rolling straight to his voicemail. His phone is off. In ten minutes flat and several broken laws we're sprinting into Swedish Medical Center climbing flight after flight of stairs to the birthing unit. Winded, I heave myself onto the reception desk.

"Cassandra Yates," I gasp. The woman in front of me types something into her computer and I see it. Her face clouds with despair. No, please no!

"Someone will be right with you, if you'll have a seat," she says professionally as she stands and moves away from the desk. I collapse hard against the floor, shaking and gasping for air. I feel like I'm drowning. Kavy's arms sweep underneath me and he carries me to a seat, keeping me in his lap.

"Kid, take a deep breath," he soothes in my ear. I desperately try to slow my breathing and my pulse. Kavy strokes my back and breathes in and out slowly, motivating my own. Once I have a hold of myself I look up into his face. He smiles my smile at me, just for me. "Good girl."

"Excuse me," a warm voice penetrates through the air. "Are you here for Miss Yates?" I unfold from Kavy's lap to face a very young looking man in scrubs. What is this bring your kid to work day?

"Yes," I answer surprisingly evenly.

"Are you family?" he asks unbelievingly scanning our odd group.

"She's our cousin," I lie easily. The doctor looks to Rodger first.

"She's my niece," Rodger lies just as easily as I did. The doctor's gaze swings to Thomas.

"I'm adopted," he lies. Cally smothers a laugh. The doctor's eyes bug out at the idea he may have just offended the adopted black cousin.

"If you could follow me please," the doctor says leading the way through some locked doors and again into a small office/conference looking room. We all settle into chairs waiting for what is surely going to be devastating news. I brace.

"I'm Doctor Calvert. I was the attending on staff when Miss Yates was brought in. She and the baby were in distress that indicated a plausible placental abruption upon admittance. Unable to stabilize Miss Yates I preformed an emergency cesarean section. I'm sorry to have to tell you this, but Miss Yates did not survive," Dr. Calvert says very clinically. She's dead. Cassie's dead. Fuck...she's dead. Breathe Shannon.

C-section means they tried to save the baby.

"The baby?" I whisper, thumbing Kel's pendant staring at the cherry table in front of me.

"He's stable with his father in the NICU."

"What?" I screech snapping my gaze to him.

"The baby was delivered successfully. He's premature but breathing on his own and stable," Dr. Calvert explains further.

"He's okay?" I ask Kavy for reassurance that I'm not imagining this.

"He's okay." Kavy beams my smile at me a thousand times brighter than I've ever seen. I jump up and move toward Dr. Calvert quickly causing him to jump back.

"Can we see him?" I ask impatiently.

"Only two visitors at a time. His father is with him now," Dr. Calvert says shakily worried this room of brutes is going to bludgeon him.

"Take her," the room orders briskly.

"Right this way." Dr. Calvert practically runs from the room. I follow closely behind pinching my arm to make sure I'm awake. Yeah, I'm awake and bruising myself. He takes me through a few sets of doors that I don't pay much attention to until I raise my gaze and meet the most perfect set of teal eyes ever created. Kellerman.

Chapter 42

Shannon

I heave myself into Kel's arms wrapping my legs around his waist like a vice grip. I bury my face in his neck and suck in cleansing lungfuls of his scent. His arms are holding me so tight I can hardly pull the deep breaths I desire. I start peppering his neck, jaw, cheeks, nose, eyes and forehead with kisses soaking him in. Holding his face with my hands, I lose myself in teal pools of adoration before pressing my mouth to his. It's a sweet loving soft kiss against his full pillowy lips. This is better than any kiss I've ever had with Kel, hands down. He slowly works his lips against mine never a tongue in play, just emotion pouring from each of us. Kel pulls away and buries his face in my throat.

"You wanna meet your son?" he asks quietly. I jump out of his arms as quickly as I'd jumped in. Kel grabs my hand and leads me over to an incubator where I get my first glimpse of perfection in this life. He. Is. Perfect. His tiny body is curled up into a ball as he lies peacefully on his stomach. His skin is pink and wrinkly only covered by the world's smallest diaper. The finest fuzz of golden hair tops his head. There's an IV in his hand and wires attached to sticky patches coming from his body. Tiny doesn't describe how small he is. My heart drops realizing how early he is.

"Is he okay?" I ask quietly.

"He's great. Doctor says she can't believe how well he's doin'. Breathin' on his own, no bradycardia, everything looks good," Kel explains.

"He's so little," I say pointing out the obvious.

"Four pounds seven and a half ounces, nineteen and a half inches long. He's long and skinny," Kel agrees.

"Can I touch him?"

"Yeah. You gotta do some serious scrubbin' first," Kel says pulling me away to a sink. After I scrub my skin like a surgeon prepping for the operation of a life time, I'm ready.

"Just put your hand in the porthole. Don't rub or stroke, it'll over stimulate him. That's what the nurse told me," Kel offers his first daddy wisdom confidently. I open the porthole and gently lay my hand on his back, the softest skin I've ever felt. I lay my face against the incubator and peer down through tear filled eyes at my son. I feel it wash over me in this moment. He's mine down to the depths of my soul. Kel's arms snake around my waist and his face nuzzles into the side of my neck.

"Jonathan David Kellerman," Kel murmurs into my neck and a sob breaks free from my chest. Our fathers' names. I let the tears stream as Kel holds me from behind kissing my hair. I've never shed tears filled with so much joy and love in my life, it's cleansing. I don't know how long we stand in our embrace but it's long enough for Johnny to wake up. For the first time in my life since I went to live with Uncle Mick I feel panic race through my body. I have no fucking clue what to do. He's wiggling beneath my hand and screeching like a kitten.

"I don't know what to do," I whine the panic seeping through my voice.

"Me neither," Kel says with a concerned voice. "He's just been asleep. Slept through the IV and everything else they did to him."

"Somebody's awake," coos a silver haired woman entering the room. Her face is soft and calm, thank God. "Little man's got some lungs." Kel and I back away from the incubator and watch her work. She drops open the side of the incubator, sticks a thermometer under his arm and checks the monitors. Once she has his temperature she weighs him (built-in scale in the incubator) then takes off his diaper and weighs him again (to see how much he peed she explains). Expertly wrapped back up in a diaper she turns to us with a kind smile.

"My name's Kate and I'll be his nurse today. Does he have a name yet?" Kate addresses me sweetly gauging how freaked out I am.

"Jonathan," Kel responds with a huge grin squeezing me tightly. She nods and writes his name on a card on the end of his incubator.

"Jonathan's going to need to be supplemented his meals until he learns suck-swallow-breathe. I'm going to put a nasogastric tube down his nose into his stomach. He may fuss a bit but it doesn't hurt," Kate explains measuring out a tiny tube the length of his stomach to his nose. I sit in a chair and watch through partially finger covered eyes. He screeches and throws his hands up as she inserts the tube, my little fighter. Once the tube is in place and sticky puttied (that's what it looks like) to his cheek, Kate puts him on his tummy and he curls into a tight ball again.

"Have we decided if we're breast or bottle feeding?" Kate asks closing the incubator.

"Uh," I say completely confused by her question. I must look like shit because clearly she thinks I just gave birth.

"I explained our situation to Kate a few hours ago," Kel says gently.

"I'm even more confused now," I say searching between the two of them for a clue.

"I understand you'll be adopting Jonathan and taking him home with you," Kate leads. Wow I guess Kel hasn't pulled any punches around here. I nod. "Women that adopt babies can breastfeed. We can get you set-up on a lactation induction protocol and see how you do. Until then if you'd like we can use donor milk to supplement his feedings. If you're not comfortable with that we can try him on formula and move to bottle feedings. It's really up to you." I had no idea. I don't know what to do.

"What's best for him?" I ask feeling like an idiot for not knowing.

"Breast milk offers him the best nutrients and vitamins as well as helping to build his immune system. Being preterm those things are even more important. That said formula is a good alternative," Kate informs me with her soft voice.

"Sign me up for whatever I need to breastfeed," I say emphatically. I have visions of being hooked up to a pump like a dairy cow for the next hours and days of my life.

"All right. I'll go call a lactation specialist to come down and visit with you. Would you like to supplement with donor milk until we see how you do?" I look to Kel for some help. I don't know anything about donor milk. Is it like donor blood? "I have some pamphlets I'll leave you and when I come back we can decide." She hands us the pamphlets and leaves us to start making important decisions about our son's life. I need a manual. Babies need to come with manuals!

"What do you think?" I ask Kel thumbing through the pamphlet. He doesn't respond so I look up at him. He's gazing down at me with such love and adoration my breath hitches. "Kel."

"You're a momma," he says through a giant ear to ear smile.

"A panicked clueless first time momma. Help me," I urge pulling his arm to sit next to me.

We read the pamphlets a few times in silence. It seems safe and like a good compromise until I can get my girls working. When Kate comes back we tell her to go ahead with the donor milk. I pull my chair over to the incubator and thread my hand through the porthole and place my hand on Johnny's back again. He lets out the slightest sigh of contentment and I feel tears coming again. Maybe I'm getting sympathy hormones from all the women that are around here. I keep my shit together and sit with my son.

"What happened Kel?" I ask in a whisper to not disturb Johnny.

"I don't have the full story yet, but I can tell you what I do know. Cassie went to another secret meeting for lunch...without her father. Her parents are in Europe, or were, they're flying back now. Anyway, she came back from her meeting and about thirty minutes later she collapsed in pain and started bleedin' like crazy. I rushed her here and that's when I called you. They thought she had something wrong with her placenta but couldn't tell. They couldn't get her stabilized and the baby was in distress so they took her for an emergency c-section. I wasn't in there it was so rushed. I thought I was gonna lose him. A few minutes later the NICU team came out of the room with him in the incubator and we came here. Cassie didn't make it," Kel explains softly stroking my hand. "She had cocaine in her system."

"WHAT?!" I hiss under my breath. Oh if this baby didn't need me to be calm right now. "Is he okay? What does that mean for him? That fucking BITCH!" I know, don't speak ill of the dead...fuck that!

"He's not havin' withdrawals and his tox-screen was clean. She must have just used today. That's what the doctors think at least," Kel whispers trying to keep me calm. How could she do that?! I take a few calming breaths and focus back on Johnny. I'll keep him safe now. If it kills me, I'll keep him safe.

"All right. I'll get this feeding set up and you can do some kangaroo care," Kate says walking to the incubator and dropping the side I just pulled my hand from.

"What's kangaroo care?" I ask yet again feeling stupid.

"Skin to skin holding. I'll have you take off your shirt and bra and put Jonathan on your chest while he gets his feeding. It's great for bonding, helps guard against serious illness and helps with development."

"Okay," I say excitedly. I get to hold him! I quickly disrobe slinging Kel's pendant around to the back as Kate hands me a hospital gown. I hold it to my front until she lifts Johnny and places him on my chest. I quickly cover us with two warm blankets and the gown, I fucking melt. I'm a puddle of love. I look over at Kel who is beaming brighter than the sun. He pulls his phone out and starts taking picture after picture. I close my eyes and relax fully for the first time in my life. Nothing will ever compare to this feeling.

"I love you, Johnny," I murmur into his fuzzy head. He wiggles further into my body and settles. Kate sets a syringe filled with milk in a pump thing and hooks Johnny's NG tube up. Dinner time.

"Now. You two have a large rowdy bunch out in the waiting area. There are only supposed to be two people in here at a time but considering your situation I've cleared in with the charge nurse to let the group back. If it gets to be too much for Jonathan or the other patients they'll have to go. Is that all right?" Kate asks, knowing she doesn't need too. I nod like a maniac.

"Get ready to meet your family, bud," Kel says placing his rough hand over Johnny's butt.

A few minutes later the door opens and in they file: my nine brothers, three fathers, two mothers, Nicky, Rodger, Thomas and Karl. Don't know when or how they all got here, but I couldn't be happier. I have also never heard this group be this silent. Not a peep even from Maggie and Mary who are streaming tears. One by one they all scrub their hands carefully watched by Doc and Aidan. Kel stands up and starts the longest round of hugs known to man. Now they stand in a semi-circle around me and my son staring at us like a treasure has been unveiled.

"Jonathan David Kellerman," I softly introduce. Audible breaths are sucked in around the room and Mary releases a sob quieting it with her hand over her mouth. Johnny wiggles but stays asleep. His little head peeks out from beneath our blankets and hospital gown.

I rest my lips on his fuzz and take in the murmurs and whispers in the room. Pop crouches next to us gazing at his first grandchild. He looks up at me with glistening eyes, "Best moment of my life, Kid," he whispers. He pushes a kiss into my cheek and lightly presses his hand onto Johnny's head. And so begins a trend of crouch, talk, kiss and touch.

"My daughter's a momma, perfect," Pappy says.

"Most beautiful sight these eyes have ever seen," Doc says.

"Best day ever," Ryan says.

"I wish Mom could see this," Adam says.

"You're a natural," Hugh says.

"You two are perfection," Collin says.

"Best I've ever seen you look," Finn says.

"Proud of you," Rodger says.

"Stunnin'," Thomas says making Johnny jump. I press my lips to his head and he immediately settles.

"This is where you're meant to be," Karl says.

"I will never forget this picture as long as I live. You two are magic," Maggie says.

"He's everything you deserve in life," Mary says.

"Everything I ever mourned that I thought you had lost the last twenty-two years, you now have," Nicky says.

"You are unconditional love personified," Aidan says.

I don't cry. I take in every word and let them strengthen my soul. I have more love and support in my life than any one person deserves and I cherish each morsel. After all of the affection everyone clears out of the room promising to be back tomorrow in smaller groups. My boys stay. Kavy pulls up a chair next to me, and as carefully as he ever has, sits down never taking his eyes off Johnny. He gingerly places a hand on Johnny's butt shuddering at the feel. After a few moments he drags his gaze to mine, his blue-grey eyes glistening.

"I didn't know I could love you more than I already do," Kavy admits softly. He pushes his face into my neck and we sit that way for a long silent spell. Kavy leaves his mitt on the baby's butt and places his other hand between the chair and the small of my back.

Sully pulls a chair in front of me, his knee pressing mine. He stares into my face before reaching a tentative hand toward Johnny. Sully pushes under Kavy's hand and gets Johnny's tiny foot between his forefinger and thumb, marveling at its size. He rests his other hand on my thigh before he speaks, chocolate eyes beaming love.

"I'm not gonna cry," Sully forces out, choked with emotion. "But I'm honored to share this moment in your life."

Cally pulls a chair next to Sully, his knee brushing mine that Sully isn't occupying. He stares at me with his bright twinkling blue eyes without words, communicating everything that could be said. He turns his gaze to Johnny and his breath hitches. He takes hold of Johnny's other foot similarly to Sully.

"I love you," Cally whispers to Johnny and rests his other hand on my thigh.

Kel resumes his seat next to me eyeing the men surrounding his son and his girlfriend. He leans over and brushes Johnny's head with his lips and places his rough calloused hand over the fuzzy spot he just kissed. Kel reaches under the hospital gown and intertwines our fingers before pressing a kiss to my cheek.

"Welcome to the family, Johnny," I coo. And we sit enveloped by the love that has protected me for the last thirteen years. I'm happy.

Chapter 43

Kellerman

I am in awe. Kid became a mother with the touch of her hand to our son's back. It's the most amazing thing I've ever experienced. Now she looks like a dairy cow. They have her hooked to breast pumps, taking medication and drinking weird herbal concoctions to get her producing milk. This is strange and cool as shit all at the same time. She's determined for this to work and as of this morning she's already got drops coming which the specialist says is unprecedented. That's Kid, making the unreal real.

We have a sleeping room here at the hospital to be close to Johnny. Kid was up every two hours pumping like a machine last night. When she was in bed I held her so tightly to my chest I'm sure she couldn't sleep, but having her with me I can't have any space between us. I don't know that I'll ever let her out of my sight again.

"We're going to try to get him to latch on this feeding," Kate says.

"We are?" Kid asks shocked and excited.

"Yes. We'll still give him the supplement when he's done, but it's time to start teaching him to nurse."

Kid looks at me with her eyes bugged out. My girl that doesn't panic has been the cutest mess since the first peep our son made. I'm not much better, but she's way cuter. Johnny's been asleep on her bare chest most of the morning. She doesn't put him down unless the staff needs to do something to him. I haven't held him yet, I'm letting her get her fill.

315

"Dad you wanna hold him while I get Momma set up here?" Kate asks casually. Now I'm panicked and bugging out. Kid turns her gaze to me and realizes for the first time I haven't held him yet.

"You haven't held him yet?" Kid whispers in a guilt-filled tone.

"I wanted you to do it first. You're kind of a baby hog," I joke. She giggles softly.

"You shoulda said something Kel. I figured you held him before I got here."

I shake my head no as the door to our room opens and Maggie and Mary walk in.

"Good morning," they whisper in unison beaming equally bright.

"Morning," Kid shines back.

"All right Daddy," Kate says and hands Johnny to me. He fits easily in my hand, one hand. His dark blue eyes open and he gazes at me with a question lurking in them. "Where's my momma?" I smile down into his face.

"I know I'm second best bud. You got boobs comin'," I explain in a soft voice. Probably not the best first conversation to have with my son, but I'm learning. Kid rests her hand on my thigh, thumbs the pendant I gave her (which makes me beam) and sighs a contented breath. Mary sniffles and Maggie clears her throat, those two and their crying. I lean down and place a gentle kiss to his forehead before Kate takes him back to Kid. Kid cradles him across her chest and my little man devours her nipple. Like father, like son. No help needed from Kate, Kid's a pro. We all listen and watch as he suckles away. Kid's glowing.

"This hurts so bad," Kid says in the happiest voice ever, making me chuckle. Johnny's legs shoot out in a startle. Kid turns and glares at me before going soft.

"I'll leave you to it. Leave him on for at least twenty minutes. I'll come back and start the feeding then," Kate says leaving the room.

Mary and Maggie take the chairs on the other side of Kid and watch their daughter being a mother with pride.

"How's the milk induction goin'?" Maggie asks.

"Kid's doin' great. Got a few drops this morning," I explain because Kid's in a daze.

"She sleep at all?" Mary asks.

"She was up pumpin' every two hours. The nurses told her she didn't have to but you know Kid."

"I'm sittin' right here," Kid chides. We all snicker.

"Everyone's gonna stay through the weekend. Mary and I'll stay until you can take Johnny home," Maggie explains.

"Thank you guys. It'll be nice to have the help," Kid says softly.

"We'd like to come home with you too. Stay for a few weeks until you're settled. If you'd like?" Mary says softly brushing her hand across Kid's cheek.

"Yes. God I don't know what I'm doin'. I need you two," Kid accepts gleefully.

"You may think you don't know what you're doin', but you are a star," Maggie says full of pride.

Johnny takes a long pull, swallows and gasps. We all freeze watching for I don't know what.

"He just got some milk," Maggie says excitedly silently clapping her hands. "He'll be goin' home in no time."

"They said he could be here a few weeks," Kid replies.

"We read all about it last night. He needs to be eating on his own, gaining weight, maintaining his temperature, you two have to take a CPR class and he has to pass a car seat test," Mary explains.

"That's a lot of stuff. Could take a while," I say thinking we're a long way off on some of those points.

"He'll fly through. He's your son, a fighter," Maggie says to us confidently. "Karl brought all of the essentials with him on his flight, the car seat, stroller and some clothes. Johnny's too small for those clothes so we started shoppin' online last night for preemie clothes. Wait 'til you see the things we bought."

"Ma you didn't have to do that," Kid says appreciatively.

"He's my grandson. I'll buy him as much as I want. The spoiling has begun."

"I second that," Mary chimes in.

"Kavy thinks I'm gonna put him in ballet," Kid says with a smile.

"Uh," I grunt. Kid looks at me and starts to laugh silently bouncing the baby up and down. He smiles around her nipple and goes back to eating. He's a boob man.

We sit and talk about nothing while Kid nurses. Johnny does a few more big swallows and maintains his breathing. Kate comes back and hooks up his feeding and Kid suggests I do the kangaroo care for a while. I pull my shirt off and Kate places Johnny on my chest covered in warm blankets. He squirms around a bit trying to get comfortable.

"Not as soft as Momma," I apologize to him. I rest my hand on his butt and the pressure settles him. I immediately feel a calm wash over me and my eyes drift closed. I'm happy.

Shannon

"I think there's some biological thing that happens when a man has his baby on his chest. It's like a sleeping pill in the form of skin contact," Mary says gazing at Kel and Johnny sleeping together. "You tired sweetheart?"

"I'm good," I say over the hum of the breast pump I'm eternally hooked up to.

"How are you holdin' up with everything else?" Maggie asks her chocolate eyes concerned behind her black rimmed glasses.

"I don't know. Cassie's dead and I don't know what to think about that. She had cocaine in her system. I'm so mad, I can't think of anything beyond that. Johnny will never know her and I worry how he'll deal with that as he gets older. And what about her parents? They haven't even shown up here."

"Honey they were arrested at the airport when they landed early this morning. The DEA picked them up," Maggie explains. I guess we've been living in a bubble here. "And you're his mother. Any issues that come up you'll deal with, but I wouldn't worry on that too much. Enjoy your time with him. Worry later."

"Okay." I shut off the pump, hand Mary my bottles containing more than a few drops of milk and close my eyes just for a moment.

Kavanagh

O'Sullivan, Cal and I walk into the NICU to find Kellerman asleep sitting in his chair with Johnny on his chest, Kid asleep in her chair right beside them. I thought the baby looked small before, surrounded by Kellerman's giant frame...it's unreal. Maggie and Mary come and greet me and their sons while we scrub our hands.

"They've been out a while now. She was up every two hours pumpin' overnight. They let the baby nurse almost two hours ago!" Mary explains excitedly. Can I just say this whole, I didn't have the baby but I can still breastfeed, situation freaks me the fuck out. Not that I'll utter a word to Kid about that.

"It's good they're in here because the media are outside. After the arrests this morning there was a short press conference and the Yates' lawyer announced Cassie's death. Clusterfuck out there," I tell the new grandmas in a grumble.

319

"Great," Maggie huffs. "We're gonna head out and do some shoppin' for Johnny now that you're here. We'll see you boys later." They give kisses to Kid, Kellerman and Johnny as they all continue to sleep.

The guys and I take seats and wait for them to wake up.

"Is this not bizarre?" O'Sullivan asks pointing at the breast pump (machine intended for torture).

"Beyond," Cal says with big bright blue eyes.

"Her boobs are gonna get even bigger," I chime in.

"Stop talkin' about my woman's tits," Kellerman mumbles. He sits up a little straighter palming Johnny with one hand. If I had a man crush it would be Kellerman. His body is ripped, he's fucking funny, and he's about as laid back as they come...I don't have a man crush though. He looks up at the clock.

"We've been out a while," he whispers looking over at Kid. "I'm glad she's sleepin'."

"Ma said she's been up all night," Cal says.

"Yeah, the whole pumpin' thing is a chore. You know how she is though, dedicated if it kills her. I need to take a piss. Can one of you hold him?" All three of us freeze, making no offer to hold that tiny precious life. We're not the most delicate bunch.

"I'll hold him," Cal says in something of a whisper. Kellerman sits forward pulling the blankets away from them, leans forward laying Johnny into one hand (ONE FUCKING HAND!) and passes him over to Cal like it's the most normal thing in the world. Cal's hands are shaking, but he grabs the baby laying him across his arm, careful with all the wires and tubes. Those twinkling blue eyes are working overtime.

"Be back in a sec. I'm gonna grab some water too," Kellerman says pulling his shirt over his head and pressing a kiss into Kid's hair. Cal doesn't respond, just stares at Johnny.

320

We all sit in silence watching Johnny in Cal's arms like he's going to sit up and start telling us his life story.

"This shit is un-fuckin'-real," Cal murmurs finally looking at us with a broad smile tattooed on his face his dimples painfully deep. "He doesn't weigh anything. If I wasn't lookin' at him I wouldn't know he was here."

"Somehow I don't believe that," O'Sullivan whispers as he snaps a few pictures with his phone.

"You wanna hold him and find out?" Cal dares him. There's a pause before he scoots toward Cal to take the baby. After the world's slowest baby transfer O'Sullivan looks like he might throw-up once Johnny's settled into the crook of his arm. Cal takes over picture duty.

"Okay, he doesn't weigh anything. But I'd know he was here no matter what." He doesn't take his eyes off the baby as he talks. "Dude, you have been born into the coolest fuckin' family. Your mom...you hit the jackpot. And your uncles, the three of us who have to be your favorite uncles, will teach you how to piss her off like no other." The three of us chuckle softly. "All right Kav your turn."

I don't want to hold him. I'm scared to death of him, but if these pansies did it so can I. I swallow a huge gulp and lean toward O'Sullivan scooping Johnny into the crook of my arm. I could hold ten of him at once, he's so small. Whatever that cunt Cassie did to make him come early, I'm glad she's dead. We're lucky he's healthy...so goddamned lucky.

"You know little man you grow up to be the size of your dad no one will believe you started out like this," I say softly gazing down at his little pink body. Cal snaps a couple of pictures.

"We'll have proof," he says waving the phone at me.

"How is it possible to love something you just met?" I ask the guys.

"No fuckin' clue. Never loved anyone like I love Kid, until I saw him yesterday. Just saw him...that's all it took," Cal says surprising all of us. He's a man of few words and they're never about love.

"No shit. Holdin' his foot yesterday...I don't know man, that shit did somethin' to me," O'Sullivan agrees staring down at the baby with gooey non-man love in his face. We've turned into pussies over a baby. Johnny starts to squirm and I go stiff looking to the guys for help. They look at me pleading for me to make it stop somehow and then he squeals like a piglet. Fuck me I'm freaking the fuck out.

"Hand him here, Kavy," Kid calls quietly from next to me. Thank Christ! I quickly hand him to her. She lays him across her arm, pulls her boob out, and he goes at it like a champ. Weirdest thing I've ever seen. All three of us are staring at him suckling away (I'm shockingly not turned on by Kid's naked tit).

"That was the sweetest thing to wake up to guys. You three passin' him around like that," Kid says with a giant smile. "I want those pictures. And Sully you teach him to piss me off and I'll teach him how to break your neck." She offers an idle threat, making all four of us chuckle.

"How ya feelin'?" Cal asks.

"Amazing," she sighs. "Didn't know this existed. Can't imagine life without it now."

Kellerman comes back in with bottles of water smiling at the sight of his woman and child.

"Just saw Kate comin' this way with his next supplement," Kellerman tells Kid kissing her hair before he takes his seat. He opens a water and hands it to Kid. Johnny makes a weird sound and takes a deep breath. Before we can freak Kellerman explains, "He's learnin' how to breathe while he eats. Don't freak." We relax as ordered. I didn't know babies had to learn to breathe and eat but again, he's not supposed to be here for another six weeks. That's a long time in the baby cooking department.

"Where'd the mas go?" Kid asks.

"Shoppin'," we all say in unison. Kid smiles and shakes her head. This baby is going to be so spoiled.

"They offered to come home with us. I think it's a good idea, but if you all don't want 'em to they don't have to," Kid explains rubbing a nervous hand across her forehead.

"You know we don't care. Why are you even askin'?" O'Sullivan scoffs.

"I don't know. I don't want to put you guys out with a baby and grandmothers."

"Kid, stop worryin' about us. We're good. Havin' him around is not an imposition. I feel like we've gone back in time thirteen years," Cal says shoving a frustrated hand through his hair.

"What?" Kellerman asks confused.

"When we were tryin' to get her to move in with us back in the day she always acted like she was an imposition. Drove us nuts," O'Sullivan fills Kellerman in. Kid grins.

"Sounds like her," Kellerman says smiling at his woman. "Always thinkin' about everyone else."

"Somebody's gotta think about these idiots, they sure as shit don't," Kid huffs.

The nurse walks in halting our conversation.

"How's he doin'?" she asks.

"He latched on great and he's taken a few deep draws. I didn't get him weighed or changed yet." Kid tells her. "My brother was holdin' him and needed a quick reprieve when Johnny started fussin'."

"Boob in the mouth shuts me up too," O'Sullivan says under his breath. Making all the men in the room snicker while the ladies roll their eyes.

"Like father, like son," Kellerman says confidently. That makes everyone laugh. When we got here yesterday I didn't know what to expect so I prepared for the worst and hoped for the best. Sitting in a room laughing while Kid nurses her son...better than anything I hoped for.

Chapter 44

Shannon

June 15, 2014

We get to take Johnny home today! He has met all of his discharge requirements including a pulmonary exam clearing him to fly home (private jet). I am ecstatic and freaked the fuck out in equal measure. Maggie and Mary are with us so it's not like Kel and I are on our own, but still we're first time parents. My boys have also stayed here with us despite me trying to convince them to go back home. And of course Thomas has stayed dutifully watchful in the waiting room every day. The man knows no bounds and I love him for it. The media have tried to come up here twice and met his giant scary enforcement. I think the hospital wants to hire him at this point. Rodger has also stayed with us, driving my brood around Seattle. The level of commitment the people in my life have to me is unreal. I'll take it and then some right now because I feel like a damn basket case!

"What is that?" Kel asks as Maggie and Mary enter the room.

"It's called a stroller, Dylan. I didn't think you were this ill informed," Maggie explains shocked by Kel's question.

"I know what a stroller is Ma," he chides. "That's a damn tank. Who bought that?"

"I did. It's an Emmaljunga. It Swedish and safe. And you're right, it's pretty much a tank," I inform him moving over to check it out.

"It's a what?" Kel looks at me like I'm speaking a foreign language (I guess I am). He's holding Johnny in one hand which has become his thing. I don't think we ever put the baby down between him and me and the rest of the family.

"It's an em-uhl-young-uh," I enunciate the name to help him out.

"Okay," he stretches the word out. "Where's the seat? That just looks like a bed."

"This is a bassinet. We have the seat at home for when he can sit up better."

"Ooh, nice stroller," Kate compliments as she comes in the room. I lift an eyebrow at Kel and he smirks back. "European?"

"Swedish. I imported it," I say moving to Kel to hold my baby. It's my turn.

"You imported it?" Kel repeats.

"Yes. Is that a problem?" I ask warningly.

"You never cease to amaze me, Kiddo," he responds placing Johnny on my chest and a quick kiss on my lips. We need to have sex. The tension between us is completely sex based. Good thing we'll be home by tonight.

"All right guys. You're all set to head out. Any last questions before you go?" Kate asks.

"Will you come home with us?" I ask seriously. She laughs and wraps Johnny and me in a sweet embrace. She pulls back and looks me in the eye.

"You don't have any need for me. You're just fine. But if you feel it necessary don't hesitate to call."

"Okay," I say meekly feeling like a wimp. "Thanks for everything, Kate."

She nods as I walk over to the stroller, lay Johnny down and swaddle him like a burrito which he loves. Kel pushes a cart full of our hospital stuff behind me as we walk through the hospital. I know the media are here, but Thomas has assured me he's got Rodger waiting somewhere safe. Cassie's parents have been put in protective custody until their trial. The Yates' empire is crumbling further daily and the media is having a field day with it. The Yates' have lost their freedom, their daughter and their grandson all because they were greedy.

The meeting Cassie had the day she died was to check on new product from Mexico. Nicky's been able to track down some of the cartel she was dealing with and may be able to shut down some of their operations. Cassie could have killed my son...I don't know how to get beyond that, other than to be thankful that she made me a mother. Kel is convinced she did cocaine the day her and her father had that meeting but we have no proof of that. He won't really talk about her...he's too mad. He's also gone a bit primitive since Johnny was born. He speaks in grunts and single word sentences a lot. It'll be good to get home and away from the media for all of us.

We end up walking out an ambulance bay where no one but hospital staff is allowed. There's Rodger beaming from ear to ear. I climb into the SUV and Kel hands me the baby. I strap him in to the car seat securely making sure he's breathing and comfortable. He's swallowed up in this thing. He's able to ride in a normal car seat instead of a preemie car seat because he's so tall (long). He's the longest baby born at thirty-four weeks gestation the hospital has ever had. He's going to be big like his daddy. I take the seat next to the baby while everyone else piles in. Kel sits behind Johnny able to keep a watchful eye.

"I dropped the guys at the plane already. We'll be to the airport shortly, Shannon," Rodger says as he eases the SUV into traffic. It's the most careful he's ever driven me and I smile at the back of his head in thanks. Johnny's eyes are open and he's staring at his daddy. They do this a lot. While Johnny sometimes looks at me, I seem to put him to sleep more often than not. I watch Kel reach his hand over the seat and place one giant rough finger in his son's grasp. Johnny grasps it and keeps staring.

"We're goin' home bud," Kel beams. "I get to eat home cooked food for the first time in months and work out on a regular basis again."

"Lord knows you need it," Maggie snarks watching Kel and her grandson with a grin.

"Gotta look good for Momma," Kel says to Johnny. I snort and shake my head.

"Don't think that's a problem, Dylan," Maggie says looking at me with a knowing smile. Yeah that's definitely not a problem. The man is simply gorgeous and fatherhood agrees with him. Johnny yawns, bored with his father's conversation.

We pull up to the tarmac and climb out. Kel carries Johnny in his car seat onto the jet while my boys, Thomas and Rodger unload the SUV. Tanner and the other pilot are there to greet us. I wave at them and climb onto the jet.

"That dude can't be old enough to fly this plane," Kel says removing Johnny from his car seat before flopping down into a leather seat. I climb into the seat next to them and buckle myself in before reaching for the baby. Kel hands him to me one-handed. I scoop him up and lay him on my chest. Everyone gets in the plane and takes their seats. My guys take the long couch next to Kel and I, everyone else heads behind us. I hope Thomas is okay.

We taxi and quickly take off. I can't wait to be home. Johnny starts to fuss so I pull my boob out and let him nurse. I was able to produce enough milk to nurse him exclusively for now. Everyone in the hospital was quite impressed with that feat. I don't think he's hungry but the doctors said it would help his ears if he suckled.

"I'll never get used to that," Kavy says motioning at my boob.

"I figured that's why you need so many randoms. Tryin' to find a good pair," I snark.

"Uh, it's the pussy I'm after not the tits. But starin' at yours and not getting' a semi is new," Kavy says in a low grunt.

"Sorry to ruin your fun," I snark back.

"I'm not," Kel huffs and we all chuckle.

Johnny settles and falls asleep still latched on. He does this all the time. I cover myself with my shirt and lean my head back to nap. The cockpit door opens pulling me from my nap attempt. Tanner walks out and brings sandwich trays and drinks. When he approaches us I give him a megawatt smile.

"Best group yet," he says as a blush covers his face and neck.

"Thank you," I respond sweetly. I can't help but flirt a little. He's too responsive. Though, I do have my boob out and my boyfriend next to me. I'm a classy broad.

He smiles nervously before returning to the cockpit.

"Really?" Kel says. I turn to look at him and catch my boys looking at me too. They all look perturbed.

"What?" I scoff, feigning innocence.

"You need to get your woman on a tighter leash," Sully instructs Kel.

"I see that," Kel responds darkly.

"Oh please. I smiled at the kid and said thank you. I didn't offer to blow him in the bathroom."

"Shannon!" Mary scolds. Oops, forgot about the parentals. I stretch the corners of my mouth down making the uh-oh face.

"Don't smile at the pilot, Shannon," Thomas demands.

"Jesus Christ people," I huff. "I've been cooped up in a hospital ten days. I was just bein' nice. You could learn that skill."

I pull Johnny up to my chest and right my clothing before unbuckling my seat belt. I stand up and move away from the guys and Kel who are still glaring at me. I hand Johnny to Mary who beams at the offer. I gift her a small smile before heading to the bathroom at the back of the plane.

If it's possible the guys and Kel are more annoying than they were before Johnny was born. Protective, possessive, overbearing and every other caveman characteristic you can imagine is what they are. I roll my shoulders, thumb Kel's pendant and try not to be annoyed as I sit on the toilet. I know they're being this way because they love us and they're scared something is going to happen to us, but a smile and a thank you does not make me a villain. I'm washing my hands when the bathroom door slides open. I'm met with the most stunning stern face and hard teal eyes. Kellerman.

Chapter 45

Kellerman

I'm pissed. I have absolutely no reason to be pissed, but I'm pissed. She smiled and said thank you in her sweet soft voice to Tanner the twelve-year-old who turned an abnormal shade of red. Not to mention her tit was out (not that he could see anything because she was completely covered). Kid gets up and leaves, handing the baby to an excited Mary, before going into the bathroom. She's pissed that I'm pissed. Perfect.

"She's pissed at us now," O'Sullivan says sheepishly.

"Can't help it. I feel like a fuckin' caveman or something," Kav says.

"Imagine how I feel," I grumble running a hand through my hair.

"You better go get us outta trouble," Cal instructs. Nobody wants to be in trouble with Kid.

I stand up to take his advice because I sure as shit don't want to be in trouble. I move down the plane checking on Johnny as I pass. He's out cold on his grandmother's chest. I walk up to the bathroom, flip up the panel hiding the locking mechanism and unlock the door. I slide it open to find Kid washing her hands with a scowl on her stunning face.

"What?" she seethes looking back down at her hands. "Did I not breathe correctly? Or maybe I need assistance washin' my fuckin' hands."

I slide the door closed and lock it before stalking over to her.

"You smiled at him," I growl in her personal space.

331

"Forgive me, I didn't know smiling had become a sin," she snarks. She shuts off the water and turns toward me glaring into my face. "Move."

"No," I growl.

"You better get outta my fuckin' way or I'm gonna kick your ass." I take a step into her and she takes a step back.

"No."

"Kel, we've had a rough few months. You really wanna end it gettin' your ass handed to you by a girl? I swear on everything that's holy if you don't move I'm movin' your ass," she seethes. Okay I'm supposed to be in here making shit better and I'm clearly making it worse. I take another step toward her and she doesn't budge. She narrows her glare even more warning me that I'm entering dangerous territory.

"No," I say and as she rears back to knock the shit out of me I grab her and smash my mouth onto hers. She struggles against me for a moment and then melts against my body. This is not sweet and tender, it's rough and animalistic. She runs her hands into my hair dragging her nails sharply over my scalp. I reach down grabbing fistfuls of her ass and plunder her mouth with my tongue. She moans in my mouth and I lift her off the ground by her ass, her legs immediately wrapping around my waist. I turn and set her on the vanity and run my mouth along her jaw and neck nipping and suckling. She pulls at the back of my shirt ripping it roughly over my head. I grab the hem of hers and remove it a little more gently, but only just. Her pendant gleams in the light and I smile feeling like I've already marked her with it. My hands engulf her larger plump tits and begin to massage.

Kid throws her head back and sucks in a deep ragged breath. I reach around and unclasp her bra and replace it with my hand on one and my mouth on the other. I don't suck so as not to steal my son's lunch but I nip and lick and tug and pull. Kid arches her back pushing her firmly in my face. I reach down and undo her button on her jeans. She takes the lead and lifts her ass off the vanity and rips her jeans and thong down her legs. I follow her lead and do the same.

As my cock springs free, Kid grabs it and strokes me vigorously. This is not going to last long. I pull her hips toward me ending her stroking and capture her mouth in a slower loving kiss. This is not how I wanted our first time back together to go, but I'm not stopping. I run my fingers through her folds and she whimpers at the touch. I groan at the back of my throat and move my hips. Palming my dick I enter her slowly, knowing between my size and the amount of time it's been since she's had me in her this will hurt a little. She gasps as my head breaches her and I fight to be still, letting her adjust.

When her breathing slows and she bites my lower lip I continue to push forward slowly inch by inch. When I'm buried to the hilt I stop and pull away from our kiss.

"You okay?" I ask my voice dripping with sex. She smiles her seductive lip curl at me and starts to rock her hips in an answer. Fuck yes! I take over and start to power into her before I capture her mouth again aggressively. I stroke her tongue tasting every bit of her mouth before she moves to my jaw and my neck. I reach between us and lightly rub her clit and her legs begin to shake around my waist. I pick up the pace with my thrust feeling the pressure build in my nuts.

I wrap my arm around her waist to get more leverage and plow myself deeper inside her. She moans and throws her head back as I work my thumb harder on her clit. She comes undone silently panting and whispering cuss words. As she clinches around me I lose control and come violently inside her. I move in and out slowly a few more times before collapsing against her.

Heaving and panting we both stay connected waiting for the other to calm down. I know I'm smashing her so I stand up pulling out, immediately wanting back in. She sits up and moves instantly to wrap her arms around my neck, burying her head in my chest. She smells like sex and me. I've marked her.

"Mine," I growl into her hair. Her arms and body start to shake with laughter.

"Caveman," she accuses. I have to agree. I do feel like a caveman.

"Yes," I agree in a softer murmur.

"You could've just asked me for sex instead of pickin' a fight with me and fuckin' me in an alpha male markin' ceremony."

"I didn't pick a fight with you for sex, Kiddo. I'm sorry about bein' a dick but I don't seem to have much control right now. I really didn't like you smilin' at that kid or talkin' to him." She pushes back from my chest and looks up into my eyes.

"Kel I may be a mother now, but I'm still me. A little flirtatious and sayin' sexually inappropriate shit is who you fell in love with. I'm not gonna change just because Johnny's here."

"I know," I growl stepping back from her. I grab a towel and clean off while handing her another towel to do the same. Though, the idea that she's rubbing me off of her makes me mad again. Fucking shit I'm like a crazy person all of a sudden. "I don't know how to explain how I feel right now. I feel like my IQ has dropped well below a hundred and I can only think eat, sleep, sex and protect."

She hops off the counter and pulls her thong and jeans back up, clasps her bra, and pulls her T-shirt over her head. I just stand there naked watching the show. She's as sexy putting her clothes on as she is taking them off. She quirks her brow at me.

"Enjoyin' the show?" she snarks. I smile a seductive panty dropping smile. She shakes her head at me but smirks. "I know you're havin' some caveman tendencies and I get that. I'm weirdly hormonal too. You and the guys have to back the fuck off a bit though. You guys smotherin' me and growlin' like feral animals because I

smile at some guy is not gonna end up good for you all."
I grab my clothes and pull them on quickly before I answer.

"I'm sorry, Kiddo. I can't help it. Kav and the guys just said they feel the same way. I'll try to rein it in but cut me some slack and try not to be such a MILF."

"Did you just call me a MILF?" she asks unbelieving. I wrap my arms around her waist and kiss her hard on the mouth.

"Yeah."

She tips her head back and lets out a loud boisterous sexy belly laugh. When she calms down her laughing she looks up at me with mischievous green eyes. I know she's about to say something that will likely piss me off.

"I'll have to use that to my advantage when I'm trolling for fresh eighteen year old meat," she purrs. Yeah, she's trying to piss me off. I growl and pull her tighter into me and grab her ass in both hands.

"You want me to fuck you again to shut you up?" Her eyes hood and she leans up onto her tiptoes.

"Promise?" she whispers.

I reach to rip her clothes off again when we hear Johnny scream. She smiles and pulls away from me.

"Duty calls," she says brightly moving to the door. I wrap my arms around her from behind and nuzzle into her neck.

"I love you," I murmur. She wraps her arms over mine.

"I love you too."

Kavanagh

Kid comes out of the bathroom with a blinding after sex glow. They were quiet, but I know what a woman looks like after she's gotten it good and Kid's gotten it good. Kellerman walks out behind her with a triumphant smile smeared on his face and no visible body damage. Thank God those two finally fucked, the sexual tension around them has been giving me wood.

Kid grabs Johnny who's wailing for a boob in the mouth. She hops in her seat and obliges her son's wishes. Kellerman flops in the seat next to her ready for a post-coital nap.

"Feel better?" Cal questions Kid brightly.

"Much," Kid matches his enthusiasm.

"It's good to have you back Kellerman," O'Sullivan mumbles behind a panty dropping smile at Kid. She turns her gaze away from him and smiles as she looks at the baby.

"Good to be back," Kellerman says as he grins at us. Can't fault the guy for being pleased with himself, he finally got laid for the first time in seven months. My dick would have shriveled up and fallen off after three weeks. I once had to go two weeks without pussy because I had mono...pure torture. Now Kellerman's coming home so I don't have to sleep with Kid anymore. Pussy will be a plenty! I'm a little bummed though, I love sleeping with Kid. I don't sleep as well when I'm not with her. Maybe Kellerman will give me a night a month, like a visitation schedule or something. I look up at him and he's got his arm around Kid's shoulders and his other hand resting on Johnny's butt, I doubt I'll get visitation...maybe a nap on a Sunday.

I feel happy and content for the first time since December. Johnny's with us. His grandparents are facing the trial of the century. Kid's safe for the most part. I can breathe so much easier. I'm ready to get back to our weird yet normal lives in Kansas City. It'll be different from before...better than before. I'm happy.

Part Four

Chapter 26

Shannon
August 30, 2014

Life is brilliant! Johnny is twelve weeks old and thriving. We went to the pediatrician yesterday and he couldn't be more pleased with my son's progress. Legally and officially my son as of two weeks ago when the adoption went through! Anyway, my little bruiser has tripled his weight and is off the charts in height (over fourteen pounds and twenty-four inches long). He's caught up and surpassed most full term babies. Breast milk does his body good apparently. My arms and back are ripped from carrying him around and I absolutely love it.

I decided to take a year off from the practice. I want to be home with Johnny, after everything...I just couldn't leave him. Karl is working as Kavy's assistant now...that's an interesting combination let me tell you, but they oddly work well together. Kel got his old job back at QD (Quintessential Design) but was adamant that his working hours stay within normal business hours. So he's home every evening with us and never works weekends. After our heated argument on the plane followed by greatly needed sex, he and I have been solid. We work so well together you'd never know we haven't been together very long. It's been over ten months since I met Kel, but we've spent more than half that time separated. Somehow we have it figured out though. We don't fight, he's amazingly helpful with and attentive to Johnny, we laugh all the time, and the sex is amazing. All is well on the Kel front.

Maggie and Mary stayed here with us for three glorious weeks. They cooked and cleaned and helped and taught and loved...I couldn't have done it without them. Everyone has been here from Chicago at least twice now. Our house has become a revolving door of visitors. Kel and Kavy started talking about extending the house after a month of our house being full to the brim. I think they're actually serious because now Sully and Cally are in on the talks.

My boys have taken to being uncles like ducks to water. We have a routine. I get up in the morning and feed Johnny. Then I take him downstairs to Kavy and Sully while Kel gets ready. Kel relieves Kavy and Sully so they can get ready. Cally and I workout together then Cally watches the baby while I take a shower and get dressed and often have morning sex with Kel. I go relieve Cally so he can get ready. Then everyone leaves us at home when Thomas arrives. It's like clockwork. Finn comes over every night to see his nephew which usually consists of him holding Johnny while we watch sports. Butch comes over on Saturdays after we visit Mia. We have a family meal that day with everyone including my boys, Finn, Karl, Rodger, Thomas and Butch. Then the guys go out and hunt for pussy and Kel and I enjoy a quiet evening with our son.

I just got Johnny to sleep through the night in the nursery. I hate having him a room away but I know it's necessary. Having him sleeping in the bassinet in our room made having sex with Kel at night nonexistent (hence the morning sex and naptime sex). Now our nocturnal activities are back to normal.

Like I said life is brilliant.

"Kavy put his hat back on. I don't want him burnt," I scold from the doorway heading out to the pool. Kavy's in the pool with Johnny floating around.

"This thing makes him look like a girl. Could you've gotten him a frillier hat?" Kavy asks swinging around Johnny's sun hat.

"It's not a fashion show. Put it on!" He grumbles something at me about ballet and puts the hat on the baby. Kavy has Johnny cradled against his tattooed chest and the baby keeps rooting on him for food. It makes me laugh.

"Put your nipple in his mouth. See if your maternal instincts kick in," Sully teases from the grill.

"Don't you dare. I saw what rolled outta here this morning. I don't want my baby to catch whatever she might've had," I warn sitting in a lounger next to Butch who throws his head back and laughs. Kavy chuckles too knowing I'm right...she was nasty, pretty but dirty.

Kavy climbs out of the pool and hands the baby to Butch before leaning down dripping pool water all over me.

"Jealous?" Kavy growls.

"Of you gettin' crabs? Very," I snark.

He grabs me around my waist heaving me over his shoulder. I squeal and flail to no avail. He reaches up and smacks my bikini clad ass before jumping into the pool with me. I push off the bottom of the pool and breach the surface just as Kavy is roaring with laughter. Kel, Sully and Cally are laughing too. Fuckers. Butch is smirking but more intent on Johnny than me being thrown in the pool. Thomas is blank as he usually is when someone fucks with me. Karl walks to the side of the pool and hands me a hair-tie rolling his eyes at the comedians.

"Kel come help me out," I call sweetly from the side of the pool. I reach my hand up and he leans down wrapping his strong less than originally calloused hand around my wrist. I wrap mine around his, plant my feet on the side of the pool and heave his big ass into the pool. He almost smashes me as he falls. Now it's my turn to laugh like a maniac. I look up and Karl is standing behind Sully and Cally as they point and laugh in Kel's direction. Karl gives them each a good shove in the back and they both come tumbling in. Points for Kid and Karl! I quickly try to climb out of the pool but big strong arms engulf my midsection before I make it out.

"That wasn't very nice," Kel purrs into my neck.

"You shouldn't have laughed at me," I fake pout. He spins me around and I wrap my legs around his middle and my arms around his neck. He is stunning. His surfer hair style is wet and swept to the side. His chiseled chest and eight-pack are tanned and glistening with beads of water that are crying out to be licked off. His teal eyes are glimmering with desire as his tongue sweeps out and swipes water from his fat bottom lip. Shudder.

I hear a shout and then Karl hits the water with a huge splash pulling me out of my reverie. Sully and Cally are dying laughing as they dive in after hurling Karl. He and the guys start playing water basketball and I turn my attention back to my man. His hand slips into the back of my bikini.

"We have an audience, Kel," I admonish pulling his hand from my ass. He growls and crushes his mouth to mine in a not appropriate in public kiss. I go right along with him massaging his tongue with mine rocking my hips against him and releasing a small whimper when he pulls away. He places a quick chaste kiss on my mouth before pulling back.

"Just a preview," he rumbles as he puts me down to go play with his friends. At least I'm not the one with a hard on. As I climb out of the pool and wrap myself in a towel Finn comes outside.

"Hey Finn," I call. His face is dark as he watches me walk toward him. "What's wrong?" He nods his head indicating I follow him inside. I look at Butch who smiles at me to go ahead. I follow Finn inside, shivering a little as the air conditioning hits my wet body.

"Just got off with Cooper," Finn says flatly.

"Okay," I encourage him to go on.

"Did you kill someone?" I gasp and wait to catch my breath before I respond.

"What?" I say because I honestly don't know what else to say.

"When Mancini's crew had you. Did you kill one of his guys?" he asks pointedly.

"Yes," I answer blankly because I still don't feel shit about it.

"Well someone got word to what's left of the Mancini Crime Family and they're lookin' for retribution. Why didn't you tell us?" His voice is pained as he pulls me into his chest. I wrap my arms around his waist and let him hold me. "I can't do this again, Kid. I can't fuckin' have you in danger again."

"Kiddo?" I hear Kel's concerned voice call from the other side of the room. I look over to him and he stalks toward Finn and me sensing there's a problem. Finn squeezes me once more and passes me off to Kel who looks into my eyes with a little fear dancing in the teal pools.

"We've got a problem," I whisper and he engulfs me in his arms smashing me into his godly chest.

"I'll get everyone so we can talk," Finn says moving away from us. Kel holds me close, rubbing his hands up and down my back until everybody makes their way into the great room.

"Fuck it's cold in here." Karl cringes. Kel let's go of me, turns me to face the group and then wraps both his arms around my shoulders pulling me roughly into him. Butch sits on the couch with Johnny asleep on his shoulder while everyone else stands and waits to listen to Finn.

"Cooper called me. What's left of the Mancini family are lookin' for Kid," Finn explains quickly.

"NO!" every voice in the room booms causing my son to jump. Kel's arms constrict around me tighter.

"Why?" Kel asks in a heaved breath.

"I killed someone while they had me," I say in something resembling a whisper. The room is silent other than the whir of the air conditioning. I wait.

"What?" Kavy asks the horrified question the whole group wants to know.

"When Nicky first got there he immediately had to stop the almost rapist," I wince at the memory as does the room. "He put me in the bathtub right after that incident because my backside was raw. Unfortunately, Mancini's team came back while Nicky was in the bathroom with me. Mancini was on the phone and Nicky had to play Scarso. That meant I was left alone in the bathroom with a guy from the team. Nicky gave him a warning not to touch me but the language Nicky used in that threat wasn't specific enough." My vague language isn't helping here. All of the eyes on me are demanding details.

"Nicky told him not to put his dick in me. The guy figured he could still touch me. When he tried I touched him first and drowned him." And I still feel nothing.

"Good girl," Butch calls from the couch cradling Johnny a little tighter.

"I got some other bad news," Finn pipes before anyone else can get started. "You've been subpoenaed as a defense witness for Governor Grady. You have to be back in Chicago September twenty-second," Finn finishes in a grumbled huff.

"That's a convenient fuckin' coincidence. The Mancini family gunnin' for me and Grady's people leadin' me to 'em," I growl glancing around the room at my protective men. "I'll get to be home for my birthday." I try to lighten the mood but it has absolutely no effect on my men.

"No fuckin' way Kiddo. Not happenin'," Kel growls in my ear. All eyes are on us now.

"Kid you can't be considering this," Cally shakes his head in disbelief.

"Absolutely not! There's no way in hell I'm lettin' you do that," Sully bellows staring straight into my soul with his chocolate eyes.

"Over my dead fuckin' body are you doin' that," Kavy seethes moving toward me. He bends to my face only inches away. "You're not fuckin' doin' it."

"Aaron, get outta her face," Karl orders strongly. "She hasn't even done anything and you're all over her. Back the hell off." Kavy grunts but backs away.

"Shannon, what do you think?" Karl asks politely.

"I don't know," I answer honestly. I don't know what to do. Obviously, Gov. Grady and Mancini are still working together and want something from me again. What threat could I possibly be to them at this point? I have the feeling now that me killing the guy in the bathroom is out, shit just got a lot more dangerous for me. I look at my son and see Butch is thinking the same thing as me. He's cradling Johnny even closer and tighter than he was a minute ago.

"If they've subpoenaed me you all know I have no choice. I have to be in Chicago for the trial. We can try to motion for my removal but you know it won't work. They're comin' for me regardless if I'm here or in Chicago," I say without waver.

"No one will get you," Thomas snarls. I look at his face and see his determination is infallible, but I know he can't keep me safe if they want me.

"What do you guys want me to do?" I ask the group of caveman panting around me.

No one responds. They know I'm right but they aren't going to admit it out loud. We all stand in silence letting our brains get a handle on this.

"Let's sleep on it guys. We don't have to figure everything out this minute. Let me talk to Nicky and Pappy. Nothing's gonna happen this weekend anyway with it bein' a holiday Monday. We can go back outside and enjoy our barbecue and deal with this tomorrow," I say confidently.

"I agree with Shannon. We aren't gonna figure it out freezin' are balls off in here," Karl responds with a shiver in his voice. The guys grumble but move back outside.

Butch offers me a sad smile before heading back out to the lounger leaving Kel and me to some privacy.

I turn around in Kel's arms and gaze up into his stormy eyes. I cup his cheek with my hand and he turns placing a kiss on my palm.

"Kiddo, I can't fuckin' do this. I'm serious. I know you wanna think about it, but I can't let you do this," he says in a soft pained voice. I don't respond because I don't have a choice. If I don't go to Chicago, someone from Chicago is coming here, plus a warrant for my arrest will be issued if I don't show for the trial. I prefer to be on offense in life. I'll talk to Nicky and Pappy, but I know I have to do this. I have to go back to Chicago so I don't end up in a blackness I can't fight my way out of.

Chapter 47

Kellerman

My inner caveman that I pushed deep within after our conversation on the way home from Seattle has broken free with a vengeance. After the barbecue shut down all the guys headed to Flannery's and Butch went home. Kid put Johnny to bed and I attacked her. I kissed and licked every inch of her body before burying myself inside her. I laid on top of her pinning her to the bed beneath me growling and panting like an animal as I thrust. Kid submitted (I use that term beyond loosely) to my aggression and held me tightly against her. I came hard as soon as her orgasm peaked and collapsed on top of her staying buried within nuzzling into her neck.

"Feel better?" Kid asks with a hint of teasing in her voice.

"No," I say in a pout. That earns me a snicker.

"Well I feel good and marked, caveman."

"Good."

"Has your IQ dropped down to a single word sentence capability?"

"Yeah."

"Well I'm gonna go to the bathroom while you go search for your club." She moves to slide from beneath me, but I press my hips into hers forcing her to remain attached to me.

"No," I grunt. She runs her hands gently over my cheek pulling at me to look at her. When I meet her gaze I know she's already decided about Chicago. I know I've lost before I even start.

"I love you," she says softly. "Everything will be fine." Her face changes to a pale washed shade quickly before I have the chance to respond. She pushes me hard in the chest before cupping a hand over her mouth. She's going to puke. I jump off the bed as she flies past me barely making it to the toilet.

I grab a washcloth wetting it in the sink before laying it across her neck. I pull her hair from her fist that's holding it from her face and tie one of her hair things around it. I'm no professional but it does the trick. She keeps trying to stand up but immediately doubles back over each time emptying her stomach more. Five times she does that as I stand behind her and watch. When she collapses against the cool tiled walls, I figure she's done for now. I hand her a small glass of water so she can rinse her mouth. As she swishes it around she starts to shake all over. Fuck she's sick.

I scoop her up in my arms and carry her back to bed, gently laying her down. Grabbing some sweats I pull them up over my hips before running down the stairs to get some supplies. I'm back in a couple of minutes with a puke bowl, saltines, water and some fever medicine. She's back in the toilet puking. When I make my way into the bathroom she's curled in a ball on the floor naked and shaking. I scoop her up again putting her in bed. I go to the dressing room and get out a long sleeve T-shirt and some yoga pants for her. I pull her into my lap and dress her as fast as I can without causing too much disruption. Once dressed she stays in my lap pressed against my chest. I scoot across the bed and lean against the headboard holding her to me. Her shaking has stopped and her breathing is more even now.

"Stomach flu?" I ask softly.

"Came outta nowhere," she huffs. "You'll have to feed Johnny the frozen milk. I don't want him gettin' this."

"I've got it. Don't worry about the baby. You feel any better?"

"I feel fine actually, just wiped."

350

"Let's get some sleep and maybe it'll pass quickly," I suggest hoping she doesn't stay sick long. My son loves me, but I'm a distant second to his momma. If he doesn't have access to boobs things get ugly. She nods in agreement and I slide down keeping her close to my body. She's asleep before I turn the lamp out.

Kavanagh

"Oh yes...fuck yes...give me that big dick! Yeah just like that...ugh yes...I love the way you fuck me...yes...YES!" Brittney (Whitney?) screams as I fuck her from behind. I keep a hold of her hips and pound into her wishing she'd stopping talking. Her voice is high and shrill, she makes Fran Drescher sound appealing. Sweat drips from my brow landing on the small of her back where a tramp stamp of something that was surely meant to be sexy (that isn't) stares back at me. I close my eyes and focus. Two minutes later I find my release. Finally! I brought this chick home at 3:30 a.m. and it's past 5:00 a.m. now...too much work or actually, too many dicks before mine.

"Thanks. You want me to call you a cab?" I ask pulling the condom off and dropping it on the floor. I'll remember to pick it up.

"I'll just sleep a while and call one when I wake up," she says in a voice that should be sweet but is grinding on my nerves.

"No slumber party tonight, Brittney," I say handing her dress to her.

"It's Whitney," she huffs. Well there you go. Good reason not to want to sleep in my bed. "And I'm tired. I'll leave later."

"Yeah, not gonna happen. You need to go." I hear Johnny screaming and hope that freaks her the fuck out.

"What's that?" she asks like it's a sound never heard by human ears before.

"A baby," I say with a questioning tone.

351

"Yours?"

"Kind of."

"Kind of?"

Fuck I don't have the energy for this and Johnny's still wailing. Kid always has a boob in his mouth by now. I feel concern creeping up my spine. I grab sweats off the floor and pull them up my hips quickly.

"You need to go. Now," I command darkly. She rolls her eyes and pulls her dress over her head and slides her fuck me heels on. I open the door to my room to see a half naked Kellerman struggling with Johnny down the hall.

"Wow. He's next," Whitney purrs from beside me ogling Kellerman's back as he descends the stairs. This chick has a death wish. O'Sullivan and Cal come out of their rooms at the same time as I'm leading the trash down the hallway.

"What's wrong with the baby?" Cal asks pulling a T-shirt over his head.

"Is this some kind of hot playground for women or something?" Whitney asks eye fucking my roommates. I push my hand into the small of her back a little more firmly causing her to stumble forward. "Hey," she protests.

"Move faster," I bark.

"Are you always an asshole after you come?" she seethes starting down the stairs.

"Nope, only after I have to fake it," I snark. She gasps and moves quicker. Johnny is screaming like a banshee at this point and I see Kellerman pulling frozen milk out. Something's wrong. Kellerman's calm as he starts to heat a pot of water on the stove with one hand, the baby cradled in the other.

As the guys and I hit the bottom stair I point Whitney toward the front door and walk away from the clinger. Fuck I hope she gets a clue.

"What's goin' on? Where's Kid?" I ask Kellerman as O'Sullivan takes Johnny trying to calm him down with shushing and bouncing (not working).

"Kid got sick last night. She doesn't want Johnny to get sick so I'm on duty. As you can hear he's not happy," Kellerman says in a chuckle. Johnny is the biggest tit man in the house. If he's too far away from a pair he lets you know about it, otherwise the kid's silent and happy all the time or sleeping. "Your random doesn't seem to know your rules." Kellerman indicates with his chin over my shoulder.

I turn to see her standing there with a hand on her hip waiting. For what, I don't know.

"Your phone dead?" I ask curtly.

"No," she huffs.

"Your brain dead?" I ask with a small amount of threat in my voice. My patience is gone, my nephew needs attention and Kid's sick...bitch needs to go. Cal takes Johnny to try his hand at calming the screams.

"I'm not a hooker you can just throw outta here like trash," she spouts louder than I'm comfortable with.

"Coulda fooled me," I say taking steps toward her. "Get the fuck outta my house before I remove you myself. You were willin' to let me fuck you after I said two words to you last night. Not the way to get a guy to want you to stick around. You've served your purpose...now go."

I'll never understand women like her. Behave like a slut and I'll treat you like one. Why are you shocked by that? I don't expect a woman to treat me like anything but the asshole I am. I offer nothing and don't expect anything in return. Just fucking. Maybe I need to put a sign on my door that stipulates the rules of entry.

"You fucking piece of shit!" she wails at the top of her lungs and swings an arm out to smack me. I step out of her reach easily causing her to stumble in her heels. Her screaming has ramped up Johnny's hysteria.

"Kav," O'Sullivan growls in a warning to me to get this shit under control. I haven't had a crazy like this in years. I'm a little out of practice. She swings at me again and I dodge it again. What the fuck?

"HEY!" Kid screams from the top of the stairs. Oh shit! She's seething. Whitney stops in her tracks at the sound of a female voice and quirks an eyebrow in her direction. Bad idea. Kid thunders down the stairs and stops only inches from Whitney. Kid's tall and even in heels Whitney's at a disadvantage.

"Who the fuck are you?" Whitney scoffs. Kid glances at me and I shrug giving her the go ahead to lay this chick out.

"I'm the person that's about twenty seconds from beating the shit outta you. Get the fuck outta my house," Kid seethes quietly trying not to alarm her son that is screaming ten feet away.

"Which one do you belong to? I'm thinkin' about comin' back for round two, three and four," Whitney says condescendingly. Yeah the bitch definitely has a death wish. Kid is completely calm like always, but I can tell she's on a razor's edge right now. She's also sick so I'm a little worried about her having to wipe the floor with this bitch.

"I don't have the energy for this shit, Kavy," Kid says still pinning her gaze on Whitney.

"Sorry, Kid," I say softly.

"Oh so you do have manners when it comes to this slut. She yours?" Whitney spits. O'Sullivan and Kellerman are moving toward us and I feel pretty certain this slut is in for a world of hurt. Kid starts laughing throwing all of us off base.

"They're all mine. Now are you gonna leave or do you want help?" Kid asks in a nice tone, but I hear the threat. Johnny's quieter now that he can hear his momma. I get the feeling he's tuning up for an encore though.

"Some creepy five-way orgy shit you're into huh, bitch? You even know which one that kid came from?" Kid moves before the slut finishes her sentence. She grabs Whitney's wrist, twists it behind her body and drives the bitch face first into the wall. Pulling up hard, Whitney screams for Kid to stop before she breaks her arm.

"Get me my gun," Kid orders. I move to her bag on the counter and pull out a gun (there are two in there) and hand it to Kid. Kid presses the barrel of the gun to the back of Whitney's head and she starts crying. Kid lets Whitney's arm go but keeps the gun in place. Kid removes the safety and the click makes the crying stop and intent listening begin.

"I'm gonna count to ten and then I'm gonna shoot you if you're still in this house. One, two, three..." I've never seen a woman run in heels faster than that in my life. She could be an athlete if that was a sport. The front door slams and Kid hands me her gun after reengaging the safety.

"Good morning," Kid coos at Johnny as she scoops him out of Cal's arms. Johnny beams a huge smile at her before rooting on her chin. Boob time. She walks him over to the couch and assumes the position. We all follow. With Johnny eating away and Kellerman protectively swathing her in his arms, I know she won't attack me right now.

"Need to be a little choosier in the random department, Kavy," she says sweetly. I figured an ass chewing was coming...I'll take this any day.

"No shit. That one was off the fuckin' charts, Kav," O'Sullivan chimes in. "Chick I brought home was pretty much like fuckin' a dead fish. A cute dead fish though." I snort at that image.

355

"Sorry guys. She seemed normal. Slutty normal," I apologize. "You feelin' better?" I try to change the subject feeling like an ass.

"I feel fine actually. Food poisoning probably. Once I got it out I felt fine."

"That's good because your tits are in high demand lately," Cal says brightly.

"Haven't they always been?" she questions suggestively.

"Yeah, but he takes it to a whole new level. I never cried because you didn't have 'em out," Cal continues the conversation like it's normal.

"True," Kid replies gazing lovingly at the baby...who's fucking huge by the way. He'll be kicking our asses by the time he's two.

"Want some toast, Kiddo?" Kellerman murmurs into her hair.

"Yeah, that's probably good to start with. Maybe some juice instead of coffee."

"Decaf doesn't really do it for you anyway," Kellerman says moving off the couch and into the kitchen. I follow him so I can apologize.

"Sorry about that," I say tightly. Not really the scene you want around your baby.

"Don't worry about it. I know how it goes. Plus watchin' Kid put that chick in her place...fuckin' hot as hell."

"I have a man crush on you," I say and wrap my arms around him in an overly affectionate hug. He bursts out in a deep booming laugh grabbing the attention of the room.

"Break it up you two. The baby doesn't need to see that shit," O'Sullivan calls over the back of the couch.

"You're next," I threaten releasing Kellerman from my grip. He and I go about making toast and oatmeal for breakfast for everyone. Once we've eaten and cleaned up the doorbell rings. I go to answer it fearing it's Whitney coming back with the cops or something. I open the door and am greeted by Nick Cooper.

"Hey," I say a little shocked to see him here at the ass crack of dawn. I move to the side to let him in the house.

"Hey. I figured I needed to be here after Finn filled you all in," he explains moving down the hall to the great room.

"Nicky," Kid calls sweetly from the kitchen as we enter.

"Hey, Shanny," he murmurs wrapping her in a tight hug. I'm cool with Cooper but every time he calls her that and touches her it makes my skin crawl. I'm a jealous little girl and I'm okay with that. I look at O'Sullivan and Cal; they feel the same way as I do by the looks on their faces. Kellerman isn't jealous, he's possessive, and doesn't want any other man touching her. He's fine with us and the rest of the family...he's used to that. Cooper is too new to get free passage. I don't want Cooper here because he's going to try to convince Kid to go to Chicago and dive back into that shit storm. I have to keep my head on because a fight is coming and I plan on winning.

Chapter 48

Shannon

Kavy, Cally and Sully are gearing up for a fight. As soon as Nicky walked in the house their hackles came up. Kel is just pissed. I unfold from Nicky's embrace and lead him over to the couch. Johnny's taking his morning nap so he'll be shielded from any outbursts that are surely to come.

"So they found out about the incident in the bathroom?" I ask in a huff plopping down on the couch. Nicky sits next to me so I angle toward him as Kel pulls me snugly into his body from behind. The boys sit on the sectional behind me so they too can face Nicky.

"Wasn't expectin' this, Shanny. Mancini's crew has held together stronger than we anticipated. The trials should squash that though," Nicky explains to the group.

"Try to get her outta the subpoena with your super special agency connections," Kavy says sternly.

"I don't want her involved either guys. I tried to pull every string I could to get her free of this. It's not fuckin' workin'. And Mancini's crew...I'm still runnin' down that threat. I'm on the outside of the family now that I'm 'dead'. It's trickier." Nicky says to the group but keeps his eyes on mine. I know what he's saying. Mancini will come for me again, this time without Nicky to keep me safe.

"It's a little hard to kill someone and have 'em testify," Sully chides.

"I'm not sure killin' her is the play. My concern is they want to influence her testimony," Nicky warns.

359

"What the fuck does that mean Cooper?" Kel growls from behind me.

"Shanny is loyal to you guys and Mancini knows it. He could take one of you to force her to testify how they want. I don't think that's the play he'd use though. My bigger concern is Johnny." Kel's arm tightens around my shoulders and the guys let out a unified growl. I feel calm wash over me. I don't panic (just the first two and a half weeks of Johnny's life).

"I don't leave the baby and I'm never unarmed. They can't get him Nicky so don't worry about that," I say confidently. I'm not worried about that happening. They'd have to kill me to get him and that would fuck their plans up. Mancini going after one of my family or Kel...that worries me.

"They have ways, Shanny," Nicky says softly letting me know that I'm not as safe as I think I am.

"What if I go to Chicago and meet with Mancini? Maybe I could negotiate or something?" I ask quickly. The attorney in me says try and figure this out, the Uncle Mick in me says prepare for war.

"No fuckin' way! Kid you can't be thinkin' this," Kel admonishes from behind me. I pull away from his arms and turn to face him. His teal eyes are raging in protectiveness.

"Kel, what else am I gonna do? If I stay here and something happens to you or someone in my family I'll still have to go to Chicago to testify and one of you will die. If I stay here and something happens to Johnny...I can't take that risk. If I'm on the offensive I can keep us all safe. I can't do that hidin' here not knowin' what's comin' for me," I say in a soft yet firm tone.

"None of our lives is worth riskin' yours. We'll keep Johnny safe. We'll keep you both safe." Kel is pleading with his entire being for me not to do this. "Please." He pulls at the nape of my neck and lays his forehead against mine with his eyes closed.

"Okay," I relent. As the words leave my lips the tension drops from his shoulders and he presses his plump pillows against my mouth in a tender kiss.

"Thank you," he whispers against my lips and I nod. I pull from Kel's embrace to face Nicky again.

"So what's the next move," I ask Nicky just as Johnny starts to fuss on the baby monitor. "Hold that thought." I bound up the stairs to the nursery and over to the walnut sleigh crib.

"Is my big boy hungry again?" I coo as I peer down at his chubby cheeks. His dark blue eyes are getting lighter and flecks of green are showing up more and more. He's the spitting image of Kel. Look out ladies.

I carry him over to the cream plush fabric rocker and let him nurse. I'm sure leaving the guys alone with Nicky will be fine now that I agreed not to go to Chicago to meet with Mancini. I have the feeling that no matter what was decided...this won't be the last of it.

"If they come for you I'll leave a bloodbath in my wake that will leave Mancini wishing he'd stayed to his mafia comfort zone," I whisper to my son in a loving voice knowing the threat I speak is more real than anything I've ever uttered. Never again will my life be changed at the hands of others. Never again.

Kellerman

Instant relief floods me as Kid agrees not to go to Chicago to *negotiate* with Mancini. I press my lips to hers and thank her. She turns back to face Cooper to ask him what we do next when Johnny wakes up. Perfect timing. As she runs up the stairs I watch her perfect ass bounce with each step. Yes even during serious moments I'm a pervert.

"Is my big boy hungry again?" Kid coos to Johnny in the sweet sugar coated way she always talks to him when he wakes up. Cooper grins as he listens to her. I can hear her moving around in the nursery, she'll stay up there to feed him. She likes her bonding time.

"If they come for you I'll leave a bloodbath in my wake that will leave Mancini wishing he'd stayed to his mafia comfort zone," she coos in the same voice. The smile leaves my face and everyone else's in the room. I wait for her to say something else, nothing comes. She didn't sound scared or panicked, just confident.

"I'm afraid that's a promise she may end up keepin'," Cooper breaks the silence.

"What the fuck does that mean?" Kav barks.

"It means if they want her, they'll come for her no matter what. The only reason they haven't come back after Shanny is because she was all over the media when she was rescued and all over the media again after Johnny was born. Her bein' visible is not good for them. Now they have a reason to try something else. As much as I'd like to believe this is just a threat, I'm not fuckin' stupid. I've got days at the most, more likely hours. They will come. For one of you most likely but my bet is still on the baby. It's the way to play it," Cooper explains professionally making my damn skin crawl.

"You would know wouldn't you?" O'Sullivan sneers.

"Yeah I fuckin' do. I know what they wanted done to her in December. I know what I did undercover for over a decade. I've seen shit that would turn you into to a goddamn puddle and I don't want that for her. I love that woman and would do anything to keep her safe. Don't question that!" Cooper leans back against the couch his barely hiding the fury simmering beneath the surface.

"How would you do it?" I ask pointedly.

"What?" Cooper huffs.

"You know how this shit works and we don't. If Mancini gave you the job how would you do it?"

Cooper studies my face for a long moment before answering. I see the mask of Scarso slip over him that

I'm sure he needs to think through my question. It's an unnerving thing to witness.

"She's alone durin' the day with Johnny and Thomas. It's an easy grab. Wait until nap time. Take Thomas out right at the door with a silencer. Immobilize Shanny. Grab the baby. Two minutes in and out tops," Cooper explains with no emotion in his voice.

"Then what?" Kav growls.

"She'll go wherever they tell her to go. She'll say whatever they want her to at the trial. They'll kill her and sell Johnny."

"Fuck," Cal coughs out leaning forward to catch his breath.

"We'll get more security here at the house. Keep her completely locked down," O'Sullivan says tightly.

"Might work. If I had time on my side I could keep her safe here with my team. I don't have time to set that in motion before they start comin'. I can try again to get her outta the subpoena, but with Grady and Mancini's connections to judges and politicians I doubt it'll happen."

"My pop could help," Kav cuts in quickly.

"Yeah we could try to use him," Cooper agrees with a small amount of hope in his voice. "With the holiday our hands are tied until Tuesday. I'd stay and help out with security, but I need to be in Chicago workin' this. You guys all right on your own until we can move on this?"

The garage door opens and the alarm chirps. I look over my shoulder to see Finn and Thomas striding in with purpose. I offer chin lifts to each before returning my gaze to Cooper.

"Texted them when he showed up," Cal informs the group nodding toward Cooper. I figured as much.

As Finn and Thomas take seats on the couch and get filled in I try to think this through. The picture that Cooper just painted was mild I'm guessing. This could end up much worse. I don't know what the right thing to do is, but I know she's safer here than in Chicago. I can keep her safe.

"I'll call in a few guys I know to help out," Thomas booms in his deep voice. "She'll be fine here in the house with the baby." He's confident which only helps me to feel more confident. My woman is surrounded by aggressive alpha men. I'm not sure how this works for all of us. You'd think we'd butt heads trying to be at the top of the heap but we don't. We're all content with our spots in this pack as Cooper often refers to it. I guess the reason it works is because Kid is really the alpha. She runs this pack and allows us to think we have some say in it. I know her game and I play it willingly. Here she comes now, looking pale again.

"Kiddo?" I say standing up to meet her at the bottom of the stairs.

"Not feelin' great again," she mumbles passing me the baby. I push my hand against her forehead as I scoop Johnny up to my shoulder. No fever but she looks like shit. She shuffles past me and flops on the couch next to O'Sullivan who scoops her into his side.

"Got any ginger snaps?" Cooper asks the group.

"Maybe in the bottom of the pantry," Cal replies for the group before going to search.

"Ginger snaps," Kid repeats through a weak smile with her eyes closed. I sit on the end of the sectional away from her with the baby. I know she was just holding him but he can't get sick. "Nicky I can't believe you remember that."

"I remember everything, Shanny," Cooper says sweetly scooping her hand into his. Here's the thing...I'm used to sharing Kid. The guys are all over her all the time. I'm cool with that because that was the package she arrived with. They don't want in her pants they're part of her heart. Cooper on the other hand...I don't like him touching Kid. I don't like him around her calling her

Shanny. He doesn't want her. He's not looking at her hungry or making a play for her, but she's mine (yes, I'm a caveman) and I don't like to share anymore than I already have to. And I share a lot!

Chapter 49

Kavanagh

Kid's really sick. I swear her skin is a pale shade of green. She's been puking her guts out all damn day. We finally got her into bed about ten minutes ago, but I doubt she's going to stay here long. She can't even keep water down. It's all hands on deck, including Cooper. I'm lying in bed with Kid. Kellerman's trying to get Johnny to eat a bottle which the baby has decided he's not having. So Johnny's giving us the performance of a lifetime screaming his head off.

Cooper went to help with the baby because O'Sullivan is occupied cleaning up the vomit covered bathroom where Kid didn't quite make it last time and Cal is on the phone with Doc trying to figure out what we should do. Finn ran to the pharmacy to try to buy some supplies for us and Thomas is in the shower cleaning off the puke he was sprayed with when Kid missed the toilet earlier.

Can I just say when one of us is sick Kid takes care of us all on her own like it's the easiest thing in the world. There are seven of us and we all look like a bunch of idiots running around here trying to make sure she's okay. We're an embarrassment to the caretaking community. Johnny's screams are becoming hysterical and Kid is stirring. I have a puke bowl at the ready because I don't want her to not make it again.

"Get me the baby," she croaks.

"We don't want him to get sick. Kellerman'll get it under control," I whisper smoothing my giant paw over her sweaty brow.

"Get. Me. My. Son," she growls. And I'm off the bed and running down the stairs.

Cooper is holding Johnny while Kellerman is fucking with the bottle in the kitchen. There is a mess of monstrous proportions considering they are trying to make a bottle. The counters are covered in different bottles, nipples, empty milk storage bags, a bottle warmer and two pots...what the fuck are they doing?

"What the fuck are you doin'?" I yell over Johnny's screams to the men. They're both sweating and look terrified. I get it. They've been down here almost a half hour at this point and obviously they can't get it under control. I walk to Cooper and scoop Johnny out of his arms. Cooper sags in relief. The baby is covered in sweat and shaking from crying so hard.

"Kid wants him," I yell to Kellerman who drops his head in defeat. We're all second best to Kid. I cradle Johnny's fiercely protesting body as best I can and fly back up the stairs.

When I burst in the room Kid is on the floor in a heap. She was trying to get to the baby since she's headed toward the door and not the bathroom.

"CALLAGHAN!" I bellow at the top of my lungs. He's the closest to help and not covered in vomit. He's in the room before I can call him again. Cal scoops Kid off the ground with ease cradling her like I'm cradling Johnny.

Cal sits against the headboard and keeps Kid in his lap. Weakly she starts to pull her shirt up and I lay Johnny across her lap and support his head in my hand. That baby knows what to do and gets to it. Kid's eyes shut and I can tell she's no longer conscious.

"We need to get her to the hospital. I couldn't get a hold of my dad but I finally got Aidan. He said to get her to the ER," Cal explains quietly struggling to support Kid's now limp body. Kellerman runs in the room and takes in the odd situation in front of him. Cal holding Kid while Johnny nurses and I support his head. Surely a Kodak moment.

"Aidan says we need to get her to the ER," I say softly as Johnny's finally going limp as he eats. Thomas, Cooper, Finn and O'Sullivan all walk in the room together and give us curious stares before figuring out what's going on.

"Need to get her to the hospital," Kellerman directs Thomas who leaves the room quickly. We have to wait until Johnny's done eating before we can do anything. Kid's breathing isn't right and her color is worse now. A little trickle of fear is creeping up my spine. Kellerman moves to the bed without a word and pulls Kid and Johnny into his arms away from Cal and I. He's cradling Kid to his chest with an arm around her back and his huge mitt palming Johnny. Kellerman's other arm is under her legs. I don't know how he has the strength to pull it off but Kid and Johnny look secure.

"Let's go," Kellerman commands and moves from the room at a brisk pace. He walks out the front door where Thomas has my SUV running alongside Cal's. Thomas opens the back door of my SUV and stares stunned as Kellerman climbs in seamlessly barely jostling his family. The rest of us pile into the SUVs and take off to Overland Park Regional Medical Center. She's just sick and needs fluids. There is no need to panic. So why am I shaking from head to toe like I do when I'm afraid I'm going to lose her?

Kellerman

Kid's still out. We've been in the ER for an hour trying to figure out what's wrong with her. She's dehydrated so they started an IV and are running tests. Johnny's passed out cold in his stroller (tank) thank God because he wore my ass out. All seven of us are smashed in this tiny room and refuse to leave until they can tell us what's wrong with her. My mind is racing with worst case scenarios and I can't make it stop. This has to be a horrible flu or food poisoning from hell. I can't consider any other option. The universe couldn't be so cruel as to hand her something else to battle in this life.

She's not puking anymore but that's surely because there is nothing left in her. Kid's been at it more than twenty-four hours. Her skin is sallow and lifeless, nothing like Kid usually is. The door to the ER room opens and we all come to attention. Doogie Howser (Dr. Jenkins) walks in (yes this is becoming something of a bad joke in my world between pilots and doctors) scanning the room with a question forming on his brow.

"Is one of you Aaron Kavanagh?" Dr. Jenkins asks still confused as to why this woman is surrounded by men that all seem to have claim on her. All of our brows furrow in the direction of Kav.

"I am," Kav responds confidently while standing from the chair on the other side of her bed from me.

"According to Miss Kelly's chart you're her power of attorney. Is that correct?" Dr. Jenkins asks tentatively not knowing who in the room may take offense to his statement.

"That's correct," Kav again answers confidently more in attorney mode.

"Would you mind if we spoke in private concerning Miss Kelly's condition? You're son can stay so you don't have to disturb him," Dr. Jenkins says clinically earning a low menacing growl from me. Before I can inform the good doctor of his grievous error the door opens again.

"I'm sorry, Doctor Jenkins, but these men insisted on bein' allowed back here. One claims to be the baby's father and the other the grandfather," a nurse says with a shrug before Karl and Butch push past her. Cal spits out a laugh while the rest of us try to hide our grins. Leave it to Karl to find a way to get in here that is impressive and entertaining. Butch's face is sick at the sight of Kid. She's like a second daughter to him and with one daughter in a coma I can only imagine what this view of Kid is doing to him. I grab his shoulder and squeeze as he takes the seat next to mine his eyes never leaving Kid.

"What's wrong with her?" Karl demands.

"I was just going to speak with Mister Kavanagh regarding her condition before you arrived," Dr. Jenkins replies to Karl looking sheepish.

"Well," Karl prompts.

"Mister Kavanagh would you care to step out of the room for a moment?" Dr. Jenkins questions his baby-face becoming wary.

"There's no need. Feel free to enlighten all of us," Kav says before retaking his seat and offering me an apologetic look. I don't give a shit who has her power of attorney or whatever else, no one in this room would dare cross me right now.

"All right. Miss Kelly is severely dehydrated and at this point we believe her vomiting and nausea may stem from hyperemesis gravidarum. This is just the onset for her based on your estimations that she has been healthy as of late. Can you tell me how many weeks she is?" Dr. Jenkins asks Karl.

"How many weeks she is what?" Karl returns.

"Pregnant?" Dr. Jenkins looks at Karl like he's an idiot. Every eyeball in the room snaps to me and I freeze. She's pregnant and there's something wrong that I don't understand, much less could any of us even pronounce it. Time for me to speak up.

"Doctor Jenkins Shannon is my girlfriend and Johnny is our son. I'm sorry for the confusion, but I need you to explain whatever the hell you just said in plain English. She's pregnant?" I ask pointedly.

"Yes Mister," he leaves the space for me to fill in.

"Kellerman."

"Mr. Kellerman. How old is your son?"

"Twelve weeks and four days. He was six weeks preterm."

371

"Were there any complications during or following the birth for Miss Kelly?"

I don't want to answer his question. I don't know why, but saying Johnny didn't come from Kid makes me sick to my stomach. I hold the doctor's gaze for a long moment.

"No. She didn't have any issues," Karl answers for me. It's not a lie per se, and I feel relieved not to have to tell this doctor our very strange circumstances.

"Well I've put in a call to a maternal fetal specialist to have a look at Miss Kelly. I'd like to do a quick scan just to check the fetus if that's all right with you Mister Kavanagh?" Kav looks at me waiting for me to give the go ahead. I nod and squeeze Kid's hand. She's pregnant with my baby. But she's really fucking sick too.

"Can you explain what's wrong with her again please?" I ask Dr. Jenkins quietly.

"She appears to be suffering from hyperemesis gravidarum, HG. It's extreme morning sickness. The severity varies on a case by case basis. At this point we need to ensure that she stays hydrated and the specialist will work out a nutrition plan with her. Once I've done the scan we'll transfer her to a room on the maternity unit until we get her rehydrated and tolerating food and fluids orally."

For a teenager Dr. Jenkins is taking every weird thing in the room in stride. He doesn't seem intimidated or horrified, though he's giving Karl a bit of the stink eye.

"Thank you," Karl addresses the doctor. "Sorry for lyin' to get back here but I needed to be with her." Karl's voice has an edge of pain to it and I understand completely. He didn't know what was wrong with her and the staff was trying to keep him away. I would have told any lie I could have come up with to get to Kid if I were him.

"I didn't know they were having an affair until the baby was born," Karl finishes with a fake sniffle. The whole room bursts into laughter waking up Kid and Johnny. I laugh so hard that the tears I've been holding at bay spill over as I lock eyes with the most stunning emerald jewels the world has ever known.

Chapter 50

Shannon

Waking up to the cacophonous sound of laughter might be the greatest thing in the world. Opening my eyes to find a teary eyed Kel might be the sweetest since they appear to be happy tears.

"Hey," Kel soothes squeezing my hand.

"Hi," I croak my throat in pain from the vomiting. I must have eaten something really nasty to be this sick. I don't think I've ever been this sick in my life. I feel better now though (good drugs?).

"Miss Kelly?" a foreign voice calls from the end of my bed. I look toward the voice and find a teenager in scrubs addressing me. Are there no adults working in important roles anymore? I offer him a sweet smile and he blushes. I really wish I was eighteen again when these boys do this. Kel growls and I smile because he doesn't realize that I have the jackpot of hotness in my bed every night. I still like messing with the young ones.

"Miss Kelly," the doctor clears his throat and tries to regain his composure. Inward shimmy of I've still got it! "I'm Shane Jenkins. Your doctor," he stutters a bit realizing he didn't do a bang up job of introducing himself professionally. I hear Cally and Finn snicker in the corner.

"What's wrong with me Doctor Jenkins?" I ask hoarsely. I could use a drink but I'm afraid I'll throw up with just a drop hitting my tongue. Johnny starts to fuss and Butch grabs him from his pram. Butch is so good with the baby and I'm glad Johnny has a "grandparent" around all the time. The baby settles immediately into

375

Butch's shoulder and I return my gaze to the young cute doctor.

"I believe you're suffering from hyperemesis gravidarum," he informs me.

"What's that?" I ask hoping it's not some rare incurable cancer because that's just how my fucking luck works.

"It's extreme morning sickness."

"I'm sorry?" I ask disbelieving. Did he just tell me I'm pregnant?!

"HG is what people often refer to as extreme morning sickness," he repeats to me like I'm an idiot.

I look at Kel and he's beaming with pride.

"I'm pregnant?" I ask Kel in a whisper.

"Yeah, Momma," he replies sweetly kissing my cheek gently.

I look to Kavy, Sully, Cally, Finn and Nicky (Nicky fits in this line up of my boys perfectly).

"I'm pregnant?"

All four nod in unison with perfect smiles and Cally's dimples to top it off.

I look at Thomas.

"I'm really pregnant?" I ask in a tone that says please wake me up from this dream.

"You're really pregnant," he replies in his luxurious deep bass tone.

I look at Karl.

"You're pregnant, Shannon. It's okay to be happy," Karl says soft and sweet.

I look at Butch who is streaming pride from his eyes.

"I'll have to start workin' out more to be able to hold two of these guys," he says through his smile.

I smile back and reach out to take Johnny from him. I want to hold my baby. I'm going to have two babies. Holy shit balls!

"When am I due? Is the HG dangerous for me or the fetus? When can I go home? Can I continue to breastfeed?" I rapid fire questions at the doctor giving him a look that says get fucking answering. He smiles kindly at my crazy.

"HG can be managed. We're still not certain that's what you're suffering from. HG can be difficult to diagnose. I've called a maternal fetal specialist and she'll be able to answer more about that and when you can go home. You can continue to breastfeed as long as you aren't prescribed any medications that counter indicate. I was hoping you could help me out with the due date. Have you had menstrual cycle since giving birth?" Say what? I look at Kel with a questioning glance. He looks at our intertwined fingers guiltily. Kel didn't want to tell the doctor our crazy background. I get it. This is not an easy story to tell and frankly there's no reason for an ER doctor to know. He won't be treating me or looking at my lady parts (I hope).

"No," I answer swiftly. I haven't. I quit taking the pill as part of the lactation induction and Kel and I have been using symptothermal method for birth control as recommended by our lactation specialist in Seattle. Who knew you could prevent pregnancy just paying attention to your body? I guess I didn't pay attention well enough if I'm knocked up. Whoops!

"Well let's do a quick scan and see if we can get you a due date before you head to your room on the maternity unit. Would you like your...friends to step out for a few moments?" he asks trepidatiously.

"My family can stay," I say strongly. I squeeze Kel's hand and offer him a broad smile. I don't feel sick at all. I hope the young doctor is wrong about the extreme morning sickness. I don't want to be sick like I have been. Please let him be wrong.

"And your family would be?" Dr. Jenkins is struggling.

"All of them," I reply pressing a soft kiss into Johnny's fuzzy head. The doctor studies me for a brief moment and then leaves the room.

"You're such a hussy!" Karl laughs from the end of my bed. I burst into laughter as the rest of the room follows.

"We're gonna have to start construction on the extension next week. You two keep making a baby every nine months we'll have to move to a compound and let Kid home school and sew all our clothes," Kavy jokes with Kel.

"You're serious about extending the house?" I ask Kavy in shock.

"Fuck yeah, Kid. I hired an architect and Kellerman hired a contractor last week," Kavy scoffs at me. I told them to do whatever they wanted. Apparently, they did.

"How big is the extension?" I ask realizing maybe I should have some details now.

"Just about twelve hundred square feet off the back of the house. I'm thinkin' we need to adjust now though," Kel answers silently communicating with Kavy's eyes. They so have man crushes on each other.

"Was it a twelve hundred square foot stripper room?" I snark.

"Only half was for the strippers. I put two bedrooms and a bathroom on the top floor," Kavy answers with no waver in his voice. Fuck he's serious.

"You're serious," I say in disbelief.

"Kid," Kavy says harshly. "You really think I'd have a stripper room in our house where you and my nephew sleep at night?" Kavy's offended. He's never offended.

"No," I respond sheepishly. "You just sounded serious."

"I almost lost you a few months ago, then you lost Kellerman, then we all almost lost Johnny, and now you're sick. Why the fuck would I bring strippers into the place where I kccp you all safe? Give me a little

378

fuckin' credit!" Okay now Kavy's just pissed. I pass Johnny off to Butch again and pull Kavy toward me. I don't want him too close because I reek of vomit, but I need him near me.

"Kavy, I know you would never endanger me or the baby," I say firmly.

"Babies," he corrects me in a snort. I smile at him and cup his cheek forcing his gaze to mine. He's not pissed. He's scared out of his mind and leading with anger.

"I'm okay, Kavy. Don't freak out on me. Women get pregnant every day and have babies every day. I'm okay," I stress firmly. I feel fine right now. Not nauseous in the least. Kind of hungry actually.

"People are after you again and you're sick," he whispers and presses his head further into my palm. All eyes in the room are on us and I can feel Kel's anxiety at my side.

I brush my thumb across Kavy's cheek before I sit back in my uprighted bed. I look to Kel who is just as freaked as Kavy and has been tryin to hold it in. Before I can assuage any of their worry Dr. Jenkins returns with a cart carrying an ultrasound machine. Butch stands up with the baby to make room for the machine yet allowing him a view of the monitor.

"Can you roll your pants down a bit for me and raise your shirt?" Dr. Jenkins asks clinically while switching the lights off in the room and messing with the ultrasound. The men in the room have tensed like the young doctor just asked me to perform a striptease. These boys never quit. I do as the doctor asked and grab Kel's hand to get him to calm the hell down. I hear the faintest growl at the back of his throat and roll my eyes.

"This gel should be warm for you," the doctor says as he squirts goo on my belly. And then he has the wand in his hand and starts moving it around. It's just a bunch of white noise and black and grey on the monitor as he moves around clicking away at the keyboard. Then he stops and rotates his wrist just slightly before pausing.

"There we are," Dr. Jenkins says softly. "Here, Miss Kelly."

"Shannon," I correct quietly focusing on the monitor to try and decipher what I'm seeing.

"Shannon, see here and here," he points to two blobs blinking on the screen.

"Yeah." I look for a long while and then it starts to hit me. "Twins?"

"Yes. And probably the cause for your severe nausea and vomiting. Some women carrying twins have worse morning sickness than others but it usually fades by the second trimester."

I know he just said something important, but I quit hearing after yes. I look at Kel who looks a little pale.

"Kel, you okay?" He nods slightly still staring at the screen. I look at my boys and family around the room and they're all staring at the screen with the same scared as shit face that Kel has. I start to giggle.

"It's not funny, Kid," Kavy admonishes me with a grin in his voice.

"You're all scared of two babies," I say through a louder laugh. They snort and humph at me as the doctor starts moving and clicking again.

"I'm just taking some measurements here so we can get a ballpark due date for you," he explains. I watch the screen and my flickering blobs. I'm going to have three babies. Maybe this isn't funny. But I feel nothing but happiness so I keep my smile plastered on my face. Kel kisses my palm and I look over to him.

"Hey," I say tenderly.

"Hi." Kel's face breaks into a face splitting smile.

"Well from these measurements it looks like you're due date is March eighth. Which puts you at about thirteen weeks, conception date around the fifteenth of June." Dr. Jenkins furrows his brow at his math. That would mean I got pregnant only a few days after giving "birth".

"They didn't waste much time breaking my heart again," Karl sniffs from the end of the bed. WHAT? All my boys bend in half laughing as I watch in utter confusion. I'm left out of an obviously very comical inside joke. Dr. Jenkins looks beyond uncomfortable. He quickly hands me a few pictures with arrows pointing at the babies, hands me a towel to clean the goo off and pulls the machine from the room. As soon as the door shuts I'm on them.

"Spill," I command Karl.

Chapter 51

Kavanagh

"Spill," Kid orders Karl who is still laughing along with the rest of us.

"The hospital Nazi's wouldn't let me back here so I told them that I was the father of your baby and Butch was my dad," Kid's eyes are huge but there's a smile playing at the edges of her mouth.

"I'm still a little lost," Kid says trying to piece the rest together.

"Well, when the baby-faced doctor, who is yummy by the way," Karl raises his brows suggestively at Kid.

"I get all the luck with young good looking doctors and pilots," Kid purrs. Kellerman growls and squeezes her hand that he's not letting go of in the near future.

"Kiddo," he warns in a threatening tone.

"What? Karl said he was hot too." Kid pouts. She's trying to lighten the mood of this room but it's not working. We're all worried and tense.

"No," Kellerman says harshly.

"Here we go again with the caveman IQ and the toddler vocabulary." Kid rolls her eyes and looks back at Karl. He's just as worried about her as the rest of us but they communicate in snark so he'll give her the levity she needs right now.

"Anyway, the hot doc started freakin' the room out talkin' about whatever he thought was wrong with you and then assumed we knew you were pregnant. Nice job by the way hussy. Dylan ended my lie then so that we could get some straight answers because the doc was askin' Aaron about your medical treatment and me about your lady bits."

"You love talkin' about my lady bits," Kid snarks (told you).

"Your lady bits are the things my dreams are made of...oh wait no. They're the things my nightmares are made of." And the snark fest begins.

"I informed the hot doc that you and Dylan had an affair and I didn't find out until Johnny was born." Karl finishes with a shrug. Kid pauses for a moment and then bursts into a full belly laugh bringing the room to life and Johnny to a wakeful state.

Kid reaches out to Butch for the baby. Butch presses a kiss to his head before handing him off. With all our parents living in Chicago Butch has become the resident grandparent. If you would have told me last year that Butch Rossi would be the surrogate grandparent to Kid's baby I would have throat punched you and laughed about it. Kid's life has never been predictable but the last year has been a new level of bizarre.

Boob in the mouth and Johnny's settled. Time to talk.

"We need to talk about stuff, Kid," I say quietly watching Kellerman. He hasn't said much but I can hear the wheels grinding in his head. I can see he wants to scoop up his family and run. I don't blame him and at this point I'd drive them to the damn airport.

If we find out Kid has whatever illness they are concerned with we can get her out of the subpoena. I don't want her to be sick but I'd take sick and safe over not sick and in Chicago.

"Let's talk tomorrow boys. It's late and I'm tired. I don't think Mancini's gonna come and get me in the hospital. That would be profoundly stupid. You guys go home and get some rest. Maybe you can talk and work through some ideas because my brain is zapped right now." Kid closes her eyes but continues to talk. "Thank you guys for takin' care of me. Can I talk to Kel for a few minutes?"

"Sure Kid," Cal answers for the room. There are collective murmurs of agreement even though none of us want to leave her right now. We'll just go to the waiting room. I'm in the back corner of the room nearest to Kid across the bed from Kellerman. Everyone leans over me to kiss her before they leave and I wait patiently (not really) for my turn. I go to stand up but Kid's hand darts out grabbing my wrist firmly.

"I know you're scared shitless right now and you feel out of control. I see your hands shaking. Nothing is gonna happen to me. Nothing." Kid's gaze is penetrating my soul as she speaks. I believe her. Fuck if I should but I do. I give her a chin lift and a long kiss on the forehead before walking away.

"Kav," Kellerman calls before I open the door. "Thanks for deferring to me earlier."

He's talking about when the baby-faced doctor asked about her scan or whatever. I was never going to make any medical decisions without consulting him. I've had Kid for almost fourteen years but she's Kellerman's now. I haven't lost her to him. I've given her to him. And in giving Kid to Kellerman I get to keep every piece of her I've had since the day I met her because Kellerman hasn't taken a thing away from me. He's given me more of her. There's a light to her now that never existed all those years she was with me and that light stems from him. So no, I haven't lost Kid. I've gained Kellerman.

I offer him a chin lift and leave the room. It's time to keep my sister safe.

Kellerman

"Hey," Kid whispers as Kav shuts the door behind him.

"Hi," I say through a small smile.

"So, your swimmers do good work Dylan Kellerman," she jokes quietly.

"I aim to exceed expectations, Miss Kelly," I joke in return. "How are you feelin'?"

"Tired. I don't feel sick anymore, at least not right now."

"That's good, Kiddo. Twins?" I ask because I'm still shocked. We haven't been as careful as we should have been. I refuse to wear condoms (I've never used one with her and I wasn't about to start after being kept away from her for months) and Kid had to quit taking the pill to bring her milk in. I understand where babies come from yet I'm still shocked right now.

"Irish triplets," Kid whispers. I hate that I know what Kid is referring to because Cassie explained it to me.

Kid picks Johnny up and hands him to me. It's way past his bedtime and dude is out cold. I lay him in his stroller and then sit on the edge of Kid's bed. She looks better, not green and pale.

"Scared the shit outta me, Kiddo," I say gazing into her green pools.

"Sorry," she says meekly. "I had no clue I was pregnant. I've been tired, but I'm takin' care of Johnny all the time so I figured it was that. I've been queasy some days, never sick though. I just brushed it off."

"You never told me you didn't feel well. Why didn't you say anything?"

"I didn't really think anything of it. It would come and then go. I'd go back to doing whatever I was doing. It really didn't seem unusual. I figured it was hormones from nursing or eating too late or eating too little. I really wasn't worried about it." Kid shrugs and runs her hand over her flat stomach.

"I'm pregnant," she says in a whisper. "I never wanted to be pregnant."

Shit. That's not what I want to hear right now. I should have worn condoms. I should have stayed off her when she said she might be ovulating. I shouldn't have flipped and fucked her in the bathroom on the plane. I'm a selfish bastard and now she has to carry two of my babies that never wanted.

"I'm sorry, Kiddo," I apologize placing my hand on top of hers on her stomach. She looks at me with her arresting gaze.

"Cassie got this with you and with Johnny. She threw it away without care or consideration for either of you. I was jealous of her. She got a part of you that I'll never have. She got the first ultrasounds. The first kicks. The first sound of a heartbeat you two created. From that jealousy came desire. I wanted to be that. I wanted to carry your babies. I wanted to pick out baby names and make you rub my feet at night. I wanted to swell with life that you and I created. Now I get it. Now I get all the things in life I never thought I'd get," she says in maybe the sweetest voice I've ever heard spill from her lips.

"Cassie didn't get shit. I never felt Johnny kick. When I went to appointments with her I stared at the monitor and never looked at Cassie because I was imagining you there. You were Johnny's mother whether or not he was in your womb. Everything we experience will be a first for me, Kiddo. Cassie took nothing from you," I reply softly. I pull Kid's hand from her belly and raise her shirt just a sliver. Leaning down I press my lips to her soft skin just above her bellybutton. Kid's breath hitches as she places her hand on my hair. The touch makes me want to devour her this instant. The feel of her skin against my lips mixed with her shallow breathing is the biggest turn on, but I'm not a heartless bastard. I also won't risk the "hot doctor" walking in on me burying myself in Kid.

"Kel," she purrs.

"Don't," I command and sit back up pulling her shirt over her exposed skin. "I'm barely controlling myself."

"You mean you don't wanna fuck a pregnant, nursing, vomit covered lady?" she snarks.

387

"You're a pain in the ass," I huff.

"Pain in the dick is what Sully says."

"He's fuckin' right," I snort.

"I'm gonna get huge with twins. I'll be the size of a house! You won't be able to fuck me," Kid say through a laugh.

"I'm sure I can get creative," I purr and wiggle my eyebrows at her.

Before we can get completely out of hand the door opens.

"We've got a bed for you upstairs now, Shannon. They'll keep you overnight for monitoring and then the specialist will meet with you in the morning. I'm less concerned with HG at this point. You haven't shown any signs of illness since waking up so that's very encouraging. They'll see how you tolerate small amounts of water overnight and then move on from there. It was nice meeting you and congratulations," Dr. Jenkins says professionally.

"Thank you for everything Doctor Jenkins. I know my family can be a bit much to handle so thank you for letting them stay with me. It was nice meeting you," Kid fucking purrs at him in her sexy as hell voice. The doctor has now turned a cartoon shade of red, so much for being professional. Kid is incorrigible! It's like she can't not be irresistible. I growl and she rolls her eyes as the doctor leaves.

"Will your IQ get even lower now that I'm pregnant, caveman?" she asks sweeping her fingers through my hair.

"Yes," I grunt in my best caveman voice.

"I love you, Kel," she says quietly through a giant smile that brings her eyes to their sparkling best.

"Love you too, Kiddo," I reply knowing no truer words have ever been spoken. I'm not this man. I'm not the man that finds the girl and ceases to be all things he believed he was...yes I am. I am this man. I'm the man that my father raised me to be. I'm the man that I always hoped I could be to make my father proud. I'm the man that got lucky in this world and made Shannon Kelly mine.

Chapter 52

Shannon

I was moved up to the maternity unit for observation late last night. I was able to keep small amounts of water down throughout the night and have now been upgraded to juice. The juice is harder to keep down but I'm managing. The specialist just left and she agrees with hottie ER doctor that I'm not suffering from HG. Thank all that's holy! I read about it and that sounds like nasty business. I feel awful for any woman that has to endure that. Yuck!

Kel and Johnny stayed here in the room with me last night. Luckily I'm in a maternity unit so Kel has a father bed and they brought in a crib for Johnny to sleep in. I convinced my boys, Butch, and Karl to go home once I was settled in. That was not an easy argument to win, but I finally won. Nicky and Thomas were non-negotiable so I relented early in allowing them to stay in the hospital. They stayed out in the waiting room and are surely wrecked today.

"Shannon, you're lookin' better," Thomas calls from the door.

"The shower and some juice helped. I'm sorry I puked on you," I apologize sincerely.

"I'm sorry I didn't get you to the toilet faster," he says gruffly. Only he would blame himself for my vomit pyrotechnics.

"I've never seen puke spray like that," Nicky says in a laugh next to Thomas as they come in the room.

"I didn't think she had any left in her," Kel chimes in finishing changing Johnny's diaper.

"I didn't think I did either," I snort. "Never been that sick in my life."

"Well you look better," Nicky compliments leaning in for a quick kiss on my cheek.

"You wanna hang out with me a while so Kel and Thomas can take Johnny on a little walk?" I ask Nicky.

"Kiddo," Kel warns.

"Kel, he can't be stuck in this damn room all day. I'll be out of here tonight or tomorrow once I can eat something. Johnny needs some fresh air. Take him out with you and Thomas. Nicky will watch me and never leave my side," I instruct coolly. I'm not looking forward to my caveman during this pregnancy. He's a damn nightmare already and we're only hours in. He stood next to the shower while I washed myself because he was afraid I would fall. I was sitting on the shower bench when he told me this. He's going to drive me insane.

"You got this?" Kel asks Nicky.

"Without question," Nicky answers confidently. He's not going to let anything happen to me. They stare at each other for a few moments until Kel offers him a chin lift and loads the baby into the stroller.

"I love you. I'll be back soon. You want anything?" Kel murmurs into my hair.

"I'm good." I smile tipping my head back to meet his gaze.

Slowly Kel meets his fat pillowy lips with mine. I open my freshly cleaned mouth to his and savor the taste of him mixed with spearmint. A small hum purrs from my throat as he works his tongue passionately across mine. I fist his T-shirt pulling him to me as a smile stretches across his lips.

"I think that's enough for now, Kiddo," Kel whispers into my lips placing a chaste kiss at the corner of my mouth.

Pregnancy hormones are pretty awesome. Well they'd be awesome if there wasn't an audience now and we weren't in a hospital. I'm going to make Kel sore from head to toe when we get out of here.

"Have a nice walk," I say in a chipper tone as Kel stands up.

"Bye, Kiddo," he says shaking his head at me. I truly am a pain in the dick.

Nicky pulls a chair to my bedside as Kel and Thomas leave pushing Johnny in his stroller. That might be the cutest sight in the world, two giant alpha males pushing a baby around.

"All right Nicky let's talk shop while we're alone. If we try to go through this with any of my boys around it's gonna turn into a caveman convention," I snark.

"I can't promise I'm any better than your family, Shanny," Nicky responds honestly.

"I know but you can at least put on a tactical hat on top of your Neanderthal skull."

"I'll do my best," he snorts his fake brown eyes show concern but his sculpted body is confident. In a pale yellow polo and tan cargo shorts you'd never know he was Jason Bourne. He's good at hiding in plain sight.

"From what I can figure Mancini is comin' for me for Governor Grady. They don't give a shit if I killed that guy...they want me for the trial. I'm not sure what they think I can offer, but they obviously think I can do good things for him." Nicky nods at my assertion.

"It's the only thing that makes sense. If they wanted you dead..." I nod at Nicky's pause understanding if they wanted me dead they would have sent someone to kill me months ago. They need me alive.

"The thing that's tricky here is how will they come at you? They can't kidnap you again so they need to be able to manipulate you instead. Comin' after one of the guys, your family, Kellerman, or Johnny seems the logical play to me. That's a lot of people to keep safe. I worry less about the guys. They're all quite proficient at protecting themselves. Your family in Chicago can be protected by the O'Sullivans. That leaves you and Johnny as the weak links," Nicky finishes quietly.

"If I wasn't pregnant I'd take off and hide me and the baby until the trial. I'm worried about the twins and my health now though. I can't be in some cabin in the woods with Johnny and my armory. It's too dangerous. If I wasn't so sick I'd take the risk."

"I could hide you and the baby, Shanny. But you're right it wouldn't be near the medical facilities you may need. I don't wanna exchange one risk for another."

"I know. I can't go to Chicago and try to meet with Mancini now either. It was a risky proposition to begin with but sick and pregnant makes it a death wish."

"You'll wait it out here. I have three guys comin' in tomorrow morning and I'll head up to Chicago to try and get you out of the subpoena. With the connections your family has and strings I can try to pull we might be able to get you out of it. I don't want you steppin' foot in Chicago when it's due to their manipulation."

"I'm worried about you bein' in Chicago, Nicky. You're supposed to be dead. What if Mancini's people see you?" I'm really worried about that. He's been in Virginia or elsewhere on the east coast since I left Chicago. I don't want his life at risk to save mine.

"I'll be fine, Shanny. I know Chicago well enough to avoid anyone that may notice me. I don't look like Scarso anymore so I'm not worried about bein' noticed in the streets. Don't worry about me. Worry about you and all your babies. Twins, Shanny. I can't believe it," Nicky says through a bright smile.

"I'm so happy, Nicky. It's nothing I ever thought I'd want. I never wanted kids when I was a little girl."

"I remember. You told me after you finished your baseball career you were gonna be the president. I asked who would take care of your babies while you were playin' baseball and you told me you wouldn't have any babies like that was the stupidest question anyone had ever asked you."

"I guess growin' up with a mother that hated me made me not want to be one. When I started workin' in family law that changed. I wanted to adopt in a few years. I still didn't want to get married or have babies though. The men I've loved in my life have been taken from me...I couldn't imagine willingly subjecting myself to that. If I never loved a man and spent my life with my boys and an adopted child or two I would have been truly content in this life. But after I met Kel things started to change. I could see spending my life with him, loving him the way I swore I never would. Then Johnny came and my perspective changed completely. Avoiding the possibility of heartbreak by closing myself off to another level of joy was unjustifiably punishing me. I'm happy now in a way I didn't think I could be. These twins are just the icing on the cake," I finish with a pleased tone and swipe of my hand over my soon to be giant belly. I'm hoping I get so big none of the guys can pick me up. They'll be stuck listening to me with no recourse.

"You deserve every happiness in this world. I hate that you ever closed yourself off from the possibilities of a future. If Kellerman brought that hope back into your life I need to thank him," Nicky says softly stroking my cheek with the backs of his fingers.

"Kel didn't bring hope back into my life. He brought me back to life. After Daddy died Uncle Mick pulled me from the ashes and started my life over but it wasn't a full life. After Liam attacked me the boys and their families brought me back to life even more than I was with Uncle Mick. But when Kel walked into my life the blackness that had lived in me for twenty-two some odd years turned to light. Kel did that. Kel brought me back to life."

Tears prick my eyes as I finish but I hold them at bay. I refuse to turn into a puddle of mushy hormone blubbering. Instead I smile because I'm happy. I'm filled to the brim with life and love. No one can take that from me now. No one.

"You're gonna make me cry with that shit, Shanny," Nicky says with choked emotion in his throat. "I can't be cryin'. I'm gonna take a piss. Take my piece," he instructs holding his .45 out to me. I grab it and slide it under the covers next to my thigh (don't want to freak out the hospital staff). I can't explain the added calm that washes over me with the feel of a gun in my hand, but it's the best feeling I get other than holding Johnny. I know Nicky's got his secondary weapon on him so I'm not worried about him being in the bathroom unarmed. Nicky presses a kiss to my forehead and disappears into the bathroom. I'm so fucking sick of hospitals.

The hair on my arms raise and I know something's wrong. Horribly wrong. Then I hear his voice.

"Keep your hand where I can see them."

Chapter 53

Kellerman

Kid was right, getting out of the hospital for a few minutes feels good. Johnny is happy and cooing away as Thomas and I stroll around. He and I have to look like quite the odd couple. There's a park right next to the hospital so we're strolling around enjoying the temperate weather on Labor Day. I wonder what kind of tank stroller Kid will import for the twins. This pregnancy is going to be such a positive change from what I experienced with Cassie. I'm happy Kid is pregnant...no elated is a better term. Once the trial is over in Chicago I'm taking Kid away for a while. She needs a break and I need some serious caveman time; Kid, Johnny, my unborn twins and me in a cave sounds pretty good right now. Alarm bells go off in my head before I hear his voice.

"Both of you keep your hands where we can see 'em," his rodent voice commands from behind Thomas and me. I keep my hands on the stroller bar and Thomas balls his fists at his sides. I feel the pressure of a gun muzzle pressed into my back as another man reaches into the back of Thomas's pants and removes his gun. I keep my eyes forward checking down to Johnny every two seconds.

"Walk," the guy behind Thomas commands. I take a tentative step forward. "Make any move or noise to alert anyone and I'll blow that baby's brains out."

I'm pulsing with adrenaline and forcing my mind to calm down and figure out a way free from these two. I assume it's just two because I can only hear their footsteps and see two shadows behind us when I look to the side. The park is pretty empty so I doubt anyone will see what's happening to us.

"Back to the parking lot," the voice commands again.

We're at the far end of the park if I stick to the trails I can buy us some more time. They try to push us into the grass to cut across.

"If he gets bumped around too much he'll start screamin'. I doubt you want that," I caution them with a lie. Johnny wouldn't give a shit but they don't know that.

"Fine. Move faster," the voice growls. I move a fraction faster and try to think. If I take off running are they really going to open fire in the middle of a park? I don't think they would but I have no clue. They could have other men out here or back in the hospital or in the parking lot waiting. If they have Kid...fuck I bet they have someone with Kid. I can't run.

Okay no running. That leaves me with fight. How do I fight them and keep Johnny safe? If I push the stroller out of the way it'll surely fall over or ram into something. If I just turn around and the gun goes off it'll be aimed near the baby. I could go for the gun but there's no assurance that I'll get it before it goes off. Fuck!

We're almost to the parking lot where there's a waiting SUV running. I see one man behind the wheel but that's it. I'm running out of time. I won't let us be taken. I'd rather us be shot and fighting for a chance. If they take us we're dead.

Kavanagh

As Cal, O'Sullivan and I pull into the hospital parking lot I feel goose bumps cover my body. Something's wrong.

"Something's wrong," O'Sullivan steals the words from my lips. I look to Cal in the passenger seat and his hands are showing a tremor. FUCK!

I whip the SUV into a parking spot and we all dash out toward the hospital when something catches my eye and I stop dead in my tracks.

"What the fuck, Kav?" O'Sullivan yells as he smashes into my back. I point to my right. Cal and O'Sullivan track my line of sight and tension pours over us.

Kellerman and Thomas are being led to an SUV pushing Johnny's stroller. There is a man behind each of them though they're shorter than Kellerman and Thomas so I can't make them out. The looks on Thomas and Kellerman's faces tell me all I need to know. They're pissed and scared and furious and thinking.

O'Sullivan takes off in a sprint across the parking lot using cars as cover. He's going to try to come around the back of them. Cal heads straight for the SUV. We're on the opposite side of it so in theory he could open the door and pull them through, at least Johnny. I move down the sidewalk in plain sight of the group of men. I'll be a good distraction.

"Kellerman!" I shout. He'd already seen me, but the guys behind hadn't. All eyes are now on me as I continue moving toward them at the side forcing them all to look my way allowing Cal and O'Sullivan free passage. I see the men have guns in the backs of Thomas and Kellerman.

"You headin' in?" I yell playing dumb like I can't see what's going on. Cal is almost to the SUV and I've lost sight of O'Sullivan.

Kellerman listens to what the guy holding the gun on Thomas says before responding.

"Nah, not yet. We'll meet you in a bit," Kellerman bellows in a voice I've never heard come out of him. It's fueled with fury and pain. He's trapped with his son and Kid's not here so I'm guessing she's in danger too. He's spread too thin with nowhere to go. I fucking hope Cooper is good at his goddamn job and has Kid safe. I can't think about her now. I have to get the baby.

399

"I'll take the baby up to Kid for you," I yell picking up my pace a bit. I can see the men behind clearer now. They look rough. They look nervous. They look fucking tiny.

"Stop where you're at," the guy behind Thomas yells jamming his gun into Thomas's back harshly. Thomas doesn't move. He locks eyes with me letting me know he'll take the bullet if I can get the baby safe. I see O'Sullivan break through some trees behind the group as Cal makes it to the side of the SUV.

"You're makin' a fuckin' mistake man. Let them go," I command moving another step. The guy is shaking from the adrenaline and nerves. He doesn't know what he's bought himself today. I can see there's a driver waiting in the SUV but he's made no move to get out and assist. O'Sullivan is moving silently toward the group. I'm only fifteen feet away now. The guy can't take his gun off Thomas to point it at me so he's stuck. I keep moving in.

"I said fuckin' stop where you're at!" he screams. "I'll drop this motherfucker!"

"Go ahead and drop me bitch," Thomas roars.

I'm ten feet away now. In a good lunge I'm at them in three steps. O'Sullivan is the same distance from behind. I can't see Cal but he's the closest at the end of the SUV. Someone is going to get shot. I can't stop it so I need to make sure it's not Johnny.

"Kellerman, put the baby in the SUV," I instruct. His eyes bug out and I try with every magical power I possess to convey to him with my eyes that Cal is waiting for Johnny. I hear the scrape of the asphalt as Cal moves his feet in position. This is our chance.

Kellerman looks over his shoulder at the guy behind Thomas who nods his head in agreement. They only want the baby. That driver is going to take off once Johnny's in the SUV. Kellerman looks back at me for a moment and I offer the slightest of nods confirming we've got this.

400

Kellerman scoops Johnny into his arms tightly and moves to the back door of the SUV. I hear the locks open. The guy with the gun in Kellerman's back moves with him. Kellerman opens the door as O'Sullivan moves within five feet of the guy behind Thomas. Kellerman opens the door and climbs into the SUV with Johnny in his arms and all hell breaks loose.

Cal rips the door open from the other side of the SUV simultaneously as O'Sullivan lands a single blow to the back of the guy's head behind Thomas. His gun goes off and Thomas hits the ground. O'Sullivan continues to wail on the guy's head that is obviously unconscious. The guy behind Kellerman swings his gun on me and then back at Kellerman as Kellerman kicks a leg out knocking the gun wielder off balance. The SUV takes off at the same time and Kellerman topples out the door without Johnny in his arms. FUCK! Kellerman is on his back on the asphalt and sweeps the legs of the lone gunman as I sprint to get to the SUV. Cal is in there with Johnny.

The SUV is flying through the parking lot when I hear shots in the distance. I don't know where they're from and I don't give a shit I keep motoring toward the SUV. Suddenly the SUV banks hard to the left and smashes into a row of parked cars. I reach the backdoor in a matter of seconds ripping it open. The airbags are deployed and the driver is out cold. Cal is curled in the floor of the backseat with Johnny smashed to his chest. I don't think Cal's conscious.

"CAL!" I scream surging into the backseat. He's out cold. I grab Johnny and pull him from Cal's iron clad grip. He's still sleeping like nothing ever happened. There's not a mark on him.

"KAV!" Kellerman screams in the distance. I slide out of the SUV as he sprints toward me.

"He's fine," I reassure Kellerman as he grabs Johnny crushing him to his chest. "Cal's out cold."

I see movement coming toward us from the front of the SUV and push Kellerman behind me.

"Sorry I was late to the party. Traffic was murder," Kieran fucking Delaney calls out to us shoving a gun in the back of his pants. "Baby okay?" he asks when he reaches us.

"Yeah," I reply confidently.

"Good," he says as he passes us by and heads to O'Sullivan. I follow.

O'Sullivan is covered in blood. His fists are mangled and his arms are shaking. Thomas is laying on the ground on his back gasping for air as I see hospital workers running in our direction. The guy that had been holding the gun on Kellerman was O'Sullivan's second victim by the looks of what's left of his face.

I look to Kellerman to see a little blood on his knuckles but not enough to cause that damage. As we reach the group a pain runs through my middle and I stop dead in my tracks. Before I can speak Kellerman runs to Kieran, forces Johnny into his arms, rips the gun from the back of Kieran's pants before racing toward the hospital with me hot on his heels.

Kid.

Chapter 54

Shannon

I keep my hands where they are and stare down the man that's entered my room. His hair is grey and age appropriately smoothed to the side. His face is regal and distinguished with crystal blue eyes. He's wearing a tailored charcoal three piece suit, a crisp white shirt and a patterned American flag hued tie. His shoes gleam from the shine he no doubt pays too much money for. The cufflinks at his wrist bare his initials, "S. G.". I see no weapon other than a smart phone gripped tightly in his left hand. His gate is purposeful and his face stone cold. He stops his entry into my room at the foot of the bed pulling the privacy curtain around us.

Once shielded he is at my bedside facing me with a peculiar grin on his lips.

"You've grown into a lovely woman, Shannon," he states matter-of-factly in a tone that suggests that fact annoys him. I don't respond.

"Your 'son' and that Neanderthal you call a boyfriend have been taken. If you assault me, alert anyone to my presence, or in general do anything that displeases me one of them will die."

Never show weakness. It only offers others strength.

Uncle Mick's words glide through me with a warming timber dragging calm behind it. My breathing slows as does my heart rate and everything in the room fades to the background as this man becomes my only focus.

"You don't seem bothered by my information. Have I misread your connections to the child and its father?" He's trying to goad me. It won't work. I don't panic.

"No matter. I have some things to discuss with you and then our business will conclude." The formality he speaks with shows me his nerves. He's playing a character...poorly. The character I'm about to play I've been coveting my whole life. Everything Uncle Mick taught me is about to flow.

"Governor Grady, you have misread the connections I have with my child and his father," I state blankly.

"So I should have had your roommates taken or the women you refer to as your mothers?" he asks in a cocky smarmy tone.

"You shouldn't have taken anyone that belongs to me. Now you've sealed your fate in this life and that of your wife and children. I'm sorry you made such a grievous error. It's truly unfortunate."

There's the crack in the character at the mention of his family. A tremor appears at the hand that cradles his phone and his eyes dart to it willing it to be still.

"You're in no position to threaten me. And you certainly have no ability to hurt my family," he growls in a menacing tone.

"No? Funny I feel very confident with the information I just provided you," I remark dismissively. "You're unarmed, old, slow and much less intelligent than I am. You won't leave this room. Your wife will be tortured and raped to death. Your daughter sold as a sex slave. Your son will be fed to pigs while he's still clinging to life. Anything you love will feel my wrath until there is not a speck of you left on earth."

I try to make my voice loud enough for Nicky to hear yet seem like I'm doing nothing untoward. I have heard not a sound from the bathroom and based on Grady's body language he thinks I'm alone.

"Your mother should have aborted you when I told her to," he fumes. That catches my attention.

"She wasn't a very good listener as I recall," I reply with no hint of the questions that rumble in my head.

"She was quite helpful if providing me the information necessary to get rid of John Murphy. If only she hadn't been fooled into believing you were dead."

My mind is spinning to catch up with what he's saying. He thinks I know what he's talking about so I have to play along while I simultaneously analyze.

"She was stupid," I say in a joking manner. This throws him. We're playing a game and I have the advantage. While he stumbles, I think.

My father and I weren't caught in a turf war crossfire. Grady ordered a hit, no doubt Mancini had a hand in that. A hit made possible by information my mother offered. Did I ever see her again after the shooting? My mind is trying to pull the memories when he speaks again.

"She was easy enough to deal with later," he says trying to goad me again.

"I don't doubt that." My mother is dead. I feel nothing. She was at the hospital...fuck I can't remember seeing her face. Didn't she put me in a car with that driver to send me to Uncle Mick?

"This is becoming a trip down memory lane that I'd prefer not visit. I'm here to discuss your testimony at my trial next month." I meet his gaze with an icy stare that informs him I'm not doing shit for him.

"You can posture all you'd like, but you and I know you'll let no harm come to that *boyfriend* of yours or his child. Really Shannon with your pedigree you should be in a relationship with someone worthy of your breeding." What the fuck does that mean?

"I wasn't aware of any such pedigree, Governor."

He cocks his head at me and a wry smile covers his lips.

"I figured you'd see the resemblance now that I'm here in front of you."

NO! No fucking way! I'm not falling for this. Fuck him for trying to make me.

405

"The only thing I see in front of me is prey."

"So you'd kill the only remaining family you have?"

"Yes," I answer quickly. He wasn't expecting that. My soft spot for family is not dictated by blood. He's misread me. I reach up to thumb my pedant realizing it's at home. Kel must have taken it off me when I was sick. That piece of jewelry has become my connection to him in his absence. I imagine the feel of the gold and diamonds beneath my fingers and ready my mind for a battle.

"That's unfortunate. I've managed to put together quite a case for you and I. See you were hidden away from me by your uncle for so many years that when you returned to Chicago to go to college and I finally found you, you couldn't wait to reconnect. As our relationship grew so did your need to please me and it overwhelmed your sense of morals. It took a great deal of time and money but I found a brilliant forger that did an amazing job of producing your signature on multiple documents showing your willing cooperation in racketeering, money laundering, and campaign funding fraud."

I don't react. I sit and wait for him to finish. I only hope that Nicky is in the bathroom recording this entire conversation. It's silent on his side of the door so I know he's listening.

"You'll take the stand at my trial and admit to your hand in my demise. You'll do this so your child and boyfriend can keep their lives."

"No. I won't. You won't do anything to my son or my boyfriend. You will release anyone that you actually have now or I'll put a bullet between your eyes in the next thirty seconds. I'm done playing your games."

I move quickly retrieving the gun from beneath the covers and aim between his eyes. I begin to count internally as his face pales. His thumb moves across the screen of his phone and without looking he presses a key.

"I've just texted the men that have them and told them to kill one. Now you're down to your last chance," his voice shakes.

"I'm at twenty on your count down." I don't react to what he says. I don't believe him. I can't believe him.

"I've told them to torture and maim them if I don't make contact every thirty minutes. If you kill me you seal their fates."

"The only fate sealed in this room is yours. Ten, nine, eight, seven, six, five, four, three..."

Chapter 55

Kellerman

I'm running through the corridors as fast as my legs will carry me desperate to get to Kid. Kav is in step with me as we pant and heave. Kav is screaming for people to get out of the way and I'm brandishing a gun. People are moving.

We get onto the maternity unit and people are screaming and ducking away from us. I'm three doors from Kid's room when I hear the gunshot.

"NOOOOOO!" I roar and tear into the room. I rip back the privacy curtain to see Kid is sitting in her bed, gun aimed at a man on the floor. Cooper is standing in the doorway of the bathroom gun drawn aiming at the same man.

"Kiddo?" I call.

"I'm fine, Kel." She turns her gaze to meet mine and I see fury stream through her face. "Where's the baby?!" she screams leaping from the bed charging at me. I engulf her in my arms and crush her to my chest, but she fights against me just as hard.

"He's fine. Kieran has him," I explain and her fight stops. She tips her head up at me in confusion.

"I don't know why he's here, but he was the only one qualified to take the baby so I could get to you."

"Kavy, go get my son," her tone has an air of threat and pain. Kav hesitates for half a second before running back down the corridor.

"Drop your weapons!" a man yells from down the corridor in the opposite direction of Kav. Kid and I slowly turn laying our guns on the ground as multiple police officers rush toward us guns drawn. Cooper jumps in front of us before the cops can take us down.

"I'm agent Nick Cooper." Cooper flashes a badge. "Miss Kelly is in my protective custody. There was an intruder in her room that I have shot. He requires medical assistance. Neither Mister Kellerman nor Miss Kelly have committed any crimes. Please lower your weapons," he commands in a professional yet authoritative tone.

"I'm sorry agent Cooper but this guy ran through the hospital with a gun," the officer says approaching me with an ominous look on his face.

"While I understand that's against hospital policy, he's broken no laws by carrying a gun unconcealed with a valid permit. His family was in danger and he was trying to protect them. I think that warrants his behavior. I believe the news outlets would love a story about it." Cooper has won based on the look on the cop's face.

"I'm really sorry for scaring people, officer. My son was almost kidnapped while I was held at gunpoint in the parking lot. Once I was able to get away I knew my girlfriend's life was in danger. I acted on instinct." I shrug trying to play off the fact that I was running through this hospital preparing to commit murder.

Kid goes completely rigid at my explanation. Not the best way to learn about what just happened to us. Kav comes running in with the baby cradled to his massive chest. Sweat is pouring into his eyes when he reaches us. Kid rips Johnny from his arms and starts checking every inch of him for an injury. Some nurses ran around us at some point when Cooper was talking to the cops to work on whoever is bleeding all over the floor.

O'Sullivan, Kieran and Cal run up two seconds behind Kav. When their eyes land on Kid they all relax.

"Gentlemen I believe you're needed outside at a crime scene. Federal agents are en route to clear this scene. Thank you for your assistance." They've been dismissed.

410

Cooper changes his gaze to a nurse hovering behind our bunch. "We need a new room immediately for Miss Kelly." She nods and runs down the hall.

Kid is still feverishly looking over the baby who's starting to fuss at being jacked with.

"Kiddo, he's fine." I try to convince her but she ignores me. The cops leave the area and the onlookers start to return to their original locales. Kid won't stop messing with the baby so I pick her up in my arms and hold her to my chest and she does the same with the baby.

Cooper nods down the hall and I see the nurse waiting for us outside a new room. I walk down the corridor cradling all the life that belongs to me in this world to my chest. I feel peace roll through my body knowing they're all safe. Safe in my arms.

Kavanagh

Holy. Fucking. Shit! That was absolute insanity. I flop into a chair in Kid's new room and catch my breath. I'm not doing cardio for a week! Cal, O'Sullivan, Kieran and Cooper drop into chairs around the room while Kellerman crawls in bed with his family. I'm tempted to crawl in with them, but I stay in my chair at the bedside.

"Someone tell me what the fuck happened. Where's Thomas?" Kid demands quietly as she shoves her boob in Johnny's mouth. I don't think he needs to eat, Kid needs him there.

"Surgery. Took a shot to the lung," Kieran replies for the group.

"What're you doin' here?" she asks in a nicer tone than her words convey.

"Followed Mancini's guys here. They weren't too careful. All the smart ones are still locked up. Grady had to bring dummies along," Kieran explains scrubbing his hands over his face.

"That was Grady in your room?" I ask concerned that Kid just killed a state governor.

"Yeah. He's bat shit fuckin' crazy too," Kid scoffs. Kellerman is sitting behind her in the bed one arm wrapped possessively around her shoulders the other around Johnny. If he could drag them into a cave he would right now. I'd take the cave next door.

"Did you kill him?" I ask tentatively getting ready to call my pop. He could get her out of it.

"Nicky shot him before I had the chance."

"Easier clean up for me than her," Cooper explains typing away on his phone. He's working now. He's sitting there in fucking flip flops, shorts and a polo. You'd never know he was a federal agent that just shot a state governor.

"Did he have a weapon?" O'Sullivan asks pulling his blood covered shirt over his head. The tat across the back of his shoulders stretches as his arms move and my eye is drawn to our family clover dotting the i of his last name. A little bit of Kid in all of us.

"Just his fuckin' mouth," Cooper answers gruffly.

"Huh?" Cal pipes in. He took a good hit to the head when the SUV crashed that Kieran took the tires out on. He refused medical attention to get up here to Kid, but I'm worried he may have a concussion.

"It's a long damn story, but I have it here on my phone. Have a listen to this shit," Cooper says turning up the volume as he plays the conversation Kid had with Grady.

When the recording finishes I feel sick to my stomach. I can't believe this motherfucker. I look to Kid's face and it's a stone veil of no emotion.

"I can't remember if my mother put me in the car with the driver at the airport. I always thought she did but now I can't fuckin' remember." Kid's tired, sick, pregnant, freaked and so many other things I'm not surprised she can't remember.

"I don't think she did. My nurse told me about my father bein' dead not my mother. I don't remember her ever visiting me. I think it was the nurse that put me in the car. I think Uncle Mick faked my death to keep me safe. Do you think he coulda done that Nicky?" she rambles trying to track everything down.

"He had the skills and the resources. I don't see why not," Cooper says confidently.

"She hated me that much. She hated me so much that she told them how to kill us. Where we'd be. Why did she hate me?" There's choked emotion in Kid's voice as she gazes down at Johnny. He's no longer nursing just sleeping using her boob as a pillow. Good man.

"Because she was a fuckin' idiot. An evil piece of shit that got what she deserved. You're a damn gift!" Kellerman growls into her neck. I'm going to look at caves when we get out of here. He'd look good in a cave with a loin cloth. So would I.

"Kid," Cal calls to her quietly. "You remember when you told us about your dad that day at the breakfast table?" She nods. "I told you about my mom dyin' that day and you crawled in my lap and made me feel good for the first time in a way I'd never felt. Your mother couldn't stand you because you burned so bright you out shined her. Even when she tried to remove you from this world you fought your way through and burned brighter than before. Don't let her touch that light now. You burn brighter today than you did yesterday knowin' that you bring light to everything you touch. Even a fucked up soul like mine."

They sit and stare at each other for a long time after he finishes. This is what they do. They communicate through their eyes and it's creepy and mesmerizing to witness.

413

"You're not fucked up," Kid repeats the same words to Cal that she said almost fourteen years ago as tears prick the back of her eyes. Kid doesn't cry but pregnancy hormones are going to make that hard on her. Cal nods and sits back in his chair.

"Cal I think you should have a doctor take a look at you," I say concerned in tone.

"I'm good, Kav," he dismisses me.

"What's wrong with him?" Kid asks with more concern in her voice than I had.

"He got knocked out holdin' Johnny in the back of the SUV," Kieran explains. "My bad. I had to take out the tires to get it to stop. Crashed into a row of parked cars."

"I think it's time I heard the whole story," Kid says with an edge to her voice. Kellerman clears his throat and launches into the story. Watching the fear, anger, pain, nausea and love wash over her face as she listens is almost too much to bear. This chapter in her life has to be over now. She's had enough. It's time for her to live the life she's always deserved filled with nothing but unconditional love.

Chapter 56

Shannon
September 20, 2014

"Happy Birthday, Momma," Kel whispers into my neck holding me from behind his hands resting on my barely-there baby bump.

In front of me is a huge three tiered cake covered in cream fondant decorated with stunning sugar flowers in every color possible. It's breathtaking and in danger of melting from all of my candles. I close my eyes and make my wish...blow. It takes a few tries, but I get them all out and applause erupts from my party goers.

Everyone is here at Flannery's to celebrate my thirty-first birthday. After we eat heavenly cake, I scan the room and take in the faces of the incredible people that fill my life.

Maggie and Mary are fussing over Johnny and he's loving every minute of it laughing and spitting bubbles at them. Pop, Doc and Pappy are huddled together discussing something very important (football from what I can hear). Ryan and Adam are laughing at Collin and Hugh trying to pick up one of the waitresses working tonight. She's not giving any one of the guys in the room the time of day. Good for her! Aidan and Finn are discussing Aidan's move here in a few weeks. He took a job at the University of Kansas Medical Center. He's moving into our house of course, which is under major construction currently. By the time it's done I think the house will almost double in size and Kavy assures me it'll be done before the twins are born.

Karl is at a table talking to Kieran. Those two are the strangest pairing in the world but they have formed a weird friendship. Thomas is at the bar talking to Nicky. Thomas is still my bodyguard even though there are no longer any threats to my life. I love having him around and he keeps me safe. Nicky is the same old secret agent telling me nothing but always around. Butch and Rodger are playing pool together smiling over at Johnny more often than not.

Kavy, Sully and Cally are standing here talking to Kel over my shoulder about how much cake I could put away in my teens. They aren't lying. Kel's deep laugh rumbles through my body and I smile at the warm tickle it sends through me.

A year ago I had almost none of this. I had my family and that was it and it was enough then. Now looking around this room I can't imagine living a day without all of these people in it. My life is fuller, richer and happier than I ever imagined life could be. I'm safe. I'm happy. I'm loved.

Kavanagh

Standing here in Flannery's for Kid's birthday is nothing short of a miracle. For the last year people have been trying to kill or take her from me and she's done nothing but fight against it. Amazing is too small a word to describe her.

She's glowing brighter than I've ever seen her. Pregnancy agrees with her. Who knew the world's most stunning woman could look even better? It took a week or so for her to bounce back after the hospital incident with Grady. But she's back and better than ever!

Former Governor Grady lived through surgery only to be shipped off to a federal penitentiary. He'll never see the light of day again. Mancini pled guilty to various charges but got a good deal because he cooperated against Grady.

Mancini gave the whole story about what happened to Kid and her dad. Kid's "mother" (the evil witch that gave birth to her, she was no mother) gave Mancini the route the driver would take to Wrigley Field so that he could ambush the car. Mancini was to eliminate Kid and her father. He's the one that took the final shots at Kid while she hung in the backseat of the burning town car. There's a special place in hell for that motherfucker.

Grady is not Kid's father. Why he thought that (lied about it) we'll never know but a DNA test proved that was a fucking lie. Mancini took out Kid's "mother" a few months after the ambush. She never saw Kid at the hospital. Kid's memory of her mother putting her in a car with a driver was wrong. It was a nurse that did that. Uncle Mick orchestrated the entire thing. We have no proof of that but it's the only thing that makes sense. He kept her safe and trained her to stay that way for the rest of her life. That man is a God send that I'm thankful for every day.

So that's it. Kid's safe. Kid's pregnant. Kid's loved. All is right in the world.

Kellerman

The size of Kid's family makes it a long ass process saying goodnight to everyone. But I finally have her to myself.

I push her down to the mattress and capture her mouth in a fervent kiss. She moans in the back of her throat and arches her back into me. Pregnancy has made her a vixen. I unclasp her bra and move my mouth along hers tasting and nipping at her mouth. She pushes her hands into my hair smashing her mouth hungrily to mine. I massage my tongue against hers as a groan thunders through my chest.

I move my mouth across her jaw and down her long slender neck. She tastes like milk and honey. I cup her tit with one hand as my mouth devours the other nipple, nibbling and tugging.

"Kel," rasps from her lips urging me further.

I whisper kisses down the plain of her torso to her slight bump and stop. I cup it in both hands and press my lips to the home of my children. I can't wait to feel them move inside her. It's time.

I sit up on my knees and pull Kid to a seated position.

"Kel," she protests until she meets my eyes. She can see the seriousness of my gaze and waits. Her green orbs aglow.

"Marry me," I demand. Not how I had planned this. "Be my wife, Kiddo. You're everything good about me and I can't spend another day in this world without everyone knowing you're mine. Marry me." She just stares at me for a long time, studying my face. Her face is soft. Her auburn waves are a mess falling around her shoulders brushing across her breasts framing her pendant. Her high cheek bones are flushed with desire and her plump lips are swollen from my assault on them. Her beauty knows no bounds.

"That was quite the caveman proposal, Kel," she admonishes. She's right, it was.

"I didn't plan it to be like this. I have a better plan, but I couldn't wait any longer. I need you to be my wife like I need to take my next breath. You turned my world upside down when you walked into Mia's room. My life was nothing but a shell until I saw your stunning green eyes alight with fierce protection at the sight of me. I was dead on the inside and you brought me back to life and made that life something people everywhere are envious of. You are the greatest gift any man could dream of and I have you. I want you to be by my side for eternity. Please, Kiddo. Will you marry me?"

"Yes," she answers immediately and smiles her panty dropping smile at me that makes my fucking toes curl.

I push her back on the bed and plunder her mouth while removing both our underwear. In one glorious movement I fill her and shudder when I bottom out. Kid wraps her arms around my shoulders and her long sexy

418

legs around my waist and I begin to rock into her slowly. With each stroke I match my tongue in her mouth and she begins to tremble.

"I love you," I murmur against her mouth before capturing it again and increasing my pace. Thundering into her she gasps and constricts her legs as her fingernails score my skin. A long deep moan flows from her mouth to mine as her orgasm rocks her to the core fueling my tension. I bury my face in her neck and thrust tirelessly as sweat mists our bodies.

"I love you too," she whispers into my ear and I come undone, powering forward emptying myself inside her. I slow my strokes as we both come down and temper our breathing. I press long kisses to her forehead, cheeks, nose and chin before I press firm to her mouth. Then I collapse onto her smashing her beneath me. She always lets me until she can't breathe anymore. I break the connection this time to finish what I started.

"Don't move," I say climbing off the bed and opening my dresser drawer. I fish out the black velvet box and come back to the bed. I lie down beside her and scoop her body to my side. She throws her leg over mine and her hand goes to my abs her face tipped up glowing at me.

I crack open the box and remove the ring. She never looks at it. I know she doesn't give a shit about a ring, but I do. I want there to be no question she's mine and well taken care of. I grab her left hand off my abs and slide the ring on her finger and wait for her reaction. After a moment she finally looks down and sits straight up grabbing her left hand with her right.

"What the fuck is this?!" she screeches.

"A ring," I say nonchalantly.

"No Kel, this is not a ring. This is a fucking skating rink. I'll need a crane to lift my hand!"

I have gone completely overboard with the ring, I'm aware of this. It's a little over ten carats (cushion cut whatever the fuck that means) with smaller diamonds around it and down the sides of the slim setting. It covers her finger almost knuckle to knuckle. Yeah, no one will question whether she's taken, not ever again. She can flirt and smile at guys all she wants now.

"Kav told me I had to get you a moon sized rock and propose at Super Bowl half time. I figured I better get half of the equation right. I asked your dads' permission too. And all your brothers and Karl and Thomas and fuckin' Cooper and Kieran and Butch and Rodger. Maggie and Mary were cryin' too hard to answer."

A lone tear drops from her eye and I sit up to quickly wipe it away.

"Don't cry Kiddo," I soothe. She never cries and it makes my stomach churn when she does.

"I love you so much. You asked everyone?" she questions her emerald eyes glistening.

"I asked everyone."

"I'll wear this horrible monstrous ring every day with pride, Dylan Kellerman. You're the only man in this world that would share me with my family and love me more because of them. I hit the jackpot with you," she finishes with a soft kiss on my lips.

"I'll never have to be a caveman again as long as that thing's on your finger," I explain pulling her back down to the bed.

"I love you, Kiddo," I murmur into her hair.

She gazes up at me and I see it. There's nothing left behind her eyes other than radiance shining brightly. The blackness is gone. Only light awaits us.

The End...

(or maybe just the beginning)

Upcoming Releases...

Kieran's story will be available Summer 2014.

Follow Norma Jeanne at the links below to receive updates on all her upcoming projects.

www.normajeannekarlsson.com
https://twitter.com/NormaJKarlsson
www.facebook.com/AuthorNormaJeanneKarlsson
www.goodreads.com/normajeannekarlsson

If you or someone you know has been the victim of a violent crime please contact your local authorities. Minority groups in particular are at higher risk for being silent victims, please don't suffer in silence. If you are unsure who to contact, call one of the national hotlines listed below and they will get you in contact with the appropriate resources.

In the United States
The National Domestic Violence Hotline
1-800-799-SAFE (7233)
1-800-787-3224 (TTY)
http://www.thehotline.org/
The National Sexual Assault Hotline
1-800-656-HOPE
https://ohl.rainn.org/online/
In the United Kingdom and Ireland
English National Domestic Violence Helpline
0808 2000 247
www.nationaldomesticviolencehelpline.org.uk
Wales Domestic Abuse Helpline
0808 80 10 800
http://www.allwaleshelpline.org.uk/
Women's Aid Federation (Northern Ireland)
0800 917 1414
www.womensaidni.org
Women's Aid (Republic of Ireland)
1800 341 900
http://www.womensaid.ie/
Scottish Women's Aid
0800 027 1234
www.scottishwomensaid.org.uk
Men's Advice Line
0808 801 0327
www.mensadviceline.org.uk
Broken Rainbow

(for lesbian, gay, bisexual and transgender people)
0300 999 5428
www.broken-rainbow.org.uk
In Australia
1800RESPECT
National Sexual Assault, Domestic and Family Violence Counselling Service
1800 737 732
https://www.1800respect.org.au/
MensLine Australia
1300 78 99 78
http://www.mensline.org.au
In New Zealand
Women's Refuge
(Domestic Violence Helpline)
0800 REFUGE (733 843)
https://womensrefuge.org.nz
Rape Prevention Education
09 360 4001
http://www.rpe.org.nz/
OUTLineNZ
(Supporting the rainbow community)
0800 OUTLINE (6885463)
http://www.outline.org.nz/